CROSS BONES

Also by Kathy Reichs

MONDAY MOURNING

BARE BONES

GRAVE SECRETS

FATAL VOYAGE

DEADLY DÉCISIONS

DEATH DU JOUR

DÉJÀ DEAD

CROSS BONES

KATHY REICHS

WILLIAM HEINEMANN : LONDON

Published in the United Kingdom in 2005 by William Heinemann

1 3 5 7 9 10 8 6 4 2

Published by arrangement with the original publisher, Scribner, an imprint of Simon & Schuster, Inc.

William Heinemann
The Random House Group Limited
20 Vauxhall Bridge Road, London, SW1V 2SA

The Random House Group Limited Reg. No. 954009
www.randomhouse.co.uk

A CIP catalogue record for this book is available from the British Library

Addresses for companies within The Random House Group Limited can be found at www.randomhouse.co.uk/offices.htm

The Random House Group Limited makes every effort to ensure that the papers used in its books are made from trees that have been legally sourced from well-managed and credibly certified forests. Our paper procurement policy can be found at: www.randomhouse.co.uk/paper.htm

FSC
Mixed Sources
Product group from well-managed forests and other controlled sources
www.fsc.org Cert no. TT-COC-2139
© 1996 Forest Stewardship Council

Printed and bound in the United Kingdom by
Clays Ltd, St Ives plc

ISBN 978 0 4340 1967 0

ACKNOWLEDGMENTS

As usual, I am deeply indebted to many of my colleagues, family, and friends for their time, expertise, and advice.

Dr. James Tabor, Chair, Department of Religious Studies, University of North Carolina at Charlotte, lit the initial spark for *Cross Bones,* shared his personal notes and research findings, checked a thousand fine points, and gallantly squired me around Israel.

Dr. Charles Greenblatt and Kim Vernon, Science and Antiquity Group, The Hebrew University of Jerusalem, and Dr. Carney Matheson, Paleo-DNA Laboratory, Lakehead University, coached me on ancient DNA. Dr. Mark Leney, DNA Coordinator, CILHI, Joint POW-MIA Accounting Command, and Dr. David Sweet, Director, Bureau of Forensic Dentistry, University of British Columbia, answered questions about modern DNA.

Azriel Gorsky, Head (Emeritus), Fibers and Polymers Laboratory, Division of Identification and Forensic Science, Israel National Police, gave advice on hair and fiber analysis, and on the workings of Israeli law enforcement.

Dr. Elazor Zadok, Brigadier General, Director, Division of Identification and Forensic Science, Israel National Police, allowed a tour of their Forensic Science facility. Dr. Tzipi Kahana, Chief Inspector, Forensic Anthropologist, Division of Identification and Forensic Science, Israel National Police, familiarized me with the Israeli medical examiner system.

Dr. Shimon Gibson, Jerusalem Archaeological Field Unit, took me to sites throughout Israel, and answered many questions about his homeland.

Debbie Sklar, Israel Antiquities Authority, provided a private tour of the Rockefeller Museum.

Officer Christopher Dozier, Charlotte-Mecklenburg Police Department, and Sergent-détective Stephen Rudman, Superviseur, Analyse et Liaison, Communauté Urbaine de Montréal Police (retired), supplied information on obtaining phone records.

Roz Lippel helped keep the Hebrew honest. Marie-Eve Provost did the same for the French.

Special thanks go to Paul Reichs for his insightful comments on the manuscript.

Credit must be given to two books mentioned in the text: *Masada: Herod's Fortress and the Zealots' Last Stand* by Yigael Yadin, George Weidenfeld & Nicolson Limited, 1966; *The Jesus Scroll* by Donovan Joyce, Dial Press, 1973.

Last, but far from least, heartfelt thanks to my editor, Nan Graham. Her advice made *Cross Bones* a far better book. Thanks also to my editor across the pond, Susan Sandon.

And, of course, to Jennifer Rudolph Walsh, Co-Head of the Worldwide Literary Department, Executive Vice President, and one of the first two women appointed to the Board of Directors of the William Morris Agency. Way to go, girl! Thanks for hanging in as my agent.

For Susanne Kirk, editor, Scribner, 1975–2004
and
For Dr. James Woodward, chancellor,
University of North Carolina at Charlotte, 1989–2005

Thanks for the years of support and encouragement.

Enjoy your retirements!

km 0 25 50
mi 0 25 50
LEBANON
Golan Heights
SYRIA
Mediterranean Sea
West Bank
Tel Aviv
Beit Hanina
Route 1
Jerusalem
JUDEAN DESERT
Qumran
Dead Sea
Gaza Strip
Ein Gedi
Masada
ISRAEL
JORDAN
EGYPT
Gulf of Aqaba
JERUSALEM
km 0 0.5
mi 0 0.25 0.5
Route 1
Jerusalem Post
American Colony Hotel
Mt. Scopus Campus of Hebrew University
Police Headquarters/ Russian Compound
Rockefeller Museum
Mount of Olives
Temple Mount
OLD CITY
KIDRON VALLEY
Tomb
SILWAN
HINNOM VALLEY
ABU TOR

CROSS BONES

Depart from evil, and do good. Seek peace, and pursue it.

—Jewish Holy Scripture,
Psalm 34:14

The fruit of righteousness is sown in peace for them that make peace.

—New Testament, James 3:18

And make not Allah because of your swearing (by him) an obstacle to your doing good and guarding (against evil) and making peace between men, and Allah is Hearing, Knowing.

—Koran 2:224

THE FACTS

- From 1963 to 1965, Masada, site of a first-century Jewish revolt against the Romans, was excavated by Israeli archaeologist Yigael Yadin and a team of international volunteers. Yadin's workers recovered the fragmentary and commingled remains of approximately twenty-five skeletons from a cave complex, designated Loci 2001/2002, located below the casement wall at the southern tip of the summit. Unlike other human remains found within the main complex of ruins at the northern end of Masada, these bones were not immediately reported to the press.

  In the 1990s, a photo surfaced of a single intact skeleton that was also recovered from Loci 2001/2002 during the 1963 to 1965 excavation. That skeleton was never mentioned or described by the project's physical anthropologist, Nicu Haas. It was not discussed by Yadin in his published reports or interviews.
  - Formal field notes were not kept during the Masada excavation, but oral briefings took place regularly between Yadin and his staff. Transcripts of these sessions are archived at the Mount Scopus Campus of Hebrew University. Pages covering the period of the discovery and clearing of Loci 2001/2002 are missing.
  - Neither the bones from the twenty-five commingled individuals, nor the articulated skeleton, nor the contents of Loci 2001/2002, are described in the six volumes of the final Masada excavation publication.
  - Though Nicu Haas was in possession of the bones for more than five years, he published nothing on the commingled individuals or on the complete skeleton recovered at Loci 2001/2002. Haas's handwritten notes, including a full bone inventory, indicate he never received the complete skeleton.

  - In the late 1960s, Yigael Yadin stated in press interviews that carbon-14 dating was seldom done, and that it was not his job to initiate such tests. The journal *Radiocarbon* indicates that Yadin sent samples for carbon-14 dating from other Israeli excavations during that period. Despite uncertainty concerning the age of the Loci 2001/2002 remains, Yadin never sent samples for radiocarbon dating.

- In 1968, the skeletal remains of a "crucified man" were found during road construction north of the Old City of Jerusalem. The deceased, Yehochanan, died at approximately twenty-five years of age, during the first century. A nail and wood fragments were embedded in one of Yehochanan's heel bones.

- In 1973, Australian journalist Donovan Joyce published *The Jesus Scroll* (Dial Press). Joyce claimed to have visited Israel, met a volunteer from Yadin's excavation team, and seen a stolen first-century scroll from Masada containing the last will and testament of "Jesus, son of James." According to Joyce, the scroll was smuggled out of Israel, presumably to the USSR.

- In 1980, roadworkers uncovered a tomb in Talpiot, just south of the Old City of Jerusalem. The tomb contained ossuaries inscribed with the names Mara (Mary), Yehuda, son of Yeshua (Jude, son of Jesus), Matya (Matthew), Yeshua, son of Yehosef (Jesus, son of Joseph), Yose (Joseph), and Marya (Mary). The coexistence of the names in one tomb is rare. Skeletal materials have been submitted for DNA testing.

- In 2000, American archaeologist James Tabor and his team discovered a freshly robbed tomb in the Hinnom Valley, outside Jerusalem. The tomb contained twenty ossuaries, all but one shattered. The lower chamber held a burial shroud wrapping a fragmentary human skeleton and hair. Carbon-14 testing showed the shroud was first-century in age. Microscopic examination revealed the hair was clean and vermin-free, indicating the deceased had been of high status. Anthropological analysis determined the remains were those of an adult male. DNA sequencing demonstrated a familial relationship among most of the other individuals buried in the tomb.

- In 2002, Israeli antiquities collector Oded Golan revealed the existence of a first-century ossuary inscribed "James, son of Joseph, brother of Jesus." That fall, the ossuary was made public. While experts agree that the small stone coffin is first-century in age, controversy surrounds the authenticity of the inscription. Circumstantial evidence suggests the ossuary came from the vicinity of the Hinnom, possibly from Tabor's "shroud" tomb.

  A formal request was submitted to the Israel Antiquities Authority for DNA testing of bone material found in the James ossuary. DNA sequencing would allow comparison of the James ossuary remains with those recovered from Tabor's Hinnom "shroud" tomb. The request was denied.

As this book went to press:

- In January of 2005, indictments were issued against Oded Golan and several others for the forgery of antiquities. Mr. Golan maintains his innocence, and continues in his insistence that the James ossuary is authentic. Experts remain divided.

1

FOLLOWING AN EASTER DINNER OF HAM, PEAS, AND CREAMED potatoes, Charles "Le Cowboy" Bellemare pinched a twenty from his sister, drove to a crack house in Verdun, and vanished.

That summer the crack house was sold up-market. That winter the new homeowners grew frustrated with the draw in their fireplace. On Monday, February seventh, the man of the house opened the flue and thrust upward with a rake handle. A desiccated leg tumbled into the ash bed.

Papa called the cops. The cops called the fire department and the Bureau du coroner. The coroner called our forensics lab. Pelletier caught the case.

Pelletier and two morgue techs were standing on the lawn within an hour of the leg drop. To say the scene was confused would be like saying D-day was hectic. Outraged father. Hysterical mother. Overwrought kids. Mesmerized neighbors. Annoyed cops. Mystified firefighters.

Dr. Jean Pelletier is the most senior of the five pathologists at the Laboratoire de sciences judiciaires et de médecine légale, Quebec's central crime and medico-legal lab. He's got bad joints and bad dentures, and zero tolerance for anything or anyone that wastes his time. Pelletier took one look and ordered a wrecking ball.

The exterior wall of the chimney was pulverized. A well-smoked corpse was extracted, strapped to a gurney, and transported to our lab.

The next day Pelletier eyeballed the remains and said, "*ossements.*" Bones.

Enter I, Dr. Temperance Brennan, forensic anthropologist for North Carolina and Quebec. La Belle Province and Dixie? Long story, starting with a faculty swap between my home university, UNC-Charlotte, and McGill. When the exchange year ended, I headed south, but continued consulting for the lab in Montreal. A decade later, I'm still commuting, and lay claim to the mother lode of frequent flyer miles.

Pelletier's *demande d'expertise en anthropologie* was on my desk when I arrived in Montreal for my February rotation.

It was now Wednesday, February 16, and the chimney bones formed a complete skeleton on my worktable. Though the victim hadn't been a believer in regular checkups, eliminating dental records as an option, all skeletal indicators fit Bellemare. Age, sex, race, and height estimates, along with surgical pins in the right fibula and tibia, told me I was looking at the long-lost Cowboy.

Other than a hairline fracture of the cranial base, probably caused by the unplanned chimney dive, I'd found no evidence of trauma.

I was pondering how and why a man goes up on a roof and falls down the chimney, when the phone rang.

"It seems I need your assistance, Temperance." Only Pierre LaManche called me by my full name, hitting hard on the last syllable, and rhyming it with "sconce" instead of "fence." LaManche had assigned himself a cadaver that I suspected might present decomposition issues.

"Advanced putrefaction?"

"*Oui.*" My boss paused. "And other complicating factors."

"Complicating factors?"

"Cats."

Oh, boy.

"I'll be right down."

After saving the Bellemare report on disk, I left my lab, passed through the glass doors separating the medico-legal section from the rest of the floor, turned into a side corridor, and pushed a button beside a solitary elevator. Accessible only through the two secure levels comprising the LSJML, and through the coroner's office below on eleven, this lift had a single destination: the morgue.

Descending to the basement, I reviewed what I'd learned at that morning's staff meeting.

Avram Ferris, a fifty-six-year-old Orthodox Jew, had gone missing a week earlier. Ferris's body had been discovered late yesterday in a storage closet on the upper floor of his place of business. No signs of a break-in. No signs of a struggle. Employee said he'd been acting odd. Death by self-inflicted gunshot wound was the on-scene assessment. The man's family was adamant in its rejection of suicide as an explanation.

The coroner had ordered an autopsy. Ferris's relatives and rabbi had objected. Negotiations had been heated.

I was about to see the compromise that had been reached.

And the handiwork of the cats.

From the elevator, I turned left, then right toward the morgue. Nearing the outer door to the autopsy wing, I heard sounds drifting from the family room, a forlorn little chamber reserved for those called upon to identify the dead.

Soft sobbing. A female voice.

I pictured the bleak little space with its plastic plants and plastic chairs and discreetly curtained window, and felt the usual ache. We did no hospital autopsies at the LSJML. No end-stage liver disease. No pancreatic cancer. We were scripted for murder, suicide, accidental and sudden and unexpected death. The family room held those just ambushed by the unthinkable and unforeseen. Their grief never failed to touch me.

Pulling open a bright blue door, I proceeded down a narrow corridor, passing computer stations, drying racks, and stainless steel carts on my right, more blue doors on my left, each labeled SALLE D'AUTOPSIE. At the fourth door, I took a deep breath and entered.

Along with the skeletal, I get the burned, the mummified, the mutilated, and the decomposed. My job is to restore the identity death has erased. I frequently use room four since it is outfitted with special ventilation. This morning the system was barely keeping up with the odor of decay.

Some autopsies play to an empty house. Some pack them in. Despite the stench, Avram Ferris's postmortem was standing room only.

LaManche. His autopsy tech, Lisa. A police photographer. Two uniforms. A Sûreté du Québec detective I didn't know. Tall guy, freckled, and paler than tofu.

An SQ detective I *did* know. Well. Andrew Ryan. Six-two. Sandy hair. Viking blue eyes.

We nodded to each other. Ryan the cop. Tempe the anthropologist.

If the official players weren't crowd enough, four outsiders formed a shoulder-to-shoulder wall of disapproval at the foot of the corpse.

I did a quick scan. All male. Two midfifties, two maybe closing out their sixties. Dark hair. Glasses. Beards. Black suits. Yarmulkes.

The wall regarded me with appraising eyes. Eight hands stayed clasped behind four rigid backs.

LaManche lowered his mask and introduced me to the quartet of observers.

"Given the condition of Mr. Ferris's body, an anthropologist is needed."

Four puzzled looks.

"Dr. Brennan's expertise is skeletal anatomy." LaManche spoke English. "She is fully aware of your special needs."

Other than careful collection of all blood and tissue, I hadn't a clue of their special needs.

"I'm very sorry for your loss," I said, pressing my clipboard to my chest.

Four somber nods.

Their loss lay at center stage, plastic sheeting stretched between his body and the stainless steel. More sheeting had been spread on the floor below and around the table. Empty tubs, jars, and vials sat ready on a rolling cart.

The body had been stripped and washed, but no incision had been made. Two paper bags lay flattened on the counter. I assumed LaManche had completed his external exam, including tests for gunpowder and other trace evidence on Ferris's hands.

Eight eyes tracked me as I crossed to the deceased. Observer number four reclasped his hands in front of his genitals.

Avram Ferris didn't look like he'd died last week. He looked like he'd died during the Clinton years. His eyes were black, his tongue purple, his skin mottled olive and eggplant. His gut was distended, his scrotum ballooned to the size of beach balls.

I looked to Ryan for an explanation.

"Temperature in the closet was pushing ninety-two," he said.

"Why so hot?"

"We figure one of the cats brushed the thermostat," Ryan said.

I did a quick calculation. Ninety-two Fahrenheit. About thirty-five Celsius. No wonder Ferris was setting a land record for decomposition.

But heat had been just one of this gentleman's problems.

When hungry, the most docile among us grow cranky. When starved, we grow desperate. Id overrides ethics. We eat. We survive. That common instinct drives herd animals, predators, wagon trains, and soccer teams.

Even Fido and Fluffy go vulture.

Avram Ferris had made the mistake of punching out while trapped with two domestic shorthairs and a Siamese.

And a short supply of Friskies.

I moved around the table.

Ferris's left temporal and parietal bones were oddly splayed. Though I couldn't see the occipital, it was obvious the back of his head had taken a hit.

Pulling on gloves, I wedged two fingers under the skull and palpated. The bone yielded like sludge. Only scalp tissue was keeping the flip side together.

I eased the head down and examined the face.

It was difficult to imagine what Ferris had looked like in life. His left cheek was macerated. Tooth marks scored the underlying bone, and fragments glistened opalescent in the angry red stew.

Though swollen and marbled, Ferris's face was largely intact on the right.

I straightened, considered the patterning of the mutilation. Despite the heat and the smell of putrefaction, the cats hadn't ventured to the right of Ferris's nose or south to the rest of the body.

I understood why LaManche needed me.

"There was an open wound on the left side of the face?" I asked him.

"*Oui.* And another at the back of the skull. The putrefaction and scavenging make it impossible to determine bullet trajectory."

"I'll need a full set of cranial X-rays," I said to Lisa.

"Orientation?"

"All angles. And I'll need the skull."

"Impossible." Observer four again came alive. "We have an agreement."

LaManche raised a gloved hand. "I have the responsibility to determine the truth in this matter."

"You gave your word there would be no retention of specimens." Though the man's face was the color of oatmeal, a pink bud was mushrooming on each of his cheeks.

"Unless absolutely unavoidable." LaManche was all reason.

Observer four turned to the man on his left. Observer three raised his chin and gazed down through lowered lids.

"Let him speak." Unruffled. The rabbi counseling patience.

LaManche turned to me.

"Dr. Brennan, proceed with your analysis, leaving the skull and all untraumatized bone in place."

"Dr. LaManche—"

"If that proves unworkable, resume normal protocol."

I do not like being told how to do my job. I do not like working with less than the maximum available information, or employing less than optimum procedure.

I *do* like and respect Pierre LaManche. He is the finest pathologist I've ever known.

I looked at my boss. The old man nodded almost imperceptibly. *Work with me,* he was signaling.

I shifted my gaze to the faces hovering above Avram Ferris. In each I saw the age-old struggle of dogma versus pragmatics. The body as temple. The body as ducts and ganglia and piss and bile.

In each I saw the anguish of loss.

The same anguish I'd overheard just minutes before.

"Of course," I said quietly. "Call when you're ready to retract the scalp."

I looked at Ryan. He winked, Ryan the cop hinting at Ryan the lover.

The woman was still crying when I left the autopsy wing. Her companion, or companions, were now silent.

I hesitated, not wanting to intrude on personal sorrow.

Was that it? Or was that merely an excuse to shield myself?

I often witness grief. Time and again I am present for that head-on collision when survivors face the realization of their altered lives. Meals that will never be shared. Conversations that will never be spoken. Little Golden Books that will never be read aloud.

I see the pain, but have no help to offer. I am an outsider, a voyeur looking on after the crash, after the fire, after the shooting. I am part of the screaming sirens, the stretching of the yellow tape, the zipping of the body bag.

I cannot diminish the overwhelming sorrow. And I hate my impotence.

Feeling like a coward, I turned into the family room.

Two women sat side by side, together but not touching. The younger could have been thirty or fifty. She had pale skin, heavy brows, and curly dark hair tied back on her neck. She wore a black skirt and a long black sweater with a high cowl that brushed her jaw.

The older woman was so wrinkled she reminded me of the dried-apple dolls crafted in the Carolina mountains. She wore an ankle-length dress whose color fell somewhere between black and purple. Loose threads spiraled where the top three buttons should have been.

I cleared my throat.

Apple Granny glanced up, tears glistening on the face of ten thousand creases.

"Mrs. Ferris?"

The gnarled fingers bunched and rebunched a hanky.

"I'm Temperance Brennan. I'll be helping with Mr. Ferris's autopsy."

The old woman's head dropped to the right, jolting her wig to a suboptimal angle.

"Please accept my condolences. I know how difficult this is for you."

The younger woman raised two heart-stopping lilac eyes. "Do you?"

Good question.

Loss is difficult to understand. I know that. My understanding of loss is incomplete. I know that, too.

I lost my brother to leukemia when he was three. I lost my grandmother when she'd lived more than ninety years. Each time, the grief was like a living thing, invading my body and nesting deep in my marrow and nerve endings.

Kevin had been barely past baby. Gran was living in memories that didn't include me. I loved them. They loved me. But they were not the entire focus of my life, and both deaths were anticipated.

How did anyone deal with the sudden loss of a spouse? Of a child?

I didn't want to imagine.

The younger woman pressed her point. "You can't presume to understand the sorrow we feel."

Unnecessarily confrontational, I thought. Clumsy condolences are still condolences.

"Of course not," I said, looking from her to her companion and back. "That was presumptuous of me."

Neither woman spoke.

"I am very sorry for your loss."

The younger woman waited so long I thought she wasn't going to respond.

"I'm Miriam Ferris. Avram is . . . was my husband." Miriam's hand came up and paused, as if uncertain as to its mission. "Dora is Avram's mother."

The hand fluttered toward Dora, then dropped to rejoin its counterpart.

"I suppose our presence during the autopsy is irregular. There's nothing we can do." Miriam's voice sounded husky with grief. "This is all so . . ." Her words trailed off, but her eyes stayed fixed on me.

I tried to think of something comforting, or uplifting, or even just calming to say. No words formed in my mind. I fell back on clichés.

"I do understand the pain of losing a loved one."

A twitch made Dora's right cheek jump. Her shoulders slumped and her head dropped.

I moved to her, squatted, and placed my hand on hers.

"Why Avram?" Choked. "Why my only son? A mother should not bury her son."

Miriam said something in Hebrew or Yiddish.

"Who is this God? Why does he do this?"

Miriam spoke again, this time with quiet reprimand.

Dora's eyes rolled up to mine. "Why not take me? I'm old. I'm ready." The wrinkled lips trembled.

"I can't answer that, ma'am." My own voice sounded husky.

A tear dropped from Dora's chin to my thumb.

I looked down at that single drop of wetness.

I swallowed.

"May I make you some tea, Mrs. Ferris?"

"We'll be fine," Miriam said. "Thank you."

I squeezed Dora's hand. The skin felt dry, the bones brittle.

Feeling useless, I stood and handed Miriam a card. "I'll be upstairs for the next few hours. If there's anything I can do, please don't hesitate to call."

Exiting the viewing room, I noticed one of the bearded observers watching from across the hall.

As I passed, the man stepped forward to block my path.

"That was very kind." His voice had a peculiar raspy quality, like Kenny Rogers singing "Lucille."

"A woman has lost her son. Another her husband."

"I saw you in there. It is obvious you are a person of compassion. A person of honor."

Where was this going?

The man hesitated, as though debating a few final points with himself. Then he reached into a pocket, withdrew an envelope, and handed it to me.

"This is the reason Avram Ferris is dead."

2

THE ENVELOPE HELD A SINGLE BLACK-AND-WHITE PRINT. Pictured was a supine skeleton, skull twisted, jaw agape in a frozen scream.

I flipped the photo. Written on the back were the date, October 1963, and a blurry notation. *H de 1 H.* Maybe.

I looked a question at the bearded gentleman blocking my way. He made no move to explain.

"Mr.—?"

"Kessler."

"Why are you showing this to me?"

"I believe it's the reason Avram Ferris is dead."

"So you've said."

Kessler crossed his arms. Uncrossed them. Rubbed palms on his pants.

I waited.

"He said he was in danger." Kessler jabbed four fingers at the print. "Said if anything happened it would be because of this."

"Mr. Ferris gave this to you?"

"Yes." Kessler glanced over his shoulder.

"Why?"

Kessler's answer was a shrug.

My eyes dropped back to the print. The skeleton was fully extended, its right arm and hip partially obscured by a rock or ledge. An object lay in the dirt beside the left knee. A familiar object.

"Where does this come from?" I looked up. Kessler was again checking to his rear.

"Israel."

"Mr. Ferris was afraid his life was in danger?"

"Terrified. Said if the photo came to light there'd be havoc."

"What sort of havoc?"

"I don't know." Kessler raised two palms. "Look, I have no idea what the picture is. I don't know what it means. I agreed to keep it. That's it. That's my role."

"What was your connection to Mr. Ferris?"

"We were business associates."

I held out the photo. Kessler dropped his hands to his sides.

"Tell Detective Ryan what you've told me," I said.

Kessler stepped back. "You know what I know."

At that moment my cell sounded. I slipped it from my belt.

Pelletier.

"Got another call about Bellemare."

Kessler sidestepped me and moved toward the family room.

I waggled the print. Kessler shook his head no and hurried down the hall.

"Are you ready to release the Cowboy?"

"I'm on my way up."

"*Bon.* Sister's busting her bloomers for a burial."

When I disconnected and turned, the hall was empty. Fine. I'd give the photo to Ryan. He'd have a copy of the list of observers. If he wanted to follow up, he could get contact information for Kessler.

I pressed for the elevator.

By noon I'd completed my report on Charles Bellemare, concluding that, however strange the circumstances, the Cowboy's last ride had been the result of his own folly. Turn on. Tune in. Drop out. Or down, in Bellemare's case. What had he been doing up there?

At lunch, LaManche informed me there'd be difficulty viewing Ferris's head wounds in situ. X-rays showed only one bullet fragment, and indicated the back of the skull and the left half of the face were shattered. He also informed me that my analysis would be critical since mutilation by the cats had distorted the patterning of metallic trace observable on X-ray.

In addition, Ferris had fallen with his hands beneath him. Decomposition had rendered gunshot-residue testing inconclusive.

At one-thirty I descended again to the morgue.

Ferris's torso was now open from throat to pubis, and his organs floated in covered containers. The stench in the room had kicked into the red zone.

Ryan and the photographer were there, along with two of the morning's four observers. LaManche waited five minutes, then nodded a go-ahead to his autopsy tech.

Lisa made incisions behind Ferris's ears and across his crown. Using scalpel and fingers, she then teased off the scalp, working from the top toward the back of the skull, stopping periodically to position the case label for photographs. As fragments were freed, LaManche and I observed, diagrammed, then gathered them into containers.

When we'd finished with the top and back of Ferris's head, Lisa retracted the skin from his face, and LaManche and I repeated the procedure, examining, sketching, stepping back for pics. Slowly, we extracted the wreckage that had been Ferris's maxillary, zygomatic, nasal, and temporal bones.

By four what remained of Ferris's face was back in position, and Y-shaped stitching held his belly and chest. The photographer had five rolls of film. LaManche had a ream of diagrams and notes. I had four tubs of bloody shards.

I was cleaning bone fragments when Ryan appeared in the corridor outside my lab. I watched his approach through the window above my sink.

Craggy face, eyes too blue for his own good.

Or mine.

Seeing me, Ryan pressed his palms and nose to the glass. I flicked water at him.

He pushed back and pointed at my door. I mouthed "open," and waved him through, a goofy smile spreading across my face.

Okay. Maybe Ryan isn't so bad for me.

But I had reached that opinion only recently.

For almost a decade Ryan and I had butted heads in an on-again, off-again nonrelationship. Up-down. Yes-no. Hot-cold.

Hot-hot.

I've been attracted to Ryan since the get-go, but there have been more obstacles to acting on that attraction than there were signers of the Declaration.

I believe in the separation of job from play. No watercooler romance for this señorita. No way.

Ryan works homicide. I work the morgue. Professional exclusion clause applies. Obstacle one.

Then there was Ryan himself. Everyone knew his bio. Born in Nova Scotia of Irish parents, young Andrew ended up on the wrong end of a biker's shattered Budweiser bottle. Switching from the dark side, the boy signed on with the good guys and rose to the rank of lieutenant-detective with the provincial police. Grown-up Andrew is kind, intelligent, and strictly straight arrow where his work is concerned.

And widely known as the squad room Lothario. Stud muffin exclusion clause applies. Obstacle two.

But Ryan sweet-talked the loopholes, and, after years of resistance, I finally jumped through. Then obstacle three roared in with the Yule.

Lily. A nineteen-year-old daughter, complete with iPod, belly ring, and Bahamian mother, a flesh-and-blood memento of Ryan's long-ago ride with the Wild Ones.

Though mystified and somewhat daunted by the prospect, Ryan embraced the product of his past and made some decisions about his future. Last Christmas he'd committed to long-distance parenting. That same week he'd asked me to be his roomie.

Whoa, bucko. I gave that plan a veto.

Though I still bunk with my feline compadre, Birdie, Ryan and I are dancing around a preliminary draft of a working arrangement.

So far the dance has been good.

And strictly home turf. We keep it to ourselves.

"How's it going, cupcake?" Ryan asked, coming through the door.

"Good." I added a fragment to those drying on the corkboard.

"That the chimney stiff?" Ryan was eyeing the box holding Charles Bellemare.

"Happy trails for the Cowboy," I said.

"Guy take a hit?"

I shook my head. "Looks like he leaned to when he should have leaned fro. No idea why he was sitting on a chimney ledge." I stripped off my gloves and squeezed soap onto my hands. "Who's the blond guy downstairs?"

"Birch. He'll be working Ferris with me."

"New partner?"

Ryan shook his head. "Loan-over. You think Ferris offed himself?"

I turned and shot Ryan a you-know-better-than-that look.

Ryan gave me an expression of choirboy innocence. "Not trying to rush you."

Yanking paper towels from the holder, I said, "Tell me about him."

Ryan nudged Bellemare aside and rested one haunch on my worktable.

"Family's Orthodox."

"Really?" Mock surprise.

"The Fab Four were here to ensure a kosher autopsy."

"Who were they?" I wadded and tossed the paper towels.

"Rabbi, members of the temple, one brother. You want names?"

I shook my head.

"Ferris was a bit more secular than his kin. Operated an import business from a warehouse out near Mirabel airport. Told the wife he'd be out of town on Thursday and Friday. According to . . ." Ryan pulled out and glanced at a spiral pad.

"Miriam," I supplied.

"Right." Ryan gave me an odd look. "According to Miriam, Ferris was trying to expand the business. He called around four on Wednesday, said he was heading out, and that he'd be back late on Friday. When he didn't arrive by sundown, Miriam figured he'd been delayed and preferred not to drive on the Sabbath."

"Had that happened before?

Ryan nodded. "Ferris wasn't in the habit of phoning home. When he hadn't shown up Saturday night, Miriam started working the speed dial. No one in the family had seen him. Neither had his secretary. Miriam didn't know which accounts he was planning to hit, so she decided to sit tight. Sunday morning she checked the warehouse. Sunday afternoon she filed a missing person report. Cops said they'd investigate if hubby hadn't surfaced by Monday morning."

"Grown man extending his business trip?"

Ryan shrugged one shoulder. "Happens."

"Ferris never left Montreal?"

"LaManche thinks he died not long after his call to Miriam."

"Miriam's story checks out?"

"So far."

"The body was found in a closet?"

Ryan nodded. "Blood and brains all over the walls."

"What kind of closet?"

"Small storage space off an upstairs office."

"Why would cats be in there with him?"

"The door's outfitted with one of those little two-way flaps. Ferris kept food and litter in there."

"He gathered the cats to shoot himself?"

"Maybe they were in there when he took the bullet, maybe they slipped in later. Ferris may have died sitting on a stool, then tumbled off. Somehow his feet ended up jamming the kitty door."

I thought about that.

"Miriam didn't check the closet when she visited on Sunday?"

"No."

"She didn't hear scratching or meowing?"

"The missus is *not* a cat lover. That's why Ferris kept them at work."

"She didn't notice any odor?"

"Apparently Ferris wasn't real fastidious about feline toilette. Miriam said if she'd smelled anything she'd have figured it was Kitty Litter."

"She didn't find the building overly warm?"

"Nope. But if a cat brushed the thermostat after her visit, Ferris would still have been cooking from Sunday till Tuesday."

"Did Ferris have other employees besides the secretary?"

"Nope." Ryan consulted the notes in his spiral. "Courtney Purviance. Miriam calls her a secretary. Purviance prefers the term 'associate.'"

"Is the wife downgrading, or the help upgrading?"

"More likely the former. Appears Purviance played a pretty big role in running the business."

"Where was Purviance on Wednesday?"

"Left early. Bad sinuses."

"Why didn't Purviance find Ferris on Monday?"

"Monday was some kind of Jewish holiday. Purviance took the day off to plant trees."

"Tu B'Shvat."

"Et tu, Brute."

"The festival of trees. Was anything missing?"

"Purviance insists there's nothing in the place worth stealing. Computer's old. Radio's older. Inventory's not valuable. But she's checking."

"How long has she worked for Ferris?"

"Since ninety-eight."

"Anything suspicious in Ferris's background? Known associates? Enemies? Gambling debts? Jilted girlfriend? Boyfriend?"

Ryan shook his head.

"Anything to suggest he was suicidal?"

"I'm digging, but so far zip. Stable marriage. Took the little woman to Boca in January. Business wasn't blazing, but it was producing a steady living. Especially since Purviance hired on, a fact she's not hesitant to mention. According to the family, there were no signs of depression, but Purviance thought he'd been unusually moody in recent weeks."

I remembered Kessler and slipped the photo from the pocket of my lab coat.

"A gift from one of the Fab Four." I held it out. "He thinks it's the reason Ferris is dead."

"Meaning?"

"He thinks it's the reason Ferris is dead."

"You can be a real pain in the ass, Brennan."

"I work at it."

Ryan studied the photo.

"Which of the Fab Four?"

"Kessler."

Floating a brow, Ryan laid down the photo and flipped a page in his spiral.

"You sure?"

"That's the name he gave me."

When Ryan looked up the brow had settled.

"No one named Kessler was cleared for that autopsy."

3

"I'M CERTAIN KESSLER'S THE NAME HE GAVE."

"He was an authorized observer?"

"As opposed to one of the multitudes of Hasidim who haunt these halls?"

Ryan ignored my sarcasm.

"Did Kessler say that's why he was here?"

"No." For some reason Ryan's questions were irking me.

"You'd seen Kessler earlier in the autopsy room?"

"I—"

I'd been distressed over Miriam and Dora Ferris, then distracted by Pelletier's call. Kessler had glasses, a beard, and a black suit. My mind had settled for a cultural stereotype.

I wasn't irked at Ryan. I was irked at myself.

"I just assumed."

"Let's take it from the top."

I told Ryan about the incident in the downstairs corridor.

"So Kessler was in the hall when you left the family room."

"Yes."

"Did you see where he came from?"

"No."

"Where he went?"

"I thought he was going to join Dora and Miriam."

"Did you actually see him enter the family room?"

"I was speaking to Pelletier." It came out sharper than I intended.

"Don't be defensive."

"That was not defensive," I said defensively, and did a two-handed pull to unsnap my lab coat. "That was enlargement of detail."

Ryan picked up Kessler's print.

"What am I looking at?"

"A skeleton."

Ryan's eyes rolled up.

"Kessler—" I stopped. "The mysterious bearded stranger told me it came from Israel."

"The photo *came from* Israel, or was shot there?"

Another screw-up on my part.

"The picture's over forty years old. It's probably meaningless."

"When someone says it caused a death, it's not meaningless."

I reddened.

Ryan flipped the photo as I had. "What's *M de 1 H*?"

"You think that's an *M*?"

Ryan ignored my question.

"What was going on in October of sixty-three?" he asked, more of himself than of me.

"Oswald's thoughts were on JFK."

"Brennan, you can be a real—"

"We've established that."

Crossing to Ryan, I reversed the photo and pointed at the object to the left of the leg bones.

"See that?" I asked.

"It's a paintbrush."

"It's a cocked-up north arrow."

"Meaning?"

"Old archaeologist's trick. If you don't have an official marker to indicate scale and direction, place something in the shot and point it north."

"You think this was taken by an archaeologist?"

"Yes."

"What site?"

"A site with burials."

"Now we're getting somewhere."

"Look, this Kessler's probably a crackpot. Find him and grill him.

Or talk to Miriam Ferris." I flapped a hand at the print. "Maybe she knows why her husband was freaked over this thing." I slipped off my lab coat. "If he *was* freaked over the thing."

Ryan studied the photo for a full minute. Then he looked up and said, "Did you buy the tap pants?"

My cheeks flamed. "No."

"Red satin. Sexy as hell."

I narrowed my eyes in a "not here" warning look. "I'm calling it a day."

Crossing to the closet, I hung up my lab coat and emptied the pockets. Emptied my libido.

When I returned, Ryan was on his feet, but again staring at Kessler's photo.

"Think any of your paleo pals might recognize this?"

"I can make a few calls."

"Couldn't hurt."

At the door Ryan turned and flashed his brows.

"See you later?"

"Wednesday's my tai chi night."

"Tomorrow?"

"You're on."

Ryan pointed one finger and winked. "Tap pants."

My Montreal condo is on the ground floor of a U-shaped low-rise. One bedroom, one study, two baths, living-dining room, a walk-through kitchen narrow enough to stand at the sink and pivot to reach the fridge behind you.

Through one kitchen archway, I cross a hall to French doors opening onto a central courtyard. Through the other kitchen archway, I cross through a living room to French doors opening onto a tiny enclosed yard.

Stone fireplace. Nice woodwork. Ample closets. Underground parking.

Nothing fancy. The building's selling point is that it's smack downtown. Centre-ville. Everything I need is within two blocks of my bed.

Birdie didn't appear at the sound of my key.

"Hey, Bird."

No cat.

"Chirp."

"Hey, Charlie."

"Chirp. Chirp."

"Birdie?"

"Chirp. Chirp. Chirp. Chirp. Chirp." Wolf whistle.

Stuffing my coat into the closet, I dropped my laptop in the study, deposited my take-out lasagna in the kitchen, and continued through the far archway.

Birdie was in his sphinx pose, legs tucked, head up, front paws curled inward. When I joined him on the love seat, he glanced up, then refocused on the cage to his right.

Charlie tipped his head and eyed me through the bars.

"How are my boys?" I asked.

Birdie ignored me.

Charlie hopped to his seed dish and gave another wolf whistle followed by a chirp.

"My day? Tiring, but disaster-free." I didn't mention Kessler.

Charlie cocked his head and viewed me with his left eye.

Nothing from the cat.

"Glad you two are getting along."

And they were.

The cockatiel was this year's Christmas present from Ryan. Though I'd been less than enthused, given my cross-border lifestyle, Birdie had been smitten at first sight.

Upon my rejection of his bid for cohabitation, Ryan had proposed joint custody. When I was in Montreal, Charlie would be mine. When I was in Charlotte, Charlie and Ryan would batch it. Birdie usually traveled with me.

This arrangement was working, and cat and cockatiel were firmly bonded.

I moved to the kitchen.

"Road trip," Charlie squawked. "Don't forget the bird."

I was lousy at tai chi that night, but afterward I slept like a rock. Okay, lasagna isn't great for "Grasp Sparrow's Tail" or "White Crane Spreads Its Wings," but it kicks ass for "Internal Stillness."

I was up at seven the next morning, in the lab by eight.

I spent my first hour identifying, marking, and inventorying the fragments from Avram Ferris's head. I wasn't yet undertaking an in-depth examination, but I was noticing details, and a picture was emerging. A baffling picture.

That morning's staff meeting ran the usual roster of the brainless, the brutal, and the sadly banal.

A twenty-seven-year-old male electrocuted himself by urinating in the track bed at the Lucien-L'Allier metro.

A Boisbriand carpenter bludgeoned his wife of thirty years during an argument over who would go out for logs.

A fifty-nine-year-old crackhead overdosed in a pay-by-the-night flophouse near the Chinatown gate.

Nothing for the anthropologist.

At nine-twenty, I returned to my office and phoned Jacob Drum, a colleague at UNC-Charlotte. His voice mail answered. I left a message asking that he return my call.

I'd been with the fragments another hour when the phone rang.

"Hey, Tempe."

In greeting, we Southerners say "hey" not "hi." To alert, draw the attention of, or show objection to another, we also say "hey," but air is expelled and the ending is truncated. This was an airless, four-A "hey."

"Hey, Jake."

"Won't get above fifty in Charlotte today. Cold up there?"

In winter, Southerners delight in querying Canadian weather. In summer, interest plummets.

"It's cold." The predicted high was in negative figures.

"Going where the weather suits my clothes."

"Off to dig?" Jake was a biblical archaeologist who'd been excavating in the Middle East for almost three decades.

"Yes, ma'am. Doing a first-century synagogue. Been planning it for months. Crew's set. Got my regulars in Israel, meeting up with a field supervisor in Toronto on Saturday. Just finalizing my own travel arrangements now. Pain in the gumpy. Do you have any idea how rare these things are?"

Gumpies?

"There are first-century synagogues at Masada and Gamla. That's about it."

"Sounds like a terrific opportunity. Listen, I'm glad I caught you. Got a favor to ask."

"Shoot."

I described Kessler's print, leaving out specifics as to how I'd obtained it.

"Pic was shot in Israel?"

"I'm told it came from Israel."

"It dates to the sixties?"

"'October '63' is written on the back. And some kind of notation. Maybe an address."

"Pretty vague."

"Yes."

"I'll be glad to check it out."

"I'll scan the image and send it by e-mail."

"I'm not optimistic."

"I appreciate your willingness to take a look."

I knew what was coming. Jake reran the shtick like a bad beer ad.

"You gotta come dig with us, Tempe. Get back to your archaeological roots."

"There's nothing I'd like better, but I can't take off now."

"One of these days."

"One of these days."

After our call, I hurried to the imaging section, scanned Kessler's photo, and transferred the .jpg file to the computer in my lab. Then I hurried back, logged on, and transmitted the image to Jake's in-box at UNCC.

Back to Ferris's shattered head.

Cranial fractures show tremendous variability in patterning. The successful interpretation of any given pattern rests on an understanding of the biomechanical properties of bone, combined with a knowledge of the intrinsic and extrinsic factors involved in fracture production.

Simple, right? Like quantum physics.

Though bone seems rigid, it actually has a certain amount of elasticity. When subjected to stress, a bone yields and changes shape. When its limits of elastic deformation are exceeded, the bone fails, or fractures.

That's the biomechanical bit.

In the head, fractures travel the paths of least resistance. These paths are determined by things such as vault curvature, bony buttressing, and sutures, the squiggly junctures between individual bones.

Those are the intrinsic factors.

Extrinsic factors include the size, speed, and angle of the impacting object.

Think of it this way. The skull is a sphere with bumps and curves and gaps. There are predictable ways in which that sphere fails when walloped by an impacting object. Both a .22-caliber bullet and a two-inch pipe are impacting objects. The bullet's just moving a whole lot faster and striking a smaller area.

You get the idea.

Despite the massive damage, I knew I was seeing an atypical pattern in Ferris's head. The more I looked, the more uneasy I grew.

I was placing an occipital fragment under the microscope when the phone rang. It was Jake Drum. This time there was no leisurely "hey."

"Where did you say you got this photo?"

"I didn't. It—"

"Who gave it to you?"

"A man named Kessler. But—"

"Do you still have it?"

"Yes."

"How long will you be in Montreal?"

"I'm leaving for a quick trip to the States on Saturday, but—"

"If I divert to Montreal tomorrow, can you show me the original?"

"Yes. Jake—"

"I've got to phone the airlines." His voice was so taut it could have moored the *Queen Mary.* "In the meantime, hide that print."

I was listening to a dial tone.

4

I STARED AT THE PHONE.

What could be so important that Jake would change plans he'd been making for months?

I centered Kessler's photo on my blotter.

If I was right about the paintbrush, the body was oriented north–south with the head facing east. The wrists were crossed on the belly. The legs were fully extended.

Except for some displacement of the pelvic and foot bones, everything looked anatomically correct.

Too correct.

A patella sat perfectly positioned at the end of each femur. No way kneecaps stay in place that well.

Something else was off.

The right fibula was on the inside of the right tibia. It should have been on the outside.

Conclusion: the scene had been doctored.

Had an archaeologist tidied the bones for a pic, or did the repositioning reflect some meaning?

I carried the photo to the scope, lowered the power, and positioned the fiber-optic light.

The soil around the bones was marked with footprints. Under magnification, I could make out at least two sole patterns.

Conclusion: more than one person had been present.

I took a shot at gender.

The skull's orbital ridges were large, the jaw square. Only the right half of the pelvis was visible, but the sciatic notch looked narrow and deep.

Conclusion: the individual was male, more probably than not.

I shifted to age.

The upper dentition looked relatively complete. The lower dentition had gaps and teeth in poor alignment. The right pubic symphysis, one of the surfaces at which the pelvic halves meet in front, was tipped toward the lens. Though the photo was grainy, the symphyseal face looked smooth and flat.

Conclusion: the individual was a young to middle-aged adult. Possibly.

Terrific, Brennan. A grown-up dead guy with bad teeth and rearranged bones. Possibly.

"Now we're getting somewhere," I mimicked Ryan.

The clock said one-forty. I was starving.

Removing my lab coat, I clicked off the fiber-optic light and washed up. At the door, I hesitated.

Returning to the scope, I collected the photo and slid it under an agenda in my desk drawer.

By three I was no clearer on the Ferris fragments than I'd been at noon. If anything, I was more frustrated.

People can reach only so far. They shoot themselves in the forehead, the temple, the mouth, the chest. They do not shoot themselves in the spine or the back of the head. It's too hard to position a barrel there and keep a finger or toe on the trigger. So bullet path can often be used to distinguish suicide from homicide.

Blasting through bone, a bullet dislodges small particles from the perimeter of the hole it creates, beveling an entrance wound internally, and an exit wound externally.

Bullet in. Bullet out. Trajectory. Manner of death.

So what was the problem? Did Avram Ferris put a gun to his own head, or did someone else do the honors?

The problem was that the affected parts of Ferris's skull looked like puzzle pieces dumped from a box. To consider beveling, I'd first have to determine what went where.

Hours of jigsawing had allowed me to identify one oval defect behind Ferris's right ear, near the junction of the parietal, occipital, and temporal sutures.

Within Ferris's reach? A stretch, but you betcha.

Another problem. The hole was beveled on both its endocranial and ectocranial surfaces.

Forget beveling. I was going to have to rely on fracture sequencing.

A skull is designed to house a brain and a very small quantity of fluid. That's it. No room for guests.

A bullet to the head sets up a series of events, each of which may be present, absent, or appear in combination with any other.

First, a hole is created. As that happens, fractures starburst outward and wrap the skull. The bullet tunnels through the brain, pushing aside gray matter and creating space where space isn't meant to be. Intracranial pressure rises, concentric heaving fractures develop perpendicular to the fractures radiating from the entrance, and plates of bone lever outward. If heaving and radiating fractures intersect, blam-o! That section of skull shatters.

Another scenario. No shattering, but the bullet says adios on the far side of the skull. Fractures barrel backward from the exit hole and slam into those hotfooting it around from the entrance hole. Energy dissipates along the preexisting entrance fractures, and the exit fractures go no farther.

Think of it this way. A bullet to the brain imparts energy. That trapped energy has to go somewhere. Like all of us, it looks for the easy out. In a skull that means open sutures or preexisting cracks. Bottom line: fractures created by a bullet's exit will not cross fractures created by its entrance. Sort it out and you've got sequence.

But sorting out the dead ends requires reconstruction.

There was no getting around it. I'd have to put the pieces back together.

That would take time and patience.

And a lot of glue.

I got out my stainless steel bowls, my sand, and my Elmer's. Pair by pair I joined fragments and held them until the bonding set. Then I placed the mini-reconstructions upright in the sand, positioned so they'd dry without slippage or distortion.

The lab techs' boom box went silent.

The windows darkened.

A bell sounded, indicating the house phones had rolled to night service.

I worked on, selecting, manipulating, gluing, balancing. Silence settled around me, grew loud within the after-hours-big-building emptiness.

When I looked up, the clock said six-twenty.

Why was that wrong?

Ryan was due at my condo at seven!

Flying to the sink, I washed my hands, tore off my lab coat, grabbed my belongings, and bolted.

Outside, a cold rain was falling. No. That's being kind. The stuff was sleet. Icy slush that clung to my jacket and burned my cheeks.

It took ten minutes to hack through the glacier on my windshield, another thirty to make a drive that was normally fifteen.

When I arrived, Ryan was wall-leaning outside my door, a bag of groceries beside his feet.

There exists some indissoluble law of nature. When encountering Andrew Ryan, I look my worst.

And Ryan looks like something sketched out by a matinee-idol planning committee. Always.

Tonight he wore a bomber jacket, striped woolen muffler, and faded jeans.

Ryan smiled when he saw me, purse drooping from one shoulder, laptop in my left hand, briefcase in my right. My cheeks were chapped, my hair wet and plastered to my face. Runoff had turned my mascara to an Impressionist study in sludge.

"Dogs got tangled in the traces?"

"It's sleeting."

"I think you're supposed to yell 'mush.'"

Ryan pushed from the wall, relieved me of the computer with one hand, and with the other brushed aside my bangs. Several held form as a solid clump.

"Close encounter with Dippity-do?"

"I've been gluing." I dug out my keys.

Ryan moved to the cusp of a comment, held back. Bending, he snatched up his bag and followed me into the condo.

"Chirp?"

"Charlie, boy," Ryan called out.

"Chirp. Chirp. Chirp. Chirp. Chirp."

"You and Charlie spend some quality time," I said. "I'm going to de-glue."

"Tap pant—"

"I didn't even order them, Ryan."

In twenty minutes I'd showered, shampooed, blow-dried, and applied subtle but artful maquillage. I sported pink cords, a body-molding top, and Issey Miyaki behind each ear.

No tap pants, but a man-killer thong. Dusty rose. Not the undies my mother would have worn.

Ryan was in the kitchen. The condo smelled of tomatoes, anchovies, garlic, and oregano.

"Making your world-famous puttanesca?" I asked, stretching to tiptoes to kiss Ryan on the cheek.

"Whoa." Ryan wrapped me in his arms and kissed me on the mouth. Fingering my waistband, he pulled outward, and peered down my back.

"Not tap pants. But not bad."

I did a two-handed push from his chest.

"You really didn't order them?"

"I really didn't order them."

Birdie appeared, looked disapproving, then strolled to his bowl.

During dinner, I described my frustration with the Ferris case. Over coffee and dessert, Ryan gave an update on his investigation.

"Ferris was an importer of ritual clothing. Yarmulkes, talliths."

Ryan misread my expression.

"The tallith's the prayer shawl."

"I'm impressed you know that." Like me, Ryan was raised Catholic.

"I looked it up. Why the face?"

"Seems it would be a very small market."

"Ferris also handled ritual articles for the home. Menorahs, mezuzahs, Shabbat candles, kiddush cups, challah covers. I plan to look those up."

Ryan offered the pastry plate. There was one *mille feuille* left. I wanted it. I shook my head. Ryan took it.

"Ferris sold throughout Quebec, Ontario, and the Maritimes. It wasn't Wal-Mart, but he made a living."

"You talked again with the secretary?"

"Appears Purviance really is more than a secretary. Handles the books, tracks inventory, travels to Israel and the States to evaluate product, schmooze suppliers."

"Israel's tough duty these days."

"Purviance spent time on a kibbutz back in the eighties, so she knows her way around. And she speaks English, French, Hebrew, and Arabic."

"Impressive."

"Father was French. Mother was Tunisian. Anyway, Purviance tells the same story. Business doing well. Not an enemy in the world. Though she did feel Ferris had been more moody than usual in the days leading up to his death. I'll give her a day to finish with the warehouse, then we'll have another little chat."

"Did you find Kessler?"

Ryan crossed to the couch and dug a paper from his jacket. Returning to the table, he handed it to me.

"These were the people cleared for autopsy patrol."

I read the names.

Mordecai Ferris
Theodore Moskowitz
Myron Neulander
David Rosenbaum

"No Kessler." I stated the obvious. "Did you locate anyone who knows the guy?"

"Talking to the family's like talking to cement. They're doing *aninut.*"

"*Aninut?*"

"First stage of mourning."

"How long does *aninut* last?"

"Until interment."

I pictured the cranial segments taking shape in my sand bowls.

"Could be a long one."

"Ferris's wife told me to come back when the family's finished sitting shiva. That lasts a week. I suggested I'd be dropping by sooner."

"This must be a nightmare for her."

"Interesting sidebar. Ferris was insured for two million big ones, with a double-up clause for accidental death."

"Miriam?"

Ryan nodded. "They had no kids."

I told Ryan about my conversation with Jake Drum. "I can't imagine why he's coming here."

"Think he'll really show?"

I'd wondered that myself.

"The hesitation tells me you've got your doubts," Ryan said. "This guy a flake?"

"Jake's not flaky. Just different."

"Different?"

"Jake's a brilliant archaeologist. Worked at Qumran."

Ryan gave me quizzical look.

"Dead Sea scrolls. He can translate a zillion languages."

"Any that are spoken today?"

I threw a napkin at Ryan.

After clearing the table, Ryan and I stretched out on the sofa. Birdie flopped by the fire.

We talked of personal things.

Ryan's daughter in Halifax. Lily was dating a guitarist and considering a move to Vancouver. Ryan feared the items were not unrelated.

Katy. For her twelfth and final semester at the University of Virginia, my daughter was taking pottery, fencing, and a class on the feminine mystique in modern film. Her independent study involved interviewing patrons of pubs.

Birdie purred. Or snored.

Charlie squawked and resquawked a line from "Hard-Hearted Hannah."

The fire crackled and popped. Ice ticked the windows.

After a while everyone drifted into silence.

Ryan reached back and pulled the lamp chain. Amber light danced the familiar shapes in my home.

Ryan and I lay molded like tango dancers, my head nestled below his collarbone. He smelled of soap and the logs he'd carried in for the fire. His fingers caressed my hair. My cheek. My neck.

I felt content. Calm. A million miles from skeletons and shattered skulls.

Ryan is built on sinewy, ropelike lines. Long ones. Eventually I felt one line grow longer.

We left Birdie in charge of the hearth.

5

RYAN LEFT EARLY THE NEXT MORNING. SOMETHING ABOUT ALL-weather radials and balance and a warped rim. I am not a good listener at 7 A.M. Nor am I the least bit interested in tires.

I am interested in air routing between Charlotte and Montreal. I can recite the entire USAirways flight schedule. Knowing the daily direct flight had been eliminated, I was certain Jake wouldn't arrive before midafternoon. I rolled over and went back to sleep.

A bagel and coffee around eight, and I headed to the lab. I was leaving for five days, and knew the Ferris family was anxious for information.

And for the body.

I spent another Elmer's morning joining the dozens of segments I'd built the day before. Like assembling atoms into molecules into whole cells, I built larger and larger sections of vault.

The facial bones were a different story. Splintering was extensive, either due to the cats, or simply due to the fragile nature of the bones themselves. There would be no reconstructing the left side of Ferris's face.

Nevertheless, a pattern emerged.

Though the lines were complex, it appeared that no break crossed the starburst radiating from the hole behind Ferris's right ear. Fracture sequencing pointed to that wound as the entrance.

But why were the hole's edges beveled on the outside of the skull? An entrance site should have been beveled on the inside.

I could think of one explanation, but fragments were missing from the area immediately above and to the left of the defect. To be certain, I'd need those fragments.

At two I wrote LaManche a note, explaining what I lacked. I reminded him that I was going to the annual meeting of the American Academy of Forensic Sciences in New Orleans, and that I would return to Montreal Wednesday night.

For the next two hours I ran errands. Bank. Dry cleaner. Cat chow. Birdseed. Ryan had agreed to take Birdie and Charlie, but the man has interesting views on pet care. I wanted to raise the odds in favor of proper feeding.

Jake phoned as I was driving underground into my garage. He was in the outer vestibule. Hurrying upstairs, I let him in the front door and led him down the corridor to my condo.

As we walked, I remembered the first time I'd laid eyes on Jake Drum. I was new to UNCC, and had met few faculty members outside my discipline. None from the Department of Religious Studies. Jake appeared in my lab late one evening, at a time when assaults on female students had caused security announcements to be broadcast campus-wide.

I was nervous as a mouse staring across a tank at an underweight python.

My fears were ungrounded. Jake had a question concerning bone preservation.

"Tea?" I offered now.

"You bet. I got pretzels and Sprite on the plane."

"The dishes are behind you."

I watched Jake select mugs, thinking what a terrible perp he'd make. His nose is thin and prominent, his brows bushy and dead straight above Rasputin black eyes. He stands six feet six, weighs 170, and shaves his head.

Witnesses would remember Jake exactly as he is.

Today I suspected he'd caused strangers on the sidewalk to circle wide. His agitation was palpable.

We exchanged small talk while waiting for the kettle.

Jake had checked into a small hotel off the western edge of the

McGill University campus. He'd rented a car to drive to Toronto the next morning. On Monday he'd leave for Jerusalem, where he and his Israeli crew would excavate their first-century synagogue.

Jake proffered his usual invitation to dig. I proffered my usual thanks and regrets.

When the tea was ready, Jake settled at the dining room table. I retrieved a magnifier and Kessler's print and laid them on the glass.

Jake stared at the photo as though he'd never seen one before.

After a full minute, he took up the lens. As he scanned the print his movements grew measured and deliberate.

In one way Jake and I are very much alike.

When annoyed, I grow churlish, snap, counter with sarcasm. When angry, truly white-hot livid irate, I go deadly calm.

So does Jake. I know. I've heard him debate issues at faculty council.

The ice facade is also my response to fear. I suspected this was also true of Jake. The change in his demeanor sent a chill scurrying through my mind.

"What is it?" I asked.

Jake raised his head and stared past me, lost, I could only guess, in a moment of probes, and trowels, and the smell of turned earth.

Then he tapped the photo with one long, slender finger.

A disjointed thought. Were it not for the calluses, Jake's hands might have been those of a concert pianist.

"Have you spoken with the man who gave this to you?"

"Only briefly. We're trying to locate him."

"What exactly did he say?"

I hesitated, debating what I could ethically divulge. Ferris's death had been reported by the media. Kessler had not asked for confidentiality.

I explained the shooting, the autopsy, and the man who called himself Kessler.

"It's supposed to have come from Israel."

"It does," Jake said.

"That's a hunch?"

"That's a fact."

I frowned. "You're that certain?"

Jake leaned back. "What do you know about Masada?"

"It's a peak in Israel where a lot of folks died."

Jake's lips did something approaching a smile.

"Please expand, Ms. Brennan."

I dug back. Way back.

"In the first century B.C.—"

"Politically incorrect. The term is B.C.E now. Before the Common Era."

"—the whole area from Syria to Egypt, anciently known as the land of Israel, which the Romans called Palestine, came under Roman rule. Needless to say, the Jews were pissed. Over the next century, a number of rebellions arose to throw the Roman bastards out. Each was a bust."

"I've never heard it put in quite those terms. Go on."

"About sixty-six A.D., sorry, C.E., yet another Jewish revolt steamrolled across the region. This one scared the sandals off the Romans, and the emperor deployed troops to suppress the insurgents."

I tunneled deep for dates.

"About five years into the revolt the Roman general Vespasian conquered Jerusalem, sacked the temple, and routed the survivors."

"And Masada?"

"Masada's a giant rock in the Judean desert. At the start of the war a group of Jewish zealots hiked it to the top and hunkered in. The Roman general— I'm blanking on the name."

"Flavius Silva."

"That's the guy. Silva was not amused. Masada was a pocket of defiance he would not tolerate. Silva set up perimeter camps, constructed an encircling wall, then an enormous ramp up the side of Masada. When his troops finally rolled a battering ram up the incline and breached the fortress, they found everyone dead."

I didn't mention my source, but I remembered all this from an early-eighties miniseries on Masada. Peter O'Toole as Silva?

"Excellent. Though your telling lacks a certain sense of scale. Silva didn't just march a few platoons to Masada. His operation was massive, including his entire Tenth Legion, its auxiliary troops, and thousands of Jewish prisoners of war. Silva didn't intend to leave until the rebels were subjugated."

"Who was in charge up top?"

"Eleazar ben Ya'ir. The Jews had been up there seven years, and were as committed to staying as Silva was to ousting them."

More miniseries memory bytes. Decades earlier, Herod had been into major development at Masada, ordering a casement wall around the top, defense towers, storehouses, barracks, arsenals, and a cistern system for catching and storing rainwater. Seventy years after the old king's death, the warehouses were still stocked, and the zealots had everything they needed.

"The main source on Masada is Flavius Josephus," Jake went on. "Joseph ben Matatyahu, in Hebrew. At the beginning of the sixty-six revolt, Josephus was serving as a Jewish commander in Galilee. Later he went over to the Romans. Regardless of his loyalties or disloyalties, the guy was a brilliant historian."

"And the only reporter in town at the time."

"There is that. But Josephus' descriptions are amazingly detailed. According to his account, the night the fortress was breached, Eleazar ben Ya'ir gathered his followers."

Jake leaned forward and set the scene.

"Picture this. The wall was burning. The Romans would pour in at dawn. There was no hope of escape. Ben Ya'ir argued that a death of glory was preferable to a life of slavery. Lots were cast, and ten men were elected to kill all the others. Another set of lots determined who among the ten would kill his fellow assassins, and, finally, himself."

"There were no dissenters?"

"If so, those opinions were overruled. Two women and several children did hide out and survive. Most of Josephus' information came from them."

"How many died?"

"Nine hundred and sixty men, women, and children," Jake said, his voice soft. "Jews view Masada as one of the most dramatic episodes in their history. Especially Israeli Jews."

"What does Masada have to do with Kessler's photo?"

"The fate of the remains of the Jewish zealots has always been a mystery. According to Josephus, Silva established a garrison on the summit immediately after Masada's conquest."

"Surely Masada has been excavated."

"For years, every digger on the planet was drooling for a permit. An

Israeli archaeologist named Yigael Yadin finally got the nod. Yadin worked for two field seasons using a team of volunteers. The first lasted from October of sixty-three until May of sixty-four, the second from November of sixty-four until April of sixty-five."

I had my first inkling where Jake was going.

"Yadin's team recovered human remains?"

"Three skeletons. On the lower terrace of Herod's palace villa."

"Palace villa?"

"The periodic uprisings kept the old boy nervous, so he fortified Masada as a sort of safe house should he and his family ever need to escape. And Herod wasn't into discomfort. In addition to the wall and defensive towers, he commissioned palaces complete with colonnades, mosaics, frescoes, terraces, gardens, the whole nine yards."

I pointed to the photo. "This is one of the three?"

Jake shook his head. "According to Yadin, one was the skeleton of a male in his twenties. Not far away lay the bones of a young woman, her sandals and scalp perfectly preserved. I'm not kidding. I've seen the pictures. The woman's hair looked like she'd braided it the morning she was unearthed."

"Aridity makes for great preservation."

"Yes. Though the remains weren't exactly as Yadin interpreted them."

"What do you mean?"

"It's not important. According to Yadin, the third skeleton was that of a child."

"What about this guy?" Again, I pointed at Kessler's photo.

"This guy." Jake's jaw muscles bunched, relaxed. "This guy wasn't supposed to be up there at all."

6

"NOT SUPPOSED TO BE UP THERE?"

"That's my theory."

"Anyone share it?"

"Some."

"Who is he?"

"That's the puzzler."

I sat back and assumed a listening posture.

"Following their victory, Silva's troops would have thrown the zealots' bodies over the cliffs, or buried the corpses communally somewhere on the summit. Yadin's team dug some test trenches, but found no evidence of a mass grave. Wait a sec."

Jake pulled two items from a battered leather briefcase, and placed them on the table. The first was a map.

I scooted my chair close and we both leaned in.

"Masada is shaped like a Stealth aircraft, with one wing pointing north, the other pointing south, and the cockpit pointing west."

My mind Rorschach-ed an amoeba, but I kept it to myself.

Jake indicated the upper edge of the summit, near the tip of his Stealth's southern wing.

"There's a network of caves here, a few yards below the casement wall."

Jake slid the second item from under the map.

Old black-and-white print. Human bones. Boot-scuffed dirt.

Kessler déjà vu.

But not quite.

In this photo the bones of many people were scattered and jumbled. Also, this shot had an official north arrow/scale marker, and, in the upper right corner, an arm and knee could be seen as an excavator brushed something lying in the dirt.

"Yadin's team found skeletal remains in one of the southern summit caves," I guessed, not taking my eyes from the print. "This shot was taken during excavation."

"Yes." Jake indicated a spot on the Masada diagram. "The locus was designated Cave 2001. Yadin mentions it in his preliminary report on the Masada project, and includes a brief description by Yoram Tsafrir, the supervising excavator of the locus."

"Minimum number of individuals in the cave?" I asked, counting at least five skulls.

"Depends on how you read Yadin."

I looked up, surprised. "MNI shouldn't be that tough to determine. Did a physical anthropologist examine the bones?"

"Dr. Nicu Haas of Hebrew University. Based on Haas's evaluation, in his first field season report, Yadin gave a total of twenty-five individuals: fourteen males, six females, four children, and one fetus. But, if you read his wording carefully, he treated one very old male as separate from the other males."

"Bringing his actual total to twenty-six."

"Exactly. In his popular book—"

"The one that came out in sixty-six?"

"Right. *Masada: Herod's Fortress and the Zealots' Last Stand.* In that publication, Yadin does basically the same thing, saying Haas found fourteen males aged twenty-two to sixty, one male over seventy, six females, four kids, and a fetus."

"So it's unclear whether the total count was twenty-five or twenty-six?"

"You're quick."

"Blistering. Could be an honest error."

"It could be." Jake's voice suggested he didn't believe it.

"Ages of the women and children?"

"The kids were eight to twelve years. The women were all young, fifteen to twenty-two."

Sudden insight. "You think our fellow here is the septuagenarian?" I tapped Kessler's photo.

"I'll get to him in a minute. For now, let me focus on the cave. In their reports, neither Tsafrir nor Yadin indicated when Cave 2001 was discovered or when it was cleared."

"Could be just sloppy—"

He cut me off.

"The find was never announced to the media."

"Perhaps that was done out of respect for the dead."

"Yadin called a press conference when the three palace skeletons were found." Jake shook his hands, fingers splayed like E.T. "Big excitement. We've got remains of the Jewish defenders of Masada. This was late November of sixty-three. Cave 2001 was discovered and cleared in October of sixty-three, one month *before* that press conference."

Jake's index finger augured into the photo.

"Yadin knew about the cave bones and never brought them up."

"If the dates weren't made public, how do *you* know when the cave was discovered or excavated?"

"I've spoken with a volunteer who worked the site. The guy's trustworthy, and he'd have no reason to lie. And believe me, I've researched the media coverage. It wasn't just *that* press conference. Throughout both dig seasons the media reported regularly on what was being found at Masada. The *Jerusalem Post* keeps topical archives, and I've spent hours with their Masada file. Articles mention mosaics, scrolls, the synagogue, the *mikvehs,* the three skeletons from the northern palace. There's not a single word on the remains from Cave 2001."

Jake was on a roll.

"And I'm not just talking the *Post.* In October of sixty-four the *Illustrated London News* published an extensive spread on Masada, pictures and all. The palace skeletons are mentioned, no respect for the dead there, but there's zilch on the cave bones."

Charlie chose that moment to yodel.

"What the hell is that?"

"My cockatiel. He doesn't usually do that unless you give him beer."

"You're kidding." Jake sounded shocked.

"Of course." I stood and gathered our mugs. "Charlie gets quite maudlin when he drinks. More tea?"

Jake smiled and held out his mug. "Please."

When I returned, Jake was working a kink from his neck. I thought of a goose.

"Let me get this straight," I said. "Yadin talked freely about the palace skeletons, but never once discussed the cave bones publicly?"

"The only mention I've ever found of Cave 2001 is in coverage of Yadin's press conference following the second season's excavation. In the *Jerusalem Post* on March 28, 1965, Yadin is quoted as lamenting that only twenty-eight skeletons had been found at Masada."

"Twenty-five from the cave, and three from the northern palace."

"If it was twenty-five."

I rolled that around in my head.

"Who did Yadin think these cave burials were?"

"Jewish zealots."

"Based on what?"

"Two things. Associated artifacts, and similarity of the skulls to a type unearthed in the Bar Kochba caves in Nahal Hever. At the time, those burials were thought to be Jews killed in the second Jewish revolt against Rome."

"Were they?"

"Turned out the bones were Chalcolithic."

Mental Rolodex. Chalcolithic. Stone and copper tools. Fourth millennium B.C.E., after the Neolithic, before the Bronze Age. Way too early for Masada.

"Physical anthropologists hold little confidence in skull typing," I said.

"I know. But that was Haas's conclusion, and Yadin accepted it."

There was a long, thoughtful silence. I broke it.

"Where are the bones now?"

"Allegedly, everyone's back in the ground at Masada."

"Allegedly?"

Jake's mug clunked the tabletop.

"Let me fast-forward a bit. In his popular book, Yadin touched briefly on the human remains recovered in Cave 2001. Shlomo Lorinez, an ultra-Orthodox member of the Knesset, read the thing and went ballistic. He'd missed the one press report back in sixty-five in which the skeletons were mentioned. Lorinez mounted a protest in the Knesset, charging that cynical archaeologists and medical researchers were violating Jewish law. He demanded to know where the remains were, and insisted on proper burial for the defenders of Masada.

"Major public controversy. The religious affairs minister and the chief rabbis proposed placement of all Masada bones in a Jewish cemetery on the Mount of Olives. Yadin objected, and suggested interment of the three palace skeletons at Masada, but reburial of the Cave 2001 folks in the cave in which they'd been found. Yadin was trumped, and in July of sixty-nine, all remains went back into the ground near the tip of the Roman ramp."

I was finding this very confusing. Why would Yadin have opposed reburial of the cave bones on the Mount of Olives? Why suggest reburial of the palace skeletons on Masada, but return of the cave bones to the cave? Was it a question of keeping the cave folks off holy ground? Or was he uncomfortable with the idea of the cave folks and the palace folks sharing the same grave?

Charlie broke my chain of thought with a line from "Hey, Big Spender."

"Did anything else turn up with the cave bones?" I asked.

"A lot of domestic utensils. Cooking pots, lamps, basketry."

"Suggesting the caves had been lived in."

Jake nodded.

"By whom?"

"It was wartime. Jerusalem was toast. All sorts of refugees might have fled to high ground. Some might have lived apart from the zealot community."

Ah-hah. "So those in the cave could have been non-Jews?"

Solemn nod.

"Not what Israel wanted to publicize."

"Not at all. Masada had become its sacred emblem. Jews making their last stand, choosing suicide over surrender. The site was a metaphor for the new state. Until recently, the Israeli military held special ceremonies inducting troops into their elite units on top of Masada."

"Ouch."

"According to Tsafrir, the cave bones were in disarray, with clothing fragments intermingled among them, as though the bodies had been dumped," Jake said. "That's not a typical pattern for Jewish burial."

Birdie chose that moment to hop onto my lap.

I made introductions. Jake scratched the cat's ear, then picked up his thread.

"To date, the Israel Exploration Society has published five volumes on the Masada excavation. Volume three notes that the caves were surveyed and excavated, but, aside from that, and a map with an outline drawing of Cave 2001, there's no mention anywhere of anything found at that locus, human or material."

Jake leaned back and picked up his mug. Lowered it.

"Wait. Change that. There is an addendum at the back of volume four. A carbon-fourteen report on textiles found in the cave. That testing was done years later. But that's it."

Displacing Birdie to the floor, I slid Kessler's photo from below Jake's Masada diagram.

"So where does this guy fit in?"

"That's where things get really weird. Cave 2001 contained the remains of one fully intact skeleton completely separate from the intermingled bones. The individual was supine, with hands crossed, head turned to the side." Jake impaled me with a look. "Not a single report mentions that articulated skeleton."

"I assume you learned about the skeleton from this same volunteer who worked the cave back in the sixties."

Jake nodded.

"This is the part where you tell me that the articulated skeleton wasn't reburied with the others," I guessed.

"This is the part." Jake drained his mug. "Press coverage of the reinterment consistently refers to twenty-seven individuals, three from the northern palace, and twenty-four from the cave."

"Not twenty-five or twenty-six. Maybe they left out the fetus."

"I'm convinced they left out the fetus *and* the articulated skeleton."

"Let me get this straight. You're saying a volunteer excavator, an eyewitness, told you personally that he and Tsafrir recovered a fully articulated skeleton from Cave 2001. But no such skeleton was ever mentioned in press coverage, or in Yadin's official report or popular book."

Jake nodded.

"And you think that skeleton was not reburied with the rest of the cave and palace bones?"

Jake nodded again.

I tapped the Kessler photo. "Did this volunteer remember if photos were taken?"

"He snapped them himself."

"Who had possession of the remains during their five years aboveground?" I asked.

"Haas."

"Did he publish?"

"Nothing. And Haas typically wrote exhaustive reports, including drawings, tables, measurements, even facial reconstructions. His analysis of the burials at Giv'at ha-Mivtar is incredibly detailed."

"Is he still alive?"

"Haas took a bad fall in seventy-five. Put him in a coma. He died in eighty-seven without regaining consciousness. Or writing a report."

"So Haas won't be clearing up the body count or the mystery of the intact skeleton."

"Not without a séance."

"Hey, big spender . . ." Charlie was sticking with a winner.

Jake changed tack. "Let me ask you this. You're Yadin. You've got these strange cave bones. What's the first thing you do?"

"Today?"

"In the sixties."

"I was still losing baby teeth."

"Work with me."

"Carbon-fourteen testing. Establish antiquity."

"I've told that back then carbon-fourteen dating wasn't done in Israel. So tally this into the picture. In his rants to the Knesset, Lorinez insisted that some Masada skeletons had been sent abroad."

"Lorinez was the ultra-Orthodox MK pushing for reburial?"

"Yes. And what Lorinez was saying makes sense. Why wouldn't Yadin request radiocarbon dating on the cave burials?"

"So you think Lorinez was right," I said.

"I do. But according to Yadin, no Masada bones left the country."

"Why not?"

"In one *Post* interview I read Yadin said it wasn't his job to initiate such tests. In the same article an anthropologist laid it off to cost."

"Radiocarbon dating isn't that expensive." Even as long ago as the early eighties, testing only ran about $150 per sample. "Surprising Yadin didn't order it, given the importance of the site."

"Not as surprising as Haas's failure to write up the cave bones," Jake said.

I let things percolate a moment in my head. Then, "You suspect the cave folks may not have been part of the main zealot group?"

"I do."

I picked up Kessler's photo.

"And that this is the unreported articulated skeleton."

"I do."

"You think this skeleton may have been shipped out of Israel, and not reinterred with the others."

"I do."

"Why not?"

"That is the million-dollar question."

I picked up the print.

"Where's this fellow now?"

"That, Dr. Brennan, earns a million more."

7

EACH YEAR, ONE HAPLESS BURG BECOMES JAMBOREE CENTRAL for the American Academy of Forensic Sciences. For a week, engineers, psychiatrists, dentists, lawyers, pathologists, anthropologists, and myriad lab geeks converge like moths on a rolled-up rug. New Orleans drew the short straw this year.

Monday through Wednesday are given over to board, committee, and business meetings. On Thursday and Friday, scientific sessions offer insider tips on cutting-edge theory and technique. As a grad student, then as a tenderfoot consultant, I attended these presentations with the ardent zeal of a religious fanatic. Now, I prefer informal networking with old friends.

Using either approach, the conference is exhausting.

Partly my fault. I volunteer for too much. Translate that to I do not struggle sufficiently against impressment.

I spent Sunday working with a colleague with whom I was coauthoring an article for publication in the *Journal of Forensic Sciences.* The next three days passed in a blur of Robert's Rules, rémoulade, and rounds of drinks. Hurricanes for my booze-rational colleagues. Perrier for me.

Conversations centered on two topics: previous escapades and odd cases. Topping this year's register of the bizarre and the baffling were skeletonized gallstones the size of Cocoa Puffs, a jailhouse suicide with a telephone cord, and a sleepwalking cop with his own bullet in his brain.

I floated a description of the Ferris case. Opinions differed concerning the peculiar beveling. Most agreed with the scenario I'd been considering.

My schedule did not permit sitting through the scientific papers. By the time I cabbed it to the New Orleans airport Wednesday, I was beat.

Mechanical problem. Forty-minute delay. Welcome to air travel in America. Check in a minute late and your flight has departed. Check in an hour early and your flight has been delayed. Mechanical problems, crew problems, weather problems, problem problems. I knew them all.

An hour later I'd finished entering committee minutes into my laptop, and my five-forty flight was posted for eight.

So much for the Chicago connection.

Frustrated, I dragged myself to customer services, stood in line, and obtained new routing. The good news: I would get to Montreal tonight. The bad news: I would land shortly before midnight. The additional bad news: I would visit Detroit on the way.

Frothing accomplishes little in these situations, other than raising one's blood pressure.

At the airport bookstore, only a few million copies of the year's blockbuster bestseller barred my way. I plucked one from the pyramid. The flap blurbed a mystery that would shatter an "explosive ancient truth."

Like Masada?

Why not? The rest of the universe was reading the thing.

By wheels-down, I'd gotten through forty chapters. Okay. They were short. But the story was intriguing.

I wondered if Jake and his colleagues were reading the book, and if so, how they were rating the premise.

Thursday's alarm was as welcome as a case of pinkeye. And almost as painful.

Arriving on the twelfth floor of L'édifice Wilfrid Derome, the building that serves as mother ship for the provincial police and forensics labs, I hurried straight to the staff meeting.

Only two autopsies. One went to Pelletier, the other to Emily Santangelo.

LaManche informed me that, following the request I'd made in my note, he'd asked Lisa to revisit Avram Ferris's head. She'd retrieved additional fragments and sent them upstairs from the morgue. He asked when I anticipated finishing my analysis. I estimated early afternoon.

Sure enough, seven shards lay beside the sink in my lab. Their LSJML number matched that assigned to Ferris's corpse.

After grabbing a lab coat, I played my phone messages, and returned two calls. Then I settled at my sand bowls and began jockeying the newcomer fragments into my reconstructed segments.

Two called the parietal home. One locked into the right occipital. One was a loner.

Three filled in the edge of the oval defect.

It was sufficient. I had my answer.

I was washing up when my cell warbled. It was Jake Drum with a miserable connection.

"Sounds like you're calling from Pluto."

"No service . . ." the line crackled and spit ". . . ince Pluto's been demoted from planet to . . ."

Demoted to what? Moon?

"You're in Israel?"

"Paris . . . nd changed plans . . . the Musée de l'Homme."

I listened to a long stretch of transatlantic popping and sputtering.

"Are you phoning on a cellular?"

". . . ocated an accession number . . . missing since the . . . eventies."

"Jake. Call me back on a land line. I can hardly hear you."

Apparently Jake couldn't hear me either.

". . . eep looking . . . all you back on a land line."

My phone beeped and went dead.

I clicked off.

Jake had gone to Paris. Why?

To visit the Musée de l'Homme. Why?

Mental head slap.

I took Kessler's photo to the scope, flipped it, and viewed the notation under magnification.

October, 1963. M de l'H.

What I'd taken to be the digit 1 was a lowercase *L.* And Ryan had been right. The first *H* was actually a smeared *M. M de l'H. Musée de l'Homme.* Jake must have recognized the abbreviation, flown to Paris, visited the museum, and dug up an accession number for the Masada skeleton.

LaManche wears soft-soled shoes and keeps his pockets empty of coins and keys. No scuffs. No jingles. For his bulk, the man moves extraordinarily quietly.

My mind was shaping the next "why?" when my nose sent it the scent of Flying Dutchman.

I swiveled. LaManche had entered through the histo lab and was standing behind me.

"Ready?"

"Ready."

LaManche and I took seats, and I placed my reconstructions between us.

"I'll skip the basics."

LaManche smiled forgivingly. I bit my tongue.

Picking up the segment that had comprised the right posterior of Ferris's skull, I pointed my pen.

"Oval defect with radiating fractures."

I indicated the spiderweb of intersecting cracks on that segment and on two others.

"Concentric-heaving fractures."

"So the entrance is behind and below the right ear?" LaManche's eyes remained on the segments.

"Yes. But it's complicated."

"The beveling." LaManche zeroed in on the problem.

"Yes."

Returning to the first segment, I pointed to the external beveling adjacent to the oval defect.

"If the gun barrel is in tight contact with the skull, ectocranial beveling can be created by the blow-back of gases," LaManche said.

"I don't think that's the case here. Notice the shape of the defect."

LaManche leaned closer.

"A bullet entering perpendicular to a skull's surface usually produces a circular defect," I said. "A bullet entering tangentially produces an irregular perforation, often more oval in shape."

"*Mais, oui.* A keyhole defect."

"Exactly. A portion of the bullet actually sheared off and was lost outside the skull. Thus the external beveling at the entrance."

LaManche looked up. "So the bullet entered behind the right ear and exited the left cheek."

"Yes."

LaManche considered that.

"Such a trajectory is uncommon but possible in suicide. Monsieur Ferris was right-handed."

"There's more. Take a closer look."

I handed LaManche a magnifying lens. He raised and lowered it over the oval defect.

"The rounded end looks scalloped." LaManche studied the oval for another thirty seconds. "As though the circle is superimposed on the oval."

"Or the reverse. The border of the circular defect is clean on the skull's external surface. But check inside."

He rotated the segment.

"Endocranial beveling." LaManche grasped it immediately. "It's a double entrance."

I nodded. "The first bullet hit Ferris's skull straight on. Textbook. Outside border clean, inside border beveled. The second struck the same spot, but at an angle."

"Producing a keyhole defect."

I nodded. "Ferris's head moved or the shooter's hand twitched."

Fatigue? Sadness? Resignation? LaManche sagged as I voiced my ugly conclusion.

"Avram Ferris was shot twice in the back of the head. Execution style."

That night Ryan cooked at my place. Arctic char, asparagus, and what we from Dixie call smashed potatoes. The spuds he baked, peeled, then worked with a fork, adding green onions and olive oil as he mashed.

I watched in awe. I've been called insightful. Brilliant even. When it comes to cooking, I have the vision of a guppy. Given an eon to ponder, my brain would never conceive a road map to mashed potatoes that did not pass through boiling.

Birdie was immensely appreciative of Ryan's *fruits de mer,* and spent the evening trawling for handouts. Later, he settled on the hearth. His purring said feline life didn't get much better.

Over dinner, I shared my conclusion regarding manner of death in the Ferris case. Ryan already knew. The investigation was now officially homicide.

"The weapon's a Jericho nine-millimeter," he said.

"Where was it?"

"Way back in a corner of the closet, under a cart."

"Did the gun belong to Ferris?"

"If so, no one knew about it."

I reached for more salad.

"SIJ recovered one nine-millimeter bullet from the closet," Ryan went on.

"Only one?" That didn't fit with my double-entry scenario.

"In a ceiling panel."

Nor did that.

"What was a bullet doing overhead?" I asked.

"Maybe Ferris went for the shooter, they struggled, the gun discharged."

"Maybe the shooter placed the gun in Ferris's hand and pulled the trigger."

"Simulated suicide?" Ryan.

"Every TV viewer knows you gotta have gunshot residue."

"LaManche didn't find any."

"Doesn't mean it wasn't there."

I munched and thought.

LaManche had recovered one bullet fragment from the victim's head. SIJ had dug one bullet from the ceiling. Where was the rest of the ballistic evidence?

"You said Ferris may have been sitting on a stool when he took the shots?" I asked.

Ryan nodded.

"Facing the door?"

"Which was probably open. SIJ's going over the office and hallways. You wouldn't believe how much crap is stacked in this place."

"What about casings?"

Ryan shook his head. "Shooter must have collected them."

That didn't make sense either.

"Why leave the gun, then turn around and collect the bullet casings?"

"An astute question, Dr. Brennan."

I had no astute answer.

I offered salad to Ryan. He declined.

Ryan changed gears. "Dropped in on the widow again today."

"And?"

"The lady won't be topping my Miss Congeniality ballot."

"She's grieving."

"So she says."

"You don't buy it?"

"My gut says there's something to gnaw on there."

"Bad metaphor." I was thinking of the cats.

"Good point."

"Any suspects?"

"A plethora."

"Big word," I said. "Sexy."

"Tap pants," Ryan said.

"Small words."

Over dessert, I told Ryan what I'd learned about Kessler's photo.

"Drum actually diverted to Paris?"

"Apparently."

"He's convinced the print shows this Masada skeleton?"

"And Jake's not one to get worked up easily."

Ryan gave me an odd look.

"How well do you know this Jake?"

"More than twenty years."

"The query concerned depth, not length of acquaintance."

"We're colleagues."

"Just colleagues?"

Eye roll. "Getting a little personal?"

"Mmm."

"Mmm."

"I'm thinking maybe we should pool our tips."

I hadn't a clue what that meant.

"I also had another chat with Courtney Purviance," Ryan said. "Interesting lady."

"Congenial?"

"Until the discussion turns to Ferris or details of the business. Then she slams shut like a bank vault."

"Protecting the boss?"

"Or afraid she's going to find herself out on the street. I picked up vibes she's not all that fond of Miriam."

"What did she say?"

"It's not what she said." Ryan thought a moment. "It was more her demeanor. Anyway, I did pry loose that Ferris dealt in artifacts from time to time."

"Items from the Holy Land?" I guessed.

"Legally obtained and transported, of course."

"There's a huge black market in illegal antiquities," I said.

"Colossal," Ryan agreed.

Synapse.

"You think Ferris was involved with the Masada bones?"

Ryan shrugged.

"And that got him killed?"

"Kessler thought so."

"Have you tracked Kessler down?"

"I will."

"Could all be coincidence."

"Could be."

I didn't think so.

8

RYAN WOKE ME SHORTLY AFTER SIX FOR SOME PRE-SUNRISE BONDING. Birdie slipped from the bedroom. Down the hall, Charlie squawked a line from Clarence Carter's "Strokin'."

While I showered, Ryan toasted bagels and made coffee. Over breakfast we discussed the cockatiel's reeducation process.

Though unmentioned on the occasion of our Yuletide exchange, I'd quickly noted Charlie's unorthodox *répertoire noir.* Upon questioning, Ryan had admitted that our feathered darling came to him via a vice squad raid on a female enterprise. The ladies' taste had been lusty, and the bird had absorbed.

For months I'd been working to redirect Charlie's musical and oratorical talents. With mixed results.

At eight, I popped in a cockatiel-training CD and Ryan and I rode together to L'édifice Wilfrid Derome. He headed to the *crimes contre la personne* squad room on the first floor, and I took the LSJML elevator to the twelfth.

After shooting close-ups and composing a summary report, I told LaManche that the remains in my possession could be released to the Ferris family. Though burial had taken place while I was in New Orleans, arrangements had been made for placement of the cranial fragments in a coffin-side pit.

At ten-thirty, I phoned Ryan. He said he'd meet me in the lobby in five. I waited ten. Bored, I slipped into the cafeteria for a Diet Coke roadie. At the counter, I made an impulse buy of Scottish shortbreads. One never knew.

Ryan was waiting when I returned to the lobby. Popping the soda, I stashed the cookies in my shoulder bag.

For twenty-seven years Avram Ferris had run his import business out of a light-industrial park off the autoroute des Laurentides, midway between Montreal island and the old Mirabel airport.

Constructed in the seventies, Mirabel was envisioned as Montreal's once-and-future aviation jewel. Though thirty miles out, a high speed rail line was to connect the airport with the city center. Lickety-split. You'd be at the gate!

The rail line never happened.

By the early nineties the commute was intolerable and getting worse. Sixty-nine bucks for a taxi downtown.

Frustrated, officials finally threw in the towel and mothballed Mirabel in favor of its geographically friendlier rival. Mirabel now gets cargo and charters. All other domestic, North American, and international flights arrive and depart Dorval, recently rechristened Pierre Elliott Trudeau International.

Avram Ferris didn't care. He'd started Les Imports Ashkenazim near Mirabel, and that's where he'd kept it.

And that's where he'd died.

He'd lived in Côte-des-Neiges, a middle-class residential neighborhood tucked behind the Jewish General Hospital, just northwest of le centre-ville.

Ryan took the Décarie expressway, cut east on Van Horne, then north on Plamondon to Vézina. Pulling to the curb, he pointed to a two-story redbrick box in a row of two-story redbrick boxes.

I scanned the block.

Each building was identical, its right side a mirror image of its left. Wood-framed doors jutted in front, balconies hung from upstairs windows. All walks were shoveled. All shrubs were wrapped. In the driveways, Chevy and Ford station wagons waited under tubular-framed, plastic-shrouded shelters.

"Not the Jaguar and SUV set," I said.

"Looks like the homeowners held a meeting and banned any trim that ain't white."

Ryan chin-cocked the building directly opposite. "Ferris's unit is upstairs on the left. His brother's down, Mama and another brother are in the duplex next door."

"Ferris's commute must have been hell."

"Probably stayed here out of love of architectural self-expression."

"You said Avram and Miriam had no kids?"

Ryan nodded. "They married late. The first wife had health problems, died in eighty-nine. Ferris remarried in ninety-seven. So far, no progeny."

"Isn't that against the rules?"

Ryan gave me a quizzical look.

"The mitzvot."

The look held.

"Jewish law. You're supposed to have babies. Not waste your seed."

"You're thinking of the farmer's almanac."

Ryan and I walked to the small front stoop.

Ryan stepped up and rang the top bell.

We waited.

Ryan rang again.

We waited some more.

An old woman trudged by behind us, grocery cart rattling in cadence with her boots.

"Isn't the widow supposed to hunker in?" Ryan asked, hitting the bell a third time.

"Shiva only lasts a week."

"And then?"

"You say daily kaddish, don't party, don't shave or snip and clip for a while. But basically you get on with your life."

"How do you know all this?"

"My first boyfriend was Jewish."

"Star-crossed love?"

"He moved to Altoona."

Ryan opened the storm door and pounded.

The cart woman stopped, turned, and stared unabashedly over her triple-wrapped muffler.

To the right, a curtain moved. I touched Ryan's arm and tipped my head. "Dora's home."

Ryan smiled brightly.

"Avram was a nice Jewish boy who went eight years between marriages. Maybe he and Mama were close."

"Maybe he told her stuff."

"Or Mama noticed things on her own."

I thought of something.

"Old ladies like cookies."

"They're known for it."

I reached into my purse and pulled out the shortbreads.

"Mama might warm to us, feel chatty."

"Damn." Ryan turned. "We're good at this."

Only, Dora didn't answer the door. Miriam did. She wore black slacks, a black silk blouse, a black cardigan, and pearls.

As on our first meeting, I was struck by Miriam's eyes. There were dark hollows beneath them now, but it didn't matter. Those lavender irises were showstoppers.

Miriam was not unaware of the effect her eyes had on men. After flicking a glance at me, she shifted to Ryan and leaned forward slightly, one hand wrapping her waist, the other gathering the cardigan at her throat.

"Detective." Soft. A little breathy.

"Good morning, Mrs. Ferris," Ryan said. "I hope you're feeling better."

"Thank you."

Miriam's skin was ghostly. She looked thinner than I remembered.

"There are a few points I'd like to clear up," Ryan said.

Miriam's focus shifted to a point between and beyond us. The old woman's cart cranked up.

Miriam reengaged on Ryan, and her head tipped slightly.

"Can't this wait?"

Ryan let the question hang in the triangle of space between us.

"Who is it?" A quavery voice floated from inside the house.

Miriam turned and said something in Yiddish or Hebrew, then reoriented to us.

"My mother-in-law is unwell."

"Your husband is dead," Ryan said, not too gently. "I can't delay a murder investigation for the comfort of the bereaved."

"I live with that thought every moment of the day. So you believe it's murder, then?"

"As do you, I think. Are you avoiding me, Mrs. Ferris?"

"No."

Lavender and blue met head-on. Neither gave way.

"I'd like to ask you again about a man named Kessler."

"I'm going to tell you again. I don't know him."

"Might your mother-in-law?"

"No."

"How do you know that, Mrs. Ferris? Kessler claimed to know your husband. Have you discussed Kessler with your mother-in-law?"

"No, but she has never mentioned that name. My husband's business brought him into contact with many people."

"One of whom may have pumped two rounds into his head."

"Are you trying to shock me, Detective?"

"Are you aware that your husband dealt in antiquities?"

Miriam's brows dipped almost imperceptibly. Then, "Who told you that?"

"Courtney Purviance."

"I see."

"Is that statement untrue?"

"Ms. Purviance has a tendency to exaggerate her role in my husband's affairs." Miriam's voice was edged like a scythe.

"Are you suggesting she'd lie?"

"I'm suggesting the woman has little in her life but her job."

"Ms. Purviance suggested your husband's demeanor had changed prior to his death."

"That's ridiculous. If Avram had been troubled, surely I'd have noticed."

Ryan circled back to his point.

"Is it not true that your husband dealt in antiquities?"

"Antiques formed a very small part of Avram's trade."

"You know that?"

"I know that."

"You've told me you know little about the business."

"That much I know."

The day was clear with a temperature just above freezing.

"Might those antiquities have included human remains?" Ryan asked.

The violet eyes widened. "Dear God, no."

Most people are uncomfortable with gaps in conversation. When faced with silence, they feel compelled to fill it. Ryan uses this impulse. He did so now. He waited. It worked.

"That would be *chet,*" Miriam elaborated.

Ryan still waited.

Miriam was opening her mouth to say more, when the voice again warbled behind her. She swiveled and spoke over her shoulder.

When she turned back, sunlight glinted off moisture on her upper lip.

"I must help my mother-in-law prepare for Shabbat."

Ryan handed Miriam a card.

"If I think of anything I will call." Again, the widened eyes. "I really do want Avram's killer brought to justice."

"Have a nice day," Ryan said.

"*Shabbat shalom,*" I said.

As we turned to go, Miriam reached out and laid a hand on Ryan's arm.

"Regardless of what you think, Detective, I did love my husband." There was a chilling bleakness to her voice.

Ryan and I didn't speak until we were back in his car.

"Well?" Ryan asked.

"I don't know," I said.

We both thought about that.

"*Chet?*" Ryan asked.

"Kind of like sin," I said.

"The lady's not into the power of sisterhood," Ryan said.

"She acted like I wasn't there," I agreed.

"You were," Ryan said.

"I thought so," I said.

"She's definitely not one of Purviance's fans."

"No."

Ryan started the engine and pulled from the curb.

"I'd say I'm pretty good at character analysis," he said.

"I'd say that's a fair assessment," I agreed.

"But I can't figure Miriam. One moment she's bereaved. The next she's broadcasting this fuck-you attitude. Protecting something?"

"She was perspiring," I said

"On a cold day," Ryan said.

We rolled to a stop at the corner.

"Now what?" Ryan asked.

"You're the detective," I said.

"The gun was an orphan. Can't trace it. My canvass of Ferris's neighbors in the industrial park turned up zip. Ditto for statements by family and business associates. I'm still waiting for tax records and a phone dump on the warehouse. I've got a Kessler query into every synagogue in town."

"Sounds like you've been doing some serious detecting."

"I've been detecting my ass off, but progress is halting," Ryan said.

"What now?"

"SIJ's still working the scene. Purviance is still checking to see if anything was stolen. That leaves lunch."

I'd barely settled with my Whopper when my cell phone warbled. It was Jake Drum. This time the connection was clear.

"You actually diverted to Paris?" I asked, then mouthed the name Jake Drum to Ryan.

"No big deal. Instead of driving to Toronto and catching a flight to Tel Aviv, I'm connecting through Charles de Gaulle."

"The skeleton's that important?"

"It could be huge."

"What have you learned?"

Ryan partially unwrapped my burger and handed it to me. I took a one-handed bite.

"My hunch was right," Jake said. "A Masada skeleton arrived at the Musée de l'Homme in November of 1963. I located a specimen file and an accession number."

"Go on."

"What are you eating?"

"Whopper."

"Fast food is sacrilege in a city like Montreal."

"It's fast."

"The gastronomic slippery slope."

I compounded the blasphemy with a sip of Diet Coke.

"Are the bones still there?"

"No." Jake sounded frustrated.

"No?"

I went for more Whopper. Ketchup dribbled my chin. Ryan blotted it with a napkin.

"I found a woman named Marie-Nicole Varin who helped inventory collections in the early seventies. Varin recalls coming across a

Masada skeleton. But it's not at the museum now. We searched everywhere."

"No one's seen it since the seventies?"

"No."

"Aren't records kept on the movement of every specimen?"

"Should be. The rest of that file's missing."

"What's the museum's explanation?"

"*C'est la vie.* Few of the current staff were here back then. Varin did the inventory with a graduate student named Yossi Lerner. She thinks Lerner may still be in Paris. And here's an interesting twist. Varin thinks Lerner's either American or Canadian."

That stopped the Whopper midway to my mouth.

"I'm trying to track him down."

"*Bonne chance,*" I said.

"I'll need more than luck."

I told Ryan what Jake had said.

He listened without comment.

We finished our fries.

Back on Van Horne, we watched a man in a long black coat, black hat, knickers, and pale stockings pass a kid in jeans and a Blue Jays jacket.

"Shabbat's coming on fast," I said.

"Probably won't increase the warmth of our welcome in these parts."

"Probably won't."

"Ever done surveillance?"

I shook my head.

"Gets the blood pumping," Ryan said.

"So I've heard," I said.

"Miriam might go out."

"Leaving Dora alone."

"I've yet to speak to Dora alone."

"We could pick up flowers," I suggested.

We hit a florist and were back at the Ferris duplex forty minutes after leaving it.

An hour later Miriam walked out Dora's front door.

9

DORA ANSWERED ON THE SECOND RING. IN THE BRIGHT SUNlight, her wrinkled skin looked almost translucent.

Ryan reintroduced us.

The old woman regarded us blankly. I wondered if she was on medication.

Ryan held out his badge.

Dora looked at it, her expression passive. It was obvious she didn't know who we were.

I offered the bouquet and cookies.

"*Shabbat shalom,*" I said.

"*Shabbat shalom,*" she said, more reflex than greeting.

"We're so very sorry about your son, Mrs. Ferris. I've been away, or I would have called sooner."

Dora took my offerings and bent to smell the flowers. Straightening, she inspected the cookies, then returned them to me.

"Sorry, miss. They are not kosher."

Feeling like an idiot, I put the cookies in my purse.

Dora's eyes floated to Ryan, then back to me. They were small and moist and frosted with age.

"You were there at my son's autopsy." Slight accent. Maybe Eastern European.

"Yes, ma'am. I was."

"There's no one here."

"We'd like to talk to you, Mrs. Ferris."

"To me?" Surprise. A little fear.

"Yes, ma'am."

"Miriam's gone to market."

"This will only take a moment."

She hesitated, then turned and led us through a smoky-mirrored entry to a plastic-covered grouping in a small sunny living room.

"I'll find a vase. Please sit."

She disappeared down a hallway to the right of the entrance. I looked around.

The place was a testimonial to sixties bad taste. White sateen upholstery. Laminated oak tables. Flocked wallpaper. Wall-to-wall gold semishag.

A dozen smells bickered for attention. Disinfectant. Garlic. Air freshener. From somewhere a closet or chest threw in a bid for cedar.

Dora shuffled back and we spent a few moments flower arranging.

Then, dropping into a wooden rocker with pillows strapped to its seat and back, she spread her feet and arranged her dress. Blue cross-trainers poked from below the hem.

"The children are with Roslyn and Ruthie at the synagogue."

I assumed those were the daughters-in-law from the other duplexes.

Dora clasped her hands in her lap and looked down at them. "Miriam has returned to the butcher for something she left behind."

Ryan and I exchanged glances. He nodded that I should begin.

"Mrs. Ferris, I know you've already talked with Detective Ryan."

The frosted gaze came up, level and unblinking.

"We hate to disturb you again, but we're wondering if anything new has come to mind since those conversations."

Dora shook her head slowly.

"Did your son have any unusual visitors in the weeks before his death?"

"No."

"Had your son argued with anyone? Complained about anyone?"

"No."

"Was he involved in any political movements?"

"Avram's life was his family. His business and his family."

I knew I was repeating the same questions Ryan had asked. Interrogation 101. Sometimes the ploy works, triggers previously forgotten recollections or details initially deemed irrelevant.

And this was the first time Dora had been questioned alone.

"Did your son have enemies? Anyone who might have wished him harm?"

"We are Jews, miss."

"I was thinking of a specific individual."

"No."

New tack.

"Are you acquainted with the men who observed your son's autopsy?"

"Yes." Dora pulled on an ear and made a gurgling sound in her throat.

"Who chose those individuals?"

"The rabbi."

"Why did only two men return in the afternoon?"

"That would have been the rabbi's decision."

"Do you know a man by the name of Kessler?"

"I once knew a Moshe Kessler."

"Was he in attendance at your son's autopsy?"

"Moshe died during the war."

My cell phone chose that moment to sound.

I checked the screen.

Private number.

I ignored the call.

"Were you aware that your son sold antiques?"

"Avram sold many things."

My phone rang again.

Apologizing, I turned it off.

Impulse. Frustration. Inspiration. A name in my head like an unwanted jingle. I'm not sure why I asked the next question.

"Do you know a man named Yossi Lerner?"

The furrows cornering Dora's eyes deepened. The wrinkled lips tucked in.

"Does that name mean something to you, Mrs. Ferris?"

"My son had a friend named Yossi Lerner."

"Really?" I kept my face neutral, my voice calm.

"Avram and Yossi met as students at McGill."

"When was that?" I didn't look at Ryan.

"Years ago."

"Did they keep in touch?" Casual.

"I have no idea. Oh, dear." Dora gulped air into her lungs. "Is Yossi involved in all this?"

"Of course not. I'm just throwing out names. Do you know where Mr. Lerner lives now?"

"I haven't seen Yossi in years."

The front door opened, closed. Seconds later Miriam appeared in the living room.

Dora smiled.

Miriam stared at us, face so devoid of expression she could have been studying moss. When she spoke, it was to Ryan.

"I told you my mother-in law is unwell. Why are you bothering her?"

"I'm fin—" Dora started to speak.

Miriam cut her off.

"She's eighty-four and has just lost her son."

Dora made a *tsk* sound.

As before, Ryan gave Miriam silence, waited for her to fill it. This time she didn't.

Dora did.

"It's all right. We were having a nice discussion." Dora flapped a blue-veined hand.

"What are you discussing?" Miriam's gaze stayed on Ryan as though Dora hadn't spoken.

"Euripides," Ryan said.

"Is that supposed to be humorous, Detective?"

"Yossi Lerner."

I watched Miriam carefully. If I expected a reaction, there was none.

"Who's Yossi Lerner?"

"A friend of your husband's."

"I don't know him."

"A school friend."

"That would be before my time."

I looked at Dora. The old woman's gaze had gone fuzzy, as though she were viewing memories outside the room.

"Why are you asking about this man? This Yossi Lerner?" Miriam pulled off her gloves.

"His name came up."

"In your investigation?" The violet eyes showed the slightest surprise.

"Yes."

"In what context?"

Outside, I heard the *beep beep* of a car alarm. Dora didn't stir.

Ryan looked at me. I nodded.

Ryan told Miriam about Kessler and his photo.

Miriam's face registered nothing as she listened. It was impossible to guess her interest or emotions.

"Is there a link between this skeleton and my husband's death?"

"Straight or sugar-coated?"

"Straight."

Ryan raised digits as he ticked off points.

"A man is murdered. A guy produces a photo, claims the skeleton in that photo is the reason for the shooting. That guy is now missing."

Ryan's pinky joined the others.

"There's evidence the skeleton in the photo came from Masada."

Thumb.

"The victim dealt in Israeli antiquities."

Ryan started over with his index finger.

"The skeleton was once in the possession of one Yossi Lerner. The victim was once pals with one Yossi Lerner."

"The other was a priest."

We all turned to Dora.

She spoke to the air.

"The other boy was a priest," she repeated. "But he was later. Or was he?"

"What other boy?" I asked gently.

"Avram had two friends. Yossi, and then later this other boy." Dora tapped a fist to her chin. "He was a priest. He surely was."

Miriam crossed to her mother-in-law, but did not reach out to her.

I was reminded of the scene in the morgue family room. The women had been side by side but distant. They had not touched. They had not embraced. The younger had not shared her strength with the older. The older had not sought comfort from the younger.

"They were very close," Dora went on.

"Your son and his friends?" I encouraged.

Dora smiled the first smile I'd seen on her face. "Such inquisitive minds. Always reading. Always questioning. Arguing. All night, some times."

"What was the priest's name?" I asked.

Dora gave a tight shake of her head.

"He was from the Beauce. I remember that. He called us *zayde* and *bubbe.*"

"Where did your son meet this priest?"

"Yeshiva University."

"In New York?"

Dora nodded. "Avram and Yossi had just graduated from McGill. Avram was much more spiritual back then. He was studying to be a rabbi. This priest was taking courses in Near Eastern religions, or some such thing. They were drawn to each other, being the only Canadians, I suppose."

Dora's eyes drifted.

"Was he a priest then?" she said more to herself than to us. "Or did he become a priest later?" Dora's fingers tightened. Her hand trembled. "Oh, dear. Oh, my."

Miriam stepped toward Ryan.

"Detective, I really must object."

Ryan caught my eye. We both rose.

Miriam sent Ryan off with a carbon copy of her earlier adieu.

"Find who did this, Detective, but please don't upset my mother-in-law when she is alone."

"First, she seemed more in reverie than upset. Second, I can't have such limits on my investigation. But we will attempt to be kind."

Nothing for me.

Back in the car Ryan wondered why I'd asked about Lerner.

"I haven't a clue," I said.

"Good impulse," he said.

"Good impulse," I agreed.

We also agreed that Lerner deserved follow-up.

While Ryan drove, I listened to my messages.

Three.

All from Jake Drum.

I've got contact information for Yossi Lerner. Call me.

I've talked to Yossi Lerner. Call me.

Amazing news. Call me.

Each "call me" was more agitated than the one before.

I told Ryan.

"Call the man," he said.

"You think?"

"Yes. I want more on Lerner."

"I'm anxious to hear what Jake's learned, but I'll be home shortly. I'd rather wait and talk on a land line. Mobile to mobile is worse than phoning Zambia."

"Have you phoned Zambia?"

"I can never get through."

Ten minutes later, Ryan dropped me at my condo.

"I've got a stakeout this weekend, and I'm already late." He took my chin in his hands and thumbed my cheeks. "Stay on this Lerner thing. Let me know what Jake's got."

"Heart-thumping surveillance," I said.

"You know what I'd rather surveil," he said.

"I'm not sure that's a word."

Ryan kissed me.

"I'll owe you," he said.

"I'll collect," I said.

Ryan headed back to Wilfrid Derome. I headed inside.

After greeting Birdie and Charlie, I changed into jeans, and made a cup of Earl Grey. Then I took the handset to the sofa and punched in Jake's number.

He answered on the first ring.

"You're still in France?" I asked.

"Yes."

"You're going to be late for your own dig."

"They won't start without me. I'm the boss."

"I forgot that."

"What I'm finding here is much more important."

Birdie hopped into my lap. I stroked his head. He shot a leg and started licking his toes.

"I've spoken with Yossi Lerner."

"I guessed that from your messages."

"Lerner still lives in Paris. He's from Quebec."

It had to be the Yossi Lerner that Dora remembered.

"Lerner was working at the museum when the Masada skeleton was there as a part-timer while researching his doctoral thesis. Are you ready for this?"

"Cut the drama, Jake."

"This'll grab you by the throat."

It did.

10

"LET ME BACK UP A MINUTE. THIS LERNER'S KIND OF A STRANGE duck. No family. Lives with a ferret. Does pickup archaeology. Israel. Egypt. Jordan. Goes in on grant money, runs a dig, writes a report, moves on. Does a lot of salvage work," Jake said.

"Save what you can before they bulldoze for the bypass."

"Exactly."

"Is Lerner affiliated with any institution?"

"He's had some temporary appointments, but says he's never been interested in a permanent position. Finds it too confining."

"That regular income can be a burden."

"The guy's definitely not into money. Lives in a seventeenth-century walk-up built as a barracks for musketeers. Whole apartment's about the size of a Buick. Access is via a winding stone staircase. Nice view of Notre-Dame, though."

"So you went to see him?"

"When I phoned, he said he worked nights, invited me over. We spent two hours celebrating the Sun King."

"Meaning?"

"We did serious damage to a bottle of Martell VSOP Medaillon."

"How old is this guy?"

"Late fifties, maybe."

Avram Ferris was fifty-six.

"Jewish?"

"Not as fervently as in his youth."

"What's his story?"

"Lerner?"

"No, Jake. Louis the Fourteenth."

I leaned back. Birdie scootched up onto my chest.

"Lerner was cool initially, but after the fourth snifter he was talking like a convert at Betty Ford. You don't want to hear about the thing with the pianist, do you?"

"No."

"Lerner worked at the Musée de l'Homme from seventy-one until seventy-four, while researching his dissertation."

"Topic?"

"The Dead Sea scrolls."

"Probably didn't take the Essenes that long to write them."

"Lerner takes things slowly. And seriously. Back then he was taking Judaism very seriously."

"Miss pianist change that?"

"Who said anything about a miss?"

"Get to the Masada bones."

"In seventy-two Lerner was asked to assist in inventorying a number of museum collections. In doing so he came across a file containing a shipping invoice and the photo of a skeleton."

"The invoice suggested the bones came from Masada?"

"Yes."

"Was it dated?"

"November 1963."

Locus 2001, the cave below the casement wall on Masada's southern summit. The jumbled bones. The isolated skeleton. According to Jake's volunteer-informant, Cave 2001 was discovered and cleared in October of '63, one month before the museum's invoice date. I felt a spark of excitement.

"Was it signed?"

"Yes, but Lerner doesn't remember by whom. He searched the museum's collections, found the skeleton, made a notation in the file indicating the specimen's condition and storeroom location, as per protocol, and moved on. But something bothered him. Why had that one set of bones been sent to the museum? Why had the bones remained boxed up and out of sight? Are you purring?"

"It's the cat."

"The following year Lerner read a book by an Australian journalist, Donovan Joyce. Joyce's premise was that Jesus survived the cross."

"And retired to a nice little place in the islands?"

"He lived to be eighty and died fighting the Romans at Masada."

"Novel."

"That's not all. While at Masada, Jesus produced a scroll containing his last will and testament."

"And how was Joyce privy to these little gems?"

"In December of sixty-four, Joyce was in Israel researching a book. While there, he says he was approached by a man calling himself Professor Max Grosset, a volunteer excavator on Yigael Yadin's team. Grosset claimed to have stolen an ancient scroll from Masada, and solicited Joyce's help in smuggling his booty out of the country. Grosset swore the scroll had fantastic importance, its authorship alone making it priceless. Joyce refused to become involved, but swears he saw and handled Grosset's scroll."

"And later wrote a book about it."

"Joyce had gone to the Holy Land to view Masada, but the Israelis refused his request for a permit to visit the summit. Forced to abandon his original book idea, he regrouped and began investigating the plausibility of Grosset's scroll. Astounded by his findings, Joyce ended up devoting eight years to the project. While he never again saw Grosset, Joyce claims to have unearthed startling new information about Jesus' paternity, marital status, crucifixion, and resurrection."

"Uh-huh."

"In his book, Joyce mentions the skeletons found in Cave 2001."

"You're kidding."

"According to Joyce, the twenty-five individuals in the cave represented a very special group, separate from the Jewish zealots. He concludes that, following Masada's conquest, out of respect for these individuals, General Silva would have ordered his soldiers to leave the cave burials undisturbed."

"Because the remains were those of Jesus and his followers."

"That's the implication."

"Lerner believed this crackpot theory?"

"The book's out of print now, but I managed to lay my hands on a copy. I've got to admit, if you're open to such thinking, Joyce's arguments are persuasive."

"Jesus."

"Exactly. Back to Lerner. After reading Joyce's book, our pious young scholar decided there was a good possibility the bones he'd uncovered at the museum were those of Jesus."

"Christ and his followers at Judaism's most sacred site."

"You've got it. The possibility rocked Lerner's world."

"Would have rocked Israel, too, not to mention all of Christendom. What did Lerner do?"

"Major angst. What if it was Jesus? What if it wasn't Jesus, but someone else of importance in the fledgling Christian movement? What if the bones fell into the wrong hands? What if the press got wind of the story? The sanctity of Masada would be disturbed. The Christian world would be enraged over what was sure to be labeled a Jewish hoax. Night after night he agonized.

"After weeks of mental torment, Lerner decided the skeleton had to go. He spent days planning ways to snatch and destroy it. He considered burning the bones. Smashing them with hammers. Weighting them and dropping them into the sea.

"Then his conscience would flip. Theft is theft. If the skeleton was Jesus he was still a Jew and a holy man. Lerner hardly slept. In the end, he couldn't bring himself to destroy the skeleton, but he couldn't live with the thought someone else might find it. To preserve religious culture and tradition, he resolved the skeleton had to disappear."

"Lerner trashed the file and stole the bones."

"Smuggled them out of the museum in an athletic bag."

"And?" I sat up.

Birdie jumped to the floor, turned, and fixed me with round yellow eyes.

"That's the throat-grabber. What's the name of your gunshot victim?"

"Avram Ferris."

"That's what I thought." Jake's next words jolted me like a bottle rocket. "Lerner gave the bones and the photo to Avram Ferris."

"His boyhood buddy," I breathed.

"Ferris had spent two years kibbutzing in Israel, and was passing through Paris on his way back to Montreal."

"Sonovabitch."

"Sonovabitch."

When we disconnected I tried Ryan. No answer. The heart-thumping surveillance had probably begun.

Too agitated to eat, I headed for the gym. Questions looped through my head as I pounded out flight after flight on the StairMaster. I tried arranging them into a logical progression.

Did Kessler's photo really show the missing Masada skeleton?

If so, did Ferris have the Masada skeleton when he was killed?

Who else knew he had it?

Was Ferris planning to sell the skeleton on the black market? To whom? Why now?

Or was he perhaps offering to destroy it for a price? To be paid by whom? Jews? Christians?

If not, why was Ferris shot?

Where was the skeleton now?

Where was Kessler?

Who was Kessler?

Why would Ferris accept a stolen skeleton?

I could conjure some possibilities for that one. Loyalty to a friend? Shared concern about the disturbance of the sanctity of the Masada legend or fear over a colossal Jewish-Christian theological confrontation at a time when Western Christian support was essential to the preservation of Israel? Dora said her son was quite pious back then. Jesus living after the crucifixion and dying during the siege of Masada? It would have been a nightmare for Christians and Jews alike.

Or would it? Jesus was a Jew. Why shouldn't he or his followers have been at Masada?

No. Jesus was a heretic Jew. He outraged the high priests.

Back to questions.

What would Ferris have done with the bones?

The logical repository would have been his warehouse.

SIJ had found no bones.

Might he have concealed them in such a way that a search would never turn them up?

I made mental notes. Ask Ryan. Ask Courtney Purviance.

Wiping sweat from my face, I pumped on.

Something was wrong with the warehouse idea.

The Torah forbids leaving a body unburied overnight. Deuteronomy or someone. Wouldn't Ferris have felt polluted having human remains in his work area? At least uncomfortable? I moved from the StairMaster to the bench press machine.

Maybe Ferris was only a transporter. Maybe he gave the bones to someone else.

To who?

Whom?

Someone who shared his and Lerner's concern?

But any Jew would be bound by the Torah prohibition.

Someone with other reasons for wanting the skeleton to disappear?

Christian reasons?

If Jesus didn't die on the cross, if Jesus lived, and his bones ended up in the Musée de l'Homme, such a finding would rock the Vatican and all of Protestant Christianity as well. The suggestion would have to be absolutely refuted, or it would blow the most basic tenet of the Christian faith right out of the water. No empty tomb. No angels. No resurrection. No Easter. The investigation and the controversy would be headline news around the globe for months. Years. The debate would be unprecedented. The passion and acrimony would be devastating.

I stopped in midpump.

The third friend! The priest from the Beauce!

Dora said the two men were very close.

Priests have no hang-ups with human bones. They wear them as relics. Embed them in altars. Display them in churches all over Europe.

Suddenly, I was in a froth to locate that priest.

I looked at my watch. Six-thirty. Grabbing my towel, I headed for the locker room.

My cell phone was barely registering a pulse. Throwing on sweats and my jacket, I hurried outside.

Jake answered after four rings, voice thick with sleep.

As I walked along Ste-Catherine, I explained about Ferris, Lerner, and the priest.

"I need a name, Jake."

"It's after midnight here."

"Doesn't Lerner work at night?"

"Okay."

I heard a yawn.

"And anything else you can find out about this priest. Was he involved in the theft of the skeleton? Where was he living back in seventy-three? Where is he living now?"

"Boxers or briefs?"

"That kind of thing."

"Calling this late might tick Lerner off."

"I have confidence in your persuasive abilities."

"And my boyish charm."

"And that."

I was stepping out of my shower when the phone rang.

Wrapping myself in a towel, I did a slip-'n'-slide across the tile, bolted to my bedroom, and grabbed the handset.

"Sylvain Morissonneau."

"You're a rock star," I said, jotting the name on the back of a bank statement.

"You have me confused with Sting," Jake said.

"Was Morissonneau involved in the skeleton heist?"

"No."

"Where is he now?"

"Lerner never knew Morissonneau all that well. Says he left for Paris shortly after the other two met at Yeshiva. Hasn't seen or heard from Morissonneau since seventy-one."

"Oh."

"I did learn one thing."

I waited.

"Morissonneau's a Cistercian."

"A Trappist monk?"

"If you say so."

After a defrosted dinner of Thai chicken and rice, I booted my computer and began a Web search.

Charlie kept squawking "Get Off of My Cloud." Birdie purred on the desk to my right.

In the course of my research, I learned several things.

In 1098 C.E., a renewal movement began within Benedictine monasticism, at the monastery of Cîteaux, in central France. The idea was to restore, as far as possible, the literal observance of the Rule of Saint Benedict. I never learned what that meant.

The Latin word for Cîteaux is *Cistercium*, and those who signed on to the reform movement came to be known as Cistercians.

Today there are several orders within the Cistercians, one of which is the OCSO, Cistercian Order of the Strict Observance. Trappist, the nickname for the OCSO, came from another reform movement at another French monastery, La Trappe, in the seventeenth century.

Lots of reform movements. Makes sense, I guess. Monks have a lot of time to reflect and decide to do better.

I found three Cistercian monasteries in Quebec. One in Oka, near Lac des Deux-Montagnes, One at Mistassini, near Lac Saint-Jean. One in the Montérégie region, near Saint-Hyacinthe. Each had a website.

I spent two hours working through endless cyberloops explaining the monastic day, the spiritual journey, the meaning of vocation, the history of the order. Search as I might, I found no membership listing for any of the monasteries.

I was about to give up when I stumbled on a brief announcement.

> On July 17, 2004, the monks of l'Abbaye Sainte-Marie-des-Neiges, with Fr. Charles Turgeon, OCSO presiding, chose their eighth abbot, Fr. Sylvain Morissonneau, 59. Born in Beauce County, Quebec, Fr. Morissonneau attended university at Laval. He was ordained a priest in 1968, then pursued academic studies in the United States. Fr. Morissonneau entered the abbey in 1971. For eight years prior to his election, he served as the monastery's business manager. He brings to the office skills both practical and academic.

So Morissonneau had stuck with the contemplative life, I thought, clicking from the monastery's website to MapQuest Canada.

Sorry, Father. Your solitude's about to be busted.

11

THE MONTÉRÉGIE IS AN AGRICULTURAL BELT LYING BETWEEN Montreal and the U.S. border. Composed of hills and valleys, crisscrossed by the rivière Richelieu, and outlined by the banks of the fleuve Saint-Laurent, the region is lousy with parks and green space. Parc national des Îles-de-Boucherville. Parc national du Mont-Saint-Bruno. Le Centre de la Nature du Mont Saint-Hilaire. Tourists visit the Montérégie for nature, produce, cycling, skiing, and golf.

L'Abbaye Sainte-Marie-des-Neiges was located on the banks of la rivière Yamaska, north of the town of Saint-Hyacinthe, in the center of a trapezoid formed by Saint-Simon, Saint-Hugues, Saint-Jude, and Saint-Barnabe-Sud.

The Montérégie is also lousy with saints.

At nine-twenty the next morning, I turned from the two-lane onto a smaller paved road that wound through apple orchards for approximately a half mile, then made a sharp turn and cut through a high stone wall. A discreet plaque indicated I'd found the monks.

The monastery sprawled beyond an expanse of open lawn, and was shaded by enormous elms. Constructed of Quebec gray stone, the place looked like a church with metastatic disease. Wings shot from three sides, and subsidiary winglets shot from the wings. A four-story round tower stood at the junction of the easternmost wing and the church proper, and an ornate square spire shot from its westernmost counterpart. Some windows were arched. Others were square and shuttered. Several outbuildings lay between the main structure and the cornfields and river at its back.

I took a moment to assess.

From my cybertour I'd learned that many monks make concessions to economic necessity, producing and selling baked goods, cheese, chocolate, wine, veggies, or items of piety. Some host visitors seeking spiritual rejuvenation.

These boys didn't appear to be of that mind-set. I saw no welcoming shingle. No gift shop. Not a single parked car.

I pulled to the front of the building. No one appeared to greet or challenge me.

My time on the Web had also taught me that the monks of Sainte-Marie-des-Neiges rise at 4 A.M., observe multiple rounds of prayer, then labor from eight until noon. I'd planned my visit to coincide with the morning work period.

In February that didn't involve apples or corn. Other than sparrows and ground squirrels, there wasn't a sign of life.

I got out and softly clicked the car door shut. Something about the place demanded quiet. An orange door to the right of the round tower looked like my best bet. I was walking in that direction when a monk rounded the far end of the spire wing. He wore a brown hooded cape, socks, and sandals.

The monk didn't stop when he saw me, but continued more slowly in my direction, as though giving himself time to consider the encounter.

He halted three yards from me. He'd been injured at some point. The left side of his face looked slack, his left eyelid drooped, and a white line diagonaled that cheek.

The monk looked at me but didn't speak. He had hair mowed to his scalp, sharpness to his chin, and a face gaunt as a musculoskeletal diagram.

"I'm Dr. Temperance Brennan," I said. "I'm here to speak with Sylvain Morissonneau."

Nothing.

"It's a matter of some urgency."

More nothing.

I flashed my LSJML identity card.

The monk glanced at the ID but held his ground.

I'd anticipated a cool reception. Reaching into my shoulder bag, I withdrew a sealed envelope containing a photocopy of Kessler's print, stepped forward, and held it out.

"Please give this to Father Morissonneau. I'm certain he'll see me."

A scarecrow hand snaked from the robe, snatched the envelope, then signaled that I should follow.

The monk led me through the orange door, across a small vestibule, and down a lavishly paneled hall. The air smelled like Monday mornings in the parochial schools of my youth. A mélange of wet wool, disinfectant, and wood polish.

Entering a library, my host gestured that I should sit. A flattened palm indicated that I should stay.

When the monk had gone I surveyed my surroundings.

The library looked like a set transported from a Harry Potter movie. Dark paneling, leaded-glass cabinets, rolling ladders going up to third-story shelves. Enough wood had been used to deforest British Columbia.

I counted eight long tables and twelve card catalogs with tiny brass handles on the drawers. Not a computer in sight.

I didn't hear the second monk enter. He was just there.

"Dr. Brennan?"

I stood.

This monk was wearing a white cassock and a brown overgarment made up of rectangular front and back panels. No cape.

"I am Father Sylvain Morissonneau, abbot of this community."

"I'm sorry to come unannounced." I held out my hand.

Morissonneau smiled but kept his hands tucked. He looked older, but better-fed than the first monk.

"You are with the police?"

"The medical-legal lab in Montreal."

"Please." Morissonneau made a hand gesture identical to that of his colleague. "Follow me." English, with a heavy québécois accent.

Morissonneau led me back down the main corridor, across a large open space, then into a long, narrow hall. After passing a dozen closed doors, we entered what appeared to be an office.

Morissonneau closed the door, and gestured again.

I sat.

Compared with the library, this room was spartan. White walls. Gray tile floor. Plain oak desk. Standard metal file cabinets. The only adornments were a crucifix behind the desk, and a painting above one row of cabinets. Jesus talking to angels. And looking considerably more fit than in the carved wooden version hanging over the desk.

I glanced from the canvas to the cross. A phrase popped into my head. *Before and after.* The thought made me feel sacrilegious.

Morissonneau took the straight-back desk chair, laid my photocopy on the blotter, laced his fingers, and looked at me.

I waited.

He waited.

I waited some more.

I won.

"I assume you have seen Avram Ferris." Low and even.

"I have."

"Avram sent you to me?"

Morissonneau didn't know.

"No."

"What is it Avram wants?"

I took a deep breath. I hated what I had to do.

"I'm sorry to be the bearer of bad news, Father. Avram Ferris was murdered two weeks ago."

Morissonneau's lips formed some silent prayer, and his eyes dropped to his hands. When he looked up his face was clouded with an expression I'd seen too often.

"Who?"

"The police are investigating."

Morrissonneau leaned forward onto the desk.

"Are there leads?"

I pointed at the photocopy.

"That photo was given to me by a man named Kessler," I said.

No reaction.

"Are you acquainted with Mr. Kessler?"

"Can you describe this gentleman?"

I did.

"Sorry." Morissonneau's eyes had gone neutral behind his gold-rimmed glasses. "That description fits many."

"Many who would have access to this photo?"

Morissonneau ignored this. "How is it you come to me?"

"I got your name from Yossi Lerner." Close enough.

"How is Yossi?"

"Good."

I told Morissonneau what Kessler had said about the photo.

"I see." He arched his fingers and tapped them on the blotter. For a moment his focus shifted to the photocopy, then to the painting to my right.

"Avram Ferris was shot in the back of the head, execution style."

"Enough." Morissonneau rose. "Please wait." He gave me the palm-stay gesture. I was beginning to feel like Lassie.

Morissonneau hurried from the room.

Five minutes passed.

A clock bonged somewhere down the hall. Otherwise, the building was silent.

Ten minutes passed.

Bored, I rose and crossed to examine the painting. I'd been right but wrong. The canvas and crucifix did constitute a before-and-after sequence, but I'd reversed the order.

The painting depicted Easter morning. Four figures were framed by a tomb. Two angels sat on an open stone coffin, and a woman, probably Mary Magdalene, stood between them. A risen Jesus was to the right.

As in the library, I didn't hear Morissonneau's entry. The first thing I knew he was circling me, a two-by-three-foot crate in his hands. He stopped when he saw me, and his face softened.

"Lovely, isn't it? So much more delicate than most renderings of the resurrection." Morissonneau's voice was altogether different than it had been earlier. He sounded like Gramps showing photos of the grandkids.

"Yes, it is." The painting had an ethereal quality that really was beautiful.

"Edward Burne-Jones. Do you know him?" Morissonneau asked.

I shook my head.

"He was a Victorian English artist, a student of Rossetti. Many Burne-Jones paintings have an almost dreamlike quality to them. This one is titled *The Morning of the Resurrection.* It was done in 1882."

Morissonneau's gaze lingered a moment on the painting, then his jaw tightened and his lips went thin. Circling the desk, he set the crate on the blotter and resumed his seat.

Morissonneau paused a moment, collecting his thoughts. When he spoke his tone was again tense.

"The monastic life is one of solitude, prayer, and study. I chose that." Morissonneau spoke slowly, putting pauses where pauses wouldn't normally go. "With my vows, I turned my back on involvement in the politics and concerns of this world."

Morissonneau placed a liver-spotted hand on the crate.

"But I could not ignore world events. And I could not turn my back on friendship."

Morissonneau stared at his hand, engaged, still, in some inner struggle. Truth or dare.

Truth.

"These bones are from the Musée de l'Homme."

A match flared in my chest.

"The skeleton stolen by Yossi Lerner."

"Yes."

"How long have you had it?"

"Too long."

"You agreed to keep it for Avram Ferris?"

Tight nod.

"Why?"

"So many 'whys.' Why did Avram insist that I take it? Why did I consent? Why have I persisted in this shared dishonesty?"

"Start with Ferris."

"Avram accepted the skeleton from Yossi because of loyalty, and because Yossi convinced him that its rediscovery would trigger cataclysmic events. After transporting the bones to Canada, Avram hid them at his warehouse for several years. Eventually, he grew uncomfortable. More than uncomfortable. Obsessed."

"Why?"

"Avram is a Jew. These are the remains of a human being." Morissonneau caressed the box. "And . . ."

Morissonneau's head cocked up. Light reflected from one lens.

"Who's there?"

I heard the soft swish of fabric.

"Frère Marc?" Morissonneau's voice was sharp.

I swiveled. A form filled the open doorway. Placing fingers to lips, the scar-faced monk raised his one good brow.

Morissonneau shook his head. "*Laissez-nous.*" Leave us.

The monk bowed and withdrew.

Lurching to his feet, Morissonneau strode across the office and closed the door.

"Avram grew uncomfortable," I prompted when he'd resumed his seat.

"He believed what Yossi believed." Hushed.

"That the skeleton is that of Jesus Christ?"

Morissonneau's eyes flicked to the painting, then down again. He nodded.

"Did you believe that?"

"Believe it? No, I didn't believe it, but I didn't know. Don't know. I couldn't take a chance. What if Yossi and Avram were right? Jesus not dead on the cross? It would be the death knell for Christianity."

"It would undercut the most fundamental tenets of the faith."

"Just so. The Christian faith is based on the premise of our savior's death and resurrection. Belief in the Passion is pivotal to a creed around which one billion souls fashion their lives. One billion souls, Dr. Brennan. The consequences of the undermining of that belief would be unthinkable."

Morissonneau closed his eyes, imagining, I could only guess, unthinkable consequences. When he opened them, his voice was stronger.

"Avram and Yossi were probably wrong. I don't believe these are the bones of Jesus Christ. But what if the press picked up on the story? What if the cesspool that is today's mass media engaged in one of their nauseating spectacles, selling their souls for a larger share of the audience for the six o'clock news? The ensuing controversy alone would be a catastrophe."

He didn't wait for a reply.

"I'll tell you what would happen. A billion lives would be wrenched out of joint. Faith would be subverted. Spiritual devastation would be rampant. The Christian world would be cast into crisis. But it wouldn't end there, Dr. Brennan. Like it or not, Christianity is a powerful political and economic force. Collapse of the Christian church would lead to global upheaval. Instability. World chaos."

Morissonneau punched the air with one finger.

"Western civilization would be torn loose at the roots. I believed that then. I believe that even more fervently now, with Islamic extremists pushing their new brand of religious fanaticism."

He leaned forward.

"I am Catholic, but I have studied the Muslim faith. And I have watched closely developments in the Middle East. Even back then, I saw the unrest and knew a crisis was looming. Do you remember the Munich Olympic games?"

"Palestinian terrorists kidnapped part of the Israeli team. All eleven athletes were killed."

"The kidnappers were members of a PLO faction called Black September. Three were captured. A little over a month later, a Lufthansa jet was hijacked by more terrorists demanding the release of the Munich killers. The Germans complied. That was 1972, Dr. Brennan. I watched the news coverage, knowing it was just the beginning. Those events took place one year before Yossi stole the skeleton and gave it to Avram.

"I am a tolerant man. I have nothing but the highest regard for my Islamic brethren. Muslims generally are hardworking, family-centered, peace-loving people who adhere to the same values you and I hold dear. But, among the good, there exists a sinister minority driven by hate and committed to destruction."

"The jihadists."

"Are you familiar with Wahhabism, Dr. Brennan?"

I wasn't.

"Wahhabism is an austere form of Islam that blossomed on the Arabian Peninsula. For over two centuries it's been Saudi Arabia's dominant faith."

"What distinguishes Wahhabism from mainstream Islam?"

"Insistence on a literal interpretation of the Koran."

"Sounds like good old Christian fundamentalism."

"In many ways it is. But Wahhabism goes much further, calling for the complete rejection and destruction of anything and everything not based on the original teachings of Muhammad. The sect's explosive growth began in the seventies when Saudi charities started funding Wahhabi mosques and schools, called madrassas, everywhere from Islamabad to Culver City."

"Is the movement really that bad?"

"Was Afghanistan that bad under the Taliban? Or Iran under the Ayatollah Khomeini?"

Morissonneau didn't pause for an answer.

"Wahhabis aren't simply interested in minds and souls. The sect has an ambitious political agenda focused on the replacement of secular leadership with a fundamentalist religious governing group or person in every Muslim country on the planet."

Jingoist paranoia? I kept my doubts to myself.

"Wahhabis are infiltrating governments and the military throughout the Muslim world, positioning themselves in anticipation of ousting or assassinating secular leaders."

"Do you really believe that?"

"Look at the destruction of modern Lebanon leading to the Syrian occupation. Look at Egypt and the murder of Anwar Sadat. Look at the attempts on the lives of Mubarak of Egypt, Hussein of Jordan, Musharraf of Pakistan. Look at the repression of secular leaders in Iran."

Again, Morissonneau raised a hand and pointed a finger at me. It now trembled.

"Osama bin Laden is Wahhabi, as were the members of his nine-eleven teams. These fanatics are engaged in what they call the Third Great Jihad, or holy war, and anything, *anything* is fair game if it advances their cause."

Morissonneau's hand dropped to the crate. I saw where he was going.

"Including the bones of Jesus Christ," I said.

"Even the *purported* bones of Jesus Christ. These madmen would use their power to manipulate the press, twisting and distorting the issue to suit their purposes. A media circus over the authentication of Jesus' bones would maim the faith of millions, and hand these jihadists the means to erode the foundation of the Church that is my life. If I could prevent such a travesty I felt obliged to do so.

"My primary reason for taking these bones was to protect my beloved Church. Fear of Islamic extremism was secondary back then. But as the years passed, that fear grew."

Morissonneau drew air through his nose and leaned back.

"It became the reason I kept them."

"Where?"

"The monastery has a crypt. Christianity has no prohibition against burial among the living."

"You felt no obligation to notify the museum?"

"Don't misunderstand me, Dr. Brennan. I am a man of God. Ethics mean a lot to me. This was not easy. I struggled with the decision. I have struggled with it every day."

"But you agreed to hide the skeleton."

"I was young when this began. God forgive me. I saw it as one of the necessary deceits of our time. Then, as time passed and no one, including the museum, seemed to be interested in the bones, I thought it best to let them lie."

Morissonneau stood.

"But now it is enough. A man is dead. A decent man. A friend. Perhaps over nothing more than a box of old bones and a lunatic theory in a crazy book."

I stood.

"I trust you will do everything in your power to keep this affair confidential," Morissonneau said.

"I'm not known for my warmth toward the press."

"So I've heard."

I must have looked surprised.

"I placed a call."

So Morissonneau's life wasn't all that cloistered.

"I'll contact the Israeli authorities," I said. "It's likely the bones will return to them, and it's doubtful they'll be calling a press conference, either."

"What happens now is in God's hands."

I lifted the box. The contents shifted with a soft clunking sound.

"Please keep me informed," Morissonneau said.

"I will."

"Thank you."

"I'll attempt to keep your name out of this, Father. But I can't guarantee that will be possible."

Morissonneau started to speak. Then his mouth closed and he quit trying to explain or excuse.

12

I didn't come close to keeping within ten miles of the limit, but luck was with me. Johnny Law was pointing his radar at some other road.

Arriving at Wilfrid Derome, I parked in the lot reserved for cops. Screw it. It was Saturday and I might have God in my Mazda.

The temperature had surged upward into the low forties, and the predicted snowfall had begun as drizzle. Dirty mounds were melting into cracks and puddling pavements and curbs.

Opening the trunk, I retrieved Morissonneau's crate and hurried inside. Except for guards, the lobby was deserted.

So was the twelfth floor.

Setting the crate on my worktable, I stripped off my jacket and called Ryan.

No answer.

Call Jake?

Bones first.

My heart was thumping as I slipped on a lab coat.

Why? Did I really believe I had the skeleton of Jesus?

Of course not.

So who was in the box?

Someone had wanted these bones out of Israel. Lerner had stolen them. Ferris had transported and hidden them. Morissonneau had lied about them, against his conscience.

Had Ferris died because of them?

Religious fervor breeds obsessive actions. Whether these actions are rational or irrational depends on your perspective. I knew that. But why all the intrigue? Why the obsession to hide them but not destroy them?

Was Morissonneau right? Would jihadists kill to obtain these bones? Or was the good father lashing out against religious and political philosophies he viewed as threatening to his own?

No clue. But I intended to pursue answers to these questions as vigorously as I knew how.

I got a hammer from the storage closet.

The wood was dry. The nails were old. Splinters flew as each popped free.

Eventually, sixteen nails rested by the crate. Laying aside my hammer, I lifted the lid.

Dust. Dry bone. Smells as old as the first fossil vertebrate.

The long bones lay on the bottom, parallel, with kneecaps and hand and foot bones jumbled among them. The rest formed a middle layer. The skull was on top, jaw detached, empty orbits staring skyward. The skeleton looked like hundreds of others I'd seen, spoils of a farmer's field, a shallow grave, a dozer cut at a demolition site.

Transferring the skull to a cork stabilizer ring, I positioned the jaw and stared at the fleshless face.

What had it looked like in life? Whose had it been?

Nope. No speculation.

One by one, I articulated every element.

Forty minutes later, an anatomically correct skeleton lay on my table. Nothing was missing save a tiny throat bone called the hyoid and a few finger and toe phalanges.

I was sliding a case form onto a clipboard when my phone rang. It was Ryan.

I told him about my morning.

"Holy shit."

"Maybe," I said.

"Ferris and Lerner were believers."

"Morissonneau wasn't so sure."

"What do you think?" Ryan asked.

"I'm just starting my analysis."

"And?"

"I'm just starting my analysis."

"My ass ain't mine until this stakeout's done. But I got a call this morning. I may have caught a break on the Ferris homicide."

"No kidding," I said.

"When I'm cut loose here I'll follow up," Ryan said.

"What's the lead?"

"When I'm cut loose here I'll follow up."

"Touché."

"Damn, we're professional," Ryan said.

"No reckless speculation for us," I agreed.

"Not a hasty conclusion in sight."

When we'd disconnected I dashed to the first-floor cafeteria, devoured a tuna sandwich and Diet Coke, and raced back to the lab.

I wanted to torpedo straight to the key questions. I forced myself to stick to protocol.

Gloves.

Light.

Case form.

Deep breath.

I started with gender.

Pelvis: narrow sciatic notch, narrow pelvic inlet, chunky pubic bones bridging an inverted V in front.

Skull: bulging brow ridges, blunt orbital borders, large crests, muscle attachments, and mastoid processes.

There was no wiggle room. This skeleton was all boy.

I turned to age.

Angling my light, I observed the left pelvic half where it would have joined hands with the right pelvic half in life. The surface was pitted and slightly depressed relative to the height of an oval rim circling its perimeter. Spiny growths protruded from the rim's upper and lower edges.

The right pubic symphysis looked the same.

I got up and walked to the watercooler.

I took a drink.

I took a breath.

Calmer, I returned to the skeleton and selected ribs three through five from both sides of the chest. Only two retained undamaged sternal ends. Laying the other ribs aside, I observed this pair closely.

Both ribs ended in deep, U-shaped indentations surrounded by thin walls terminating in sharp-edged rims. Bony spicules projected from the superior and inferior borders of each rim.

I leaned back and laid down my pencil.

Feeling what? Relief? Disappointment? I wasn't sure.

The pubic symphyses scored as phase six on the Suchey-Brooks age-determination system, a set of standards derived from the analysis of the pelves of hundreds of adults of documented age at death. For males, phase six suggests a mean age of sixty-one.

The ribs scored as phase six on the Iscan-Loth age-determination system, a set of standards based on the quantification of morphological changes in ribs collected from adults at autopsy. For males, this suggests an age range of forty-three to fifty-five.

Granted, Y-chromosomers are tremendously variable. Granted, I'd yet to observe the long bones and the molar roots radiologically. Nevertheless, I was certain my preliminary conclusion would hold. I jotted it on the case form.

Age at death: forty to sixty years.

There was no way this guy died in his thirties.

Like Jesus of Nazareth.

If Jesus of Nazareth died in his thirties. Joyce's theory had him living until eighty.

This guy fit neither profile.

There was also no way this man had lived into his seventies.

So he also failed to fit the profile of the old male from Cave 2001. But had the isolated skeleton described by Jake's volunteer-informant actually been the old male? Maybe not. Maybe Yadin's septuagenarian was jumbled with the commingled bones, and the isolated skeleton was another individual altogether. An individual of forty to sixty.

Like this guy.

I flipped to the next page.

Ancestry.

Right.

Most systems for racial assessment rely on variations in skull shape, facial architecture, dental form, and cranial metrics. Though I often rely on the latter, there was a problem.

If I took measurements and ran them through Fordisc 2.0, the program would compare my unknown to whites, blacks, American Indians, Hispanics, Japanese, Chinese, and Vietnamese.

Big help if crate-man lived in Israel two thousand years back.

I went through the trait list on my form. Prominent nasal bones. Narrow nasal opening. Flat facial profile when viewed from the side. Cheekbones hugging the face. On and on.

Everything suggested Caucasoid, or at least European-like ancestry. Not Negroid. Not Mongoloid.

I took measurements and ran them. Every comparison placed the skull squarely with the whites.

Okay. Computer and eyeballs were in agreement.

What then? Was the man Middle Eastern? Southern European? Jewish? Gentile? I knew of no way to sort that out. Nor did DNA testing offer any help.

I moved on to stature.

Selecting the leg bones, I eliminated those with eroded or damaged ends, and measured the rest on an osteometric board. Then I plugged the measurements into Fordisc 2.0, and asked for a calculation using all males in the database, with race unknown.

Height: sixty-four to sixty-eight inches.

I spent the next several hours scrutinizing every knob and crest and hole and notch, every facet and joint, every millimeter of cortical surface under magnification. I found nothing. No genetic variations. No lesions or indicators of illness. No trauma, healed or otherwise.

No penetrating wounds in the hands or feet.

Killing the fiber-optic light on the scope, I arched backward and stretched, my shoulders and neck feeling like someone had set them on fire.

Could it be I was getting older?

No way.

I crossed to my desk, dropped into my chair, and checked my watch. Five fifty-five. Midnight in Paris.

Too late to phone.

Jake answered sounding groggy and asked me to wait.

"What's up?" Jake had returned, whooshing a pop-top.

"It ain't Jesus."

"What?"

"The skeleton from the Musée de l'Homme."

"What about it?"

"I'm looking at it."

"What?"

"It's a middle-aged white guy of average stature."

"What?"

"You're not holding up your end of this conversation, Jake."

"You have Lerner's bones?"

"The skeleton he liberated is here in my lab."

"Christ!"

"Not this guy."

"You're sure?"

"This guy saw forty come and go. My best estimate says he was at least fifty at death."

"Not eighty."

"No way."

"Could he have been seventy?"

"I doubt it."

"So it's not the older Masada male referred to by Yadin and Tsafrir."

"Do we know for a fact that Yadin's old guy was the isolated skeleton?"

"Actually, no. The older bones could have been mixed in with the main heap. That would leave the isolated skeleton as one of the fourteen males aged twenty-two to sixty."

"Or totally unaccounted for."

"Yes." There was a long pause. "Tell me how you got the skeleton."

I told him about Morissonneau and my visit to the monastery.

"Holy shit."

"That's what Ryan said."

When Jake spoke again his voice was almost a whisper.

"What are you going to do?"

"First off, tell my boss. These are human remains. They were found in Quebec. They're the coroner's responsibility. Also, the bones may be evidence in a homicide investigation."

"Ferris?"

"Yes."

"And then?"

"Undoubtedly my boss will tell me to contact the appropriate authorities in Israel."

There was another pause. Sleet plopped against the window above my desk and ran in rivulets down the glass. Twelve floors below, traffic clogged the streets and crawled the Jacques Cartier Bridge. Taillights drew glistening red ribbons on the pavement.

"You're sure this is the skeleton in the Kessler photo?"

Good question. One I hadn't considered.

"I saw nothing to rule that out," I said.

"Anything to rule it in?"

"No." Lame.

"Is it worth another look?"

"I'll do it now."

"Will you talk to me before you contact Israel?"

"Why?"

"Please promise you'll ring me first?"

Why not. Jake had initiated this whole thing.

"Sure, Jake."

When we hung up, I sat a moment, hand resting on the receiver. Jake sounded uneasy about my notifying the Israeli authorities. Why?

He wanted first claim on rights to publish concerning the discovery and analysis of the skeleton? He feared losing control of the skeleton? He distrusted his Israeli colleagues? He distrusted the Israeli authorities?

I had no idea. Why hadn't I asked?

I was hungry. My back hurt. I wanted to go home, have dinner with Birdie and Charlie, and curl up with my book.

Instead I dug out Kessler's photo and placed it under the scope. Slowly, I moved from the top of the skull south over the face.

The forehead showed no unique identifier.

Eyes. Nothing.

Nose. Nothing.

Cheekbones. Nothing.

I twisted my head right, then left to relieve the pain in my neck.

Back to the scope.

When the mouth came into view, I stared through the eyepiece. I looked up and across my worktable at the skull.

Something wasn't right.

Returning my eyes to the scope, I increased magnification. The teeth ballooned.

I brought the central incisor into focus, then inched from the midline toward the back of the jaw.

My stomach knotted.

I got up, retrieved my magnifying glass, and picked up the skull. Rotating the palate upward, I examined the dentition.

The knot tightened.

I closed my eyes.

What the hell could this mean?

13

I CARRIED THE PHOTO FROM THE SCOPE TO THE SKULL. USING THE hand lens, I counted from the midline of the palate to a gap on the right.

Two incisors, one canine, two premolars. Gap. Two molars.

The skeleton in Kessler's print was missing its first upper molar on the right.

The skull on my worktable was not.

Was this not the skeleton pictured in the photo?

I returned to the scope, raised it, and positioned the skull. Then I directed the fiber-optic light onto the right maxillary molars.

Under magnification, I could see that the molar roots were exposed more than normal. The socket edges were pitted and porous.

Periodontal disease. No big deal.

What *was* a big deal was the condition of the right first upper molar's chewing surface. The cusps were high and rounded, while the cusps on the adjacent molars were completely ground down.

What the hell was that all about?

I articulated the jaw and noted occlusion. The first molar made contact before any other molar in the row. If anything, the first molar should have exhibited greater wear than its neighbors, not less.

I leaned back and considered.

There were two possibilities. A. This was a different skeleton from that in the Kessler photo. B. This was the same skeleton, but with a molar inserted into the gap.

If a molar had been inserted, there were two possibilities. A. It was the actual tooth that had been lost from the jaw. Teeth often fall out once the soft tissue decomposes. B. It was the tooth of another, mistakenly inserted into the jaw. This possibility would explain the differential cusp wear.

When had the tooth been reinserted? Three possibilities seemed reasonable. A. At the time of burial. B. During Yadin's excavation. C. During the skeleton's stay at the Musée de l'Homme.

My instincts said B.

Okay. If the tooth was replaced during the Masada dig, who had done it? Many possibilities. A. Yadin. B. Tsafrir. C. Haas. D. An excavator.

My gut feeling?

An excavator found the tooth beside the skeleton, tried the jaw, it seemed to fit, he stuck it in. The Cave 2001 bones were jumbled. Good records weren't kept. Mistakes happen all the time with students and unskilled volunteers.

So. Funerary act? Simple error? Neither of the above, different skeleton than that in Kessler's photo?

I was in over my head. I needed an odontologist.

It was now ten past seven on a Saturday night. I knew what Marc Bergeron, our lab's dental expert, would say.

Get apical X-rays.

I couldn't do that until Monday.

Frustrated, I spent the next hour studying Kessler's print under magnification.

I spotted no anatomical quirk or detail that could tie the skeleton in the photo unequivocally to the bones on my table.

For the rest of the evening I sat around feeling agitated and blocked. Birdie and I watched an NCAA basketball game. I was strongly for Duke. Bird was pulling for the Clemson Tigers. Probably a feline thing.

Sunday morning it took less than thirty minutes online to locate and order the Donovan Joyce book. *The Jesus Scroll.* Ads blurbed it as the most disturbing work ever written about Christianity. Good press. Too bad the thing was out of print.

Every few hours I called Jake. His mobile was off. At one, I quit leaving messages and tried his hotel. He'd checked out.

Ryan's surveillance ended with three arrests and the confiscation of a truckload of cigarettes. He showed up at six, eyes deeply shadowed, hair wet from the shower. I had a Perrier, Ryan had a Moosehead, then we walked to Katsura on rue de la Montagne.

My patch of centre-ville was quiet. Few students milled outside Concordia University. Few fun-seekers partied on rue Crescent.

There's something 'bout a Sunday.

Or maybe it was the temperature. Overnight, Saturday's sleet had given way to clear skies and arctic cold.

Over sushi, I gave Ryan the rundown on Morissonneau's skeleton, ending with my conclusion that the bones were those of a white male aged forty to sixty at the time of his death.

"So my age estimate rules out the Cave 2001 septuagenarian, the Bible's thirty-three-year-old Jesus, and Donovan Joyce's eighty-year-old Jesus."

"But you're certain Kessler's photo shows the isolated skeleton in Cave 2001, and that that skeleton is the one Lerner stole from the Musée de l'Homme and gave to Ferris, who gave it to Morissonneau?"

"Jake's certain. He's talked to someone who worked as a volunteer excavator in Cave 2001. But I can't find a single unique identifier to unequivocally tie Morissonneau's skeleton to the one in Kessler's photo. And there's something going on with one of the teeth."

I told Ryan about the odd molar.

"So you suspect it's not the same skeleton?"

"Or it is the same skeleton, but the molar was inserted after the photo was taken."

"Someone found the guy's missing tooth during recovery and stuck it back in the socket?"

"Possibly."

"You sound unconvinced."

"The cusps look less ground down to me."

"Meaning the tooth could be from another person, someone younger."

"Yes."

"Meaning?"

"I don't know. Maybe just a mix-up. Yadin used volunteers. Maybe one of them inserted the molar, thinking it belonged."

"You're going to see Bergeron?"

"Monday."

Ryan filled me in on his lead in the Ferris case.

"When I ran the name Kessler, not a lot popped out."

"Dearth of Jewish felons?"

"Meyer Lansky," Ryan said.

"I stand corrected," I said.

"Bugsy Siegel," Ryan added.

"Twice."

"David Berkowitz."

"Thrice."

"Elegant," Ryan said.

"Shakespearean," I agreed.

"When I tinkered around, what *did* pop out was a guy named Hershel Kaplan."

I was stumped. What follows thrice. Frice? Quatrice?

"Kaplan's a small-time hustler. Did a couple of bumps for white-collar stuff. Credit card fraud. Check forgery. Also goes by the names Hershel Cantor and Harry Kester."

"Let me guess. Kessler was also one of Kaplan's aliases."

"Hirsch Kessler." Ryan dug a photocopy from his back pocket. "That your boy?"

I studied the photo. Glasses. Dark hair. This guy was clean-shaven.

"Maybe." They all look alike? I felt like a moron.

I closed my eyes and conjured Kessler.

I opened my eyes and stared at the mug shot.

Subconscious ring-a-ding. What?

The craning neck. The drooping lids. A word when Kessler ambushed me outside the family room. Turtle. I'd forgotten. The same word had again flashed into my mind.

"Kessler had a beard. But I think it's the same man." I handed the paper back. "Sorry. It's the best I can do."

"It's a start."

"Where's Kessler now? Kaplan?"

"I'm looking into that."

Back home, Ryan talked with Charlie while I showered. I was standing naked by my dresser when he entered the bedroom.

"Freeze."

I turned, a lace baby doll nightie in one hand, a satin charmeuse slip in the other.

"I'm going to have to know what you're doing, ma'am."

"You a cop?"

"That's why I ask the tough questions."

I raised the lingerie and a questioning brow.

"Put down the nighties and step away from the dresser."

I did.

It was a typical Monday morning madhouse at the lab. Four dead in a house fire. One shooting. One hanging. Two stabbings. A crib death.

Only one case for me.

Objects had been found in the basement sink of an apartment high-rise in Côte Saint-Luc. Police suspected they were the skull bones of an infant or toddler.

After the morning meeting, I asked LaManche to follow me to my lab. I showed him Morissonneau's skeleton, filled him in on its history and possible provenance, and explained how it had come into my possession.

As expected, LaManche assigned the remains an LSJML number, and told me to treat them as a coroner case. Final resolution would be my call. Should I declare the bones ancient, I was free to release them to the appropriate archaeologists.

When LaManche had gone, I asked my lab technician, Denis, to X-ray the skeleton's dentition. Then I got down to the baby.

I had to admit the specimens looked like two very young and incomplete parietal bones. The concave surfaces showed the vascular patterning produced by close association with the brain's outer surface.

Cleaning resolved the issue.

The "bones" were fragments of coconut shell. The venous patterning was the result of water action on caked mud.

When I'd delivered my report to the secretary's office, Denis handed me a small brown envelope. I dumped the contents onto my light box.

One look strengthened my suspicion that the first maxillary molar had been reinserted into the skeleton's jaw. And not too skillfully. On X-ray, I could see that the tooth's angle was slightly wrong, and that the roots didn't conform properly to their sockets.

And something else.

As a tooth ages, its cusps grind down. Okay. I'd spotted the discrepancy in wear. But other features also change with time. The older a tooth, the more secondary dentin in its pulp chamber and canal.

I'm no dentist, but the right first maxillary molar looked less radio-opaque than the other molars.

I phoned Marc Bergeron. His receptionist put me on hold. I listened to a Thousand Strings play something resembling "Sweet Caroline." In my mind's eye I saw a patient, reclined, agape, tubing sucking at his mouth. I was glad it wasn't me.

Marc picked up during a mind-numbing version of "Uptown Girl." He'd squeeze me in that afternoon.

Jake called as I was packaging the skull.

"Did you get my messages?" I asked.

"I checked out Saturday and took the midnight flight to Tel Aviv."

"You're in Israel?"

"Jerusalem. What's up?"

I told him about the inconsistency between the skeleton in the photo and the skeleton in my lab, and described the seemingly aberrant molar.

"What does it mean?"

"I'm seeing our odontologist this afternoon."

There was a long, long pause. Then, "I want you to pull that molar and one or two others."

"Why?"

"For DNA testing. I also want you to cut femoral segments. Is that a problem?"

"If Ferris and Lerner are right, these bones are almost two thousand years old."

"It's possible to extract mitochondrial DNA from old bone, right?"

"It's possible. But then what? Forensic analysis is based on comparison, either to the victim's own DNA, or to that of a family member. If mtDNA *could* be extracted and amplified, to what would you compare it?"

Long Jake pause. Then, "New finds are unearthed every day. You never know what will turn up, or what will be relevant down the road. And I've got grant money specifically earmarked for this type of thing. What about race?"

"What about it?"

"Wasn't there a recent case where profilers said the perp was white and some lab predicted, correctly, that the guy was black?"

"You're thinking of the Derrick Todd Lee case in Baton Rouge. That test relies on nuclear DNA."

"Can't nuclear DNA be extracted from ancient bone?"

"Some claim to have done it. There's a growing field of study on aDNA."

"aDNA?"

"Ancient DNA. Folks at Cambridge and Oxford are working on getting nuclear DNA from archaeological material. Here in Canada, there's an institute called the Paleo-DNA Laboratory in Thunder Bay."

I remembered a recent article in *The American Journal of Human Genetics.*

"A French group reported on nuclear and mitochondrial DNA from skeletons dug from a two-thousand-year-old necropolis in Mongolia. But Jake, even if you could get nuclear DNA, racial prediction is very limited."

"How limited?"

"There's a Florida company that offers a test that translates genetic markers into a prediction of likely racial mix. They claim they can predict the percentage present of Indo-European, Native American, East Asian, and sub-Saharan-African ancestry."

"That's it?"

"For now."

"Not much help with the bones of an ancient Palestinian."

"No," I agreed.

I listened to another of Jake's pauses.

"But either mito or nuclear DNA analysis might show whether that odd molar belonged to a different individual."

"It's a long shot."

"But it might."

"It might," I conceded.

"Who does these tests?"

I told him.

"Visit your dentist, see what he says about the odd tooth. Then take samples. And cut enough bone for radiocarbon analysis, too."

"The coroner's not going to foot the bill," I said.

"I'll use my grant money."

I was zipping my parka when Ryan came through the door.

What he told me sent my thoughts winging a one-eighty.

14

"Miriam Ferris is related to Hershel Kaplan?"

"Affinal tie."

"Affinal." I was having trouble wrapping my mind around Ryan's statement.

"It's a kinship term. Means linked by marriage." Ryan gave his most boyish smile. "I use it in tribute to your anthropological past."

I sketched a mental diagram of what he'd just said. "Miriam Ferris was married to Hershel Kaplan's wife's brother?"

"Former wife."

"But Miriam denied knowing Kaplan," I said.

"We asked about Kessler."

"One of Kaplan's known aliases."

"Confusing, isn't it?"

"If Kaplan was family, Miriam would have known him."

"Presumably," Ryan agreed.

"She'd have recognized him at the autopsy."

"If she'd seen him."

"You really think Kaplan is Kessler?" I asked.

"You were reasonably convinced by the mug shot." Ryan was looking at the box on my table.

"Is Kaplan's wife's brother still alive?"

"Former wife. Before the divorce, Miriam's husband would have been Kaplan's brother-in-law. Anyway, the guy died of diabetic complications in ninety-five."

"So Kaplan and his wife split, leaving him single. And Miriam's husband died, leaving her single."

"Yep. Ferris's murder was a return engagement for the grieving widow. You'd think she'd be better at it. What's in the box?"

"I'm taking Morissonneau's skull to Bergeron for an opinion on the teeth."

"His patients should love that."

Ryan pulled his lips back in a ghoulish grimace.

I rolled my eyes.

"When did Miriam tie the knot with Avram Ferris?" I asked.

"Ninety-seven."

"Pretty quick after her first husband's death."

"Some widows bounce right back."

Miriam didn't strike me as a bouncer, but I kept the thought to myself.

"How long has Kaplan been divorced?" I asked.

"The missus bailed during his second stretch at Bordeaux."

"Ouch."

"I checked Kaplan's prison sheet. The guy caused no problems, appeared sincere in his desire to improve himself, got cut loose at half time."

"So he has a parole officer?"

"Michael Hinson."

"When was he released?"

"Two thousand and one. According to Hinson, Kaplan's been a legit businessman ever since."

"What business?"

"Guppies and guinea pigs."

I raised a quizzical brow.

"Centre d'animaux Kaplan."

"He has a pet store?"

Ryan nodded. "Owns the building. Guppies down, Kaplan up."

"Does he still meet with the PO?"

"Monthly. Been a model parolee."

"Admirable."

"Never missed a check-in until two weeks ago. He failed to call or show up on February fourteenth."

"The Monday following the weekend Avram Ferris was shot."

"Want to pet the Pomeranians?"

"Bergeron's expecting me at one."

Ryan looked at his watch.

"Meet you downstairs at two-thirty?"

"I'll bring a Milk-Bone."

Bergeron's office is at Place Ville-Marie, a multitowered high-rise at the corner of René-Lévesque and University. He shares it with a partner named Bougainvillier. I'd never met Bougainvillier, but I always pictured a flowering vine with glasses.

After driving to the centre-ville, I parked underground, and rode an elevator to the seventeenth floor.

Bergeron was with a patient, so I settled in the waiting room, box at my feet. A large woman sat opposite, thumbing a copy of *Châtelaine.* When I reached for a magazine, she looked up and smiled. She needed a dentist.

Five minutes after my arrival, the *Châtelaine* woman was invited into the inner sanctum. I suspected she'd be there awhile.

Moments later a man exited the inner sanctum. His jacket was off and his tie was loose. He was moving fast.

Bergeron appeared and led me to his office. A high whining emanated from down the hall. I pictured the *Châtelaine* woman. I pictured the plant in *The Little Shop of Horrors.*

As I unpacked my box, I sketched some background for Bergeron. He listened, bony arms crossed on bony chest, white frizz luminous in the window light.

When I'd finished Bergeron took the skull and examined the upper teeth. He examined the jaw. He articulated the jaw and studied the molar occlusion.

Bergeron held out a hand. I placed the tiny brown envelope in it.

Clicking on a light box, Bergeron arranged the dental X-rays and leaned close. His hair haloed like a dandelion in the bright fluorescence.

Seconds passed. A full minute.

"*Mon Dieu,* no question." A skeletal finger tapped the second and third right upper molars. "Look at these pulp chambers and canals. This man was at least fifty. Probably older."

The finger moved to the row's first molar.

"There's much less dentin deposition here. This tooth is unquestionably from a younger person."

"How much younger?"

Bergeron straightened, pooched air through his lips. "Thirty-five. Maybe forty. No more."

Bergeron returned to the skull.

"Minimal cusp wear. Probably the lower end of that range."

"Can you tell when the molar was reinserted?"

Bergeron looked at me as though I'd asked him to calculate quadratic equations in his head.

"A rough estimate?" I amended.

"The glue is yellowed and flaking."

"Wait." I raised a palm. "You're saying the tooth's glued in?"

"Yes."

"So it wasn't reinserted two thousand years back?"

"Definitely not. Maybe a few decades back."

"In the sixties?"

"Very possible."

Option B or C, insertion during Yadin's excavation, or at the Musée de l'Homme. My gut was still going with the former.

"Would you mind extracting those three upper molars?"

"Not at all."

Bergeron reboxed the skull and hurried from the office, his six-foot-three frame moving with all the grace of an ironing board.

I gathered the X-rays, wondering if I was making a big deal over nothing. The odd tooth came from a younger individual. Someone stuck the thing into the wrong jaw. Maybe a volunteer digger. Maybe Haas. Maybe an unskilled museum worker.

Down the hall, the whining continued.

There are myriad points at which errors of individuation can occur. Recovery. Transport. Sorting. Cleaning. Maybe the admixture took place in the cave. Maybe in Haas's lab. Maybe later at the museum in Paris.

Bergeron returned and handed me the box and a ziplock bag.

"Anything else you can tell me?" I asked.

"Whoever replaced that molar was a dental jackass."

Le centre d'animaux Kaplan was a two-story glass-fronted store in a row of two- and three-story glass-fronted stores on rue Jean-Talon. Signs in the window offered Nutrience dog and cat foods, tropical fish, and a special on parakeets, cage included.

Two doors opened directly off the sidewalk, one wood, one glass. Chimes jangled as Ryan pushed through the latter.

The shop was crammed with odors and sounds. Tanks bubbled along one wall, birdcages lined another, their occupants ranging from the drab to the flamboyant. Beyond the fish I could see other representatives of the Linnaean hierarchy. Frogs. A coiled snake. A small furry thing curled into a ball.

Up front were rabbits, kittens, a lizard with a wattle to rival my great aunt Minnie's. Puppies dozed in cages. One stood, tail wagging, front paws pressed to the wire mesh. One gnawed a red rubber duck.

Parallel shelves shot the center of the store. A kid of about seventeen was sliding collars onto hangers halfway down the side opposite the birds.

Hearing chimes, the kid turned, but didn't speak.

"*Bonjour,*" Ryan said.

"Yo," the kid said.

"Some help, please."

Dropping his carton, the kid slouched toward us.

Ryan badged him.

"Cops?"

Ryan nodded.

"Cool."

"Way cool. And you would be?"

"Bernie."

Bernie was scrupulously adhering to his interpretation of gangsta chic. Low-slung jeans with knee-level crotch, shirt unbuttoned over a grungy T. He was way too skinny to make the look work. Everyone was.

"I'm Detective Ryan. This is Dr. Brennan."

Bernie's eyes slid to me. They were small and dark and overset by brows that met in the middle. Bernie'd probably bought his share of Clearasil.

"We're looking for Hershel Kaplan."

"He's not here."

"Is Mr. Kaplan often away?"

Bernie raised one shoulder and cocked his head.

"Do you know where the gentleman is today?"

Bernie shrugged both shoulders.

"Are these questions too tough for you, Bernie?"

Bernie scraped hair from his forehead.

"Shall I start over?" Ryan's voice could have frozen margaritas.

"Don't bust my ass, man. I just work for the guy."

A puppy began yapping. It wanted out.

"Listen carefully. Has Mr. Kaplan been here today?"

"I opened up."

"Has he called?"

"No."

"Is Mr. Kaplan upstairs?"

"He's on vacation, aw'right?" Bernie shifted weight from one leg to the other. There wasn't much to shift.

"It would have been helpful if you'd said that at the outset, Bernie."

Bernie looked at the floor.

"Do you know where Mr. Kaplan has gone?"

Bernie shook his head.

"When he'll be back?"

The head shake continued.

"There's something wrong here, Bernie. I'm getting the feeling you don't want to talk to me."

Bernie kept eyeing the mud on his sneakers.

"This going to mess up that bonus Kaplan promised?"

"Look, I don't know." Bernie's head came up. "Kaplan told me to keep the place running and not talk it up that he'd split."

"When was that?"

"Maybe a week ago."

"Do you have a key to Mr. Kaplan's apartment?"

Bernie didn't respond to that.

"You still live at home, Bernie?"

"Yeah." Wary.

"We could swing by, ask Mom to help clear this up."

"Man." Whiny.

"Bernie?"

"His key might be on the ring."

Ryan turned to me.

"Do you smell gas?"

"Maybe." I sniffed. I smelled many things. "Yes, you could be right."

"How about you, Bernie? You smell gas?"

"That's the ferret."

"Smells like gas to me." Ryan moved a few feet to his left, then to his right, nose working the air. "Yeah. Gas. Dangerous stuff."

Ryan turned to Bernie.

"Would you like us to check it out?"

Bernie looked skeptical.

"Wouldn't want to guess wrong with all these creatures depending on you," Ryan said, the essence of reasonableness.

"Yeah. Sure, man."

Bernie crossed to the counter and pulled keys from below the register.

Ryan took the keys and turned to me.

"Citizen asked us to check out a gas leak."

I gave a shrug that would have made Bernie proud.

Ryan and I exited the glass door, hooked a left, and reentered the building through the wooden door. A narrow staircase rose steeply to a second-floor landing.

We clumped up.

Ryan knocked. There was no answer. Ryan knocked again, harder.

"Police, Mr. Kaplan."

No answer.

"We're coming in."

Ryan inserted key after key. The fourth worked.

Kaplan's apartment had a small kitchen, a living room, a bedroom, a bath with black-and-white tile and a freestanding tub. Venetian blinds covered the windows, and genuinely awful mass-market landscapes decorated the walls.

Some concessions had been made to evolving technology. The tub had been jerry-rigged with a handheld shower. A microwave had been placed on a kitchen counter. An answering machine had been connected to a bedroom phone. Otherwise, the place looked as if it had been ripped from a low-budget thirties movie.

"Elegant," Ryan said.

"Understated," I agreed.

"I hate it when decorators get carried away."

"Lose all appreciation for linoleum."

We moved to the bedroom.

A folding table held phone books, ledgers, and stacks of papers. I crossed to it and began poking around. Behind me Ryan opened and closed dresser drawers. Several minutes passed.

"Find anything?" I asked.

"A lot of bad shirts."

Ryan shifted to the nightstand.

He made his discovery as I made mine.

15

I PICKED UP THE LETTER AS RYAN PRESSED THE BUTTON ON THE answering machine.

I read while listening to the sugary voice: *This message is for Hershel Kaplan. Your reservation for Saturday, February twenty-sixth, has been confirmed on Air Canada flight nine-five-eight-zero, operated by El Al, departing Toronto Pearson International Airport at eleven-fifty P.M. Please be advised that, due to heightened security, El Al requires passenger check-in at least three hours prior to departure. Have a pleasant flight.*

"Kaplan's gone to Israel," Ryan said.

"Kaplan may have known Miriam Ferris better than we thought," I said. "Look at this."

Ryan crossed to me. I handed him a pale gold card.

Hersh:

You view happiness as an impossible dream. I have seen it in your eyes. Pleasure and joy have moved to a place beyond the scope of your imagination.

You are angry? Ashamed? Afraid? Don't be. We are pushing forward, slowly, like swimmers moving through an angry sea. The waves will recede. We will triumph.

Love,
M

I pointed to initials embossed on the card. "*M.F.*"

"The acronym has other meanings."

"Rarely on stationery. And *M.F.* isn't a common initial combination."

Ryan thought a moment.

"Morgan Freeman. Marshall Field. Millard Fillmore. Morgan Fairchild."

"I'm impressed." I worked it. "Masahisa Fukase."

Blank stare.

"Fukase's a Japanese photographer. Does amazing images of crows."

"Some of Fairchild's images were pretty amazing."

Eye roll. "I have a gut feeling Miriam wrote this. But when? There's no date. And why?"

"To cheer Kaplan in prison?"

I pointed to the note's last line. "*We* will triumph?"

"To encourage Kaplan to pump two slugs into hubby?"

Suddenly the room felt cold and dark.

"Time to call Israel," Ryan said.

Back at Wilfrid Derome, Ryan peeled off to the crimes contre la personne squad room, and I returned to my lab. Selecting the right femur from Morissonneau's skeleton, I descended to autopsy room four, and placed the bone on the table.

After connecting the Stryker saw, I masked, and cut two one-inch plugs from the femur's midshaft. Then I returned to my lab and phoned Jake. Once again, I was rousing him at the midnight hour.

I told Jake what Bergeron had said about the odd molar.

"How did someone else's tooth get into the jaw of that skeleton?"

"It happens. My guess is the molar somehow became incorporated with the skeleton during recovery of the bones in the cave. The roots fit the socket reasonably well, so someone, maybe a volunteer digger, slipped it into the jaw."

"And Haas later glued it."

"Maybe. Maybe someone at the Musée de l'Homme. It's probably just an error."

"Did you cut samples for DNA testing?"

I reiterated my skepticism about the value of DNA in a case in which no comparative samples existed.

"I want the tests done."

"Okay. It's your grant money."

"And carbon fourteen."

"Priority or standard delivery on the radiocarbon?"

"What's the difference?"

"Days versus weeks. And several hundred dollars."

"Priority."

I gave Jake the names of the labs I intended to use. He agreed and provided a billing account number.

"Jake, if carbon-fourteen testing indicates this skeleton is as old as you say it is, you know I'll have to contact the Israeli authorities."

"Call me first."

"I'll call. But I'd like to kn—"

"Thanks, Tempe." Quick intake of breath. I sensed Jake was about to tell me something. Then, "This could be explosive."

I started to question that, decided not to press. I wanted to get the samples ready for morning pickup.

After disconnecting, I logged onto the Net, called up the websites, and downloaded two case-submission forms for the DNA testing, and one for the radiometric testing.

The odd molar had come from a different individual than the bones and teeth of the rest of the skeleton. I wanted it treated as a single case for DNA testing. I assigned the odd molar one sample number.

I assigned a second, single sample number to one of the plugs I'd cut from the skeleton's femur and one of the molars Bergeron had extracted from its jaw.

I registered the second of the skeleton's molars and the second bone plug for radiocarbon dating.

When I'd completed the paperwork, I asked Denis to FedEx the bone and tooth samples to the respective labs.

That was it. There was nothing else I could do.

Days passed.

Frost crept across my windows. Snow capped the slats of my side-yard fence.

My casework entered a typical late winter lull. No hikers or campers. Fewer kids in the parks. Snow on the land, ice on the river. Scavengers hunkered in, waiting out winter.

Come spring, the bodies would blossom like monarchs swarming north. For now, it was quiet.

Tuesday morning, I purchased Yadin's popular work on Masada. Beautiful photographs, chapters and chapters on the palaces, bathhouses, synagogues, and scrolls. But Jake was right. Yadin devoted barely a page to the cave skeletons, and included only one lonely photo. Hard to believe the book triggered such a controversy when it was published in '66.

Tuesday afternoon, Ryan learned that Hershel Kaplan had entered Israel on February 27. Kaplan's present whereabouts were unknown. The Israel National Police were looking for him.

Ryan phoned Wednesday afternoon to ask if I'd like to accompany him on a follow-up with Courtney Purviance, then grab some dinner.

"Follow-up on what?"

"No biggie, just a detail on one of Ferris's associates. Guy named Klingman says he stopped by to see Ferris that Friday, couldn't scare anyone up. Just dotting *i*'s and crossing *t*'s."

What the hell. I had nothing better to do.

Ryan picked me up around four. Purviance lived in a typical Montreal walk-up in Saint-Léonard. Gray stone. Blue trim. Iron staircase shooting straight up the front.

The lobby was small, the tile floor filmed by salty snowmelt. Beside the interior door were four mail slots, each with a handwritten nameplate and buzzer. Purviance lived in unit 2-B.

Ryan thumbed the button. A female voice answered. Ryan gave his name. The woman responded with a question.

While Ryan cleared security, I scanned the names of the other tenants.

Purviance told Ryan to wait.

He turned. I must have been smiling.

"What's so funny?"

"Look at these names." I pointed to 1-A. "How does that translate in French?"

"'The pine.'"

I tapped 1-B. " That's 'olive' in Italian." 2-A. "That's 'oak' in Latvian. We've got an international arborist convention, right here in Saint-Léonard."

Ryan smiled and shook his head.

"I don't know how your brain works, Brennan."

"Stunning, isn't it?"

The door buzzed. We climbed to the second floor.

When Ryan knocked, Purviance again asked that he identify himself. He did. A million locks rattled. The door cracked. A nose peeked out. The door closed. A chain disengaged. The door reopened.

Ryan introduced me as a colleague. Purviance nodded and led us to a tiny living room filled with way too much furniture. Filled with way too much, period. Every shelf, tabletop, and horizontal surface was crammed with memorabilia.

Purviance had been watching a *Law & Order* rerun. Briscoe was telling a suspect he didn't know jack.

Clicking off the TV, Purviance took a seat opposite Ryan. She was short, blonde, and twenty pounds overweight. I guessed her age at just north of forty.

As the two talked, I checked out the apartment.

The living room gave onto a dining room, which gave onto a kitchen, shotgun style. I assumed the bedroom and bath were reached by a short hallway branching off to the right. With the exception of the room in which we were seated, I guessed the place received natural light a total of one hour a day.

I refocused on Ryan and Purviance. The woman looked drawn and weary, but now and then sunlight caught her face. When that happened Courtney Purviance was startlingly beautiful.

Ryan was asking about Harold Klingman. Purviance was explaining that Klingman owned a shop in Halifax. Her fingers adjusted and readjusted the fringe on a throw pillow.

"Would Klingman's visit to Ferris have been unusual?"

"Mr. Klingman often dropped by the warehouse when he was in Montreal."

"You were out sick that Friday."

"I have sinus problems."

I believed it. Purviance's speech was punctuated with frequent sniffing. She cleared her throat repeatedly. Every few seconds, a hand darted from the pillow and swiped her nose. I found myself fighting the urge to hand her a tissue.

"You said earlier that Ferris was acting moody just before his death. Can you elaborate on that?"

Purviance shrugged one shoulder. "I don't know. He seemed quieter."

"Quieter?"

"He didn't joke around as much." The fringe-straightening intensified. "Kept to himself more."

"Got any theories why that might have been?"

Purviance snorted, then abandoned the pillow for a go at her nose. "Talked much with Miriam?"

"You think there was trouble on the home front?"

Purviance raised her brows and palms in a "beats me" gesture.

"Did Ferris ever mention marital difficulties?"

"Not directly."

Ryan asked a few more questions about Purviance's relationship with Miriam, then moved on to other topics. Another fifteen minutes, and he wrapped up.

After leaving, we grabbed an early dinner on Saint-Laurent. Ryan asked my impression of Purviance. I told him the lady clearly had no love for Miriam Ferris. And she needed a good nasal spray.

Thursday, the Donovan Joyce book arrived. *The Jesus Scroll.* I opened it around noon, intending a quick scan.

At some point it began to snow. When I looked up, the sky had dimmed, and my side-yard fence caps had grown into tall, furry hats.

Joyce's theory was more bizarre than that in my airport novel. It went something like this.

Jesus was Mary's illegitimate son. He survived the cross. He married Mary Magdalene. He lived to a ripe old age, wrote his last will and testament, and was killed during the final siege at Masada.

Jake's summary of Joyce's involvement with Max Grosset had been accurate. According to Joyce, Grosset was an American professor with a British accent who'd worked as a volunteer archaeologist at Masada. Grosset told Joyce, during a chance encounter at Ben-Gurion airport in December of 1964, that he'd unearthed the Jesus scroll the previous field season, hidden it, then returned to Masada to retrieve it.

Joyce got a peek at Grosset's scroll in the airport men's room. To

Joyce, the writing looked Hebrew. Grosset said it was Aramaic, and translated the first line. *Yeshua ben Ya'akob Gennesareth.* "Jesus of Gennesareth, son of Jacob/James." The writer had added the astonishing information that he was the last in the line of the Maccabean kings of Israel.

Though offered $5,000, Joyce refused to assist Grosset in smuggling the scroll out of Israel. Grosset succeeded on his own, and the scroll ended up in Russia.

Later, unable to pursue his original book topic because he'd been denied permission to visit Masada, and intrigued by what he'd seen in the men's room at Ben-Gurion, Joyce had researched the name on the scroll. The appellation "Son of James" was used, Joyce concluded, because Joseph had died childless, and, according to Jewish law, his brother James would have raised Mary's illegitimate child. "Gennesareth" was one of history's several names for the Sea of Galilee.

Joyce was so convinced of the scroll's authenticity that he spent the next eight years researching Jesus' life.

I was still reading when Ryan arrived with enough food to feed Guadalajara.

I popped a Diet Coke. Ryan popped a Moosehead. As we ate enchiladas, I hit the main points.

"Jesus viewed himself as a descendant in the Hasmonean line."

Ryan looked at me.

"The Maccabean kings. His movement wasn't simply religious. It was a grab for political power."

"Oh good. Another conspiracy theory." Ryan dipped a finger in the guacamole. I handed him a tortilla.

"According to Joyce, Jesus wanted to be king of Israel. That pissed Rome off, and the penalty was death. But Jesus wasn't betrayed, he surrendered to authorities following negotiation by an intermediary."

"Let me guess. Judas?"

"Yep. The deal was that Pilate would release Barabas, and Jesus would turn himself in."

"And why would he do that?"

"Barabas was his son."

"I see." Ryan wasn't buying any of it.

"This prisoner exchange involved an escape mechanism, and the whole plan depended on controlling the clock."

"Life is timing."

"Do you want to hear this?"

"Is there any possibility of sex right now?"

I narrowed my eyes.

"I want to hear this."

"There were two forms of crucifixion—slow and fast. Slow, a prisoner could last up to seven days. Fast, you were dead in twenty-four hours. According to Joyce, Jesus and his followers had to time his execution so that fast was the only option."

"Fast would be my choice."

"Sabbath was approaching. And Passover. According to Jewish law, no corpse could remain on a cross."

"But crucifixion was a Roman show." Ryan went for another enchilada. "Historians agree Pilate was a tyrant and a bully. Would he have given a rat's ass about Jewish law?"

"It was in Pilate's interest to keep the locals happy. Anyway, the plot involved the use of a death-mimicking drug. *Papaver somniferum* or *Claviceps purpurea.*"

"I love it when you talk dirty."

"The opium poppy and ergot, a lysergic-acid producing fungus. In modern lingo, heroin and LSD. Both were known in Judea. The drug would have been administered via the sponge on the reed. According to the Gospels, Jesus first refused the sponge, later accepted it, drank, and immediately died."

"Only you're saying he lived."

"I'm not saying it. Joyce is."

"How do you get a live body down from a cross in front of witnesses and guards?"

"Keep the witnesses at a distance. Bribe the guards. It's not like there was a coroner standing by."

"Let me get this straight. Jesus is out cold. He's whisked to the tomb, later spirited away, nursed back to health, and somehow ends up at Masada."

"That's what Joyce says."

"What was this wingnut doing in Israel?"

"Nice to see you're keeping an open mind. Joyce went to research a book on Masada. But the Israeli authorities denied him access."

"Maybe the Grosset incident is a figment of Joyce's imagination. Or a story he invented out of spite."

"Maybe it is." I helped myself to the last of the salsa. "Or maybe it's real."

Nothing much happened for the next few days. I finished the Joyce book. I finished the Yadin book.

Jake was right on that account, too. Yadin described the remains from the Herodian period. He discussed the Romans who'd occupied Masada briefly after 73 C.E., and Byzantine monks who'd settled there in the fifth and sixth centuries. He gave detailed information on the period of the Jewish revolt, including an elaborate discussion of the three skeletons found in the northern palace. Wide-angles, close-ups, diagrams, maps. But just one photo and a few paragraphs on the cave skeletons.

Curious.

On Sunday, Ryan and I went skating on Beaver Lake, then gorged on mussels at L'Actuel on rue Peel. I had *la casserole marinière au vin blanc.* Ryan had *la casserole à l'ail.* I've got to credit the boy. He can handle garlic that would kill a marine.

On Monday I logged into my e-mail and found a report from the radiometric-testing lab.

I hesitated. What if the skeleton was only a century old? Or medieval, like the shroud of Turin?

What if it dated to the time of Christ?

If it did, it did. So what? My estimate of age at death made the individual too old to be Jesus. Or too young, if you believed Joyce.

I double-clicked to open the file.

The lab had found sufficient organic material to triple-test each bone and tooth sample. The results were presented as raw data, then calibrated to a date in years before present, and to a calendar date range, given as C.E. or B.C.E. Nothing politically incorrect about archaeology.

I looked at the dates derived from the tooth.

Sample 1: Mean Date (BP—years before present) 1,970 +/- 41 years	Calendar date range 6 BCE—76 CE
Sample 2: Mean Date (BP—years before present) 1,937 +/- 54 years	Calendar date range 14 CE—122 CE
Sample 3: Mean Date (BP—years before present) 2,007 +/- 45 years	Calendar date range 47 BCE—43 CE

I looked at the femoral dates. Total overlap with the dental dates.

Two millennia.

The skeleton dated to the time of Christ.

I experienced a moment of total blankness. Then arguments and questions bumper-car-ed through my brain.

What did it mean?

Who to call?

I dialed Ryan, got his voice mail, and left a message telling him the bones were two thousand years old.

I dialed Jake. Voice mail. Same message.

Now what?

Sylvain Morissonneau.

The urge expelled all momentary uncertainty. Grabbing jacket and purse, I bolted for the Montérégie.

Within an hour I was at l'Abbaye Sainte-Marie-des-Neiges. This time I went straight through the orange door into the lobby separating the library from Morissonneau's office corridor. No one appeared.

Muffled chanting floated from somewhere to my right. I started toward it.

I'd gone ten yards when a voice stopped me.

"Arrêtez!" More hiss than speech. Halt!

I turned.

"You have no right to be here." In the dim light, the monk's eyes looked devoid of pupils.

"I've come to see Father Morissonneau."

The hooded face stiffened.

"Who are you?"

"Dr. Temperance Brennan."

"Why do you disturb us in our sorrow?" The dead black eyes bore straight into mine.

"I'm sorry. I must speak with Father Morissonneau."

Something flicked in the gaze, like a match flaring behind darkly tinted glass. The monk crossed himself.

His next words sent ice up my spine.

16

"DEAD?"

Not a flicker in the gargoyle stare.

"When?" I sputtered. "How?"

"Why have you come here?" The monk's voice wasn't cold or warm. It was neutral, devoid of emotion.

"Father Morissonneau and I met not long ago. He seemed fine." I made no effort to mask my shock. "When did he die?"

"Almost a week ago." Flat, revealing nothing beyond the words.

"How?"

"You are family?"

"No."

"A journalist?"

"No."

I dug a card from my purse and handed it to him. The monk's eyes slid down, back up.

"On Wednesday, March second, the Abbot failed to return from his morning walk. The grounds were searched. His body was found on one of the paths."

I sucked in air.

"His heart had failed."

I thought back. Morissonneau had looked perfectly healthy. Robust, even.

"Was the abbot under the care of a physician?"

"I am not at liberty to share that information."

"Did he have a history of coronary disease?"

The monk didn't bother to answer that.

"Was the coroner notified?"

"The Lord God reigns over life and death. We accept his wisdom."

"The coroner doesn't," I snapped.

Strobe images. Ferris's shattered skull. Morissonneau stroking a box of old bones. A Burne-Jones painting *The Resurrection.* Words about jihad. Assassination.

I was growing frightened. And angry.

"Where is Father Morissonneau now?"

"With the Lord."

I gave the monk a screw-you look.

"Where is his body?"

The monk frowned.

I frowned.

A robed arm unfolded and gestured in the direction of the door. I was being ushered out.

I could have argued that the priest's death should have been reported, that by failing to do so the monks had broken the law. This didn't seem the time.

Mumbling condolences, I hurried from the monastery.

On the drive back to Montreal, my fear escalated. What had Jake said about the skeleton Morissonneau had given me? Its discovery could be explosive.

Explosive how?

Avram Ferris had possessed the skeleton and he'd been shot. Sylvain Morissonneau had possessed the skeleton and he was dead.

Now I possessed the skeleton. Was I in danger?

Every few minutes my eyes jerked to the rearview mirror.

Had Morissonneau really died of natural causes? The man had been in his fifties. He'd looked perfectly fit.

Had be been murdered?

My chest felt tight. The car seemed hot and cramped. Though the weather was frigid, I cracked a window.

Ferris had died sometime over the weekend of February twelfth. Kessler/Kaplan had entered Israel on the twenty-seventh. Morissonneau had been found dead on March second.

If Morissonneau's death was due to foul play, Kaplan couldn't have been involved.

Unless Kaplan had returned to Canada.

Again, I checked my rear. Nothing but empty highway.

I'd visited Morissonneau on Saturday, the twenty-sixth. He'd died four days later.

Coincidence?

Perhaps.

A coincidence the size of Lake Titicaca.

Time to call the Israeli authorities.

The lab was relatively calm for a Monday. Only four autopsies were in progress downstairs.

Upstairs, LaManche was leaving to lecture at the Canadian Police College in Ottawa. I stopped him in the corridor and shared my concerns over Morissonneau's death. LaManche said he'd look into it.

I then explained the carbon-14 results on the skeleton.

"Given an estimated age of roughly two thousand years, you are free to release the bones to the proper authorities."

"I'll get on it," I said.

"Without delay. We have such limited storage space."

LaManche paused, remembering, perhaps, the Ferris autopsy and its overseers.

"And it is best to avoid offending any of our religious communities." Another pause. "And, remote as the possibility may be, international incidents can arise from the most harmless of circumstances. We would not want that to happen. Please, do this as soon as possible."

Remembering my promise, I phoned Jake. He was still not answering. I left a message informing him that I was about to contact the Israeli authorities concerning turnover of Morissonneau's skeleton.

I sat a moment, wondering which agency to phone. I hadn't asked Jake because I'd promised to speak with him again before I made the call. Now he was unavailable, and LaManche wanted the case resolved.

My thoughts took a detour. Why was Jake so uneasy about my speaking to Israel? What was he afraid of? Was there someone in particular he wanted out of the loop?

Back to the question at hand. I was certain the Israel National

Police would have no interest in a death two millennia back. Though Israeli archaeology was not my bailiwick, I knew most countries have agencies to oversee the preservation of cultural heritage, including antiquities.

I logged on to the Internet, and Googled the words "Israel" and "antiquities." Almost every listing included a reference to the Israel Antiquities Authority. Five minutes of surfing got me a number.

I checked the time. Eleven-twenty A.M. Six-twenty P.M. in Israel. I doubted anyone would be working this late.

I punched the digits.

A woman answered on the second ring.

"*Shalom.*"

"*Shalom.* This is Dr. Temperance Brennan. I'm sorry, but I don't speak Hebrew."

"You've reached the offices of the Israel Antiquities Authority." Heavily accented English.

"I'm calling from the Laboratoire de sciences judiciaires et de médecine légale in Montreal, Canada."

"Sorry?"

"I'm forensic anthropologist for the medical-legal lab in Montreal."

"Yes." Boredom tinged with impatience.

"Remains have come to light here under somewhat unusual circumstances."

"Remains?"

"A human skeleton."

"Yes?" Slightly less bored.

"There is evidence to suggest this skeleton may have been unearthed at Masada during Yigael Yadin's excavation in the sixties."

"Your name, please?"

"Temperance Brennan."

"Hold please."

I did. For a full five minutes. Then the woman came back on. She did not sound bored.

"May I ask how this skeleton came into your possession?"

"No."

"Excuse me?"

"I'll explain the situation to the proper authority."

"The IAA is the proper authority."

"Who is the director, please?"

"Tovya Blotnik."

"Perhaps I should speak with Mr. Blotnik."

"He's gone for the day."

"Is it possible to reach—"

"Dr. Blotnik dislikes interruptions at home."

For some reason, I felt reluctant to divulge the full story. Jake's admonition not to call before contacting him? LaManche's reference to international relations? Irrational gut reaction? I didn't know, but there it was.

"I mean no disrespect. But I would prefer to speak with the director."

"I am physical anthropologist for the IAA. If the bones are to come here, Dr. Blotnik will direct me to handle the transaction."

"And you are?"

"Ruth Anne Bloom."

"I'm sorry, Dr. Bloom, but I'll need verification from the director."

"That's a highly unusual request."

"I'm still making it. This is a highly unusual skeleton."

Silence.

"May I have your contact information?" Glacial.

I gave Bloom my cell and lab phone numbers.

"I'll pass on the message."

I thanked her and hung up.

Logging back on to the Internet, I Googled Tovya Blotnik. The name came up in conjunction with several articles addressing a controversy over an ancient stone coffin called the James ossuary. In each, Blotnik was cited as director-general of the IAA.

Okay. Blotnik was kosher. So why the hindbrain heads-up to be cautious with Bloom?

The fact that Lerner and Ferris thought the skeleton in my lab was Jesus Christ? The fact that Jake asked me not to do what I was doing?

I wasn't sure. But again, there it was.

I was shooting the last few pictures of Morissonneau's skeleton when Ryan reappeared, looking like the cat that swallowed Big Bird. I waved him into the lab.

"They've got him," he said.

"I'll bite," I said.

"Hershel Kaplan."

"How'd they catch him?"

"Genius failed to pay for a bauble."

"He stole something?"

"Slipped a necklace into his pocket. All a terrible mistake. He intended to pay."

"Of course. What now?"

"I'd like to haul his ass back to Canada."

"Can you do that?"

"Not unless we charge him. Then we can formally request extradition through external affairs."

"Have you got enough to charge him?"

"No."

"He'd fight it anyway."

"Yes."

Ryan chin-gestured the skeleton. "What's happening with Masada Max?"

"Carbon fourteen puts his birthday somewhere around the time of the Bethlehem star."

"No shit."

"I'm trying to send him back to Israel."

I told Ryan about my conversation with the IAA.

"What got your sonar pinging?"

I thought about that.

"Jake told me not to talk to anyone in Israel until I'd spoken with him."

"So why call?"

"LaManche wants the skeleton gone."

"Why not level with Bloom?"

"Jake's caution, I suppose. I'm not sure. A little voice just told me to wait and talk to Blotnik."

"Probably a good bet."

"There's something else."

I told him about Morissonneau.

Ryan's brows dipped. He was about to speak when both my cell and his beeper erupted.

Ryan took the gizmo from his belt, checked the number, and pointed at my desk phone. I nodded and stepped into the adjoining lab.

"Temperance Brennan."

"Tovya Blotnik calling from Jerusalem." Santa voice. Rich and jolly as hell.

"I'm delighted to hear from you, sir. I wasn't expecting your call before morning."

"Ruth Anne Bloom phoned me at home."

So much for the ban on interruptions.

"Thank you for taking the time," I said.

"Not at all. Not at all. It's a pleasure to accommodate foreign colleagues." Blotnik chuckled. "You work for a coroner in Canada?"

I explained my position.

"Right, then. What's this about a skeleton from Masada?"

I described the photo that had started it all. Then, using no names, I told Blotnik how the skeleton had been stolen from the Musée de l'Homme by Yossi Lerner, then hidden by Avram Ferris and Sylvain Morissonneau.

I outlined the radiocarbon results.

I did not mention Hershel Kaplan. I did not mention the Joyce book, or the reason behind the theft and concealment of the bones. I did not mention the samples I'd sent off for DNA testing.

I did not mention the fact that Ferris and Morissonneau were dead.

"You obtained this photo how?" Blotnik asked.

"From a member of the local Jewish community." True enough.

"Probably all nonsense." The jovial chuckle now sounded forced. "But we can't ignore this, now can we?"

"I think not."

"And I'm sure you're quite anxious to be rid of this mess."

"I've been authorized to release the bones. If you'll provide a shipping address, I'll arrange with FedEx—"

"No!"

No chuckle there.

I waited.

"No, no. I can't put you to all that trouble. I'll send someone."

"From Israel to Quebec?"

"It's no problem."

No problem?

"Dr. Blotnik, archaeological materials are transported internationally all the time. I'm perfectly happy to package the materials and use any shipping service you select—"

"I must insist."

I said nothing.

"There have been some unfortunate outcomes recently. Perhaps you've heard of the James ossuary?"

The James ossuary was the ancient stone coffin mentioned in the Internet links. I vaguely recalled something in the news a few years back about damage to an ossuary on loan to the Royal Ontario Museum.

"The James ossuary was the piece broken in transport to Toronto?"

"Smashed would be a better word. En route from Israel to Canada."

"It's your call, sir."

"Please. This is best. I'll be back in touch shortly with the name of the envoy."

Before I could reply Blotnik cut me off.

"The skeleton *is* in a secure location?"

"Of course."

"Security is of the utmost importance. Make sure no one has access to those bones."

I returned to my lab as Ryan was cradling the receiver.

"Kaplan's not talking," he said.

"And?"

"Guy in major crimes over there says he'll turn up the heat."

Ryan noticed that I was disconnected from the conversation.

"What's up, sunshine?"

"I don't know."

Ryan's expression reshaped subtly.

"Too much cloak and dagger over this skeleton," I said. "Even if it *is* the missing Masada skeleton. If there *is* a missing Masada skeleton."

I recounted my conversation with Blotnik.

"A five-thousand-mile trip seems a bit drastic," Ryan agreed.

"A bit. Antiquities are routinely shipped around the globe. There are companies that specialize in doing just that."

"How about this." Ryan placed a hand on each of my shoulders. "We have a nice dinner, go back to your place, maybe slip into something derived from the art of dance."

"I didn't order the tap pants."

My gaze drifted to the window. I felt anxious and restless, and didn't know why.

Ryan stroked my cheek. "Nothing's going to change overnight, Tempe."

Ryan was dead wrong.

17

THAT NIGHT I DREAMED OF THE MAN NAMED TOVYA BLOTKIN. He was wearing dark glasses and a black hat, like Belushi and Aykroyd in their Blues Brothers act. Blotkin was on his haunches, scraping with a trowel. It was dark, and each time his head moved moonlight glinted off his lenses.

In my dream Blotkin plucked something from the ground, rose, and offered the object to a second figure whose back was to me. The second figure turned. It was Sylvain Morissonneau. He was holding a small black canvas.

Light seeped from Morissonneau's fingertips as he scratched dirt from the canvas. Slowly, a painting emerged. Four figures in a tomb: two angels, a woman, the risen Jesus.

Jesus' features dissolved leaving only a skull, gleaming and brilliant white. A new face took shape above the orbits and orifices, like fog congealing in mountain terrain. It was the face of Jesus that had hung over my grandmother's bed. The Jesus with gimmicky I'm-following-you-everywhere eyes. The Jesus that had frightened me throughout my childhood.

I tried to run. I was fixed in place.

The Jesus mouth opened. A tooth floated out. The tooth grew and spiraled toward me.

I tried to bat it down.

My lids flew up.

The room was dark save for the digits on my clock radio. Ryan snored softly beside me.

My dreams are normally not Freudian puzzlers. My subconscious takes events and weaves them into psychedelic tapestries. Morissonneau's comment about the dreamlike quality of Burne-Jones's paintings? Whatever the trigger, this one had been a beaut.

I looked at the clock. Five forty-two.

I tried sleeping.

At six-fifteen I gave up.

Birdie trailed me to the kitchen. I made coffee. Charlie wolf-whistled, broke off, and rummaged in his seed dish.

I took my mug to the sofa. Birdie settled in my lap.

Outside, two sparrows poked fruitlessly at the courtyard snow. I knew how they felt.

More questions than answers on the skeleton. No explanation of how Sylvain Morissonneau died. No progress on Ferris.

No idea why Jake hadn't returned my calls.

Or had he?

Tiptoeing into the bedroom, I retrieved my purse, returned to the sofa, and dug out my cell phone.

Jake had called. Twice.

Damn! Why hadn't I heard?

I'd been engaged in festivities with Ryan.

Jake had left a simple message. Twice. *Call me.*

I punched in Jake's number. He answered right away.

"It's a good thing you've got international coverage," I said. "All this speed-dialing to Jerusalem would force me to mortgage the place on St. Bart's."

"You've got a place on St. Bart's?"

"No. But I'd like one." Birdie reoccupied my lap. "The carbon-fourteen results came back. The skeleton's two thousand years old."

"Have you contacted anyone?" Jake asked.

"The IAA. I had to, Jake."

"Who did you speak with?" Tight.

"Tovya Blotnik. He wants to send an envoy to Montreal to collect the bones."

"Does Blotnik know you took samples for DNA testing?"

"No. You do know those results will take longer?"

Jake ignored my question.

"Does he know about the odd tooth?"

"No. I thought you might want to talk about that first. Jake, there's something else." I told him about Morissonneau.

"Holy crap. Do you think the guy's ticker really clocked out?"

"I don't know."

Empty air. Then,"Did Blotnik say anything about a tomb or an ossuary?"

"He mentioned a James ossuary."

More empty air. Charlie filled it on my end with a line from "Strokin'." I wondered briefly what the cockatiel had witnessed the night before. Jake's voice brought me back.

"You're sure he said James ossuary?"

"Yes. What's the big deal with this James ossuary?"

"Never mind that for now. Tempe, listen to me. Listen carefully. This is important. Don't mention the DNA samples. All right? Can you hold back on that for a bit?"

"Why?"

"Can you please trust me and promise you won't mention the DNA testing for now?"

"At this point there's nothing to mention."

"And I don't want you to give that skeleton to Blotnik."

"Jake, I—"

"Please. Can you do this for me?"

"Not if you won't tell me what's going on. Why *shouldn't* I cooperate with the IAA?"

"I can't discuss this by phone."

"If Masada is the place of origin, legally I must return the skeleton to Israel. I have no choice."

"Bring it yourself. I'll pay your expenses."

"I can't dance off to Israel right now."

"Why not? I'll deal with Blotnik."

"Bring it myself?"

What would I tell LaManche? Ryan? Who would take care of Birdie? Charlie?

Jesus, I was thinking like my mother.

"I'll have to think about this, Jake."

"Screw thinking. Just come to Israel and bring the skeleton."

"You don't seriously believe I've got the bones of Jesus?"

Long pause. When Jake spoke again his voice was different, lower and more guarded.

"All I can say is that I'm onto something big."

"Big."

"If I'm right, it's mammoth. Please, Tempe. Book a flight. Or I can do it for you. I'll meet you at Ben-Gurion. Don't tell anyone you're coming."

"I don't want to spoil your George Smiley moment, but—"

"Say you'll make the trip."

"I'll think about it."

I was doing that when Ryan appeared. He'd pulled on jeans. Just jeans. The jeans hung low.

My libido sat up.

Ryan noticed it do so.

"I could lose the Levi's so you can ogle the naughty bits."

Eye roll.

"I made coffee."

Ryan kissed my head, yawned, and disappeared. Birdie jumped down and padded after him.

I heard rattling, then the refrigerator. Ryan reappeared with my AAFS mug, dropped into an armchair, and thrust both legs full length.

Charlie whistled a line from "Dixie," then screeched, "Strokin'!"

"Did I hear conversation?" Ryan asked.

I waggled the cell phone. "Jake wants me to deliver Morissonneau's skeleton to Israel. He's pretty insistent."

"Land of sun and fun."

"And suicide bombers."

"And that." Ryan blew across his coffee. "Do you want to go to Israel?"

"I do and I don't."

"I love a woman who knows her mind."

"I've always wanted to visit the Holy Land."

"Things are slow. Your lab wouldn't implode if you disappeared for a week."

"What about the boys?" I swept a hand at Birdie and Charlie. "What if Katy needed me?"

I felt instantly stupid. My daughter was twenty-four and a thousand miles away. And a short drive from her father.

"Violence got you nervous?"

"I've traveled to dicier places."

"Why not go?"

I had no answer.

I *was* needed at the lab.

Two kids found bones in a trunk in their uncle's attic. Cold case! Call the cops!

The bones were human. Female, white, thirty to forty years at the time of her death.

Important detail. Every bone had been drilled with tiny holes. Some holes still sported wires.

The knee bone's connected to the ankle bone. The ankle bone's connected to the foot bone.

You get the picture. Unc was a retired physician. The kids' unknown was a teaching skeleton.

My report was completed by 9:05.

After lunch, my thoughts veered to Jake and his guarded mention of a major discovery. What discovery? And why such concern for Masada Max, as Ryan had taken to calling the skeleton? Max couldn't possibly be Jesus. Max had been too old at the time of his death.

Or too young. Wasn't that the premise of the Joyce book?

Both Jake and Blotnik had made reference to the James ossuary. Several Internet articles had mentioned it.

Curious, I did some cyber-surfing.

It yielded the following.

An ossuary is a small stone casket.

Ossuaries served an important function in Jewish burial in first-century Israel. The deceased were entombed and left to decay. One year later, their bones were collected and permanently interred in ossuaries.

Thousands of ancient ossuaries have been discovered throughout Israel and Palestine. One can be purchased on the antiquities market for a few hundred dollars.

The James ossuary is a first-century limestone box measuring approximately twenty inches in length. It is inscribed in Aramaic with the words "James, son of Joseph, brother of Jesus."

When first reported in 2002, the James ossuary made a big splash. According to many, before its discovery, no evidence of Jesus existed outside written texts. The box was heralded as the first physical link to Jesus.

Okay. That's big.

In 2003, an IAA authentication committee was formed. The committee declared the box legit, the inscription a forgery, based largely on oxygen isotope analysis of patina, an encrustation caused by surface oxidation.

The finding led to controversy. Many experts disagreed, calling the committee's work sloppy, its conclusions premature.

Bottom line? No one disputes the age of the box. Some question the inscription, in whole or in part. Some accept the whole enchilada.

Ryan came by at two. Resting a haunch on my desk, he raised his brows. I raised mine back.

"Just for kicks I ran a check on your monastery. Address kicked out something interesting."

I leaned back in my chair.

"Father André Gervais dimed the SQ post in Saint-Hyacinthe one week ago today."

"Gervais is a monk at l'Abbaye Sainte-Marie-des-Neiges?"

Ryan nodded. "Seems the boys were edgy about a car with two male occupants parked inside their wall. Saint-Hyacinthe sent a cruiser to check it out." Ryan paused for effect. "Both the driver and passenger were Palestinian nationals."

"Jesus."

"Nope. The other team." Ryan checked a spiral pad. "Jamal Hasan Abu-Jarur. Muhammed Hazman Shalaideh. Car was a rental."

"What were they doing out there?"

"Claimed they were sightseeing and got lost. Both men had valid passports. Names came up clean. The cop told them to move along."

"When was this?"

"March first."

My scalp prickled.

"Three days after my visit. One day before Morissonneau died."

"Could be coincidence."

"We're running into a lot of those."

"Now for the good news."

"Groovy."

"Hershel Kaplan made fourteen trips to Israel in the two years prior to his last jolt in Bordeaux. Turns out Kaplan's cousin to one of Jerusalem's less fastidious antiquities dealers."

"Get out!"

"Ira Friedman's the Israel National Police major crimes dick I've been dealing with. Friedman worked Kaplan pretty hard, suggested they were looking at him for violations of the Antiquities Law, the Protection of Holy Places Law, the desecration of graves, the destruction of cultural resources, tax fraud, smuggling, trespass, the rape of the lock, the mutiny on the *Bounty,* the murder of Lesnitsky, the kidnapping of Rapunzel, the theft of the golden fleece, and the wreck of the *Edmund Fitzgerald.*"

"He said that?"

"I'm paraphrasing. Friedman got Kaplan thinking seriously about his future. He also dropped my name, mentioned that Canada wanted to discuss the rubber content of some checks."

"Wily."

"Ploy worked. Kaplan's developed an enormous interest in talking to the home folks."

"Meaning?"

"Wants me, and only me."

"Man's got good instincts."

Ryan smiled a smile as wide as the Chattahoochee. "Friedman wants me in Jerusalem. The brass okayed it."

"The SQ's actually footing the bill?"

"Amazing, eh? External affairs rolled it to the Royal Canadian Mounted Police. The Mounties bumped it back to us. I'm lead investigator on the Ferris homicide, so I'm the lucky traveler."

"We'll be in high demand in Israel," I said.

"Shall we oblige?" Ryan asked.

"Hell, yeah."

18

THERE'S ONE ADVANTAGE TO FLYING INTO A WAR ZONE. SEAT availability.

As I booked with Air Canada, Denis wrapped Masada Max and packed him into a hockey bag. Then I raced home to arrange cat and cockatiel care. Winston, my building's custodian, agreed. I'd owe him a fifth of Crown Royal.

I was stuffing a suitcase when Ryan buzzed. Zipping the lid, I dug a catnip mouse from my stash, tossed it to Birdie, and flew out the door.

I have known Ryan for years and traveled with him on several occasions. The man has many fine qualities. Patience in airports is not among them.

We took the 7 P.M. shuttle to Toronto, Ryan grousing all the way about premature departures and long layovers.

He needn't have worried. Our AC flight to Tel Aviv was operated by El Al, and security was tighter than Los Alamos in the forties. By the time we explained and reexplained the contents of my carry-on and its supporting documentation, cleared the panty-by-panty luggage check, and discussed our life histories and future aspirations in the personal interrogation session, it was after ten.

Ryan used the few minutes left to sweet-talk the gate agent. Between giggles, the nice lady upgraded us to business class.

We boarded on time. We departed on time. An aviation miracle.

At cruising altitude, Ryan accepted his second champagne, and an in-air set of toothy smiles was exchanged.

I have a routine on long international flights.

Phase one. I drink the OJ and read until dinner.

Phase two. I eat sparingly. I saw *Airplane.* I remember the bad fish.

Phase three. I slap the DO NOT DISTURB sticker on my seat, lean back, and crank up as many movies as it takes to drop off.

I followed my routine, starting with a guide to the Holy Land that Winston had produced. Don't ask why. I've never known the man to travel outside Quebec.

Ryan read James Joyce's *Dubliners* and ate everything served. He was snoring by the opening credits of his first film.

I lasted through *Pirates of the Caribbean, Shrek,* and the window-box scene in *Arsenic and Old Lace.* Somewhere around dawn I drifted off, but my mind never really disengaged.

Or so I thought.

When I opened my eyes an attendant was clearing Ryan's meal tray.

I raised my seat.

"Sleep well, cupcake?"

Ryan tried brushing hair from my cheek. It stuck. I broke the saliva bond and did a two-handed ear tuck.

"Coffee?" Ryan flattened bangs that were reaching for the overheads.

I nodded.

Ryan waggled his mug at an attendant and pointed to me. I set up my tray. Coffee appeared on it.

"Thanks, Audrey."

Audrey?

"Pleasure, Detective." Audrey's smile left last night's in the dental dust.

Security at Ben-Gurion wasn't as rigorous as it had been at Pearson. Maybe Ryan's badge. Maybe the coroner's detailed paperwork. Maybe confidence that if we'd had nitro in our blow-dryers they'd have found it by now.

Exiting customs, I noticed a man wall-leaning ahead and to our left. He had shaggy hair and wore an argyle sweater, jeans, and sneakers.

Except for bushy brows and a few more years, the man was a Gilligan double.

Gilligan was following our progress.

I elbowed Ryan.

"I see him," Ryan said, not breaking pace.

"Guy looks like Gilligan."

Ryan looked at me.

"*Gilligan's Island.*"

"I hated *Gilligan's Island.*"

"But you're acquainted with the character."

"Except Ginger," Ryan amended. "Ginger had talent."

Gilligan pushed from the wall, dropped his hands and spread his feet, making no attempt to mask his interest in us.

When we drew within yards, Gilligan made his move.

"*Shalom.*" The voice was deeper than you'd expect from a guy Gilligan's size.

"*Shalom,*" Ryan said.

"Detective Ryan?"

"Who's asking?"

"Ira Friedman."

Friedman stuck out a hand. Ryan shook it.

"Welcome to Israel."

Ryan introduced me. I shook Friedman's hand. The grip was more powerful than you'd expect from a guy Gilligan's size.

Friedman led us outside to a white Ford Escort illegally parked in a taxi zone. Ryan loaded the luggage, opened the front door and offered the passenger seat.

Ryan's six-two. I'm five-five. I opted for the back.

I pushed aside papers, a manual of some kind, balled-up food wrappers, boots, a motorcycle helmet, a baseball cap, and a nylon jacket. There were French fries in the crack. I left them there.

"Sorry about the car," Friedman said.

"No problem." Brushing crumbs from the upholstery, I crawled in, wondering if declining Jake's offer of airport pickup had been a mistake.

As we drove, Friedman brought Ryan up-to-date.

"Someone up your food chain contacted one of your external affairs guys, who contacted one of our senior police representatives for the U.S. and Canada. Seems your guy knew our guy at the consulate in New York."

"A personal touch can mean so much."

Friedman stole a sideways glance, obviously unfamiliar with Ryan's sense of humor. "Our guy in New York sent paper to the International Relations Unit at national headquarters here in Jerusalem. IRU bounced the request down to major crimes. I caught it."

Friedman merged onto Highway 1.

"Normally this kind of request goes nowhere. We'd have nothing to ask your suspect, no knowledge of the crime. That's assuming we could even find him. Once a tourist enters the country, he's pretty much invisible. If we did locate him, legally he could refuse to talk to us."

"But Kaplan was kind enough to palm a choker," Ryan said.

"Herodian shekel on a gold chain." Friedman snorted. "Dumb ass. Thing wasn't even real."

"How long can you hold him?"

"Twenty-four hours, and we've already eaten that. I can push it to forty-eight with some fancy talking. Then it's charge him or kick him."

"Will the shopkeeper press charges?"

Friedman shrugged. "Who knows? Guy got his coin back. But if Kaplan walks, I'll keep him on a very short leash."

Now and then Friedman would glance in the rearview. Our eyes would meet. We'd both smile.

Between rounds of collegiality, I tried taking in the landscape. I knew from Winston's book that the route from Tel Aviv to Jerusalem was taking us from the coastal plain, through the Shephelah, or lowlands, into the Judean hill country, and up into the mountains.

Night had fallen. I couldn't see much.

We rounded curve after curve, then suddenly Jerusalem was twinkling before us. A vanilla-wafer moon grazed the top of the Temple Mount, lighting the Old City with an amber glow.

I've observed few scenes that triggered a physical reaction. Haleakala volcano at dawn. The Taj Mahal at sunset. The Masai Mara during wildebeest migration.

Moonlit Jerusalem stopped my breath. Friedman picked up on it, and our eyes met again.

"Awesome, isn't it?"

I nodded in the dark.

"Lived here fifteen years. I still get goose bumps."

I wasn't listening. My mind was shanking up images. Suicide bombers. Christmas pageants. West Bank settlements. Catechism classes at my old parish church. Newsreel scenes of angry young men.

Israel is a place where the wonder of the past slams daily into the bitter reality of the present. Driving through the night, I couldn't take my eyes from the ancient settlement forever and always at the center of it all.

A quarter hour after first seeing Jerusalem, we were in the city. Cars lined the curbs, bumper sniffing bumper, like dogs in some frozen canine parade. Vehicles crammed the streets. Pedestrians thronged the walks, women in *hijab* or full burka, men in black hats, teens in Levi 501's.

How like Quebec, I thought, with its constant clash of religion, language, and culture. French and English. The two solitudes. In Jerusalem the ante was upped to three. Muslim beside Christian beside Jew, all separate.

I lowered my window.

The air was packed with smells. Cement. Exhaust. Whiffs of flowers, spices, garbage, cooking grease.

I listened to the familiar city-night jazz. Car horns. Traffic humming on an overpass. The sound of a piano slipping from an open door. It was the melody of a thousand urban centers.

Ryan had booked us into the American Colony, a Turkish-style manse-turned-hotel in East Jerusalem. His thinking: Arab sector, no bombs.

Friedman turned from the Nablus Road into a circle drive bordered by flowers and palms. Passing a small antiquities shop, he looped around and stopped under a vine-draped portico.

Friedman alighted and retrieved our suitcases.

"Hungry?"

Two nods.

"I'll be in the bar." Friedman slammed the trunk. "Lower level."

Ryan's choice was a good one. The American Colony was all antiques, chandeliers, hanging tapestries, and hammered bronze. The floors were polished stone. The windows and doorways were arched, and the floor plan centered on a flower-filled courtyard.

Everything but the pasha himself.

We were expected. Check-in was quick.

As Ryan asked a few questions, I scanned names engraved on small marble wall plaques. Saul Bellow. John Steinbeck. Jimmy Carter. Winston Churchill. Jane Fonda. Giorgio Armani.

My room was everything the lobby promised. Mirrored armoire. Carved writing desk. Persian carpet. Bathroom aglow with gold gilt mirrors and black-and-white tile.

I wanted to shower and crawl into the four-poster. Instead, I brushed teeth and hair, changed, and hurried downstairs.

Ryan and Friedman were already seated at a low table in one of the alcoves. Each had a bottle of Taybeh beer.

Friedman signaled a waiter.

I ordered Perrier and an Arabic salad. Ryan went with spaghetti.

"This hotel is beautiful," I said.

"The place was built by some fat-cat Arab around 1860. Forget his name. Room one was his. The other downstairs rooms were his wives' summer digs, and in the winter, the ladies moved up a floor. The guy was hot for a son, but no one obliged, so he married a fourth time, and built two more rooms. The new bride disappointed him, too, so he died."

Friedman sipped his beer.

"In 1873, a big-bucks Chicago attorney named Horatio Spafford sent his wife and four daughters off on a European vacation. The ship sank and only Mama survived." Another sip.

"Couple years, couple more daughters. Then the Spaffords lost a son. They were real religious, members of some church organization, so they decided to seek consolation in the Holy Land. In 1881 they came and settled with friends in the Old City. The group became known as the American Colony, and developed quite a reputation for helping the poor.

"Long story short, others joined and the group outgrew its digs. The Spaffords rented, then eventually bought this place. Ever hear of Peter Ustinov?"

Ryan and I nodded.

"In 1902 Peter's granddaddy started sending visitors here from a hotel he owned up in Jaffa. Became the American Colony Hostel, later Hotel. The place has survived four wars and four regimes."

"The Turks, the Brits, the Jordanians, and the Israelis," I guessed.

"Bingo. But you're not here for a history lesson. Why's this toad Kaplan such a hot property in Canada?"

Ryan filled Friedman in on the Ferris investigation.

"Big leap from bad paper to homicide," Friedman said.

"Jumbo," Ryan agreed. "But the widow's got a history with Kaplan."

"Which she failed to mention," Friedman said.

"She did," Ryan said.

"And Kaplan fled the country."

"He did."

"Widow stands to collect four million," Friedman said.

"She does."

"Four million's a lot of motivation."

"Nothing gets by you," Ryan said.

"You'd like to chat with Mr. Kaplan?"

"At his earliest convenience."

"First thing in the morning?"

"Nah, let him brush his teeth."

Friedman turned to me. "My fault, I'm sure, but I didn't get your connection to the case."

I explained how I'd obtained the photo from Kaplan and the skeleton from Morissonneau, and mentioned my call to the IAA.

"Who'd you talk to?"

"Tovya Blotnik and Ruth Anne Bloom."

"Bloom's the bone lady?"

I hid a smile. I'd been given the same tag.

"Yes."

"They mention that bone box?" Friedman asked.

"The James ossuary?"

Friedman nodded.

"Blotnik mentioned it. Why?"

Friedman ignored my question. "This Drum suggest you keep a low profile once you got here?"

"Jake advised me not to contact anyone in Israel before meeting with him."

Friedman drained his beer. When he spoke again his voice sounded flat, as though he was sealing his real thoughts from it.

"Your friend's advice is solid."

Solid. But, as things turned out, futile.

19

FIVE-TWENTY A.M. OUTSIDE MY WINDOW THE TREETOPS WERE black, the mosque's minaret just a hard shadow across the street. I'd been jarred awake by its loudspeaker sounding the call to *fajr*, morning prayer.

God is great, the muezzin coaxed in Arabic. Prayer is better than sleep.

I wasn't so sure. I felt sluggish and disconnected, like a patient clawing out of anesthesia.

The mechanical wailing ended. Birdsong filled the void. A barking dog. The thunk of a car door.

I lay in bed, gripped by a shapeless sense that tragedy loomed not far off. What? When?

I watched my room ooze from silver to pink as I listened to traffic sounds merge and strengthen. I prodded my unconscious. Why the uneasiness?

Jet lag? Fear for my safety? Guilt over Morissonneau?

Whoa. There was a burrow I hadn't poked. I'd visited the monastery, four days later Morissonneau was a body on a path. Had my actions triggered the priest's death? Should I have known I was placing him in danger?

Had I placed Morissonneau in danger?

What the hell *was* this skeleton?

In part, my anxiety grew from the fact that others seemed to know what I did not.

Blotnik. Friedman. Even Jake appeared to be holding back.

Especially Jake? Did my friend have an agenda he wasn't sharing? I didn't really believe that.

And holding back on what?

The James ossuary for one thing. Everyone was skittering around the subject. I vowed to crack that mystery today.

I felt better. I was taking action. Or at least planning to take action.

At six I rose, showered, and descended to the restaurant, hoping Ryan had also awakened early. I also hoped he'd reconciled to the fact that I was in 304 and he was down the hall in 307.

We'd discussed sleeping arrangements before leaving Montreal. I'd insisted on separate rooms, arguing that we were traveling to Israel on official business. Ryan had objected, saying no one would know. I'd suggested it would be fun to sneak back and forth. Ryan had disagreed. I'd prevailed.

Ryan was seated at a table, scowling at something on his plate.

"Why would anyone serve olives for breakfast?" Ryan's tone suggested he was more jet-lagged than I.

"You don't like olives?"

"After five P.M." Ryan sidelined the offending fruit and dug into a mound of eggs the size of Mount Rushmore. "In gin."

Deducing that congenial conversation would not be forthcoming, I focused on my hummus and cheese.

"You and Friedman are off to see Kaplan?" I asked when Rushmore had been reduced to a hummock.

Ryan nodded then checked his watch.

"Masada Max is going to Blotnik?" he asked.

"Yes. But I promised Jake I'd meet with him before contacting anyone else. He'll be here any minute, then we'll head over to the IAA."

Knocking back his coffee, Ryan stood and aimed a finger at me. "Be careful out there, soldier."

I snapped two fingers to my forehead. "Roger that."

Ryan returned salute and strode from the room.

Jake arrived at seven wearing jeans, a sleeveless camouflage jacket, and a blue Hawaiian shirt open over a white T. Quite a fashion statement on a shave-headed, six-foot-sixer with hedgerow brows.

"You brought boots?" Jake asked, dropping into the chair Ryan had vacated.

"To meet with Blotnik?"

"I want you to see something."

"I'm here to deliver a skeleton, Jake."

"First I need for you to see this."

"First I need for you to tell me what the hell's going on."

Jake nodded.

"Today." It came out louder than I intended. Or not.

"I'll explain on the way."

"Starting with this ossuary?"

Two men passed speaking Arabic. Jake watched until they disappeared through the low stone arch leading from the restaurant.

"Can you lock the bones in your room safe?" Jake's voice was barely above a whisper.

I shook my head. "Too small."

"Bring them."

"This better be good," I said, tossing my napkin onto my plate.

Jake pointed at my feet.

"Boots."

Driving across the city, Jake told me the strange story of the James ossuary.

"No one disputes the authenticity of the box. It's the inscription that's in question. The IAA declared it a fake. Others say the 'brother of Jesus' part is legit, but claim the words 'James, son of Joseph' were added later. Others believe the opposite, that the Jesus phrase was added later. Still others think the Jesus phrase was forged."

"Why?"

"To goose the ossuary's value on the antiquities market."

"Didn't an IAA committee dissect every aspect of the thing?"

"Yeah. Right. First of all, there were two subcommittees. One looked at writing and content. The other looked at materials. The writing and content subcommittee contained one expert on ancient Hebrew writing, but other equally qualified epigraphers dispute her conclusions."

"An epigrapher is a specialist in analyzing and dating script?"

"Correct. Get this. One genius on the committee pointed to variations in handwriting and in thickness and depth of the lettering as proof of forgery. I won't bore you with detail, but variation is exactly what you'd expect on a nonmechanically incised inscription. Uniform lettering would be a dead giveaway of a fake. And the mixing of formal and cursive script is a well-known phenomenon in ancient engraving.

"Another issue was misspelling. Joseph was spelled *YWSP,* and James was spelled *Y'OB.* One committee member said Joseph should have been *YHWSP,* and that the *Y'OB* spelling of James had never been found on any Second Temple period ossuary."

"The Second Temple period is the time of Jesus."

Jake nodded. "I did my own survey. The James ossuary's spelling appeared in more than ten percent of the Joseph inscriptions I located. I found five occurrences of the name James. Three, a majority, had the same spelling as that on the James ossuary."

"Was the committee unaware of the existence of these other inscriptions?"

"You tell me."

Jake's eyes kept shifting to the traffic around us.

"Incidentally, the committee included not a single New Testament scholar or historian of early Christianity."

"What about the oxygen isotope analysis?" I asked.

Jake's eyes cut to me. "You've done some homework."

"Just some Web surfing."

"The oxygen isotope analysis was ordered by the materials subcommittee. It showed no patina deep down in the letters, but picked up a grayish chalk-and-water paste that shouldn't have been there. The committee concluded that the paste had been applied intentionally to imitate weathering. But it's not that simple."

Jake readjusted the rear and side-view mirrors.

"Turns out the patina on the 'Jesus' part of the inscription is identical to the overall patina on the box. In ancient Aramaic, Jesus would have been the last word inscribed. So if that word's legit, and even some members of the IAA now agree that it is, then I think the whole inscription must be legit. Think about it. Why would an ossuary be inscribed with just the words 'brother of someone'? It doesn't make sense."

"How do you explain the paste?"

"Scrubbing could have removed the patina down in the letters. And it could have altered the chemical composition of the patina by creating carbonate particles. The ossuary's owner said the thing had been cleaned repeatedly over the years."

"Who's the owner?"

"An Israeli antiquities collector named Oded Golan. Golan says he was told at the time of his purchase that the ossuary came from a tomb in Silwan." Jake jabbed a thumb at my window. "We're on the outskirts of Silwan now."

Again, Jake scanned the cars ahead and behind. His nervousness was making me edgy.

"Problem is the ossuary's not recorded as an archaeologically excavated artifact from Silwan or from anywhere else in Israel."

"You think it was looted."

"Gee. You think?" Jake's voice dripped sarcasm. "Golan claims he's had the ossuary more than thirty years, making it legal, since antiquities acquired before 1978 are fair game."

"You don't believe him?"

"Golan's reported to have floated a price tag of two million U.S. for the thing." Jake snorted. "What do you think?"

I thought it was a lot of money.

Jake pointed through the windshield at a hill rising steeply off the shoulder of the road.

"The Mount of Olives. We've come around the east side, and now we're skirting the southern edge."

Jake turned left onto a small street lined with sand-colored low-rises, many decorated with crudely drawn planes or cars, indicating an occupant had made hajj to Mecca. Boys chased balls. Dogs worked patterns around the boys. Women shook rugs, lugged groceries, swept stoops. Men conversed on rusted lawn chairs.

My mind flashed an image of the Palestinians parked outside l'Abbaye Sainte-Marie-des-Neiges. I told Jake about them, and paraphrased some of the things Morissonneau had said.

Jake opened his mouth, reconsidered, closed it.

"What?" I asked.

"Not possible."

"What's not possible?"

"Nothing."

"What is it you're not telling me?"

All I got was a head shake.

The predawn premonition of tragedy rolled over in my brainpan.

Jake made another turn and pulled into a clearing behind the village. Ahead and to the left, stone stairs descended to what appeared to be a school. Boys stood, sat, or pushed and shoved on the steps.

"Is Morissonneau's death related to—" To what? I had no idea what we were doing. "To those men?" A sweep of my hand took in the hockey bag, the village, and the valley below. "To this?"

"Forget Muslims. Muslims don't give a rat's ass about Masada or Jesus. Islam views Jesus not as a divinity, but as a holy man."

"A prophet like Abraham or Moses?"

"A messiah, even. According to Muslims, Jesus didn't die on the cross, he was taken alive to heaven, from where he will return."

That sounded familiar.

"What about Allah's Holy Warriors? The radical fringe?"

"What about them?"

"Wouldn't the jihadists love to lay their hands on the bones of Jesus?"

"Why?"

"To ransack Christianity."

A blackbird swooped to earth as we parked. We both watched it hop through garbage, wings half-spread, as though uncertain whether to stay or go.

Jake remained silent.

"I have a bad feeling about Morissonneau's death," I said.

"Don't look to Muslims."

"Who would you look to?"

"Seriously?" Jake turned to me.

I nodded.

"The Vatican."

I couldn't help laughing. "You sound like a character in *The Da Vinci Code.*"

Jake didn't say anything.

Outside my window, the bird pecked roadkill. I thought of Poe. The thought was not uplifting.

"I'm listening," I said, settling back.

"You're a product of Catholic schooling?"

"I am."

"Nuns teach the New Testament?"

"They were hall of fame on guilt, but bush league on scripture."

"The good sisters teach you Jesus had siblings?"

"No."

"Of course not. That's why the James ossuary's got the pope's panties in a twist."

The metaphor was jarring.

"The RC Church has a hard-on for virgin birth."

I didn't even want to think about that one.

"And it's stupid. The New Testament is full of references to Jesus' siblings. Matthew 13:55: 'Is not his mother called Mary and his brethren, James, and Joses, and Simon, and Judas?' Mark 6:3 repeats the same thing. In Galatians 1:19, Paul refers to his meeting with 'James the Lord's brother.' Matthew 13:56 and Mark 6:3 both indicate that Jesus had sisters."

"Don't some biblical scholars interpret these as references to half-siblings, maybe born to a previous wife of Joseph before his marriage to Mary?"

"Both Matthew 1:25 and Luke 2:7 state that Jesus was Mary's first-born son, though that does not rule out prior children of Joseph. But it's not just the Bible that refers to Jesus' siblings. The historian Josephus talks of 'the brother of Jesus—who was called Christ—whose name was James.'"

Jake was on a roll.

"In Jesus' time, virginity after marriage would have been unthinkable, a violation of Jewish law. It just wasn't done."

"So James and the others might have been later children of Mary."

"Matthew's gospel plainly states that, after Jesus was born, Joseph *knew* Mary." Jake came down hard on the word "knew." "And Matthew wasn't talking handshakes and cookies. He used the word in the biblical sense.

"Though Joseph isn't the only candidate for Daddy of Jesus' siblings. Once Jesus grows up, Joseph totally disappears. You never hear about the guy."

"So Mary might have remarried?"

"If Joseph died or left, it would have been expected."

I understood the dilemma for the Catholic Church.

"Whether by Joseph or by some other man, the implication is that Mary gave birth to other children. And one of them was James. So if the James ossuary is real, it throws into question the whole concept of perpetual virginity, and perhaps, by association, the concept of virgin birth."

Another Jake snort.

"Saint Jerome and his cronies cooked that one up in the fourth century. Jesus' pal Mary Magdalene became a prostitute. Jesus' mother became a virgin. Good women don't have sex. Bad women do. The idea appealed to the misogynist male ego. The concept became dogma, and the Vatican's been championing it ever since."

"So if the James ossuary is real, and the box actually belonged to Jesus' brother, the Vatican has some explaining to do."

"You bet. The idea of Mary as a mama is a mega-problem for the Vatican. Hell, even if the box means only that Joseph had other kids, that's still a problem. It suggests that Joseph impregnated his wives. And, again, the Vatican's credibility is screwed."

The blackbird had been joined by others. For a few moments I watched them squabble over carrion rights.

Okay. The James ossuary blew the lid on Mary's virginity. I could see how the Vatican would be concerned about that. I could see how Christian or Muslim radicals might want to get their hands on the box. Same argument Morissonneau had presented. Save the faith. Wreck the faith. But how did the ossuary link to the Masada skeleton? Or did it? Had the two finds coincidentally surfaced at the same time?

"What does the James ossuary have to do with Morissonneau's skeleton?"

Jake hesitated. "I'm not sure. Yet. But here's an interesting sidebar. Oded Golan worked as a volunteer at Masada."

"For Yigael Yadin?" I asked.

Jake nodded, again checked his surroundings. I wanted to probe the connection between Max and the James ossuary, but Jake gave me no chance.

"Let's go."

"Where?" I asked.

"The Jesus family tomb."

20

BEFORE I COULD REACT, JAKE CLIMBED FROM THE TRUCK. THE blackbirds cawed in protest and flapped skyward.

Reaching behind the seat, Jake transferred items from his pack to the zipper compartment of my hockey bag. Then he shouldered the bag's strap, scanned the area, locked the driver's-side door, and set off.

I trailed behind, a cascade of questions whirling in my brain.

The Jesus family tomb? If authenticated, such a find would be huge. CNN, BBC, around the globe mammoth.

What proof did Jake have?

Why had he waited until now to tell me?

How did this tomb relate to the bones I'd carried from l'Abbaye Sainte-Marie-des-Neiges? To the James ossuary?

I felt fearful.

I felt awestruck.

I felt totally jazzed.

Ten yards downslope, Jake stopped on a ledge.

"We're standing on the edge of the Kidron Valley." Jake indicated the gorge at our feet. "The Kidron meets the Hinnom just south of here, then veers west."

I must have looked lost.

"The Hinnom Valley runs south from the Jaffa Gate on the west side of the Old City, then eastward along the south side of Mount Zion until it meets the Kidron. The Kidron separates the Temple Mount from the Mount of Olives on the east side of the city." Jake pointed. "Over there. Know much about the Hinnom?"

"Not really."

"The place has quite a colorful history. In the pre-Christian era, babies are supposed to have been sacrificed to the gods Moloch and Baal in the Hinnom. The Jews turned the valley into a city dump—garbage, anything deemed unclean, including the bodies of executed criminals, were burned there. In later Jewish literature the valley was called Ge-Hinnom, and in the Greek of the New Testament, Gehenna. Because of the trash fires, the Hinnom provided imagery for a fiery hell in the Books of Isaiah and the New Testament. Gehenna is the source of the English word 'hell.'"

Jake stuck a thumb at an ancient tree at my back.

"Judas is supposed to have hanged himself there. According to tradition, his body fell from that tree and was disemboweled."

"You don't believe that's the actual tree—"

A small bird darted between us, moving so fast I couldn't make out its color. Jake threw up an arm, and a boot slipped. Pebbles shot downward.

My adrenals opened fire.

Regaining his footing, Jake continued with a question.

"According to the Bible, where did Christ go after his crucifixion?"

"Into a tomb."

"He descended into hell, and on the third day rose again. Right?"

I nodded.

"At the time that was written the Hinnom was constantly burning and had taken on the popular image as the place 'down there' where the wicked would be cast into the flames of destruction. Hell. Hell Valley. The biblical reference is to burial in a location in or near the Hinnom."

Jake left no gap for comment.

"These valleys were the location of the tombs of the wealthy."

"Like Joseph of Aramathea."

"You got it." Jake pointed flat-handed to our left and rear, then swept his arm in a clockwise arc. "Silwan's the village behind us. Abu Tor's across the way." Jake closed his circle on the hill to our right. "The Mount of Olives is to the north."

I sited off his fingers. Jerusalem crawled the summit westward from the Mount, its domes facing off across the Kidron with the minarets of Silwan.

"These hills are honeycombed with ancient tombs." Jake yanked out a bandanna and wiped sweat from his head. "I'm taking you to one unearthed by Palestinian roadwork a few years back."

"How far down the valley?" I asked.

"Way down."

Jake backhanded the bandanna into a jeans pocket, grabbed a bush, and hopped off the ledge. I watched him scrabble downhill, bald head shining like a copper pot.

Using the same bush, I squatted, kicked out my legs, and bellied over the edge. When my feet made contact, I let go, turned, and began picking my way downhill, sliding on loose rocks and grabbing vegetation.

The sun was climbing a brilliant blue sky. Inside my Windbreaker, I began to sweat.

Again and again I thought of the pair outside l'Abbaye Sainte-Marie-des-Neiges. My eyes kept moving from the ground at my feet to the village at my back. The slope was at least sixty degrees where Jake had chosen to descend. If anyone wanted to pick us off, we were easy targets.

On one backward glance I spotted a man walking a path on the valley rim.

My heart gunned into overdrive.

An assassin? A man walking a path on the valley rim?

I looked downhill. Jake was drawing farther and farther ahead.

I goosed the tempo.

Five yards down, I slipped and cracked my shin. Tears shot from wherever they'd been waiting on call. I blinked them back.

Screw it. If someone wanted to kill us we'd be dead by now.

I dropped back to my tenderfoot crawl.

Jake was spot-on. The tomb wasn't at the bottom, but it was way down the valley, in a grassy stretch strewn with rocks and boulders.

When I arrived he was squatting by an outcrop squinting into a rectangle the size of my microwave. I watched him roll a paper, light one end, and thrust the makeshift torch into the opening.

Oh, God.

Closing my eyes, I talked myself down.

Feel.

Wind on my face.

Smell.

Sun-heated grass. Garbage. Coal smoke.

Taste.

Dust on my teeth and tongue.

Listen.

The buzzing of an insect. Gears grinding way off up the valley.

I took a deep breath. A second. A third.

I opened my eyes.

Small red flowers bloomed at my feet.

I took another breath. Counted.

Six flowers. Seven. Ten.

I looked up to see Jake eyeing me oddly.

"I'm a bit claustrophobic." I offered the understatement of the decade.

"We don't have to go in," Jake said.

"We're here," I said.

Jake looked skeptical.

"I'm fine." The overstatement of the decade.

"The air's okay," Jake said.

"What more could one ask?" I said.

"I'll go first," Jake said.

He slid down the incline and disappeared, feet-first.

"Hand me the bones." His voice came out muffled and hollow.

My heartbeat revved as I maneuvered the bag. I breathed it back to normal.

"Come on down." Quiz-show dramatic.

Deep breath.

Turning, I thrust my feet into darkness. Jake grabbed my ankles. I inched backward until I felt hands on my waist. I dropped.

Murky dimness. One skewed rectangle of light squeezing in from outside.

"You okay?" Jake asked.

"Dandy."

Jake's flashlight clicked on.

The space was approximately eight feet square, with a ceiling so low we had to crouch. Food wrappers, cans, and broken glass littered the floor, graffiti marred the walls. The air smelled like a mix of mud and ammonia.

"Bad news, Jake. Some have come before." I pointed at a used condom.

"These tombs are popular with drifters and kids."

Jake's beam darted here and there. It looked yellow and wavery, and not reassuring.

As my eyes adjusted, I picked out details.

The tomb's entrance was to the east, facing the Old City. The northern, western, and southern walls were cut by a series of oblong recesses, each approximately two feet wide. Stones blocked the entrances to a few of the recesses, but most were wide-open. In the amber beam I could see their interiors were packed with fill.

"The little chambers are called loculi," Jake said. "*Kochim* in Hebrew. During the first century, the dead were shrouded and left in loculi until decomposed. Then the bones were collected and permanently stored in ossuaries."

I felt a tingle on one hand. I looked down. Jake noticed and shot the beam my way.

A daddy longlegs was high-stepping it up my sleeve. Gently pinching one leg, I displaced the arachnid. I freak in tight spaces, but I'm cool with spiders.

"This tomb has a lower level."

Jake duck-walked to the southwest corner. I followed.

Jake pointed his light at what I'd assumed to be a loculus. It disappeared into total darkness.

"You game for the cellar if I'm there to catch you?"

"Go," I said, not granting my amygdala time to react.

Jake rolled to his stomach, inserted his legs, and wiggled downward. Closing my eyes I did the same.

I felt hands.

I felt terra firma.

I stuck the landing.

I opened my eyes.

There wasn't a pixel of light. Jake was so close our shoulders were touching.

I became intensely interested in the flashlight.

"Light?"

A yellow shaft cut the darkness.

"Those batteries new?" I asked.

"Relatively."

The ammonia smell was stronger at this level. I recognized what it was. Urine. I made a note to keep my hands off the floor.

Jake played his beam over the wall we were facing, and then over the one to our left.

The lower chamber was smaller, but appeared to be laid out like the one above. That would mean two loculi to the north. Two to the south. Three in back.

"You say there are thousands of these tombs?" My voice sounded dead in the underground space.

"Most were robbed long ago. I stumbled onto this one while hiking with students in the fall of 2000. Kid spotted the opening, saw artifacts scattered outside. It was obvious looters had just hit, so we called the IAA."

"You did a full excavation?"

"Hardly. The IAA archaeologist couldn't have been less impressed. Said there was nothing left that was worth protecting, and left us to our own devices. We salvaged what we could."

"Why the disinterest?"

"In his opinion, the site wasn't anything special. I don't know if the guy had a hot date that night, or what. He couldn't get out of here fast enough."

"You disagree with his assessment?"

"Less than two years after we found this tomb, Oded Golan, the antiquities collector I told you about, revealed the existence of the James ossuary to a French epigrapher named André Lemaire."

"You think the ossuary was stolen from here?"

"It makes sense. The ossuary is rumored to have come from somewhere near Silwan. Within two years of the looting of this tomb the ossuary was presented to the world."

"If the James ossuary came from this tomb, that would suggest this is the place Jesus' brother was buried."

"Yes."

"Making this the Jesus family tomb."

"Awesome, eh?"

I didn't know what to say, so I said nothing.

"We found twelve boxes, all smashed, the remains tossed aside."

"Remains?"

"Bones."

Jake dropped one knee and raised the other. His movement sent shadows dancing the walls.

"But that's not the best of it. Golan's James ossuary has elaborate detailing, and the motif's a dead ringer for the boxes we found here. What's more—"

Jake's head shot up.

"What?"

His fingers wrapped my arm.

"What?" I hissed.

Jake clicked off the light and touched a finger to my lips.

Ice flooded my veins.

I remembered the man on the valley rim. Had we been followed?

How easy it would be to block the entrance! How easy it would be to shoot down the tunnel!

Beside me I felt Jake go totally still. I did the same.

Heart hammering, I strained for the faintest sound.

Nothing.

"False alarm," Jake whispered when an eon had passed. "But we left the bones topside. I'm going to grab them."

"Can't we just move on to the IAA?"

"When I tell you what else we found here, you'll want the full tour. And you'll want to see what's at my lab. It's amazing." Jake handed me the flashlight. "Back in a sec."

"Look around while you're up there," I whispered. "Make sure there's no papal vigilante crouched by the entrance." The joke sounded lame.

"Will do."

I watched Jake muscle up the tunnel, hoping I had the arm strength to do the same. When his boots disappeared, I crawled along the wall I was facing and directed the light inside the first of the loculi.

Empty, but the dirt-covered floor was gouged and scuffed. Jake's students? The looters?

I moved down the wall, then rounded the corner.

Same story in each loculus.

Duckwalking to the base of the tunnel, I looked up and listened. Not the faintest sound drifted down from above.

The air felt damp and cold. Inside my jacket, my sweat-soaked shirt adhered to my back. I began to shiver.

Where the hell was Jake?

"Jake?" I called up.

No answer.

"Probably securing the perimeter," I murmured to break the silence.

I was moving along the southern wall when the beam dimmed, strengthened, dimmed, and died.

Inky black.

I shook the flashlight. Not a flicker. I shook it again. Nothing.

I heard a sound behind me.

Had I imagined it?

I held my breath. One. Two. Thr—

I heard it again. The rub of something soft scraping stone.

Dear God! I wasn't alone!

I froze.

Moments later, I sensed, more than heard, another whisper of movement.

The tiny hairs rose on my nape and arms.

I held absolutely motionless. A second. A year.

Another sound. Different. More terrifying.

My skin went taut from scalp to sternum.

21

GROWL? PURR? GROAN?

Before I could pigeonhole it, the sound stopped.

My brain groped for a familiar image to explain what I'd heard.

It came up empty.

I thumbed the flashlight switch. Nothing. I thumbed it in the opposite direction. More nothing.

Eyes wide, I searched my surroundings.

Blackness.

I was trapped underground, surrounded by stone and hillside a thousand feet thick. It was dark. And damp.

And I wasn't alone!

Something's in here! a voice screamed in my head.

My chest felt tight. I drew air through my nose.

The stench of urine seemed stronger now. And there was something else. Fecal matter? Rotting flesh?

I tried breathing through my mouth.

My mind flew in a million directions.

Turn around? Scream? Break for the tunnel?

I was frozen in place. Afraid to move. Afraid to stay still.

Then, I heard it again. Half growl, half rumble.

My fingers death-gripped the flashlight. It might at least serve as a club.

Something scratched stone.

Claws?

Cold fear sparked my nerves.

I shook the flashlight. The batteries rattled but offered nothing.

I shook harder.

A weak yellow cone wormed into the darkness. Still squatting, I pivoted slowly and lit the corner behind me.

And caught a shadow of movement in the last loculus!

Get out! screamed the voice in my head.

I was backing toward the tunnel when the growl started again. The message was low and feral.

I froze again. Hand shaking, I refocused on the loculus.

Eyes gleamed from low in the recess, pupils round and red as neon cranberries. Below them, the outline of a scarred snout.

Wild dog? Fox? Hyena?

Jackal!

The jackal stood with neck angled down, shoulder blades shooting to bony peaks behind its ears. Its fur was mangy and matted.

I took a cautious step backward.

The jackal bared teeth that were brown and glistening. It's forelimbs flexed and its head shot up.

Every muscle in me went rigid.

The jackal swung its snout from side to side, nostrils working the air. The movement sent shadows rippling the hills and valleys of its rib cage. Though emaciated, its belly hung low.

Dear God! I was trapped underground with a starving jackal! Probably a pregnant female!

Where was Jake? What to do?

My brain coughed up facts garnered from some nature documentary.

Jackals are nocturnal in areas inhabited by humans.

The jackal had been sleeping. Jake and I had startled her awake. Not good.

Jackals are territorial and scent-mark their turf.

The urine smell. The jackal viewed the tomb as her territory, and me as an invader. Not good.

Jackals live and hunt as monogamous pairs.

The jackal had a mate.

Sweet Jesus! The male could return at any time. He could be in the loculus with her!

I couldn't wait for Jake. I had to make a move.

Now!

Waistbanding the light, I pivoted, and crawled toward the mouth of the tunnel.

Behind me I heard a snarl, then scratching. I sensed air movement. I braced and regripped the flashlight. Maybe I could jam it into the jackal's mouth, prevent teeth sinking into my flesh. Maybe I could strike a blow to the head.

The jackal didn't attack.

Get out before you're one against two!

I resnugged the flashlight in my waistband, and gripped stones jutting from opposite sides of the tunnel. Thrusting with my legs and pulling with my hands, I heaved upward with all my strength.

After repositioning my feet, I reached for another handhold, and pulled and lunged upward again.

My right-foot support held. The left broke free.

Spinning, I fell back down the tunnel and hit the floor hard. A flash-fire of pain ripped my shoulder and cheek.

The tomb went black.

My heart went stratospheric.

I lay still, taking in sound.

Blood roaring in my ears.

Stones rattling down the tunnel.

The *tic-tic-tic* of the rolling flashlight.

The *ting* of metal hitting rock.

Underlying it all, a low, rumbling growl.

Within seconds, the stones stopped falling and the flashlight lay silent.

Only my heart and the jackal played on.

The growling was no longer coming from the southeastern loculus. Or was it? The tomb was acting as an echo chamber, ricocheting sound from wall to wall. I couldn't pinpoint the jackal's location.

The darkness pressed in.

My options had tanked. The jackal now held an advantage. She could see, hear, and smell me in the dark. I had no idea where she was.

Weak as it was, my beam had confused the jackal, held her in place like a deer on a highway. It might work again.

Would my movement provoke the jackal? Would the batteries function? I took the double gamble.

Extending my left arm, I inched my hand across the tomb floor.

And found nothing.

My jacket swished, sounding like thunder in the small space.

The jackal growled louder, and then went still. I heard fast breathing. The panting was more terrible than the growling had been. Was she preparing to pounce?

I pictured eyes watching in the dark. My groping grew desperate. My hand swept right, front, left.

Finally, my fingers closed on a metal tube.

I drew the flashlight to me and hit the switch.

Sickly yellow lit my body. I almost wept with relief.

The growling kicked into high.

Heart thudding, I pushed to my elbows and played the light over the northern and eastern walls.

No jackal.

The southern wall.

No jackal.

Reorienting, I swept the beam over the western side of the tomb. Every recess was filled with dirt and rock, leaving no crevice in which a jackal could hide.

I was probing the loculus closest to me, when a trickle of dirt cascaded down the wall.

The batteries chose that moment to die.

I heard movement above my head.

Fighting back tears, I shook the flashlight. It kicked back on.

I raised the beam.

The loculi were stacked one above the other in the western wall. The jackal was crouched in one of the upper-level recesses.

When my beam hit her, the jackal drew back her lips and snarled. Her body tensed. Her limbs flexed.

Our eyes met. The jackal's were round and shiny.

A sudden realization. The jackal, too, felt trapped. She wanted out. I was blocking the tunnel.

We stared at each other. I stared a split second longer.

Snarling, the jackal launched herself at me.

I reacted without thought, dropping to the floor, wrapping my hands around my head, and tucking into a fetal curl. The weight of the jackal hit my left hip and thigh. I heard a snarl, and felt the weight shift.

Levering an elbow, I tried dragging myself away from the tunnel mouth. Paws hit my chest and moved toward my throat. I tucked my chin and crossed my arms, expecting teeth to rip my flesh. Then, the press of weight against my torso, the brush of fur against my head, and sudden release. The jackal had bounded over me and upward.

I heard panting and claws scraping stone. I turned my light toward the tunnel. The jackal was slinking out of sight.

Amazingly, the flashlight continued to shine, though weakly. Quick assessment. I gave the jackal time to put mileage between us, then crawled toward the tunnel. There had been some collapse, but the stones were nothing I couldn't handle.

I spent two minutes lifting and rolling rock, then positioned my feet as before and flexed to heave myself upward.

And realized my left hip had taken a hit. Great. All I needed was another tumble and I'd be down here for a very long time.

Dropping back, I tested my legs.

As I shifted from foot to foot, my light angled upward and caught a hollow from which rocks had been knocked free.

I let my beam sniff the scar.

It looked deep. Too deep.

I rose and wedged myself upward into the tunnel for a closer look.

The scar wasn't a scar. It was a breach.

Angling the beam, I peered into the void beyond.

It took a moment for my eyes to pick it out.

It took another for my mind to comprehend.

Oh my God! I had to show Jake!

Injuries forgotten, I pulled myself upward.

Just below the tunnel mouth, I paused and peeked out, prairie-dog style.

The upper chamber looked empty. No Jake. No jackal.

"Jake!" I hissed.

No answer.

"Jake!" I repeated as loudly as I could without bringing in vocal cords.

Same nonresponse.

I braced my feet, threw out my arms, and pulled and pushed myself onto the upper-chamber floor.

Jake didn't appear.

Ignoring the objections of my shoulder and hip, I rose to a squat and looked around in the flashlight sweep.

I was alone.

I listened.

No sound filtered in from outside the tomb.

Rotating quickly, I moved my beam through the velvety black around me.

Blue flashed in the darkness of a northern loculus.

What the hell?

I knew what the hell.

I worked the light. I was right. The hockey bag.

But why? Where was Jake?

"Jake!" Full vocal.

I dropped to all fours, crawled toward the loculus, stopped. Jake had hidden the bag for a reason. Reversing, I crawled toward the tomb's entrance.

It was then I heard the first sound since leaving the tunnel. I froze, head cocked.

A muffled voice.

Another.

Shouting.

Jake's voice. Words I couldn't make out. Hebrew?

More words I couldn't make out. Angry words.

A soft thud. Another.

Running footsteps.

The blackness grew blacker. I glanced toward the entrance.

Legs were blocking the small square of sunlight.

22

IN A HEARTBEAT, BOOTS SHOT INTO THE TOMB. A BODY FOLLOWED. A large body.

I scrabbled backward and pressed myself to a wall. Crumpled cans jabbed my knees and pop-tops gouged the palms of my hands.

My mind flashed again to the man on the valley rim. My heart pounded. Sweet Mother of God! Would I live through this day?

Tightening my grip, I raised the flashlight, ready to strike.

The body had settled onto its haunches, back to me. My beam lit coconut palms on Waikiki blue.

I took my first breath since seeing the legs. Outside I could hear shouting.

"What the hell's going on?"

"Hevrat Kadisha." Jake threw the words over one shoulder, never taking his eyes from the entrance.

"I don't speak Hebrew."

"The goddamn bone police." Jake was panting from exertion.

I waited for him to explain.

"Da'ataim."

"That clears it up."

"The ultra-Orthodox."

"They're here?" I pictured men in *shtreimel* and *peyos* rolling over the rim of the Kidron.

"In force."

"Why?"

"They think we have human bones in here."

"We do have human bones in here."

"They want them."

"What do we do?"

"Wait them out."

"Will they leave?"

"Eventually."

That was not reassuring.

"This is insane," I said after listening for a few moments to the shouting outside.

"These cretins show up at excavations all the time."

"Why?"

"To harass. Hell, we often need police protection just to do our jobs."

"Isn't access to archaeological sites by permit only?"

"These head cases don't care. They're opposed to the unearthing of the dead for *any* reason, and they'll riot in order to stop a dig."

"Is theirs a majority view?" In my mind's eye the bearded men now carried posters and placards.

"God, no."

Outside, the voices eventually stilled. Somehow, I found the quiet more disconcerting than the shouting.

I told Jake about the jackal.

"You're sure it was a jackal?"

"I'm sure," I said.

"I didn't see it run from the tomb."

"She was moving fast," I said.

"And I was focused on those morons out there. You're okay?"

"I'm fine."

"Sorry," Jake said. "I should have checked before we went down."

I agreed wholeheartedly.

Outside the tomb, the silence continued.

I shone the light on my watch. Nine-seventeen.

"What's the law in Israel regarding human remains?" I asked, still speaking in a loud church whisper.

"Bones can be excavated if they're about to be destroyed by development or plunder. Once they've been studied, they must be handed over to the Ministry of Religious Affairs for reburial."

As we spoke, Jake kept his eyes on the small opening through which he'd just slithered.

"Sounds reasonable. Similar statutes protect native burials in North America."

"These fanatics are hardly reasonable. They believe halakha, Jewish law, forbids any disturbance of the Jewish dead. Period."

"What if a site is about to be bulldozed?"

"They don't care." Jake flapped a hand at the entrance. "They say build a bridge, dig a tunnel, reroute the road, encase the whole bloody tomb in cement."

"Are they still out there?"

"Probably."

"Who decides if human remains are Jewish?" My stomach was still knotted from my encounter with the jackal. I was talking mainly to calm myself.

"The guardians of Orthodoxy, themselves. Handy, eh?"

"What if ancestry's unclear?" I was thinking of the bones in the bag behind me.

Jake snorted. "The Ministry of Religious Affairs ponies up a thousand shekels for each reburial. How many do you suppose are declared non-Jewish?"

"But—"

"The Hevrat Kadisha say prayers over the bones and, *voilà,* the dead are converted to Judaism."

I didn't get it, but I let it go.

Ominous quiet slipped in from outside. Again I checked my watch. Nine twenty-two.

"How long do we wait?" I asked.

"Until the coast is clear," Jake said.

Jake and I fell silent. Now and then one or the other of us would shift, seeking to gain a more comfortable position. Being six-six, Jake shifted most.

My hip hurt. My shoulder hurt. I was cold and damp. I was sitting in garbage in a crypt waiting out folks who would have put the Inquisition to shame.

And it wasn't even 10 A.M.

An eon later, I again illuminated my watch face. Twenty minutes had passed. I was about to suggest checking for cleared coasts, when a man shouted.

"*Asur!*"

Another took up the cry. "*Asur!*"

My stomach knot tightened. The men were close now, on the hillside just outside the tomb.

I looked at Jake.

"'Forbidden,'" he translated.

"*Chilul!*"

"'Desecration.'"

Something ricocheted off the outcrop above the tomb entrance.

"What the hell was that?"

"Probably a rock."

"They're throwing at us?" If a whisper can be shrill, mine was.

I heard another something wing off the capstone.

"*B'nei Belial!*"

"They say we're children of the devil," Jake explained.

"How many are out there?" I asked.

"Several carloads."

A fist-size stone hit the rim of the entrance.

"*Asur! Asur la'asot et zeh!*" It had now become a chant. "*Asur! Asur!*"

Jake raised his eyebrows at me. In the darkness they looked like a solid black hedge levitating skyward. I raised mine back.

"I'll have a look," he said.

"Be careful," I said, for lack of a better contribution.

Squat-walking to the entrance, Jake dropped one knee, placed a hand on it, and craned out.

What happened next happened fast.

The chanting fragmented into individual cries.

"*Shalom alaichem,*" Jake wished the men peace.

Angry voices shouted back.

"*Lo!*" Jake shouted. I understood enough Hebrew to know that meant no.

More yelling.

"*Reik—*"

There was a sickening crack, as rock hit bone.

Jake's spine arched, one leg shot backward, and he slumped to the ground.

"Jake!"

I scrabbled to him on all fours.

Jake's head lay outside, his shoulders and body inside the tomb.

"Jake!"

No response.

Reaching out, I placed trembling fingers on Jake's throat.

I felt a pulse, weak but steady.

Rising to a crouch, I leaned into the opening for a better view of Jake's head.

Jake's face was down, but I could see the back and side of his skull. Blood flecked his ear, and glistened red in the sunlit grass. Already flies were buzzing in for quick look-sees.

Cold fear barreled through my veins.

First a jackal, and now this! What to do? Move Jake and risk exacerbating his injury? Leave him and go for help?

Impossible without risking a skull fracture of my own.

Outside, the chanting started up again.

Give the bastards what they want?

They'd bury the skeleton. The truth about Max would be lost forever.

Another rock winged off the tomb's exterior. Then another.

Sonovabitch!

No ancient mystery was worth the loss of a life. Jake needed medical attention.

Setting the flashlight on the tomb floor, I scrabbled backward, took hold of Jake's boots, and pulled.

He didn't budge. I pulled again. Harder.

Inch by inch, I tugged Jake into the protection of the tomb. Then I crawled around his body and turned his head sideways. Should Jake become nauseous, I didn't want him choking on his vomit.

Then I remembered.

Jake's cell phone! Was it on him? Could I get at it?

Working my way down, I checked Jake's shirt pocket, his left front and rear jeans pockets, and every accessible opening on his camouflage jacket.

No phone.

Damn!

The hockey bag?

I angled toward the northern loculi. My hands looked bitter white as I crawled toward the bag. It was as though I were watching the hands of another. I saw them struggle with zippers, disappear into pouch after pouch.

My brain recognized the feel of the familiar shape.

Yanking the phone free, I flipped the cover. The small screen flashed a neon blue welcome.

What digits to punch? 911?

I had no idea what one dialed in an emergency in Israel.

Scrolling through Jake's directory, I chose a local listing, and hit "send."

The screen flashed the number and the word "Dialing." I heard a series of beeps, then one long beep, then the screen welcomed me anew.

I tried again. Same result.

Damn! Too deep in rock for a signal!

I was about to try again, when Jake moaned. Pocketing the phone, I crawled to him.

When I arrived, Jake had rolled to his belly, and drawn his palms in under his chest.

"Take it easy," I said, picking up the flashlight.

Moving gingerly, Jake maneuvered to a sit. A tendril of blood trickled from a gash in his forehead. He swiped at it, creating a dark smear across his nose and right cheek.

"What happened?" Groggy.

"You stopped a rock with your head."

"Where are we?"

"A tomb in the Kidron."

Jake seemed to struggle a moment, then, "The Hevrat Kadisha."

"At least one of them has a future in major league baseball."

"We've got to get out of this place."

"If it's the last thing we ever do."

"Is the bag still in the loculus?"

"Yes."

Jake hopped to a squat, swayed, dropped his head, and braced himself straight-armed against the ground.

I reached out to steady him.

"Can you climb the hill?"

"Minor setback." Whole muscle bundles went taut, then Jake dropped to all fours. "Beam me up, Scottie."

As I lit his way, Jake crawled not to the entrance, but to the northern wall, rolled a large stone toward the loculus containing Masada Max, and wedged it into the opening.

"Let's go," he said, rejoining me.

"Will they come in here?"

"Maybe. But we'd never make it past them to the truck."

"Will they notice the hockey bag?"

"I could move it to the lower level."

For the first time since crawling topside, I remembered what I'd uncovered in the lower chamber. I didn't want the Hevrat Kadisha going down there and finding it. Losing Max would be bad enough. Losing what had been walled in below would double the calamity.

"Let's leave the bag in the loculus and hope they don't spot it. If they do come in here, I don't want them poking around downstairs. I'll explain when we're in the truck. How do we do this?"

"We walk out."

"Just like that?"

"When they see that I'm injured, they'll probably back off."

"They'll also note that we're empty-handed."

"They'll also note that."

"Do you suppose they saw the hockey bag?"

"I have no idea. Are you ready?"

I nodded, and switched off the flashlight. Jake stuck his head through the opening and shouted.

Surprised? Wary? Rearming? The Hevrat Kadisha fell silent.

Extending both arms, Jake flexed his legs, and torqued himself up and out.

When Jake's boots cleared the opening, I followed. Halfway up I felt a hand on my waistband, then I was kneeling on the hillside.

The jolt to sunlight was blinding. My pupils went to pinpoints. My eyes slammed shut.

I opened them to one of the strangest scenes I've ever witnessed.

23

OUR ATTACKERS WORE BROAD-BRIMMED HATS AND LONG-COATED black suits. Bearded and side-curled, each looked hotter and angrier than the next.

Okay. My mental image had been spot-on. But I'd been way off on the numbers.

As Jake again wished the men peace and opened discussion, I took a quick count.

Forty-two, including a couple of kids under the age of twelve, and another half dozen who looked to be teenagers. Apparently ultra-Orthodoxy was a growth industry.

Hebrew flew around me. Based on my newly acquired vocabulary, I was able to grasp that Jake and I were being accused of having taken or done something forbidden, and that some thought we were the children of Satan. I assumed Jake was denying both charges.

Men and boys shouted, glasses and clothing coated with dust. Some bobbed, side curls bouncing like tethered Slinkys.

After several minutes of animated dialogue, Jake focused on a gray-hair who seemed to be the alpha male, probably a rabbi. As the two spoke, the others fell silent.

The rabbi bellowed, face raspberry, pointed finger wagging in the sunlight. I caught the word "*ashem.*" Shame.

Jake listened, replied calmly, the voice of reason.

Eventually, the foot soldiers of Orthodoxy grew restless. Some resumed shouting. Some shook fists. A few of the younger men, probably yeshiva students, picked up stones.

I kept my eye on the latter.

After a fruitless ten minutes, Jake raised his hands in an I-give-up gesture. Turning to me he said, "This is pointless. We're out of here."

I joined him, and together we circled left.

The rabbi yelled a command. The battalion split. The right flank stayed at the tomb. The left flank stuck to Jake and me.

With long strides, Jake began climbing up out of the Kidron. I followed, taking two steps to every one of his.

Yard after yard I scrambled, panting, sweating, hauling myself up on rocks, vines, and bushes. My hip screamed. My legs grew heavy.

Now and then I glanced downhill. A dozen black hats dogged my trail. My neck and back stayed stiff, anticipating the impact of cobble on cranium.

Fortunately, our pursuers spent their days in temples and yeshivas, not gyms. Jake and I left the valley well in the lead.

A half dozen cars now occupied the clearing behind Silwan. Jake's truck was where we'd left it, but the driver's side window was not. Tiny cubes of glass flashed sunlight from the ground. Both the truck's doors were open, and papers, books, and clothing lay tossed about.

"Shit!" Jake sprinted the last few yards, and began grabbing his belongings and tossing them into the back.

I joined in. Within seconds we'd gathered everything, slammed ourselves in, and hit the locks.

The first black hats crested the summit as Jake turned the key, palmed the gearshift, and hit the gas. The wheels spun, and we lurched forward, two plumes of dust following our wake.

I looked back.

The men were wiping brows, replacing headwear, shaking fists. They looked like a jittering troupe of black marionettes, momentarily tangled, but firm in their belief God was pulling the strings.

Jake made a left, then a right out of the village. I kept my eyes on the rear window.

At the blacktop, Jake slowed and put a hand on my arm to calm me.

"Think they'll follow?" I asked.

Jake's fingers closed like a vise.

I turned to him.

And felt yet another rush of fear.

Jake's left hand was gripping the wheel hard. Too hard. His knuckles protruded like bony white knobs. His face was pasty and his breath was coming in short, shallow gasps.

"Are you all right?"

The truck was losing speed, as though Jake couldn't keep his mind on both accelerating and steering.

Jake turned to me. One pupil was a speck, the other a vacant black hole.

I grabbed the wheel just as Jake collapsed forward onto it, his boot dropping full on the gas.

The truck lurched. The speedometer rose. Twenty. Twenty-two. Twenty-five.

My first reaction was panic. Naturally, that didn't slow the pickup.

My brain kicked in.

One-arming Jake against the seat back, I grabbed the wheel.

The truck continued gathering speed.

While steering with my left hand, I struggled to shift Jake's leg with my right. The leg was dead weight. I couldn't lift or jostle it sideways.

The truck was on a downslope and accelerating fast. Twenty-seven. Thirty.

I tried shoving Jake's leg. Kicking it with my heel.

My movements jerked the wheel. The truck swerved and a tire dropped onto the shoulder. I corrected. Gravel flew, and the truck hopped back up onto the pavement.

Trees were clipping by faster and faster. We hit thirty-five. I had to do something.

The Mount of Olives formed a sheer rock face on the left. Twenty yards up, I saw a recess fronted by a small clearing overgrown with brambles.

I fought the urge to spin the wheel. Not yet. Wait.

Please, God! Hold the traffic!

Now!

I swung the wheel left. The truck veered over the center line and careened on the rims of two wheels. Abandoning my attempts at steering, I wedged both hands under Jake's thigh and heaved upward. His boot lifted a few millimeters. The engine hitched and backed off.

The truck shattered a wooden guardrail, pitched sideways, and slid, spewing dirt and gravel. Brambles and cold, Cambrian rock closed in.

I yanked Jake toward me and down. Then I threw myself over him, arms covering our heads.

Branches clawed the side panels. Something popped against the windshield.

I heard a loud metallic crunch, felt a jolt, and Jake and I pitched into the wheel.

The engine cut off.

No voice called out. No bee bumbled. No car whizzed past. Just the silence of the Mount and my own frenzied breathing.

For several heartbeats, I stayed motionless, feeling adrenaline making the rounds.

Finally, one bird threw out a tentative caw.

I sat up and checked Jake. His forehead had a lump the size of a bluepoint oyster. His eyelids looked mauve, and his skin felt clammy. He needed a doc. Pronto.

Could I move him?

Would the engine turn over?

Opening my door against the resistance of the brambles, I slid to the ground, and plowed my way around the truck.

Pull Jake out? Shove him sideways?

Jake was six-six and weighed 170. I was five-five and weighed, well, less.

Fighting vegetation, I yanked the driver's side door and stepped in. I was wriggling an arm under Jake's back when a vehicle slowed and left the pavement behind me. Gravel crunched as it rolled to a stop.

A Samaritan? A zealot?

Withdrawing my arm, I turned.

White Corolla. Two men in front.

The men looked at me through the windshield. I looked back.

The men conferred.

My gaze dropped to the license plate. White numbers, red background.

Relief flooded through me.

Both men got out. One wore a sport jacket and khakis. The other wore a pale blue shirt with black epaulettes, black shoulder patch, and black braided cord looping the armpit and running into the left breast pocket. A silver pin over the right pocket proclaimed in Hebrew what I assumed to be the cop's name.

"Shalom." The cop had a high forehead capped by a thin blond crew cut. He looked about thirty. I gave him two years until he started pricing hair plugs.

"Shalom," I replied.

"Geveret, HaKol beseder?" Madam, is everything all right?

"My friend needs medical attention," I said in English.

Crew Cut approached. His partner remained behind the open door of their vehicle, right hand cocked at his hip.

Clawing free of the bushes I stepped away from the truck, non-threatening.

"And you would be?"

"Temperance Brennan. I'm a forensic anthropologist. American."

"Uh. Huh."

"The driver is Dr. Jacob Drum. He's an American archaeologist working here in Israel."

Jake made an odd gurgling sound in his throat. Crew Cut's gaze cut to him, and then to the remains of Jake's driver's side window.

Jake chose that moment to rejoin the conscious. Or perhaps he'd been awake and listening to the exchange. Bending forward, he retrieved his sunglasses from among the pedals, slipped them on, and straightened.

Glancing from the cop to me and back, Jake slid to the passenger side to facilitate conversation.

The cop circled to him.

More *shaloms* were exchanged.

"Are you injured, sir?"

"Just a bump." Jake's laugh was convincing. The blue point on his forehead was not.

"Shall I radio for an ambulance?"

"No need."

Crew Cut's face looked dubious. Perhaps it was the incongruity between the injury to Jake and the injury to Jake's window. Perhaps it was always that way. It had looked dubious upon its exit from the Corolla.

"Really," Jake said. "I'm fine."

I should have objected. I didn't.

"I must have hit a pothole, or dropped a wheel or something." Jake gave a self-deprecating laugh. "Dumb-ass move."

Crew Cut glanced at the blacktop, then back at Jake.

"I'm excavating a site near Talpiot. Working with a crew from the Rockefeller Museum."

So Jake had heard me.

"Just showing the little lady around."

Little lady?

Crew Cut's mouth moved to say something, reconsidered, merely requested the usual papers.

Jake produced a U.S. passport, an Israeli driver's license, and the truck's registration. I forked over my passport.

Crew Cut studied each document. Then, "I'll be a moment." To Jake, "Please stay in your vehicle."

"Mind if I see if this piece of junk will start?"

"Don't move the vehicle."

While Crew Cut ran our names, Jake tried the ignition, again and again, with no luck. The wounded piece of junk had gone as far as it was going that day.

A semi rumbled by. A bus. An army Jeep. I watched each recede, its taillights growing smaller and closer together.

Jake slumped against the seat back and swallowed several times. I suspected he was feeling queasy.

Crew Cut returned and handed back our documents. I checked the side mirror. The plainclothes cop was now slouched behind the wheel.

"Can I offer you a ride, Dr. Drum?"

"Yeah." Jake's bravado had evaporated. "Thanks."

We got out. Pointlessly, Jake locked the truck, then we followed Crew Cut and climbed into the Corolla's backseat.

The plainclothes cop eyed us, nodded. He wore silver-rimmed glasses on a tired face. Crew Cut introduced him as Sergeant Schenck.

"Where to?" Schenck asked.

Jake started to give directions to his apartment in Beit Hanina. I cut him off.

"A hospital."

"I'm fine," Jake protested. Weakly.

"Take us to an ER." My tone suggested not an inch of wiggle room.

"You're staying at the American Colony, Dr. Brennan?" Schenck. The boys had been thorough.

"Yes."

Schenck made a U-turn onto the blacktop.

During the ride, Jake stayed awake, but grew passive. At my request, Schenck radioed ahead to the ER.

When Schenck pulled up, two orderlies swept Jake from the car, strapped him to a gurney, and whisked him away for CTs or MRIs or whatever techno-wizardry is brought to bear in cases of head trauma.

Schenck and Crew Cut handed me a form. I signed. They sped off.

A nurse pumped me for information on Jake. I supplied what I could. I signed other forms. I learned I was at Hadassah Hospital, on the Mount Scopus campus of Hebrew University, just a few minutes north of the Israel National Police Headquarters.

Paperwork completed, I took a seat in the waiting area, prepared for a long stay. I'd been there ten minutes when a tall man in aviator shades pushed through the double doors.

I felt, what? Relief? Gratitude? Embarrassment?

Drawing close, Ryan slid the aviators onto his head.

"You good, soldier?" The electric blues were filled with concern.

"Dandy."

"Offense run scrimmages on your face?"

"I slipped in a tomb."

"I hate it when that happens." Ryan's mouth did that twitchy thing it does when I'm looking like hell.

"Don't say it," I warned.

My hair was sweaty from climbing in and out of the Kidron. My face was scraped and swollen from my tunnel dive. My jacket was smeared with paw prints. I was dirt-speckled, bramble-scratched, and my jeans and fingernails were caked with enough crypt mud to plaster a hut.

Ryan dropped into the chair beside me.

"What went down out there?"

I told him about the tomb and the jackal, and about the incoming rounds from the Hevrat Kadisha.

"Jake lost consciousness?"

"Briefly." I left out details of the runaway truck.

"Probably a mild concussion."

"Probably."

"Where's Max?"

I told him.

"Better hope these guys follow their own dictates and let the dead lie."

I explained Jake's theory that the James ossuary had been looted from this tomb, making the place the Jesus family crypt.

"This hypothesis is based on carvings on old boxes?"

"Jake claims to have more proof at his lab. Says it's dynamite."

A woman arrived with an infant. The infant was crying. The woman eyed me, kept walking, and took a seat in the farthest bank of chairs.

"I saw something, Ryan." With one thumbnail, I dug mud from under the other. "When I was in the lower chamber."

"Something?"

I described what I'd spotted through the hole created when the rock fell out.

"You're sure?"

I nodded.

Across the room the baby was picking up steam. The mother rose and began pacing the floor.

I thought of Katy. I remembered the night she spiked a temperature of 105, and the emergency-room run with Pete. Suddenly, I missed my daughter very much.

"How did you know we were here?" I asked, dragging my thoughts back to the present.

"Schenck's major crimes. He knew Friedman was working Kaplan, and that I'd come to Israel with some female American anthropologist. Schenck put two and two together and dimed Friedman."

"Any news on that front?"

"Kaplan's denying he copped the necklace."

"That's it?"

"Not quite."

24

"TURNS OUT THE ACCUSED, THAT WOULD BE KAPLAN, AND THE wronged, that would be Litvak, go way back."

"Kaplan is a friend of the shopkeeper he robbed?"

"Distant cousin and sometime supplier. Kaplan provides Litvak with the occasional, how did Litvak phrase it? Item of curiosity."

"Litvak deals in antiquities?"

Ryan nodded.

"Illegal?"

"Of course not."

"Of course not."

"Litvak and Kaplan had had words just prior to the disappearance of the necklace."

"Words over what?"

"Kaplan promised something and failed to deliver. Litvak was pissed. Things got heated. Kaplan stormed out."

"Palming the necklace on his way."

Ryan nodded. "Litvak was so peeved he called the cops."

"You're kidding."

"Litvak's not the sharpest knife in the set. And a bit of a hothead."

The infant was cranking up for a personal best. The woman walked by, patting its back.

Ryan and I smiled them past.

"What was Kaplan supposed to have delivered to Litvak?" I asked when mother and child had moved off.

"An item of curiosity."

I rolled my eyes. It hurt.

Ryan folded his shades and slid them into his shirt pocket. Leaning back, he stretched his legs and laced his fingers on top of his stomach.

"A gen-oo-ine Masada relic."

I was about to say something clever like, "No shit!" when the triage nurse entered the waiting area and strode our way. Ryan and I stood.

"Mr. Drum has suffered a mild concussion. Dr. Epstein has decided to keep him overnight."

"You're admitting him?"

"For observation. It's standard. Other than a headache and possibly some irritability, Mr. Drum should be fine in a day or two."

"When can I see him?"

"It'll be an hour or two until he's transferred upstairs."

When the nurse had gone, Ryan turned in his chair.

"How about lunch?"

"Sounds good."

"How about lunch with strong liquor, then sex?"

"You are one silver-tongued devil."

Ryan's face lit up.

"But, no."

Ryan's face fell.

"I need to tell Jake what I saw in that tomb."

Two hours later, Ryan and I were in Jake's room. The patient was wearing one of those tie-at-the-nape gowns that had seen way too much bleach. Tubing ran from his right arm. His left was thrown over his forehead, palm out.

"It wasn't the tomb," Jake snapped, voice thick, face paler than the gown.

"Then why the demonstration?"

"The Hevrat Kadisha were targeting you!"

The nurse hadn't been kidding about irritability.

"Me?"

"They know why you're in Israel."

"How could they?"

"You called the IAA."

"Not since I've been here."

"You contacted Tovya Blotnik from Montreal." Barked like one who might eat his own young.

"Yes, but—"

"The phones at the IAA are bugged."

"By whom?" I wasn't believing this.

"The ultra-Orthodox."

"Who think you are a child of the devil," Ryan inserted.

I threw him a look that said I wasn't amused.

Jake ignored the exchange.

"These people are lunatics," he went on. "They throw rocks so people can't drive on the Sabbath. They put up posters damning archaeologists by name. I get calls over and over in the middle of the night, recorded messages, cursing me to die of cancer, hoping that terrible things happen to my family."

Jake's eyes closed against the fluorescents burning overhead.

"It wasn't the tomb," he repeated. "They know that tomb's empty. And they haven't a clue about its true importance."

"Then what did they want?" I asked, confused.

Jake's eyes opened.

"I'll tell you what they wanted. The rabbi kept demanding the remains of the hero of Masada."

Masada Max.

Whom we'd left in a loculus not twenty feet from them.

"Will they search the tomb?"

"What do you think?" An ornery ten-year-old.

I refused to be sucked in by Jake's foul mood.

"I think it depends on whether they saw us with the hockey bag."

"Give the lady a big gold star."

The little lady.

Jake lowered his arm and stared at his clenched fist. For a few seconds, no one spoke.

I broke the silence.

"There's more, Jake."

Jake looked at me. I noticed that his pupils had equalized.

"I dislodged a rock climbing up from the lower chamber. There's a recess behind the tunnel wall that's completely closed off."

"Right." Scornful. "A hidden loculus."

"When I shined the flashlight inside, I saw what looked like old fabric."

"You're serious?" Jake struggled to sit up.

I nodded.

"There's no question that tomb dates to the first century. The ossuaries prove that. Textiles from that period have been found in the desert, but never in Jerusalem."

"If you promise not to take my head off, I'll tell you the rest."

Jake lay back on his pillow.

"I think the fabric may be a shroud."

"No way."

"I also saw bones."

"Human?"

I nodded.

At that moment a nurse came through the door, rubber heels squeaking on the shiny gray tile. When she'd finished checking Jake she turned to me.

"You must leave now. This patient needs rest."

Jake struggled up onto his elbows. "We've got to get back out there," he said to me.

"Lie down, Mr. Drum." The nurse placed hands on Jake's shoulders and applied pressure.

Jake resisted.

The nurse gave him a look that suggested rubber hoses were next.

Jake yielded.

The nurse looked at me.

"Now." Her tone suggested rubber hoses for visitors.

I patted Jake's arm.

"I'll go back out first thing in the morning."

"It can't wait."

Nurse Ratchet glared my way.

I stepped back from the bed.

Jake raised his head from the pillow and spit one last word.

"Now!" Sounding just like Nurse Ratchet.

* * *

Ryan phoned INP headquarters from the hospital lobby. I was too preoccupied to pay much attention.

How would I find my way back to the Kidron? Who would help me once I got to the tomb? I couldn't ask Ryan. He was here on police business. Friedman was taking time out of his schedule to help him. Ryan needed to focus on Kaplan.

"Friedman's coming," Ryan said, flipping the cover on his rented mobile.

"He's finished with Kaplan?"

"He's giving the gentleman time to reflect."

"Kaplan thinks he's been arrested because of Litvak's necklace?"

"And some bad checks in Canada."

"You haven't yet questioned him about Ferris?"

Ryan shook his head. "Friedman's got an interesting approach. Says little, lets the suspect talk, all the while watching for details and inconsistencies he can pounce on later."

"Give a liar enough rope . . ."

"Kaplan's getting enough to dangle from the top of K2."

"When does Ferris go into the mix?"

"Tomorrow."

"Will you show Kaplan the picture he gave me at the autopsy?"

"Should give him a jolt."

I experienced a sudden jolt of my own.

"Ohmygod, Ryan! Do you suppose Max could be Kaplan's gen-oo-ine Masada relic? Do you suppose Kaplan got wind of the skeleton from Ferris?"

Ryan smiled widely. "Want to come along and ask him?"

"Could help Friedman with his pounce."

"I'm sure he'd agree."

"I'm a terrific pouncer."

"I've seen you. It's frightening."

"It's a gift."

While we waited, Ryan asked how I planned to return to the Kidron.

I admitted to some uncertainty on logistics.

We'd been in the lobby ten minutes when Friedman arrived. En route to the American Colony, he updated Ryan on the Kaplan interrogation.

There was little to update. Kaplan was still saying he'd intended to pay for the necklace. Litvak was now saying maybe he'd been a bit hasty.

Ryan filled Friedman in on my morning's activities.

"You think this textile's genuine first century?" Friedman asked into the rearview mirror.

"It's definitely old," I said. "And the loculus looks undisturbed."

"And looters will be on that tomb like flies on a corpse."

Friedman thought a moment. Then, "Whoo-hoo!!"

Hebrew?

"We be tomb raiders!"

Friedman had been watching far too many movies.

"Where to?" he asked.

"Are you sure you want to do this?" I asked.

"Ab-so-fuckin-lutely," Friedman said. "I take this country's cultural heritage very seriously."

"Don't we need a permit? Or at least authorization?"

"Got it covered."

Good enough.

"The hotel, please. I'll pick up my camera."

"Anything else?" Ryan asked.

"A shovel and something to dislodge stones." My mind flashed to the blackout in the lower chamber. "And powerful flashlights with brand-new batteries."

Friedman dropped me at the American Colony, then he and Ryan set off on a supply mission. I raced to the third floor.

Jake would recover!

I would retrieve Max and, perhaps, a first-century shroud!

Wrapping whose remains?

From whose tomb?

I was pitched so high I took the stairs two risers at a time.

Soap was in my future! A hairbrush! A dry shirt!

Ryan and Friedman were helping!

Life was good! An adventure!

Then I opened my door.

And stared in disbelief.

25

MY ROOM WAS TRASHED.

The bed had been stripped, the linens tossed, the mattress flipped. The closet and armoire stood agape, with hangers, shoes, and sweaters flung in all directions.

My euphoria crumbled.

"Who's there?"

Stupid. Of course they'd gone, and wouldn't introduce themselves if they hadn't.

I checked the door for signs of forced entry. The lock was intact. The wood was not gouged.

Heart bounding, I rushed into the room.

Every drawer was open. My suitcase was upended, the contents pitched and mauled.

My laptop lay untouched on the desk.

I tried to think what that meant.

Thieves? Of course not!

Why leave the computer?

A warning?

From whom? About what?

With shaky hands, I snatched up underwear, T-shirts, jeans.

Like Jake, gathering belongings from around his truck.

My mind loosened.

I knew.

The thought carved a wedge. Anger barreled in.

"You smarmy little bastards!"

I slammed drawers. Folded sweaters. Rehung pants.

Outrage hardened me, annihilating any prospect of tears.

I finished with the bedroom, moved to the bath. Arranged my toiletries. Washed my face. Brushed my hair.

I'd just changed shirts when the phone rang. Ryan was in the lobby.

"My room's been ransacked," I said, without preamble.

"Sonovabitch."

"Probably Hevrat Kadisha looking for Max."

"You're not having a gold-star morning."

"No."

"I'll buttonhole the manager."

"I'm on my way down."

By the time I descended, Ryan had been joined by Friedman, and they'd established two things. No visitor had inquired about me. No desk clerk had given out my room key.

Or had admitted to doing so.

I believed it. The American Colony was operated and staffed by Arabs. I doubted there was a Hevrat Kadisha sympathizer among them.

The manager, Mrs. Hanani, asked if I wished to file an official police report. Her voice conveyed a decided lack of enthusiasm.

I declined.

Clearly relieved, Mrs. Hanani promised a full in-house investigation, stepped-up security, and compensation for anything stolen or damaged.

Friedman assured her that was a splendid plan.

I made a request. Mrs. Hanani hurried to the kitchen to fill it.

When she returned I slipped the items into my backpack, offered thanks, and assured her I'd lost nothing of value.

Climbing into Friedman's car, I wondered if later I'd regret my separate-rooms dictum. Professionalism be damned. Lying in bed, alone in the dark, I knew I'd want Ryan beside me.

It took almost an hour to get back to the Kidron. The Jerusalem police had been tipped that a suicide bomber was headed their way from Bethlehem. Extra checkpoints had been set up, and traffic was snarled.

On the way, I asked Friedman about the permit. Patting a pocket, he assured me he'd obtained the paper. I believed him.

At Silwan, I directed Friedman to the same clearing in which Jake had parked. As he and Ryan dug tools from the trunk, I checked the valley.

Not a black hat in sight.

I led the trek downhill. Ryan and Friedman followed.

At the tomb I stood a moment, considering the entrance. The small black portal stared back blankly.

I felt a hitch in my heartbeat. Ignoring it, I turned. Both my companions were perspiring and breathing hard.

"What about the jackal?" I asked.

"I'll announce we've come to call." Friedman pulled his revolver, squatted, and fired a bullet into the tomb. "If she's in there, she'll take off."

We waited. No jackal appeared.

"She's probably miles from here," Friedman said.

"I'll check the lower level," Ryan said, holding out his hand.

Friedman handed him the gun.

Ryan winged a shovel and crowbar through the opening, then wriggled down into the tomb. I heard a second shot, then the scraping of boots. Silence. More scraping, then Ryan's face appeared in the entrance.

"Jackal-free," he said, handing Friedman his weapon.

"I'll take first watch." Friedman's mouth looked tight. I wondered if he shared my aversion to close confinement.

I strode forward, shoved my pack then my feet into darkness and dropped, hoping to fool whatever neurons were monitoring personal space. They fell for it. I was in the tomb before my brain was wise to the move.

Beside me, Ryan was working a Mag-Lite. Our faces were jack-o'-lanterns, our shadows dark cutouts in the wash of white behind us.

"Point it over there." I indicated the northern loculus.

Ryan redirected the beam. The rock had been moved. No hint of blue leaped from the gloom.

I crawled to the loculus. Ryan followed.

The small recess was empty.

"Bloody hell!"

"They got him?" Ryan asked.

I nodded.

I wasn't surprised.

But I was crushed to see it.

Max had been taken.

"I'm sorry," Ryan said.

Southern manners. Reflex. I started to say, "It's all right," caught myself. It wasn't all right.

The skeleton was gone.

I slumped back onto my heels, feeling the oppressive weight of the tomb. The cold rock. The stale air. The velvety silence.

Had I really had a close encounter with one of Masada's dead?

Had I lost him for good?

Was I sitting in a burial place of the holy?

Was I being watched?

By the Hevrat Kadisha?

By the souls of those peopling the catechisms of my youth?

Who had Max been?

Who had lain in this tomb?

Who lay here still?

I felt a hand on my shoulder. My brain snapped back.

"Let's go below," I whispered.

Crawling to the tunnel, I used the same technique that had gotten me into the tomb.

In and down.

Ryan was beside me in seconds.

Hadn't I dumped all the fallen rocks to the right? Some now lay to the left. Was my memory faulty? Had these rocks also been moved?

Dear God, let it still be here!

Ryan crooked the Mag-Lite at the breach I'd created in my tumble. Bright white arrowed into inky black.

And fell on russet.

As before, my eyes strained to absorb. My brain struggled to sort.

Rough texture. Lumpy contour.

Peeking from one edge, barely visible, a tiny brown cylinder knobbed at one end.

A human phalanx.

I grabbed Ryan's arm.

"It's there!"

No time for proper archaeological protocol. We had to get the goods out before the Hevrat Kadisha got wise.

While I held the light, Ryan wedged the crowbar into a crack outlining a rock immediately above the breach. Ryan heaved, triggering a rainfall of pebbles.

The rock wobbled, dropped back into place.

Ryan heaved harder.

The rock shifted, settled again.

I watched as Ryan made a dozen thrusts, glad Friedman was covering our flank topside. I hoped we wouldn't need him down here.

Ryan exchanged the crowbar for the shovel. Inserting the blade, he levered backward on the handle with all his strength.

The rock popped forward and dropped with a thud.

I scrambled to the enlarged opening. It was big enough.

My heart started throwing in extra beats.

Calm. Ryan's here. Friedman's on guard at the entrance.

Leading with my head and shoulders, I pulled myself into the loculus, and wriggled to the far end, moving gingerly and hugging the wall. Ryan lit my way.

What I'd spotted was indeed textile. Two sections remained, each rotten and discolored. The larger was toward the opening of the loculus, the foot end. The smaller was farther in, near where I assumed the head lay.

Leaning close, I could make out a coarse checkerboard weave. The pieces were small, the edges ragged, indicating much of the original had been lost.

Some bones lay below the shroud. Others ringed it. In addition to the phalanx, I recognized fragments of ulna, femur, pelvis, and skull.

How to recover what remained without tearing the shroud? I ran through options. None was ideal.

Inserting my fingertips, I lifted a corner of the larger section.

The fabric rose with a soft crinkling, the sound of dry leaves being crushed underfoot.

I tested at intervals.

Portions came up easily. Portions stuck.

I dug my digital camera from my pack. With Ryan lighting the loculus like a tiny movie set, I placed my Swiss Army knife as a scale marker, and took shots from several angles.

Photos done, I dug out the Tupperware and spatula supplied by Mrs. Hanani.

Using the spatula's blade and my fingertips, I carefully separated cloth from underlying bone and rock. When I had liftoff, I gently wound each segment of cloth in onto itself, and sealed each roll in a separate tub.

Not optimal, but under the circumstances, the best I could do.

With the shroud removed, I had a clear view of the human remains.

The phalanx and one calcaneus were the only intact bones. The rest of the skeleton was fragmented and badly deteriorated.

With shadow puppets mimicking my actions on the walls around me, I spent the next hour gathering bones, teeth, and underlying fill.

My back and joints ached from working pretzeled into the cramped space. My feet went numb.

At one point Friedman called down from above, "Everything okay?"

"Hunky-dory," Ryan answered.

And later, "How long?"

"Soon."

"Should I make camp?"

"Soon," Ryan repeated.

Late afternoon was bleeding into dusk when we finally surfaced.

Ryan climbed out first. I handed up the shovel, the crowbar, and the pack containing the remnants of the shroud and the person whom that shroud had once wrapped.

The former lay coiled in a pair of shallow containers. The latter filled two small tubs. Barely. A third tub held fill from the loculus floor.

Friedman was sitting on the ground, ankles crossed, back to the hillside. He didn't look irked. He didn't look bored.

He looked like Gilligan waiting for the Captain.

On seeing us, Friedman drained his bottled water, and cranked to his feet.

"Get your man?"

Good question. I'd taken a peek. The pelvic fragments were broadcasting mixed signals on gender.

I gave a thumbs-up, then brushed dirt from my hands by rubbing them together.

"Going up?" Ryan asked Friedman in an elevator voice.

Friedman nodded, took the shovel, and began climbing. We fell in behind.

Twenty yards from the top we stopped for a group breather. Friedman's face was crimson. Sweat matted Ryan's hairline. I was far from ready for close-ups, myself.

Minutes later, we were at Friedman's car.

"Join us for dinner?" Ryan asked as Friedman pulled out of Silwan.

Friedman shook his head. "Gotta get home."

To what? I wondered. A wife? A budgie? A chop defrosting in the kitchen sink?

At the hotel, Ryan and Friedman remained outside. I went straight to the desk. The clerk managed to check out my appearance while avoiding actual eye contact. I was impressed. But not enough to explain why I looked like a train wreck.

Keys in hand, I started back toward the circle drive. Ryan had left Friedman and was walking toward me through the portico. Behind him, I could see Friedman conversing with Mrs. Hanani.

The hotel manager stood stiffly, eyes down, arms wrapping her waist.

Friedman said something. Mrs. Hanani's head jerked up and shook in negation.

While Friedman spoke again, Mrs. Hanani pulled cigarettes from a pocket and tried lighting up. The match head jigged around, finally hit its target. Mrs. Hanani drew smoke into her lungs, exhaled, again shook her head.

Friedman walked away. Mrs. Hanani took a drag and exhaled slowly, squinting through the smoke at his departing back. I couldn't read her expression.

"What is it?" Ryan asked.

"Nothing."

I held out his key.

Ryan's hand closed around mine.

"What chow would you be favorin', ma'am?"

I knew I wanted a shower. I knew I wanted clean clothes. I knew I wanted food, followed by twelve hours of sleep.

I hadn't a clue what cuisine I favored.

"Got a plan?"

"Fink's."

"Fink."

"On Histadrut. Been there since before Israel was Israel. Friedman tells me Mouli Azrieli's an institution."

"Mouli would be the owner."

Ryan nodded. "Mouli's reputed to have turned Kissinger away rather than close the doors to his regulars. But more to the point, Mouli is said to rustle up some mean beef goulash."

Rustle up? Ryan was going into his cowboy routine.

"Thirty minutes." I raised one muddy finger. "On one condition."

Ryan spread his arms. What?

"Lose the lingo."

I turned toward the stairs.

"Lock the booty in your room safe," Ryan said to my back. "Rustlers in these parts."

I stopped. Ryan was right. But my room had been burgled. It wasn't safe. I'd lost one set of bones, and didn't want to risk losing another.

I turned.

"Do you think Friedman would secure the bones at police headquarters overnight?"

"Unquestionably."

I held out my pack. Ryan took it.

Soap and shampoo. Blush and mascara. A half hour later, in soft light, from the right angle, I looked reasonably good.

Fink's boasted a total of six tables. And a million examples of bric-a-brac. Though the decor was dated, the goulash was excellent.

And Mouli did join us with his stack of scrapbooks. Golda Meir. Kirk Douglas. John Steinbeck. Shirley MacLaine. His celeb collection rivaled that at the American Colony.

In the taxi, Ryan asked, "What would you be thinking, lass?" He'd traded *Gunsmoke* for Galway.

"Mouli needs new curtains. What would you be thinkin'?"

Ryan beamed a smile as wide as Galway Bay.

"Ah, 'tis that," I said.

"'Tis," he said.

I needn't have worried about fretting sleepless alone in the dark.

26

I SLEPT THROUGH THE MUEZZIN'S CALL TO PRAYER. I SLEPT through morning rush hour humming by my window. I slept through Ryan slipping off to his room.

I awoke to my jeans playing "A Hard Day's Night."

That couldn't be right.

"*I should be sleepin' like a log . . .*"

The music cut off.

Weird dream. Lying back, I remembered the prior evening's post-prandial romp. The lyrics fast-forwarded in my mind.

"*You know I feel all right . . .*"

The tinny music blared again.

Jake's mobile!

Bolting from bed, I unpocketed the phone, and dropped the jeans back onto the floor.

"Jake?"

"*You've* got my cell."

"How are you?"

I looked at the clock. Seven-forty.

"Peachy. I love being bled and having thumbs shoved up my butt."

"Nicely put."

"I'm outa here before they take another run at me."

"You've been released?"

"Right." Jake snorted.

"Jake, you have to—"

"Uh. Huh. Did you get it?"

"The bag was gone."

"Fucking sonovabitch!"

I waited out the explosion.

"What about the other?"

"I have the shrou—"

"Don't say it over a cell phone! Can you get to my place?"

"When?"

"I've got to deal with the truck, then scare up a replacement vehicle." Pause. "Eleven?"

"Directions?" I darted to the desk.

Jake gave them. The landmarks and street names meant nothing to me.

"I have to call the IAA, Jake." To tell them I'd lost the skeleton. I was dreading it.

"First, let me show you what else I recovered from that tomb."

"I've been in Israel for two days. I have to call Blotnik."

"When you've seen what I have."

"Today," I said.

"Yeah, yeah," he snapped. "And bring my goddamn phone."

Dead air.

Obviously Jake still had irritability issues. And paranoia issues? Did he really believe his calls were being monitored?

I was standing naked, phone in one hand, pen in the other, when someone kicked my door.

Crap. Now what?

I checked the peephole.

Ryan had returned bearing bagels and coffee. He'd shaved, and his hair was wet from the shower.

Through my morning toilette, I described Jake's call.

"We'll finish with Kaplan well before eleven. Where's Jake living?"

"Beit Hanina."

"I'll get you out there."

"I've got directions."

"How is he?"

"Ferocious."

* * *

Kaplan was being held at a police station in the Russian Compound, one of the first quarters to be established outside the Old City. Originally intended as a residence for Russian pilgrims, it was now a down-at-the-heels piece of inner city deservedly slated for urban renewal.

The district headquarters and attached lockup were a collection of buildings wedged between Jaffa Street and the Russian church. Stone walls, iron window grates. Dingy and decrepit, the place blended well with the hood.

Police units pointed every which way. Friedman parked among them, by a cement barricade flanking the compound. Near it, a massive stone pillar lay half-exposed in the earth.

The pillar was fenced off with iron railings, inside of which were mounded thousands of cigarette butts. I pictured policemen and nervous prisoners taking their last open-air drags before heading or being herded inside.

Friedman noticed me eyeing the pillar.

"First century," he said.

"Herod strikes again?" Ryan said.

Friedman nodded. "They say it was intended for the royal stoa of Herod's Temple Mount."

"The old boy was quite a builder."

"Quarrymen noticed a crack, so they just left the thing in the ground. Two millennia later, it's still here."

We passed through a small guardhouse where we were electronically searched, then questioned. Inside the station, we were again quizzed by a sentry who had to have been at least a year out of high school, then led to a recently vacated office.

Smoke fouled the air. Papers littered the desk, topped by a half-drunk mug of coffee. Stacks of reports. A Rolodex flipped to *T.*

I noted a name on the mug. Solomon.

I wondered how ole Sol felt about being booted from his digs.

The air had that universal police station smell. A small fan did its best, but it wasn't enough.

Friedman disappeared, returned. Minutes later, a uniformed cop escorted the prisoner into the office. Kaplan wore black pants and a white shirt. No belt. No shoelaces.

The cop took up a position outside the door. Ryan leaned on one wall. I leaned on another.

Kaplan flashed Friedman a chamber-of-commerce smile. He was clean-shaven, and his eyes seemed pouchier than I remembered.

"I trust Mr. Litvak has come to his senses."

You picked a fine time to leave me, Lucille.

The raspy voice cinched it. Kessler and Kaplan were one and the same.

Friedman pointed to a chair. Kaplan sat.

"This is such a silly misunderstanding." Kaplan laughed a silly-misunderstanding laugh.

Friedman took Sol's desk chair and inspected his fingernails.

Kaplan turned and got his first good look at me. Something flicked in his eyes, shutter-quick.

Recognition? The first inkling of why he was here?

Ryan stepped forward. Wordlessly, he held up the photo of Max.

Kaplan's smile faltered, but hung in.

"You remember Dr. Brennan?" Ryan nodded in my direction.

Kaplan didn't reply.

"Avram Ferris?" Ryan went on. "All that nasty autopsy business?"

Kaplan swallowed.

"Tell me about it," Ryan said.

"What's to tell?"

"I didn't travel to Israel to discuss checks, Mr. Kaplan." Ryan's voice could have cut polar ice. "Or is it Kessler?"

Kaplan crossed his arms. "Yes, Detective. I knew Avram Ferris. Is that what you came here to ask?"

"Where did you get this?" Ryan tapped the photo.

"From Ferris."

"I see."

"It's true."

Ryan gave Kaplan silence. Kaplan filled it.

"Really."

Kaplan flicked a glance at Friedman. Friedman was still admiring his manicure.

"Ferris and I did occasional business."

"Business?"

"It's stuffy in here." Kaplan's bonhomie was fading fast. "I need water."

"Mr. Kaplan." Deep disappointment in Friedman's voice. "Is that how we ask?"

"Please." Exaggerated sigh.

Friedman strode to the door and spoke to someone in the corridor. Returning to his seat, he smiled at Kaplan. The smile held all the warmth of a proto-amphibian.

"Business?" Ryan repeated.

"I bought and sold things for him."

"What kind of things?"

A small guy with a big nose arrived and handed Kaplan a grimy glass. The guy was scowling. Sol?

Kaplan gulped, looked up, but didn't speak.

"What kind of things?" Ryan repeated.

Kaplan shrugged. The water trembled.

"Things."

"Protecting client confidentiality, Mr. Kaplan?"

Kaplan shrugged again.

"Skeletal things?" Ryan waggled the photo of Max.

Kaplan's face stiffened. Draining the water, he carefully placed the glass on Sol's blotter, leaned back, and laced his fingers.

"I want a lawyer."

"Do you need a lawyer?"

"You don't intimidate me."

"You hiding something, Mr. Kaplan?"

Ryan turned to Friedman.

"What do you think, Ira? You suppose Mr. Kaplan was engaged in a little black-marketeering?"

"I think that's possible, Andy."

Kaplan's face remained deadpan.

"Or maybe he decided illicit antiques were kids' stuff, embarked on a more ambitious career path."

Kaplan's fingers were thin. He clasped them so tightly the knuckles went white.

"Could be, Andy. Now that you mention it, he looks like a real Renaissance guy to me."

Ryan addressed Kaplan.

"That it? You decide to up the ante?"

"I don't know what you mean."

"I mean murder, Hersh. It is Hersh, isn't it?"

"Jesus Christ." A flush crept north from Kaplan's collar. "Are you crazy?"

"What do you think, Ira? You think Hersh capped Avram Ferris?"

"No!" Kaplan shot forward and twisted from Ryan to Friedman. "No!"

Ryan and Friedman exchanged shrugs.

"This is insane." The flush detonated across Kaplan's face. "I didn't kill anyone. I couldn't."

Ryan and Friedman waited.

"Okay." Kaplan raised both hands. "Look." Kaplan chose his words carefully. "Occasionally I secure objects of questionable provenance."

"You did this for Ferris?"

Kaplan nodded. "Ferris phoned, asked if I could find a buyer for something special."

"Special?"

"Extraordinary. Once-in-a-lifetime."

More waiting.

"Something that would cause havoc in the Christian world. Those were his words."

Ryan raised the photo.

Kaplan nodded. "Ferris gave me the photo, said not to tell anyone where I got it."

"When was this?"

"I don't know. This winter."

"That's a bit vague, Hersh."

"Early January."

Ryan and I exchanged glances. Ferris was shot in mid-February.

"What happened?"

"I floated word, found there was interest, told Ferris I'd deal, but first I'd need more than just his word and his photo for validation. He said he'd get me proof of the skeleton's authenticity. Before we could meet, Ferris was dead."

"What did Ferris tell you about the skeleton?" I asked.

Kaplan turned to me. His eyes showed something for a moment, then went neutral.

"It came from Masada."

"How'd Ferris get it?'

"He didn't say."

"Anything else?"

"He said it was a person of historic importance, and claimed to have proof."

"Nothing else?"

"Nothing else."

We all thought about that. What proof might Ferris have had? Statements from Lerner? Le Musée de l'Homme? The museum file that Lerner had stolen? Maybe the original paperwork from Israel?

In the corridor, I heard someone talking to the cop. Poor, displaced Sol?

"What about Miriam Ferris?" Ryan changed tack.

"What about her?"

"Are you acquainted with Mrs. Ferris?"

Kaplan shrugged.

"Is that a yes?"

"I know her."

"In the biblical sense?"

"That's disgusting."

"Let me rephrase, Hersh. I did ask if it was Hersh, didn't I? Did you have an affair with Miriam Ferris?"

"What?"

"First I asked confirmation of your given name. Then I asked if you were doing Miriam. Two-part questions too tough for you?"

"Miriam was married to my ex-wife's brother."

"After your brother-in-law's death, you two kept in touch?"

Kaplan didn't answer. Ryan waited. Kaplan folded.

"Yes."

"That how you hooked up with Ferris?"

Again the silence. Again the wait. Again Kaplan crumbled.

"Miriam is a good person."

"Answer my question, Hersh."

"Yes." Bitter.

"Why pony up the photo at Ferris's autopsy?"

Kaplan shrugged one shoulder. "Just trying to help."

Ryan went over it and over it. Kaplan grew restless, but stuck to his story. He knew Miriam through his former brother-in-law, and Ferris through Miriam. From time to time, he did some minor-league buying and selling of illegal goods. He'd agreed to unload the skeleton for Ferris. Before he got full background on the bones, Ferris was killed. He didn't do it. His conscience told him to surrender the photo.

Kaplan's version never changed.

That time.

27

AT HALF PAST TEN, RYAN AND I RECLAIMED POSSESSION OF THE shroud and bones, then climbed into Friedman's personal car, an '84 Tempo with a duct tape *K* on the right rear window. Friedman stayed with Kaplan.

"What's his plan?" I asked

"Give the gentleman time to reconsider his tale."

"And then?"

"Ask him to repeat it."

"Repetition is good," I said.

"Brings out inconsistencies."

"And forgotten details."

"Case in point, Mama Ferris," Ryan said.

"Got us hooked into Yossi Lerner and Sylvain Morissonneau," I agreed.

Beit Hanina is an Arab village with the timely good fortune to find itself within modern Jerusalem's new municipal boundaries. It is now Beit Hanina Hadashah, or New Beit Hanina. Jake had kept a flat here for as long as I'd known him.

Jake's directions sent us into territory that was Jordan from 1948 until 1967. Ten minutes after leaving the Russian Compound, we hit the Neve Yakov checkpoint on the Ramallah, formerly the Nablus, Road. Good timing. The queue only stretched a block and a half.

Ryan joined the line and we crept forward, car length by car length.

On our trip to the Kidron, Jake had told me that the wall designed to cocoon Israel from the rest of the world would shoot down the center of the road we were on. I scanned the stores flanking each side.

Pizza parlors. Dry cleaners. Sweet shops. Florists. We could have been in St-Lambert. Scarsdale. Pontiac. Elmhurst.

But this was Israel. To my left lay the insiders, those whose businesses would prosper despite the wall. To my right lay the outsiders, those whose businesses would wither because of the wall. Sad, I thought. These, the common folk humping to feed their families, were the real winners and losers in this disputed land.

Without Friedman, Ryan and I had anticipated a grilling. *Au contraire.* The guard glanced at our passports and Ryan's badge, bent for a look, and waved us through. Crossing into the West Bank, we made an immediate left, then another onto Jake's street.

Jake rented the top floor of a small stucco home owned by an Italian archaeologist named Antonia Fiorelli. Jake lived up. Fiorelli lived down, with seven cats.

Ryan announced our arrival via a cracked speaker in the property wall. Seconds later Jake opened the gate, led us past a chicken-wire coop housing goats and rabbits, down a winding pebble walk, and up an outer staircase. By the second floor, we'd picked up a three-cat escort.

There are several feline types. The pet-me-I-adore-you-let-me-curl-in-your-lap calico. The feed-me-don't-bug-me-I'll-call-*you* Siamese. The I'm-watching-to-see-if-your-chest-is-still-moving-while-you-sleep feral tom.

This trio fit nicely into category three.

Most of Jake's flat was taken up by a large central room with brown tile floor, white plaster walls, and brick trim arching the windows and doors. Wooden cabinets lined one end, and swooped around as an island to separate the kitchen from the living and dining areas.

Jake's bedroom was the size of a broiler oven. It contained an untidy bed, a dresser, and a cardboard box for dirty laundry.

Everything else was "office." A vestibule area had been converted to a computer and map room. An enclosed porch was used for artifact cleaning. A back bedroom was set up for cataloging, recording, and analysis.

Jake's disposition had improved since our earlier phone conversation. He greeted us and inquired about our morning before asking for the shroud. He even said please. And smiled.

"This was the best I could do under the circum—"

"Yeah. Yeah." Jake gave a come-on gesture with both hands.

Okay. The mood rally wasn't complete.

I set Mrs. Hanani's Tupperware on the counter. Jake opened and inspected the contents of the first tub.

"Oh my God."

He pried the cover from the second tub.

"Oh my God."

Ryan looked at me.

Jake moved to the shroud containers.

Oh my God, Ryan mouthed over Jake's arched back. I crimped my eyes in a knock-it-off warning.

Wordlessly, Jake stared at the larger section of shroud.

"Oh. My. God."

Jake disappeared into the back bedroom, returned with a magnifying lens, and inspected the larger remnant.

"I'll take these to Esther Getz this afternoon," he said.

Jake studied the shroud a full minute, then straightened.

"Getz is a textile expert at the Rockefeller Museum. Did you examine the bones?"

I shook my head. "There's not much to examine."

Jake set down the lens, stepped back, and made a sweeping gesture with one long arm. Ryan gave a trumpet flourish with his lips.

I moved to the counter, and gently poured the contents of each tub onto its lid.

"Do you have gloves?"

Jake started toward the back bedroom.

"And tweezers," I said to his retreating back. "And a probe or dental pick."

He got all three. As Jake and Ryan watched, I sorted, naming each fragment.

"Phalanx. Calcaneus." Those were the easy ones. No other shard was larger than my earlobe. "Ulna, femur, pelvis, skull."

"So what do you think?" Jake asked when I'd finished.

"I think there's not much to examine."

"Male or female?"

"Yes," I said.

"Damn it, Tempe. This is serious."

I inspected a chunk of occipital bone. The nuchal crest was prominent, but it wasn't a record-setter. Ditto for the linea aspera on some splinters of femoral shaft. The only thing left of the pelvis was the thick, chunky part that had formed a joint with the sacrum. No gender-specific feature remained.

"The muscle attachments are robust. I'd give it a qualified 'male,' and that's probably the best I'll be able to do. Nothing's complete enough for measurement."

I picked up and rotated the heel bone. A small, circular defect caught my eye. Jake noticed my interest.

"What?"

I pointed at the tiny tunnel on the outer side of the bone. "That's not natural."

"What do you mean, not natural?" Jake asked.

"It's not supposed to be there."

Jake repeated his come-on gesture, more impatient than before.

"It's not a foramen for a vessel or nerve. The bone's badly abraded, but, from what I can see, the hole's edges are sharp, not smooth."

I lay down the calcaneus and handed Jake the glass. He bent and brought the midpart of the bone into focus.

"What do you think it is?" Ryan asked.

Before I could answer, Jake shot into the map room. Drawers opened and slammed, then he reappeared, flipping through stapled pages.

Slapping the pages onto the counter, Jake jabbed a finger at one.

I looked down.

Jake was pointing at an article titled "Anthropological Observations on the Skeletal Remains from Giv'at ha-Mivtar." His finger was on a page of photographs. Much detail had been lost in the photocopy process, but the subject was obvious.

Four shots depicted fragments of a calcaneus and other foot bones, some before and some after separation and reconstruction. Though coated with a thick, calcareous crust, an iron nail could be seen traversing the calcaneus from side to side. A wooden plaque peeked from below the nail head.

A fifth photo showed a modern heel bone for comparison. On it was a circular lesion positioned precisely as the defect on our shroud calcaneus.

I looked a question at Jake.

"Back in sixty-eight, fifteen limestone ossuaries were found in three burial caves. Thirteen were packed with skeletal remains, and preservation was first-rate. Bunches of wildflowers. Spikes of wheat. Things like that. Trauma on the bones indicated that a number of individuals had died from violence. An arrow wound. Blunt-force trauma."

Jake tapped the photos.

"This poor bastard was crucified."

Jake positioned a second article beside the first and flipped to a sketch showing a body on a cross. The victim's arms were spread-eagle on the crosspiece, but contrary to modern images, the wrists were tied, not nailed. The legs were spread wide, with the feet nailed to the sides, not the front of the upright.

"We know from Josephus that wood was scarce in Jerusalem, so the Romans would have left the upright in place, and only the crossbar would have been carried. Both parts would have been used repeatedly."

"So the arms were tied, not nailed," said Ryan.

"Yes. Crucifixion originated in Egypt. In Egypt they tied. Remember, death wasn't caused by nailing. Hanging from a cross weakens the two sets of breathing muscles, the intercostals and the diaphragm, leading to death by asphyxiation.

"The victim would have been positioned with the legs straddling the upright and each foot nailed laterally. The calcaneus is the largest bone in the foot. That's why the nail was driven through the calcaneus, from outside to inside."

The Jesus family tomb. A crucified man in a shroud.

Realizing where Jake was going, I flapped a hand at the heel bone lying on his counter.

"There's no way to know if this is due to trauma. The defect could be the result of a disease process. It could be postmortem damage. A worm or snail hole."

"It could have been made by a nail?"

Jake's eyes burned with excitement.

"It's possible." My voice carried little conviction.

Crucifixion? Of whom? We'd already excluded one candidate. Max was too old at the time of his death, if you believed traditional scripture. Or too young, if you believed the Joyce theory based on Grosset's scroll. Was Jake suggesting *these* were the bones of Jesus of Nazareth?

As with Max, a tiny part of my brain wanted to believe. A larger part didn't.

"You said you recovered other bones from the Kidron tomb?" I asked.

"Yeah. Looters don't give a rat's ass about skeletal remains. They just dumped the bones on the tomb floor when they carted off the intact ossuaries. We got those. We also got bones that were adhered to the insides of the boxes they smashed and left behind."

"I hope those remains were in better condition than these." I pointed at the contents of the Tupperware.

Jake shook his head. "Everything was fragmentary, and preservation wasn't great. But the dumped bones were still in discrete piles with ossuary fragments mixed in. That helped in sorting out the floor individuals."

"Did someone analyze the material?"

"A physical anthropologist with the Science and Antiquity Group at Hebrew University. He was able to identify three adult females and four adult males. Said that's all the information he could get out of the assemblage. There was nothing measurable, so he couldn't calculate statures or run population comparisons of any kind. He found no indicators of specific ages, no unique individual characteristics."

"Did he spot any lesions similar to this one?"

"He mentioned osteoporosis and arthritis. That was it as far as trauma or disease."

"Were any of the other bones found in loculi, like our guy here?" I asked.

Jake shook his head. "They wanted boxes, not bones. Thank God the bastards didn't go knocking out walls. I still can't believe you found a hidden loculus. And a shroud. Oh my God! Two thousand years. Do you know how many people have been in and out of that tomb? And you found an undisturbed burial. Oh my God!"

Behind Jake, Ryan lip-synced *Oh my god.*

"Where are the other bones now?" I asked

"Back in"—Jake did the E.T. shimmy thing with his fingers—"holy ground. And the Hevrat Kadisha won't say where. But I've got the anthropology report."

Ryan imitated the shimmy thing.

A grin crawled Jake's face. "Most of them, anyway."

"Oh?" I floated one brow.

"A few little scraps might have gotten misplaced."

"Misplaced?"

"Remember our phone conversation about DNA testing on the Masada skeleton?"

I nodded.

"Nice folks at that lab."

"The IAA agreed to send samples?"

"Not exactly."

"You sent samples on your own?"

Jake shrugged. "Blotnik refused. What was I supposed to do?"

"Ballsy move," Ryan said.

"I'll ask now what I asked then," I said. "What's the point of genetic profiling when there's nothing for comparison?"

"It should still be done. Now, follow me."

Jake led us to the back bedroom, where he'd spread photos on a worktable. A few showed whole ossuaries. Many showed fragments.

"The robbers took a lot of boxes, smashed others," Jake said. "But they left enough for reconstruction."

Jake dug a five-by-seven from the stack and handed it to me. It pictured eight ossuaries. All had cracks. Many had gaps.

"Ossuaries differ in style, size, shape, thickness of stone, the way the lid fits. Most are fairly plain, but some have elaborate decoration. That of Joseph Caiaphas, for example."

"The Sanhedrin Council elder who committed Jesus for trial before Pontius Pilate," Ryan said.

"Yes. Though his Hebrew name was Yehosef bar Qayafa. Caiaphas was high priest of Jerusalem from eighteen until thirty-seven C.E. His ossuary was discovered in 1990. It's amazing, carved with unbelievably beautiful inscriptions. Also discovered around that time was an ossuary inscribed 'Alexander, son of Simon of Cyrene.' That box was also lavishly decorated."

"Simon was the gentleman who helped Jesus carry the cross on the road to Golgotha."

Ryan, the biblical scholar.

"You know your New Testament," Jake said. "Simon and his son Alexander are mentioned in Mark 15:21."

Ryan smiled modestly, then tapped the photo of Jake's reconstructions. "I like the ones with the flower petal things."

"Rosettes." Jake pulled out two more five-by-seven glossies. "Now look at these."

He handed the photos to Ryan. I leaned close.

The ossuary depicted was close to rectangular, with a fitted cover and a pocked surface. In one view, I could make out traces of carved rosettes. The circle-on-circle figures reminded me of the patterns we drew with pencil compasses when we were kids.

In the second view, a crack jagged across one end, made a hard right, and shot northwest up the box's camera-facing side.

The little bone coffin looked exactly like those Jake had glued back together.

"The James ossuary?" I asked.

"Notice the inscription." Jake handed us each a magnifying lens. "Do you read Aramaic?" he asked Ryan

Ryan shook his head. I gave him a look of feigned surprise.

Jake missed or ignored the exchange. "The astonishing thing about the James ossuary is the unusual refinement in the inscription. It's much more in keeping with inscriptions found on more lavishly styled ossuaries."

You could have fooled me. Even magnified, the message looked like a child's scratching.

Jake's finger started on the cluster of symbols at the far right end.

"The Jewish name Jacob, or Ya'akov, translates in English to 'James.'"

"Thus the term Jacobites for the supporters of King James the Second of England."

Ryan was starting to get on my nerves.

"Right." Jake's finger moved left across the famous little symbols. "'James, son of Joseph, brother of Jesus.'" He tapped the cluster of symbols at the left end. "Yeshua, or Joshua, translates to 'Jesus' in English."

Jake retrieved and lay down the photos.

"Now come with me."

He led us to the rear of the enclosed porch, unlocked a large cabinet, and spread the double doors. Limestone shards filled the top two shelves. The reconstructed ossuaries occupied the lower six.

"Apparently these weren't the brightest looters on the planet. They missed a number of inscribed fragments."

Jake handed me a triangular shard from the top shelf. The letters were shallow and nearly invisible. I brought them into focus under my lens. Ryan put his face close to mine.

"Marya," Jake translated. "'Mary' in English."

Jake pointed to an inscription on one of the reconstructed boxes. The symbols looked similar.

"Matya. 'Matthew.'"

Jake ran a finger across lettering on a larger box one shelf down.

"Yehuda, son of Yeshua. 'Jude, son of Jesus.'"

Jake dropped to the third shelf.

"Yose. 'Joseph.'"

He moved to the box next to Joe's.

"Yeshua, son of Yehosef. 'Jesus, son of Joseph.'"

Shelf four.

"Mariameme. 'The one called Mara.'"

"That writing looks different," Ryan said.

"Good eye. That's Greek. Hebrew. Latin. Aramaic. Greek. The Mideast was a linguistic mosaic back then. Marya, Miriam, and Mara are all the same name, basically, 'Miriam' or 'Mary.' And nicknames were used, just as they are today. Mariameme is a diminutive of 'Miriam.'" Jake pointed to shelf three. "And Yehosef and Yose are the same name, Joseph."

Returning to the top shelf, Jake selected another fragment, and exchanged it for the one I was holding. This inscription made Marya's look like new. The lettering was so faint it was almost invisible.

"That name is probably Salome," Jake said. "But I can't be sure."

I ran the names through my mind.

Mary. Mary. Salome. Joseph. Matthew. Jude.

Jesus.

The Jesus family? The Jesus family tomb? Everyone fit but Matthew.

I thought, but didn't say, Oh. My. God.

28

"How do biblical scholars or historians interpret the Jesus family?" I asked, keeping my voice steady.

"The historical view is that Jesus, his four brothers, James, Joseph, Simon, and Jude, and his two sisters, Mary and Salome, were the biological children of Joseph and Mary. The Protestant view is that Jesus had no human father, but Mary had other children by Joseph."

"Making Jesus the eldest sibling," Ryan said.

"Yes," Jake said.

"The Vatican sees Mary as a perpetual virgin," I said.

"No siblings allowed," Ryan added.

Jake nodded. "The Western Catholic view is that the others were first cousins, offspring of Joseph's brother Clopas, who was also married to a woman named Mary. The Eastern Orthodox view is that God is the father of Jesus, Mary remained a virgin, and the brothers and sisters are the children of Joseph, a widower, by a previous marriage."

"Making Jesus the youngest." Ryan was infatuated with birth order.

"Yes," Jake said.

My mind cataloged.

Two Mary's. Salome. Jude. Joseph. And someone named Matthew.

Something fluttered in my gut.

"Weren't these names common, like Joe or Tom today?" I asked.

"Very," Jake said. "Anyone hungry?"

"No," I said.

"Yes," Ryan said.

We trooped back to the kitchen. Jake laid out cold cuts, cheese, flat bread, oranges, pickles, and olives. The cats watched as we helped ourselves. Ryan skipped the olives.

When we'd sandwiched up, we moved to a picnic table in the dining area. We talked as we ate.

"Mary was the most common female name in first-century Roman Palestine," Jake said. "For men it was Simon, followed by Joseph. Uncovering ossuaries with these names is no big deal. What *is* a big deal is the co-occurrence, the finding of the names in a single tomb. That's the mind-blow."

"But, Jake—"

"I've studied published catalogs of Jewish ossuaries. Of the thousands of boxes stored in collections all over Israel, only six are inscribed with the name Jesus. Of those six, only one is inscribed 'Jesus, son of Joseph.' And now ours."

Jake shooed a cat.

"Ever hear of onomastics or prosopography?"

Ryan and I shook our heads.

"The statistical analysis of names." Jake popped an olive into his mouth and talked through the depitting process. "For example, among his catalog of published ossuaries, an Israeli archaeologist named Rahmani found nineteen Josephs, ten Joshuas, and five Jacobs, or James."

Jake palmed the pit and popped another olive.

"Another expert studied registered names in first-century Palestine and came up with figures of fourteen percent for Joseph, nine percent for Jesus, and two percent for Jacob. Crunching these numbers, a French paleoepigrapher named André Lemaire calculated that only 0.14 percent of the male population of Jerusalem could bear the name 'Jacob, son of Joseph.'"

Pit out. Olive in.

"Based on the assumption that every male had approximately two brothers, Lemaire calculated that roughly eighteen percent of the men named 'Jacob, son of Joseph' would have had a brother named Jesus. So over two generations, only 0.05 percent of the population would likely be called 'Jacob, son of Joseph, brother of Jesus.'"

"How many people lived in first-century Jerusalem?" I asked.

"Lemaire used a figure of eighty thousand."

"Of whom about forty thousand would have been male," Ryan said.

Nod. "Lemaire concluded that in Jerusalem during the two generations before seventy C.E., no more than twenty people could have fit the inscription on the James ossuary."

"But not everyone ended up in an ossuary," I said.

"No."

"And not every ossuary was inscribed."

"Astute points, Dr. Brennan. But the mention of a brother is rare. How many Jacobs, sons of Joseph, had a brother, Jesus, who was famous enough for that relationship to be marked on their ossuaries?"

I had no answer so I replied with a question.

"Do other name experts agree with Lemaire's estimate?"

Jake snorted. "Of course not. Some say it's high, others say it's low. But what are the chances of this whole cluster of names in one tomb? The Marys, Joseph, Jesus, Jude, Salome. The probability must become infinitesimal."

"Is this the same Lemaire to whom Oded Golan first revealed the James ossuary?" I asked.

"Yes."

My eyes drifted to the heel bone with its peculiar lesion. I thought of Donovan Joyce and his bizarre theory of Jesus living on to fight and die at Masada. I thought of Yossi Lerner and his bizarre theory of Jesus' bones ending up at the Musée de l'Homme in Paris.

Believing it was Jesus, Lerner had stolen the skeleton we were calling Max. But Max's age at death had proven Lerner wrong. My skeletal estimate put him at forty to sixty. That estimate also made Max too young to be the octogenarian who had penned Grosset's Jesus scroll.

Now Jake was suggesting another bizarre theory, and another candidate. Jesus had died by crucifixion, but his body hadn't risen, it had remained in its tomb. That tomb had become the final resting place of the Jesus family. That tomb was in the Kidron. Looters had found that tomb and stolen the James ossuary from it. Jake had rediscovered that tomb and recovered the remains of ossuaries and individuals the looters had left behind. I had blundered onto a hidden loculus in that tomb, and found a burial no one else had. The shrouded bones of Jesus.

My stomach went from a flutter to a knot.

I lay down my sandwich. One of the toms began a slow ooze toward it.

"Was James well-known in his day?" Ryan asked.

"You better believe it. Let's back up a bit. Historical evidence suggests Jesus was born to a lineage known as Davidids, direct descendents of David, a tenth-century B.C.E. king of Israel. According to Hebrew prophets, the Messiah, the final king of a restored nation of Israel, was to come from among this royal line. The Davidids, with their radical revolutionary potential, were well-known to the Herod family, who ruled Palestine at the time, and to the Romans, right up to the emperor. These 'royals' were watched very closely, and at times, hunted down and killed.

"When Jesus was crucified in thirty C.E. for his claim to messianic kingship, his brother James, next in the Davidid line, became top dog in the Christian movement in Jerusalem."

"Not Peter?" Ryan asked.

"Not Peter, not Paul. James the Just. That fact is not widely known, and rarely given proper consideration. When James was stoned to death in sixty-two C.E., for basically the same kind of messianic claims as Jesus, brother Simon stepped up to the plate. After a forty-five-year run, Simon was crucified under the emperor Trajan, specifically because of his royal lineage. Guess who came up to bat next?"

Ryan and I shook our heads.

"A *third* relative, Judas, took over the movement in Jerusalem."

I thought about that. Jesus and his brother claimants to the messianic title of King of the Jews? Okay. I could buy into a different political perspective. But what else was Jake suggesting? Jesus still in his tomb?

"How can you be certain that the Kidron tomb dates to the right period?" My voice sounded tense. I felt suddenly edgy.

"Ossuaries were only used from about thirty B.C.E. to seventy C.E."

"One of the inscriptions is in Greek." I waved a hand at the Tupperware lying on the counter. "Maybe these people weren't even Jewish."

"The mixture of Greek and Hebrew is very common in first-century tombs. And ossuaries were used only for Jewish burial." Jake anticipated my next question. "And almost exclusively in and around Jerusalem."

"I thought Christ's tomb was under the Church of the Holy Sepulcher, inside the Old City," Ryan said, rolling a slice of Muenster around a pickle.

"So do a lot of folks."

"You don't."

"I don't."

"Jesus was from Nazareth," I said. "Why wouldn't the family plot be there?"

"The New Testament indicates Mary and her children took up residence in Jerusalem following the crucifixion. Tradition has it Mary died and was buried here, not up north in Galilee."

There was a long silence during which the tom slunk to within inches of my feet.

"Let me understand this." The cat skittered backward at the sound of my voice. "You're convinced the James ossuary inscription is real."

"I am," Jake said.

"And that the thing was looted from the tomb we visited."

"Rumors have always placed the ossuary's origin in that location."

"And that that tomb was the final resting place of Jesus' kin."

"Yes."

"And that the lesion in this shroud calcaneus suggests one of the tomb's occupants was crucified."

Jake nodded silently.

My eyes met Ryan's. They found not a hint of a smile.

"Have you shared your theory on this tomb with Blotnik?"

"I have. Though obviously not the crucified calcaneus. You just found that. I still can't believe it."

"And?"

"He blew me off. The man's a pigheaded cretin."

"Jake?"

"You'll see when you meet him."

I let that go and switched tacks.

"You snitched specimens from the bones adhered to the smashed ossuaries and from the bones dumped on the tomb floor and sent them for DNA testing. When?"

"I held samples back when I turned the collection over for analysis and reburial. I sent them off for testing right after our phone conversation. Your comments confirmed what I hoped. mtDNA might show maternal relationships among individuals in the tomb, and aDNA might at least tell gender."

Again, my eyes went to the bones on the counter. A question formed in my mind. I wasn't yet ready to pose it.

"Normally, bodies were left for one year to decay, then the bones were collected and sealed in ossuaries, right?" Ryan asked. "Then why was the shroud person left in the loculus?"

"According to rabbinic law, a dead man's bones had to be collected by his son. Perhaps this man had none. Perhaps it had to do with his manner of death. Perhaps some crisis prevented the family from returning."

Crisis? Like the execution of a dissident and the suppression of his movement, forcing his family and followers underground? Jake's meaning was clear.

Ryan looked as if he might have something to say, but kept it to himself.

I got up and retrieved the article containing the foot-bone photos. Crossing back to the table, I noticed the header at the top of each page.

N. Haas. Department of Anatomy, Hebrew University–Hadassah Medical School.

My mind jumped on it. Think about Max. Masada. Anything but the heel bone and its disturbing lesion.

"Is this the same Haas that worked at Masada?"

"Yes, ma'am."

I skimmed the article. Age. Sex. Cranial metrics. Trauma and pathology. Diagrams. Tables.

"This is quite detailed."

"Flawed, but detailed," Jake agreed.

"Yet Haas never wrote a thing on the Cave 2001 skeletons."

"Not a word."

The Masada skeleton was never reported, spirited out of Israel, stolen from a museum, smuggled to Canada. According to Kaplan, Ferris claimed it was that of a person of historic importance, discovered at Masada. Jake had admitted to hearing rumors of such a skeleton. A volunteer excavator had confirmed the discovery of such a skeleton. Kaplan's photo had sent Jake flying to Montreal, then Paris. Because of Max, I'd been persuaded to come to Israel.

Lerner thought the skeleton was that of Jesus. He was wrong. The age at death didn't work. Jake was suggesting the real thing lay on the counter behind me.

So why the decades of intrigue over the Masada skeleton? Who was this man we were calling Max?

I pictured Max, stolen and probably lost forever.

I pictured my wild ride in Jake's truck.

I pictured my ransacked room.

Anger flared.

Good. Use it. Focus on Max. Avoid the impossible coincidentally found in a Kidron tomb. The impossible lying in Tupperware on a kitchen counter.

"The Masada skeleton's gone for good, isn't it?" I asked.

"Not if I can help it." Something crossed Jake's face. I couldn't say what. "I'll talk to Blotnik today."

"Blotnik has juice with the Hevrat Kadisha?" Ryan asked.

Jake didn't answer. Outside, a goat bleated.

"What are you thinking?" I asked.

Jake frowned.

"What?" I pressed.

"There's something bigger at stake." Jake rubbed his eyes with the heels of his hands.

I opened my mouth. Ryan snagged my gaze, gave an almost imperceptible head shake. I closed it.

Jake dropped his hands, and his forearms slapped the tabletop.

"This is more than the usual reburial bullshit. The Hevrat Kadisha had to have received a heads-up. They followed us to the Kidron because of the Masada bones." One long finger began worrying crumbs. "I think Yadin knew something about that skeleton that scared the crap out of him."

"What sort of something?"

"I'm not sure. But sending an emissary all the way from Israel to Canada? Trashing a hotel room? Maybe even killing a guy? That's more than Hevrat Kadisha."

I watched Jake convert a small hill of crumbs into a long, thin line. I thought of Yossi Lerner, Avram Ferris, and Sylvain Morissonneau.

I thought of Jamal Hasan Abu-Jarur and Muhammed Hazman

Shalaideh, the Palestinians parked outside l'Abbaye Sainte-Marie-des-Neiges.

I didn't know the players. I didn't know the field. But my instincts told me Jake was right. The game was deadly, the goal was Max, and the opposition was determined to win.

Always the same question. Who was Max?

"Jake, listen."

Throwing out his feet, Jake slumped back, crossed his arms, and looked first at Ryan, then at me.

"You'll get your DNA results. You'll get your textile analysis. That's the tomb. That's important. But for now, let's focus on Masada."

At that moment Ryan's cell phone sounded. He checked the screen, and strode from the room.

I turned back to Jake.

"Haas never reported on the cave skeletons, right?"

"Right."

"What about field notes?"

Jake shook his head. "Some excavators kept diaries, but notes as you and I think of them weren't protocol at Masada."

I must have looked shocked.

"Yadin met with his senior staff each evening to discuss the day's developments. The sessions were taped and later transcribed."

"Where are those transcripts?"

"The Institute of Archaeology at Hebrew University."

"Are they accessible?"

"I can make a few calls."

"How are you feeling?" I asked.

"Tip-top."

"How about we swing by the big U and poke through old files."

"How about we take the shroud to Esther Getz then hit the big U."

"Where's Getz's lab?"

"At the Rockefeller Museum."

"Isn't the IAA housed there?"

"Yes." Dramatic sigh.

"Perfect." I said. "It's time I introduced myself to Tovya Blotnik."

"You're not going to like him."

While I cleared the table, Jake placed his calls. I was screwing the lid on the pickles when Ryan reappeared. His face suggested he hadn't received the best of all possible news.

"Kaplan's changed his story," he said.

I waited.

"Claims someone hired him to cap Ferris."

29

I BLINKED, SET DOWN THE JAR, RECOVERED ENOUGH TO ASK A question.

"Kaplan was paid to kill Ferris?"

Tight nod.

"By whom?"

"He's yet to share that little detail."

"He's been claiming he's innocent as Little Bo Peep. Why talk now?"

"Who knows?"

"Friedman believes him?"

"He's listening."

"Sounds like a plot straight out of *The Sopranos.*"

"You could say that." Ryan glanced at his watch. "I've gotta get back there."

Ryan was gone five minutes when Jake surfaced. Good news. We could access the Masada transcripts. And Getz would see us. He'd told her about the shroud, but not about the bones. While I questioned the wisdom of concealment, this was Israel, his turf, not mine. And Jake assured me he was only buying a few days.

And a few purloined bone samples, I suspected.

As Jake downed two aspirin and I repackaged the shroud, we discussed what to do with the bones. The Hevrat Kadisha were obviously unaware of the bones' existence, or they'd have been screaming that we hand them over. And since the HK already had Max, they'd no longer have a reason to keep me under surveillance, or tail me. We decided Jake's flat was safe.

Locking the bones in the ossuary cabinet, we secured the doors, then the outer gate, and set off. Though the tension in his jaw suggested a headache in progress, Jake insisted on taking the wheel of his rented Honda.

Crossing back through the Nablus Road checkpoint, Jake wormed through traffic to Sultan Suleiman Street in East Jerusalem. Across from the northeast corner of the Old City wall, opposite the Flower Gate, he pulled into a driveway that led uphill to a pair of metal doors. A battered sign identified the Rockefeller Museum in English and Hebrew.

Jake got out and spoke into a rusted intercom. Minutes later the doors opened and we circled to a beautifully landscaped front lawn.

Backtracking on foot to a side entrance, I noticed an inscription on the building's exterior: GOVERNMENT OF PALESTINE. DEPARTMENT OF ANTIQUITIES.

Times change.

"When was this building constructed?" I asked.

"Place opened in 1938. Mainly houses antiquities unearthed during the time of the British Mandate."

"Nineteen nineteen to 1948." I'd read that in Winston's book. "It's beautiful."

It was. White limestone, all turrets, and gardens, and arches.

"There's some prehistoric material here as well. And some kick-ass ossuaries."

Kick-ass or not, the place was deserted.

Jake led me through several exhibit halls to a flight of stairs, our steps ricocheting hollowly off the stone walls. The air was heavy with the smell of disinfectant.

Upstairs, we passed through several arched openings and turned right into a recessed alcove. A plaque announced the office of Esther Getz.

Jake knocked softly, then cracked the door.

Across the room I saw a woman of about my age, robust, with a jaw that could have opened the iced-up St. Lawrence in spring. Seeing us, the woman left her scope and swept forward.

Jake made introductions.

I smiled and offered my hand. Getz shook it as though I might be contagious.

"You've brought the shroud?"

Jake nodded.

Getz made space on a table. Jake centered the two Tupperware containers on it.

"You're not going to belie—"

Getz cut him off. "Refresh me on provenance."

Jake described the tomb, without mentioning its specific location.

"Anything I say today will be strictly preliminary."

"Of course," Jake said.

Getz pried free one lid and studied the shroud, repeated with the second tub. Then she gloved and gently removed each remnant. Fifteen minutes later she'd managed to unroll the smaller swatch.

We spotted it simultaneously. Like kids in chem class, we all leaned in.

"Hair." Getz wasn't talking to us, she was thinking out loud.

Another fifteen minutes and she'd tweezed most strands into a vial, placed a half dozen others under a magnifying scope.

"Freshly cut. Some sheen. No signs of lice or casings."

Getz exchanged the hair for the larger segment of cloth.

"Simple one-to-one plain weave."

"Typical first century." Jake pumped an arm.

Getz repositioned the remnant, refocused. "The fibers are degraded, but I don't see the flatness and variation I would expect with flax."

"Wool?" Jake asked.

"Based on this, I'd have to say yes."

Getz moved the remnant back and forth. "No weaving faults. No holes. No mending." Pause. "Odd."

"What?" Jake's arm froze.

"This yarn was spun in the opposite direction from that typical of first-century Israel."

"Meaning?"

"It was imported."

"From?"

"My guess would be Italy or Greece."

Another half hour and Getz was scoping the smaller scrap.

"Linen." Getz straightened. "Why were the two remnants packaged separately?"

Jake turned to me.

I fielded the question.

"The small remnant came from the deepest end of the loculus, and was associated with cranial fragments. The larger came from a position closer to the opening, and was associated with postcranial fragments."

"One wrapping for the head, another for the body," Jake said. "That's exactly what Simon Peter describes in John 20:6–7. 'And seeth the linen clothes lie, and the napkin, that was about His head, not lying with the linen clothes, but wrapped together in a place by itself.'"

Getz glanced at her watch.

"You realize, of course, that the IAA must take custody. You may leave the specimens with me." Not subtle.

"Of course. Our find is fully documented." Emphasis on the "our." Jake wasn't being subtle, either. "I'll be requesting carbon-fourteen dating." Jake beamed Getz his most winning smile. "In the meantime, I'll be on pins and needles awaiting your report."

Against all odds, Getz managed to resist Jake's charm.

"Isn't everyone," she said, gesturing toward the door. We were being dismissed.

Trailing Jake into the corridor, I was sure of one thing: Esther Getz had never been dubbed the Getzster. No nicknames for this chick.

Next stop, Tovya Blotnik.

The IAA director's office was four alcoves down from Getz's. Blotnik stood when we entered, but didn't come around his desk.

It's funny. Telephone voices conjure images. Sometimes those images are dead-on. Sometimes, they're way off.

The IAA director was a short, wiry man with a gray goatee and hair that tufted around a blue silk yarmulke. I'd pictured Santa. He looked more like a Jewish elf.

Jake introduced me.

Blotnik looked surprised, recovered, and leaned forward to shake hands.

"*Shabbat shalom.*" Jittery smile. Santa voice. "Please, sit."

The choices were limited since all but two chairs were stacked with papers and books. Jake and I took them.

Blotnik sat behind his desk. For the first time he seemed to notice my face.

"You've been injured?" American English. Maybe New York.

"It's nothing," I said.

Blotnik opened his mouth, closed it, unsure what to say. Then, "But you've survived your jet lag?"

"Yes," I said. "Thank you."

Blotnik bobbed his head and spread both hands on the desktop. All his movements were sharp and hummingbird quick.

"This is extraordinarily kind, bringing the skeleton to me. Truly above and beyond." Full-blown elf smile. "You have it with you?"

"Not exactly," Jake said.

Blotnik looked at him.

Jake described the incident with the Hevrat Kadisha, omitting all detail concerning the tomb.

Blotnik's face sagged. "Such absurdity."

"Yes." Glacial. "You know the Hevrat Kadisha."

"Not really."

Jake's brows dipped, but he said nothing.

"Where is this tomb?" Blotnik steepled his fingers. Two perfect palm prints remained on the blotter.

"In the Kidron."

"This is the source of the textiles Esther mentioned?"

"Yes."

Blotnik asked several more questions about the tomb. Jake replied in vague, icy terms.

Blotnik stood.

"I'm sorry, but you caught me on my way out." Blotnik gave what I'm sure he considered a sheepish grin. "Shabbat. Slipping off early."

"*Shabbat shalom,*" I said.

"*Shabbat shalom,*" Blotnik said. "And thank you so much for trying, Dr. Brennan. The IAA is deeply indebted. Such a long trip. Such a loss. Your gesture is truly remarkable."

We were in the hall.

Driving to Hebrew University, Jake and I discussed our encounter with Blotnik.

"You really don't like the guy," I said.

"He's a self-promoting, egotistical fraud."

"Don't hold back, Jake."

"And I don't trust him."

"Why?"

"He's professionally dishonest."

"How?"

"Uses the work of others, publishes, doesn't give proper credit. Want me to go on?"

Jake abhorred senior scientists who exploited junior colleagues or students. I'd heard the rant. I let it go.

"Getz told Blotnik about the shroud."

"I figured she would, but it's a risk I'm willing to take. Esther's the best there is with ancient textiles, and I need her authentication of the thing. Besides, by going through Getz, it makes it impossible for Blotnik to piggyback onto the find."

"But you don't trust either of them with the bones."

"No way anyone sees those bones until I've got them fully documented."

"Blotnik didn't seem all that upset about the Masada skeleton," I said. "And he didn't seem as surprised to see me as I'd expected."

Jake glanced at me.

"When I called from Montreal, I never mentioned the date I was coming."

"No?"

Jake made a left.

"And what about the jet lag comment?" I asked.

"What about it?"

"It's as though Blotnik knows exactly how long I've been here."

Jake started to speak. I cut him off.

"And wouldn't anyone in archaeology in Israel know about the Hevrat Kadisha?"

"Duh!" Jake snorted. "You caught that, too?"

"Could it be that Blotnik seemed unconcerned because *he* has the skeleton?"

"Long shot. The guy's a wimp." Jake cut me a look. "But if he does, I'll kick his ass from here to Tel Aviv."

We also discussed Getz's comments.

"Not exactly garrulous, is she?"

"Esther's direct."

Not the descriptor I'd pinned on the Getzster.

"But you liked what she saw," I said.

"Damn right. Clean hair. No vermin. Imported fabric. And wool was a luxury back then. Most shrouds were exclusively linen. Whoever this boy was, he had social standing." Jake shot me another look. "And a hole in his heel bone. And relatives with names straight out of the Gospels."

"Jake, I've got to admit, I'm skeptical. First the Masada skeleton, now these shroud bones. Are you talking yourself into something because you desperately want it to be true?"

"I've never believed the Masada skeleton is that of Jesus. That was Lerner's interpretation, based on the cocked-up thinking of Donovan Joyce. But I do think the bones are those of someone who shouldn't have been up on that rock. Someone whose presence is going to make the Israelis, and maybe the Vatican, pee their shorts."

"A nonzealot."

Jake nodded.

"Who?"

"That's what we're going to find out."

We rode in silence for a while. Then I went back to the shroud.

"Is the shroud I found in the tomb similar to the shroud of Turin?" I asked.

"The Turin cloth is linen, and has a more complicated, three-on-one twill weave. Which makes sense. That shroud dates to the medieval, somewhere between 1260 and 1390 C.E."

"Carbon-fourteen dated?"

Jake nodded. "Confirmed by labs in Tucson, Oxford, and Zurich. And the Turin shroud was a single garment for the whole body. Ours is a two-part deal."

"What's current thinking on the Turin image?" I asked.

"Probably resulted from oxidation and dehydration of the cellulose fibers of the cloth itself."

Another wham-o for the Vatican.

Getting to the university took less time than finding a spot to park. Jake finally wedged his rented Honda into footage meant for a scooter, and we set off toward the eastern end of campus.

The sun beamed down from an immaculate blue sky. The air smelled of freshly cut grass.

We walked through patches of shadow and light, past classrooms, offices, dorms, and labs. Students drank coffee at outdoor tables, or strolled wearing bandannas, backpacks, and Birkenstocks. A kid tossed a Frisbee to his dog.

We could have been on any campus in any city in the world. High atop its Mount Scopus hilltop, Hebrew University was an island of tranquillity in an urban sea of sentries, barricades, smog, and cement.

But nothing in this land is immune. As we walked my mind superimposed images on the peaceful tableau. Newsreel footage: July 31, 2001. A day much like this one. Students taking exams or registering for summer courses. A parcel left on a café table. Seven killed, eighty injured. Hamas claimed responsibility, retaliation for Israel's assassination of Salah Shehadeh in Gaza City. Fourteen Palestinians dead there.

And the beat goes on.

The gatekeeper at the Institute of Archaeology was a woman named Irena Porat. A decade older, with a fashion sense that ran toward the fuzzy and the floral, Porat was considerably less menacing than Esther Getz.

Shaloms were exchanged.

Porat spoke to Jake in Hebrew.

Jake answered and, I assumed, reminded Porat of his call.

As Jake explained our purpose, Porat inspected something crumbly she'd found in her ear. I caught the word "Masada," and Yadin's name.

When Jake finished, Porat asked a question.

Jake answered.

Porat said something, then tipped her head toward me.

Jake responded.

Leaning close, Porat spoke to Jake in a lowered voice.

Jake nodded, face solemn.

Porat gave me her best welcoming smile.

I returned her smile, a trusty co-conspirator.

Porat led us down two flights of stairs to a grim, windowless room. The walls and floor were gray, the furnishings battered tables, folding chairs, and rows of floor-to-ceiling shelves. Large boxes filled two corners.

"Please." Porat pointed the ear-probe finger at me, then at a table.

I sat.

Porat and Jake disappeared into the shelving. When they emerged Jake carried three large brown corrugated files. Porat lugged another.

Dumping her file on the table, Porat gave one final instruction, one final smile, and withdrew.

"Nice lady," I said.

"A bit heavy on the angora," Jake said.

Each file was identified in Hebrew in black Magic Marker. Jake lined them up, selected the first, and removed the notebooks it contained.

Jake selected one, I took another.

European-size plain paper. Hebrew typing on one side.

I flipped a few pages.

I could read nothing.

Crash course. Jake wrote a list of phrases that would serve as flags: Yoram Tsafrir. Nicu Haas. Cave 2001. Skeleton. Bone. He also showed me how to read Hebrew dates.

Jake started with the earliest notebook. I took the next in sequence. Using my list, I scouted ahead, *Sesame Street*–style. What looks the same? What looks different?

I came up with a lot of false hits. We'd been at it an hour when I got my first real one.

"What's this?" I asked, sliding the notebook to Jake.

Jake skimmed the text, sat forward.

"It's the October twentieth, 1963, meeting. They're talking about Cave 2001."

"What're they saying?"

"Yoram Tsafrir is reporting on his progress in another cave, 2004. Listen to this."

I definitely was.

"Tsafrir says the finds are '. . . much more beautiful than the pieces found in Cave 2001 and 2002.'"

"So Cave 2001 was explored earlier than October twentieth," I said.

"Yes."

"Didn't the dig begin in early October?"

Jake nodded.

"So the cave must have been discovered in the first two weeks of excavation."

"But I found no mention of it until this entry." Jake frowned. "Keep going. I'll go back through the pages I've done."

The next reference to Cave 2001 was on November 26, 1963, over a month later. Haas had been invited to join the group.

"Haas is reporting on the three skeletons from Locus 8, that's the northern palace area, and Locus 2001, that's the cave bones." Jake's finger moved over the text. "He says there are twenty-four to twenty-six persons and a six-month fetus. Fourteen males, six females, four children, and some unknowns."

"We know the figures don't add up," I said.

"Right." Jake looked up. "But more to the point: Where is any previous discussion of the cave and its contents?"

"Maybe we missed it," I said.

"Maybe."

"Let's reread everything prior to October twentieth," I suggested.

We did.

There wasn't a single mention of the cave's exploration or excavation.

But I did learn something.

The pages were numbered. In Arabic.

I could read Arabic numbers.

I went back through the period in question.

Pages were missing from the early weeks of October.

With a growing sense of dread, we rechecked every notebook in every file.

The pages hadn't been improperly cataloged.

They were gone.

30

"CAN MATERIALS BE CHECKED OUT?" I ASKED.

"No. And Porat assured me we have everything in the collection."

"If the pages were removed, it had to be internal."

We considered in silence.

"Yadin announced the discovery of the palace skeletons at a press conference in November of sixty-three," I said. "Clearly, he was interested in human remains."

"Hell, yeah. How better to validate the Masada suicides?"

"So Yadin talked about the three people found up top, in the area occupied by the main group. His brave little zealot 'family.'" I hooked quotes around the word. "But he ignored the Locus 2001 remains, the twenty-whatever people found in the cave below the casement wall, at the southern tip of the summit. No press at all for those folks."

"Zip-o."

"What *did* Yadin tell the media?"

Jake's fingertips worked his temples. The veins hummed blue through his whitewashed skin.

"I'm not sure."

"Might he have had doubts about the age of the bones?"

"In his first season report Yadin stated that nothing from the cave pointed to anything later than the period of the first revolt. And he was right. Radiocarbon dates reported in the early nineties on bits of fabric found mixed with the bones fell between forty and 115 C.E."

Missing pages. Stolen skeletons. A murdered dealer. A dead priest. It was like peering down a hall of tilted mirrors. What was real? What was distortion? What led to what?

I sensed one thing.

Some invisible thread tied everything back to the cave bones.

And to Max.

I noticed Jake steal a glance at his watch.

"You're going to bed," I said, sliding notebooks into files.

"I'm fine." His body language disagreed.

"You're eroding right in front of me."

"I do have a bastard of a headache. Would you mind dropping me off and taking my car?"

I stood.

"No problem."

Jake provided a map, directions, and the keys to the Honda. He was asleep before I left his flat.

I'm pretty good with directions. I'm pretty good with maps. I'm lousy with signs in unfamiliar symbols in foreign languages.

The trip from Beit Hanina to the American Colony should have taken twenty minutes. An hour later I was hopelessly lost. Somehow I'd gotten onto Sderot Yigal Yadin. Then I was on Sha'arei Yerushalaim without making a turn.

Checking the name of a cross street, I pulled over, spread Jake's map on the wheel, and tried to pinpoint my location.

In the rearview, I noticed a car slide to the curb ten yards behind me. My mind did an automatic data log. Sedan. Dark blue. Two occupants.

A sign indicated I was near the exit to the Tel Aviv road. But which Tel Aviv road? My map showed two.

I looked for more landmarks.

Data log. No one emerging from the sedan.

I saw signs for the central bus station and a Holiday Inn. I could get directions at either.

I was smokin'. I had a plan.

I set off, intending to hit whichever institution first crossed my path.

Data log. Sedan pulling out behind me.

I felt a prickle of apprehension. It was Friday and moving toward dusk. The streets were Sabbath empty.

I turned right.

The sedan turned right.

I'd been tailed twice in my life. On neither occasion had the intent been to promote my good health.

I made a right, then a left one block later.

The sedan did the same.

I didn't like this.

Gripping the wheel two-handed, I sped up.

The sedan stayed with me.

I hung a left.

The sedan rounded the corner behind me.

I turned again. I was now lost in a maze of smaller streets. Only one van in sight. The sedan drew closer.

One shotgun thought: Get away!

Accelerating quickly, I swerved around the van, scanning ahead, searching for a haven.

One familiar sign. A red cross. First aid. A clinic? A hospital? No matter, either would do.

My eyes flicked to the rearview.

The sedan was closing in.

I spotted a clinic in the middle of a small strip center. Pulling into the lot, I threw the car into park, and bolted for the door.

The sedan shot past. Through the rolled-up window I got one snapshot image.

Angry mouth. Viper eyes. Untrimmed beard of a muj fundamentalist.

I met Ryan in the hotel lobby at seven. By then I wasn't sure if I'd been tailed or not. My room had been trashed. I'd been threatened by a jackal. Jake and I had been stoned. Max had been nabbed. We'd wrecked the truck. During a long, hot bath I began yielding to the view that my jangled nerves had reconfigured events.

Maybe the sedan was traveling the same route as mine. Maybe the driver was as lost as I was. Maybe the occupants were an Israeli version of our back-home testosterone-bloated, Friday-night-cruising rednecks.

"Don't be naive," I said to myself, taking a deep breath. That car had specific interest in my car.

Neither Ryan nor I was in the mood for a heavy meal. The desk clerk gave directions to an Arabic restaurant not far away.

As the woman spoke her eyes kept flicking to me. When I met them, they danced away. I had the feeling she wanted to tell me something.

I tried to cast friendly, inviting glances, but she didn't volunteer whatever was on her mind.

The restaurant was marked by a sign the size of my face soap. We found it after three stops for directions. An armed doorman checked us through.

Inside, it was dim and packed. Booths lined two walls and tables filled the center. The clientele was mostly male. The few women present wore *hijabs*. The owner didn't believe in smoke-free sections.

We were shown to a booth so dark it was impossible to make out the printed word. I glanced at the menu then gave Ryan a take-it-away gesture.

The waiter wore a white shirt and black pants. His teeth were yellowed, his face lined from years of cigarettes.

Ryan said something in Arabic. I understood the word "Coke." The waiter asked a question. Ryan gave a thumbs-up. The waiter scribbled on a pad and left.

"What did you order?" I asked.

"Pizza."

"Vocabulary à la Friedman?"

"I can also ask the location of the toilet."

"What kind?"

"American Standard?"

"Of pizza."

"I'm not sure."

I told Ryan about my visit to the Rockefeller.

"Getz thought the shroud was first century, made of both linen and wool, and probably imported."

"Meaning costly."

"Yes. And the hair was clean, trimmed, and vermin free."

Ryan got it right away. "Good threads. Good grooming. The guy in the shroud was upper crust and had a perforated heel bone. Jake thinks it's J.C."

I recounted Jake's explanation of the history of the Kidron and Hinnom. Hell Valley. Then I ticked points off on my fingers.

"High-status individual found in a Kidron tomb Jake's certain was the Jesus family tomb. The tomb held ossuaries inscribed with names out of scripture. Jake believes the tomb is the source of the James ossuary, the possible burial box of Jesus' brother."

I dropped my hand. "Jake's convinced the man in the shroud is Jesus of Nazareth."

"What do you think?"

"Come on, Ryan. What are the chances? Think of the implications."

We both did that for a moment. Ryan spoke first.

"How does Max tie in with this Kidron tomb?"

"I don't think he does. And that's another point. What's the probability that two skeletons with claims to being Jesus Christ show up at the same, exact point in time?"

"That's not quite true. Max was unearthed in the sixties. It's just recently that he's resurfaced."

"Ferris is killed. Kaplan shows me the photo. I locate Max, then rule him out. Three weeks later I find the guy in the shroud and *he's* Jesus Christ? It's preposterous."

"Jake was so hot to have Max he paid your way to Israel. Who does he think Max was?"

"Someone of importance who shouldn't have been at Masada."

I recounted my trip to Hebrew University, and told Ryan about the missing pages from the Masada transcripts.

"Curious," he said.

I also described my meeting with Tovya Blotnik, and mentioned Jake's qualms about the man.

"Curious," he said.

I debated telling Ryan about the sedan. What if the whole thing was the product of my imagination?

What if it wasn't?

Better to be wrong than to take a rock in the head. Or worse.

I described the incident.

Ryan listened. Was he smiling? Too dark to tell.

"Probably nothing," I said.

Ryan reached across the table and put a hand over mine. "You're okay?"

"More or less," I said.

Ryan rubbed his thumb back and forth across my skin. "You know I'd prefer that you didn't set out on your own."

"I know," I said.

The waiter dropped two coasters on the table and parked a can of high-test Coke on each. Apparently Ryan's Hebrew lessons hadn't included the word "diet."

"No beer?" I asked.

"Not an option."

"How do you know?"

"No beer signs."

"Always detecting," I said, smiling.

"Crime never sleeps."

"I think I'll go to the *Jerusalem Post* tomorrow, browse through the archives, see what Yadin was saying about the Masada cave skeletons back in the sixties," I said.

"Why not use the university library?"

"Jake says the *Post* keeps old articles on file by topic. Should be a hell of a lot quicker than plowing through reels of microfiche."

"The *Post* will be closed on Saturday," Ryan said.

Of course it would. I changed the subject.

"How was your interview?" I asked.

"Kaplan's insisting he was hired to hit Ferris."

"By whom?"

"Kaplan claims he never knew her name," Ryan said.

"Her?"

I think Ryan nodded.

"What did this mystery woman say to him?"

"She needed a shooter."

"Why'd she want Kaplan to kill Ferris?"

"She wanted him dead."

Eye roll. Wasted in the dark.

"When did she solicit his help?"

"He thinks it was the second week of January."

"Around the time Ferris was asking Kaplan to sell the skeleton."

"Yep."

"Ferris was shot in mid-February."

"Yep."

The waiter issued napkins, plates, and utensils, then placed a pizza between us. It was covered with olives, tomatoes, and little green things I took to be capers.

"How'd the woman make contact?" I asked when the waiter had gone.

"Called the pet shop."

Ryan served slices of pizza.

"Let me understand this. A strange woman rang up, inquired about guinea pigs, then said, 'Oh, by the way, I want you to take someone out?'"

"That's his story."

"Now *that's* curious."

"That's his story."

"This woman give a name?"

"Nope."

"Could Kaplan tell you anything about her?"

"Said she sounded like a cokehead."

The pizza was excellent. I took a moment to wade through the flavors. Tomato, onion, green pepper, olives, feta, and a spice I couldn't identify.

"What did she offer?"

"Three grand."

"What did Kaplan say?"

"Ten grand."

"He got ten thousand dollars?"

"The woman counteroffered with three grand up front, three after the hit."

"What did Kaplan do?"

"He claims he took the payout, then blew her off."

"He scammed her?"

"What's she gonna do? Call the cops?"

"She's still got three grand to have him capped."

"Good point." Ryan served up seconds.

"Did Kaplan and this woman ever meet face-to-face?"

"No. The money was left under a trash can in Jarry Park."

"How very James Bond."

"He insists that's how it worked."

We ate and watched the crowd around us. A woman sat opposite, her face a pale egg in the darkness. It was all I could see. Her *hijab* hid her hair and was pinned beneath her chin. Her shirt was dark, the sleeves long, the cuffs buttoned tight at the wrists.

Our eyes met. The woman didn't look away. I did.

"I thought Kaplan was strictly white-collar," I said.

"Maybe he got bored and decided on a career change."

"Kaplan could be making the whole thing up to throw you off."

"I've been thrown off by lesser luminaries," Ryan said, doling out the last two slices of pizza.

Again, we ate in silence. When I'd finished, I leaned back against the wall.

"Could the mystery woman be Miriam Kessler?"

"I posed that very question to Kaplan. The gentleman answered in the negative, saying the good widow was above reproach."

Ryan bunched his napkin and tossed it onto his plate.

"Got any ideas?" I asked.

"Madonna. Katie Couric. Old Mother Hubbard. Lots of women call small-time crooks with no history of homicidal behavior and offer them money to commit murder."

"Curiouser and curiouser," I said.

31

"ALLAHUU-UUU-AKBAAAAR—"

Recorded prayer exploded outside my window.

I opened one eye.

Dawn was seeping around the things in my room. One of them was Ryan.

"You awake?"

"*Hamdulillah.*" Ryan's voice was thick and fuzzy.

"Um hmm," I said.

"Praise the Lord." Mumbled translation.

"Whose?" I asked.

"Too deep for five A.M."

It *was* a deep question. One I'd considered long after Ryan fell asleep.

"I'm convinced it's Max."

"The muezzin?"

I hit Ryan with a pillow. He rolled over.

"Someone wanted Max so badly they were willing to kill for him."

"Ferris?"

"For one."

"I'm listening." Ryan's eyes were blue and sleepy.

"Jake's right. This goes beyond the Hevrat Kadisha."

"I thought the HK boys wanted everyone."

I shook my head. "This isn't about the generic Jewish dead, Ryan. It's about Max."

"So who is he?"

"Who *was* he." My voice was taut with self-recrimination.

"It's not your fault."

"I lost him."

"What could you have done?"

"Delivered him directly to the IAA. Not hauled him with me to the Kidron. Or, at least taken steps to keep him secure."

"Shouldn't have left the Uzi behind in the Bradley."

I clocked Ryan again. He confiscated the pillow, scooted up, and propped it behind his head. I nestled beside him.

"Facts, ma'am," Ryan said.

It was a game we played when stumped. I started the time line.

"In the first century C.E., people died and were buried in a cave at Masada, probably during the seven-year occupation of the summit by Jewish zealots. In 1963, Yigael Yadin and his team excavated that cave but failed to report on bones found there. Nicu Haas, the physical anthropologist detailed with analyzing those bones, stated verbally to Yadin and his staff that the remains represented twenty-four to twenty-six commingled individuals. Haas made no mention of one isolated, articulated, and complete skeleton, later described to Jake Drum by a volunteer excavator who'd helped clear the cave."

Ryan picked up the thread.

"That isolated, articulated, and complete skeleton, hereinafter to be referred to as Max, ended up at the Musée de l'Homme in Paris. Sender, unknown."

"In 1973, Yossi Lerner stole Max from the museum and gave him to Avram Ferris," I said.

"Ferris spirited Max to Canada, later entrusted him to Father Sylvain Morissonneau at l'Abbaye Sainte-Marie-des-Neiges," Ryan said.

"On February twenty-sixth, Morissonneau gave Max to Brennan. Days later Morissonneau turned up dead."

"You're jumping ahead," Ryan said.

"True." I thought about dates. "On February fifteenth, Avram Ferris was found shot to death in Montreal."

"On February sixteenth, a man named Kessler handed Brennan a photo of a skeleton that turned out to be Max." Ryan.

"Hirsch Kessler turned out to be Hershel Kaplan, a small-time hustler and dealer in illegal antiquities."

"Kaplan fled Canada and was arrested in Israel." Ryan. "Said flight took place just days before Father Morissonneau's death on March second."

"On March ninth, Ryan and Brennan arrived in Israel. The next day Drum took Brennan on a tomb crawl, and Max was stolen by the Hevrat Kadisha. Presumably. Also that same day, Brennan's room was ransacked," I added.

"The next day, March eleventh, under skilled interrogation"—Ryan grinned his humblest of grins—"Kaplan admitted that Ferris had asked him to sell Max. Kaplan claimed he floated word of the skeleton's availability in early to mid January."

"That same day, Brennan was followed by men who appeared to be Muslim. Oh, and we forgot about Jamal Hasan Abu-Jarur and Muhammed Hazman Shalaideh." Ryan.

"The men parked outside l'Abbaye Sainte-Marie-des-Neiges," I said.

"'Tourists.'" Ryan hooked quote marks around the word.

"Chronologically, that occurred about two weeks after Ferris's murder."

"Noted," Ryan agreed. "Under even more skilled interrogation, on that same day Kaplan admitted that a woman hired him to kill Ferris, but denied knowing the woman, and denied being the shooter."

"That deal was struck in early January, weeks before Ferris was shot." I thought for a moment. "Anything else?"

"Those are the facts, ma'am. Unless you want to get into the shroud bones. But they are seemingly unrelated to Max or Ferris."

"True." I moved the game to phase two. "Main players?"

Ryan began. "Yossi Lerner, Orthodox Jew and liberator of Masada Max."

"Avram Ferris, murder victim and onetime possessor of Max," I added.

"Hershel Kaplan, aka Hirsch Kessler, murder suspect and would-be seller of Max." Ryan.

"Miriam Ferris, grieving widow with ties to Hershel Kaplan," I said. "And recipient of four million in insurance money."

"Yes."

"Sylvain Morissonneau, possible murder victim and onetime possessor of Max."

"Kaplan's mystery woman."

"Good one," Ryan said.

"Minor characters?"

Ryan considered.

"Mr. Litvak, Israeli associate and accuser of Kaplan."

"How does Litvak fit in?" I asked.

"Another party with an interest in Max," Ryan said.

"All right, then Tovya Blotnik," I said.

"The IAA director?"

"Same reasoning," I said.

"Jake Drum," Ryan said.

"No way," I said.

Ryan shrugged.

"Peripherals?" I asked.

"Dora Ferris, victim's mother."

"Courtney Purviance, victim's employee."

"We're getting goofy."

"True," I agreed. "But one thing is clear. Somehow it all comes back to Max."

"Hypotheses?" Ryan opened phase three.

I started.

"Proposition one. A group of ultra-Orthodox Jews has discovered Max's identity and fear his presence at Masada will taint the image of Judaism's sacred site."

"But we know Max is not J.C. So who is he?"

"A Nazarene. Suppose this ultra-Orthodox group has learned that those living in the cave weren't with the main group of Jewish zealots. They were, in fact, Jewish followers of Jesus, maybe even members of his own extended family."

"Yadin knew this? The IAA?"

"That would explain Yadin's reluctance to discuss the cave remains, and the government's refusal to do further testing."

"Tell me again. Why are Jesus followers on Masada a bad thing?"

"The Israelis have made Masada a symbol of Jewish freedom and resistance against external forces. It turns out there were Christians living up there, Jewish or not? They think they've reinterred the bones of the last defenders of Masada, but they've got early Christians buried under their monument? It would be enormously disturbing, especially for Israeli Jews."

"Proposition one suggests some fringe group of black hats is willing to do what it takes to keep all this quiet?"

"I'm just throwing it out there."

I remembered Donovan Joyce's strange theory, and Lerner's reaction to it.

"Remember that book I read called *The Jesus Scroll*?"

"The one about Jesus going geriatric?"

"Yes." I held up two fingers. "Proposition two. A group of militant, right-wing Christians has learned of Max's existence and believes he is Jesus. They fear the skeleton could be used to invalidate scripture."

"Yossi Lerner believed that," Ryan said.

"Yes." I said. "And perhaps Ferris. And at one time, Morissonneau."

"But Max isn't J.C."

"*We* know Max can't be Jesus. But Lerner was sure he was Jesus, and look how he reacted. Maybe others think so, too, and they're playing hardball to make the bones disappear."

"Proposition three." Ryan gave my scenario a different spin. "A group of Islamic fundamentalists have learned of Max's existence and believe he is Jesus. They want to use the bones to undermine Christian theology."

"How?"

"Jesus at Masada would shatter the central concept of the resurrection. How better to kick the legs out from under Christianity?"

"And these Muslim fanatics will stop at nothing to get their hands on Max. That works."

I pictured Sylvain Morissonneau in his office at l'Abbaye Sainte-Marie-des-Neiges. I made a note to contact LaManche to find out if an exhumation and autopsy had been ordered.

"Proposition four." I offered a hybrid of my proposition two and Ryan's proposition three. "A group of Islamic fundamentalists have learned of Max's existence and believe he is a Nazarene, perhaps even a member of the Jesus family. They fear both Christians and Jews might embrace this finding, reinterpreting Masada with zealots and early Nazarenes struggling against oppression, side by side. They fear the skeleton might be used to trigger a resurgence of religious ardor in the Judeo-Christian world."

"And they've vowed to prevent that," Ryan added. "That works."

We took a moment to consider our hypotheses. Fanatic Christians, Jews, or Muslims believing the bones were those of Jesus or one of his family or followers? Each proposition was as frightening as the next.

Ryan broke the silence.

"So who is Kaplan's mystery woman?" he asked. "And how does she link to Ferris? And how does she link to Max?"

"Excellent questions, Detective."

"I expect phone records this afternoon."

Ryan pulled me closer.

"Friedman wants to let Kaplan stew for a day."

"Stewing can be productive," I said.

Ryan kissed my cheek.

"I think we're on the right track, Ryan."

"Even if you're on the right track, you'll get run over if you just sit there."

"Will Rogers," I identified the quote. Another game.

Ryan's hand went to the back of my neck.

"Not much doing on the Sabbath."

Ryan's lips brushed my ear.

"Day of rest," I agreed.

"Little we can detect right now."

"Mm," I said. I think.

"But I have another excellent question," Ryan whispered.

I had an excellent answer.

Yes!

In the Toronto airport I'd noticed a book on the tao of sex, health, and longevity. I hadn't purchased it, but at the current rate, I was guessing I'd live to be 180. The deep breathing alone must have bought me a decade and a half.

Following breakfast and an argument concerning my driving solo to Beit Hanina, Ryan headed to police headquarters and I drove solo to Beit Hanina.

Jake was in better spirits than when I'd left him.

"Got something you're going to love," he said, flapping a paper above his head.

"Beard's recipe for grouse pie."

Jake dropped his hand. "Your abrasions look better."

"Thanks."

"You have a facial or some kind of treatment?"

"Moisturizer." I cocked my chin at the paper. "What do you have?"

"A memo from Haas to Yadin containing notes on the Cave 2001 bones." Jake leaned close and squinted. "Just moisturizer?"

I squinted back. "Positively Radiant."

"No treatment?"

Not one I was going to discuss.

"Let me see the memo." I held out a hand.

Jake yielded the paper. The notes were handwritten in Hebrew.

"How long have you had this?"

"A couple of years."

I shot Jake a look.

"It came mixed in with materials I requested on these first-century synagogue ruins I'm digging. Probably because there's a first-century synagogue site on Masada. The thing popped into my mind while I was eating breakfast. I vaguely remembered skimming some memo from Haas. It had nothing to do with the Talpiot site, so I set it aside. I dug back through my files, and there it was. I'd never really read it until this morning."

"Does Haas mention an isolated articulated skeleton?"

"No. In fact it's clear from his memo he never saw that skeleton." A mile-wide smile. "But he mentions pig bones."

"Pig bones?"

Nod.

"What does he say?"

Jake translated as he read: "'This has nothing to do with the riddle of the pig tallith.'"

"What does that mean?"

"I don't know, but he refers to a pig tallith 'riddle' or 'problem' twice."

"What would pig bones be doing at Masada? And what does that have to do with Cave 2001?"

Jake ignored my questions. "Another thing. Yadin estimated there were more than twenty cave skeletons, but Haas catalogs only two hundred and twenty individual bones. He places them into two categories: those that are clear, and those that are not so clear with regard to age."

He translated again from the memo.

"In the clear category, he lists one hundred and four old, thirty-three mature, twenty-four juvenile, and seven infant." Jake looked up. "He says six of the bones belonged to ladies."

There are 206 bones in the adult human skeleton. I did some quick math.

"Haas cataloged two hundred and twenty bones. That would mean ninety-six percent of the assemblage was missing."

I watched Jake chew dead skin on the ball of his thumb.

"Do you have a copy of the photo in Yadin's book?"

Jake went to his files and returned with a three-by-five black-and-white print.

"Five skulls," I said.

"That's another inconsistency," Jake said. "Tsafrir wrote in his field diary there were ten to fifteen skeletons in the cave, not twenty-some, and not five."

I wasn't really listening. Something in the photo had caught my attention.

Something familiar.

Something wrong.

"May I take a closer look?"

Jake led me to the back room. I took a seat at the dissecting scope, clicked on the light, and brought the center skull into focus.

"I'll be damned."

"What?"

I increased magnification, shifted to the photo's upper left corner, and slowly moved across the print.

At some point Jake said something. I agreed.

At another point I noticed Jake was no longer with me.

With each grainy detail, my apprehension grew. The same apprehension I'd felt upon spotting Max's ill-fitting tooth.

Had no one noticed? Had the experts been wrong?

Was I wrong?
I began again at the upper left corner.
Twenty minutes later, I sat back.
I wasn't wrong.

32

JAKE WAS IN THE KITCHEN, KNOCKING BACK ASPIRIN.

"These bodies weren't just dumped in the cave." I flicked Yadin's print. "They were buried. Laid out in graves."

"No way!"

I placed the photo on the counter. "Notice the hands and feet."

"The bones are articulated," Jake said. "They're lying in anatomical position."

"Indicating at least some of these were primary burials."

"No one's ever interpreted the site that way. Why's everything else so helter-skelter?"

"Check out the long bones. There." With a pen, I indicated a small puncture. "And there." I indicated another.

"Tooth marks?"

"You bet they are." I tapped several bones and some long, jagged fragments. "These were splintered to extract the marrow. And look at this." I moved my pen to a hole in the base of one of the skulls. "Some critter tried to munch that brain."

"What are you saying?"

"This wasn't a body dump. This was a small cemetery disturbed by animals. Roman soldiers didn't just throw dead bodies into the cave after the siege. People took time to dig graves and place these bodies into the ground. Animals later dug them up."

"If the cave was used as a cemetery, then why the cooking pots and lamps and household debris?"

"The site may have been inhabited at one time, later used for burial. Or maybe people lived in an adjacent cave and used 2001 for burial and refuse disposal. Hell, I don't know. You're the archaeologist. But the presence of a cemetery suggests that the Roman-soldiers-dumping-bodies interpretation of the remains is wrong."

Jake still sounded skeptical. "Hyena and jackal predation has been a problem here for centuries. In antiquity, both Jewish and Christian graves in the northern Negev were covered with slabs to prevent animals from digging them up. Modern Bedouins still use stones."

"Looking at this photograph, I think there were two or three single inhumations, and maybe a common grave of five or six individuals," I said. "The disturbances probably took place shortly after the burials. That's why everything looks so chaotic."

"Hyenas are known to drag remains back to their dens." Less skeptical. "That would account for the large number of missing bones."

"Exactly."

"Okay. The cave contained graves. So what? We still don't know *whose.*"

"No," I agreed. "Haas's memo mentions pig bones. Wouldn't their presence suggest the burials weren't Jewish?"

Jake shrugged a bony shoulder. "Haas talks about a pig tallith riddle, whatever that means, but it's unclear where this pig and its prayer shawl were found. Pig bones in the cave might suggest that the bodies there were those of Roman soldiers. That interpretation has its supporters. Or they could suggest that the bones were those of Byzantine monks. Monks had a small colony on Masada in the fifth and sixth centuries."

"According to Haas, the cave remains included six women and a six-month fetus. That doesn't sound like Roman soldiers to me," I said. "Or monks."

"And remember, fabric found with the bones yielded dates of forty to 115 C.E. That's way too early for the monks."

Jake refocused on the photo.

"Your take on this as a disturbed cemetery makes a lot of sense, Tempe. Remember the palace skeletons?"

I did.

"Yadin's book gives the impression that he found three separate individuals, a young man, a woman, and a male child. He concluded, very dramatically, I might add, that the palace skeletons were those of the last defenders of Masada."

"That's inaccurate?" I asked.

"It's quite a stretch. Not long ago I was allowed to examine archival evidence pertaining to the northern palace loci, including all diaries and photos. I'd expected to see three distinct skeletons. Not so. The bones were scattered and very fragmentary. Wait a minute."

Jake lay down the photo and took up the Haas memo.

"I thought so. Haas also talks about the palace skeletons. He describes both males as adults, one about twenty-two, the other about forty years of age."

"Not the kid Yadin described."

"Nope. And, as I recall, one male was represented only by legs and feet."

I started to speak. Jake cut me off.

"And another thing. Yadin's field diary referred to animal dung at the palace locus."

"Hyenas or jackals might have dragged three partial bodies there from elsewhere."

"Quite a different picture from the brave little family taking its noble last stand."

I suddenly realized what had been bothering me about the palace skeletons.

"Think about this, Jake. After its capture, the Romans inhabited Masada for thirty-eight years. Would they have left corpses lying around in one of Herod's luxurious palaces?"

"The palaces may have fallen into disrepair during the zealot occupation. But you're right. No way."

"Yadin wanted desperately for the palace skeletons to be a Jewish rebel family. He took a few liberties in interpreting those bones, then heralded the discovery to the press. So why the wariness concerning the cave skeletons?"

"Maybe Yadin was aware of pig bones from the get-go," Jake said. "Maybe the pig bones made him uneasy about the identity of the cave people. Maybe he suspected they might not be Jewish. Maybe he thought they were Roman soldiers. Or some outsider group living on

Masada during the occupation, but separate from the main zealot group."

"Maybe Yadin was aware of more than that," I said, thinking of Max. "Maybe it was the other way around. Maybe Yadin, or one of his staff, figured out exactly who was buried in that cave."

Jake guessed my thought. "The single articulated skeleton."

"That skeleton was never sent to Haas with the rest of the bones."

"It was spirited out of Israel and sent to Paris."

"Where it was buried in the collections at the Musée de l'Homme, and discovered by Yossi Lerner a decade later."

"After happening upon the skeleton, Lerner happened upon Donovan Joyce's book, and was so convinced of the skeleton's explosive potential, he filched it."

"And now that skeleton's been filched again. Does Haas mention a complete skeleton *anywhere* in his memo?"

Jake shook his head.

"Do you think his reference to pig bones is significant?"

"I don't know."

"What did Haas mean by the 'riddle of the pig tallith'?"

"I don't know."

More questions without answers.

And still the big one.

Who the hell was Max?

Ryan picked me up at eleven in Friedman's Tempo. Again thanking me for the return of his rental car, Jake dragged off to bed.

Ryan and I headed back to the American Colony.

"His spirits have improved," Ryan said. "But he's still kind of dopey."

"It's been less than forty-eight hours. Give him time."

"Fact is, he was kind of dopey be—"

"Noted."

I told Ryan about Haas's memo, and its reference to a pig tallith riddle. I also told him it was clear from Haas's skeletal inventory he'd never seen Max.

I shared with Ryan my belief that the bodies had been buried, not dumped in the cave, and that the graves had later been disturbed by animals.

He asked what it all meant. Other than throwing doubt on traditional interpretations of Masada, I didn't have an answer.

"Did you get your phone records?"

"Yes, ma'am." Ryan patted his breast pocket.

"Does a phone dump always take so long?"

"Gotta get warrants. Once warrants are issued, Bell Canada moves at the pace of sludge. I asked for incoming and outgoing back through November, and told them to hold the lists until they'd ID'd every call."

"Meaning?"

"Ferris's home and office. Kaplan's shop and flat."

"What about mobiles?"

"Fortunately, we're not dealing with the cell phone set."

"That simplifies things."

"Considerably."

"And?"

"I just glanced at the fax. Since this place is in Sabbath lockdown, I thought we might divide and conquer this afternoon."

"You want to go over it together?"

"What do you think?"

How bad could it be?

Ninety minutes later I knew.

In one month the average person places and receives enough calls to fill two to four eight-by-ten sheets. With very small print. We were looking at two businesses and two residences, for a period of four and a half months. You do the math.

How to proceed? After some debate we'd settled the issue scientifically. Heads: by chronology. Tails: by subscriber.

The coin opted for the time-line approach.

We started with November. I took Ferris's home and Les Imports Ashkenazim, Ryan took Kaplan's flat, and le centre d'animaux Kaplan. In the first hour we learned the following.

Hersh Kaplan wasn't the most popular guy in town. The sole person to ring his flat in November was Mike Hinson, his parole officer. Ditto for dialing out.

At le centre d'animaux Kaplan most callers were pet, pet-food, or pet-product suppliers, or people from the neighborhood, presumably customers.

At the Ferris home, calls went back and forth between Dora, the brothers, a butcher, a kosher grocer, a temple. No surprises.

Out in Mirabel, calls were made to and received from suppliers, shops, and temples throughout eastern Canada. Several calls were placed to Israel. Courtney Purviance phoned the warehouse, or was phoned at home. Miriam checked in, but less frequently. Avram rarely called his condo in Côte-des-Neiges.

Hour three revealed that December's pattern deviated little from that of November. Late in the month, several calls were made from the Ferris home to a local travel agency. The Renaissance Boca Raton Hotel was also contacted. The Renaissance was also dialed twice from the warehouse.

At three, I sat back, a low-level headache seething in my temples.

Beside me, Ryan lay down his marker and rubbed his eyes.

"Break for lunch?"

I nodded.

We trooped downstairs to the restaurant. In an hour we were back at my room desk. I again took Ferris's records. Ryan resumed with Kaplan's.

A half hour later I spotted something.

"That's odd."

Ryan looked up.

"On January fourth, Ferris called l'Abbaye Sainte-Marie-des-Neiges."

"The monastery?"

I slid the sheet sideways. Ryan glanced at it.

"They talked for fourteen minutes." He turned to me. "Did Morissonneau mention contact with Ferris?"

I shook my head. "Not a word."

"Good eye, soldier." Ryan highlighted the line with yellow marker.

Ten minutes. Fifteen. A half hour.

"Bingo." I indicated a call. "On January seventh, Ferris called Kaplan."

Ryan switched from the pet shop record to Kaplan's home phone.

"Twenty-two minutes. Ferris asking Kaplan to black-market Max?"

"The call was made three days after Ferris talked with Morissonneau."

"Three days after Ferris talked to someone at the monastery."

"True." I hadn't thought of that. "But the January fourth call lasted almost a quarter of an hour. Ferris must have been talking with Morissonneau."

Ryan raised his I-am-quoting-a-quote index finger. "Assumption is the mother of screw-up."

"You made that up," I said.

"Angelo Donghia."

"And he is . . . ?"

"It's on the Internet. Simpson's Quotations. Google it."

I made a note to do just that.

"The Ferris autopsy was February sixteenth," Ryan said. "When he gave you the photo, did Kaplan say how long he'd had it?"

"No."

Back to the records. Several lines down I spotted a vaguely familiar number preceded by an Israeli country code. I got up and checked my agenda.

"On January eighth Ferris called someone at the IAA."

"Who?"

"I don't know. It's the main switchboard number."

Ryan sat back. "Any idea why he'd do that?"

"Maybe he was offering to give the Masada skeleton back."

"Or sell it back."

"Maybe he was looking for documentation."

"Why would he want that?"

"To reassure himself of the skeleton's authenticity."

"Or to goose its value."

"Authentication would do that."

"When you first made contact, did Blotnik mention knowing about the bones?"

I shook my head.

Ryan made a note.

Another half hour passed.

The fax was fuzzy, the numbers and letters barely legible. My neck ached. My eyes burned. Edgy, I got up and paced the room. I told myself it was time to quit. But I rarely listen to my own advice. Returning to the desk, I plowed on, hearing each breath in cadence to the pounding in my head.

I saw it first.

"Ferris phoned Kaplan again on the tenth."

"Someone at Ferris's warehouse phoned Kaplan again on the tenth."

Maybe it was the headache. Maybe it was the tedium. Ryan's pickiness no longer amused me.

"Am I being a liability here?" It came out sharper than I'd intended.

Ryan's eyes came up, blue and surprised. For a long moment they looked directly into mine.

"Sorry. Can I get you anything?"

Ryan shook his head.

I went to the minibar and popped a Diet Coke.

"Kaplan received another call from Ferris on the nineteenth," Ryan said to my back.

Dropping into my chair, I found the outgoing call on Ferris's warehouse record.

"Twenty-four minutes. Planning the big score, I guess."

The vessels in my head were now hammering with heavy thumping strokes. Ryan saw me press my fingers to my temples. He laid a hand on my shoulder.

"Knock off if you've had enough."

"I'm fine."

Ryan's eyes roamed my face. He brushed bangs from my forehead.

"Not as heart-pumping as surveillance?"

"Not as heart-pumping as mitosis."

"But meaningful detecting."

"Really?" I was full-out cranky now. "In five hours we've learned what? Kaplan called Ferris. Ferris called Kaplan. Big deal. We knew that. Kaplan told us."

"We didn't know Ferris called Morissonneau."

I smiled. "We didn't know Ferris called the *monastery.*"

Ryan raised a palm. "We be good."

I slapped a lifeless high-five.

And upended my Coke with an elbow. The Real Thing made a real mess, soaking the desktop and rolling cheerfully onto the floor.

We shot to our feet. While I ran for towels, Ryan plucked up and shook the phone records. I mopped, he blotted, then we lay the sheets flat on my bathroom floor to dry.

"Sorry," I said lamely.

"Drying time," Ryan said. "Let's eat."

"I'm not hungry."

"Gotta eat."

"No, I don't."

"Yes, you do."

"You sound like my mother."

"Nutrition is the key to good health."

"Good health is merely the slowest possible rate at which to die."

"You stole that."

I probably had. George Carlin?

"Gotta eat," Ryan repeated.

I gave up arguing.

We had dinner in the hotel restaurant, the mood in our little alcove stiff and unnatural. My fault. I felt jammed, my nerves tight.

We talked around things, his daughter, my daughter. No murder. No skeletons. Though Ryan tried his best, long silences played across the table.

Upstairs, Ryan kissed me outside my door. I didn't ask him in. He didn't press.

It took a long time to fall asleep that night. It wasn't the headache. Or the muezzin. Or the cats brawling in the street below.

I'm not a joiner. I don't sign on with the Junior League, the garden club, or the Sweet Potato Queens. I'm an alcoholic who's never hitched up with AA. Nothing against alliance. I'm simply a self-help sort of gal.

I read. I absorb. Bit by bit, I crack the mystery of me.

Like why, at that moment, I wanted a bellyful of Merlot.

AA dubs us once and future alcoholics. Others, naively, call us recovered. They're wrong. Capping the bottle doesn't end the alcoholic dance. Nothing does. It's in the double helix.

One day you're queen of the prom. The next you lack reasons to get out of bed. One night you slumber the sleep of the newborn. The next you're awake, anxious and tossing, and uncertain why.

That night was one of those nights. Hour after hour, I lay staring at the minaret out my darkened window, wondering for whom the spire reached. The god of the Koran? The Bible? The Torah? The bottle?

Why had I been so short with Ryan? Sure, we'd spent hours and learned almost nothing. Sure, I'd rather have been solving the mystery of Max. But why take it out on Ryan?

Why did I want a drink so badly?

And why had I been such a klutz with the Coke? Ryan would have a field day with that one.

I drifted off after midnight, and dreamed disjointed dreams. Phones. Calendars. Disembodied numbers, names, and dates. Ryan on a Harley. Jake chasing jackals from a cave.

At two, I got up for water, then sat wearily on the side of the bed. What did the dreams mean? Were they simply a replay, brought on by headache and the afternoon's tedium? Was my subconscious attempting to send up a message?

Eventually, I slept.

More than once I awoke, bedding twisted hard in my fists.

33

I CAN'T SAY I WAS UP WITH THE MUEZZIN. BUT IT WAS CLOSE.

The sun was rising. The birds were singing. The headache was gone.

The demons were gone.

After clearing papers from my bathroom floor, I showered, then went the extra mile with blush and mascara. At seven, I called Ryan.

"Sorry about yesterday."

"Maybe we can get you into a ballet class."

"I don't mean the Coke spill. I mean me."

"You are a gentle flower, a winsome sprite, a creature of loveliness and—"

"Why do you put up with me?"

"Am I not the most gallant and wonderful being in your world?"

"Oh, yeah."

"And sexy."

"I can be a pain in the ass."

"Yeah. But you're *my* pain in the ass."

"I'll make up for it."

"Tap pants?"

You have to admire the guy. He never gives up.

Friedman called during breakfast. Kaplan wanted to talk about Ferris. Friedman offered to pick Ryan up and leave me the Tempo. I accepted.

Back upstairs, I rang Jake, but got no answer. I assumed he was still asleep.

Wait? No way. I'd been waiting two days.

The *Jerusalem Post* is headquartered off Yirmeyahu Street, a main artery that begins at the Tel Aviv highway then loops toward the religious neighborhoods of North Jerusalem and joins up with Rabbi Meir Bar Ilan Street, famous for its full-contact Sabbath rock throwers. Jewish motorist or not, these guys didn't want you driving on their holy day. Ironically, in my stumblings on Friday, I'd passed within a block of the *Post*'s doors.

I parked and walked to the building, checking my back for cruisers and jihadists. From Friedman's sketch map, I knew I was in the Romema neighborhood on the far western edge of West Jerusalem. The *quartier* was definitely not a tourist destination. Actually, that's being generous. The *quartier* was ugly as hell, all garages and fenced lots stacked with tires and rusting auto parts.

I entered a long, low rectangle with JERUSALEM POST chiseled on one side. Architecturally, the place had all the charm of an airplane hangar.

After much security, and many *shalom*s, I was directed to the basement. The keeper of the archives was a woman of about forty, with a pale mustache, and dried makeup around the corners of her mouth. Her hair was fried blonde and dark for an inch out from her scalp.

"*Shalom.*"

"*Shalom.*"

"I'm told you keep old articles on file by topic."

"Yes."

"Is there a Masada dossier?"

"There is."

"I'd like to view it, please."

"Today?" Her tone suggested she'd rather release files to kindergarteners with finger paints.

"Yes, please."

"My staff is primarily here to get the archives online."

"That is such overwhelming work." My shoulders sagged in sympathy. "But so valuable."

"We've got materials going back to the days when the paper was the *Palestinian Post.*"

"I understand." I smiled my warmest greeter-at-the-Wal-Mart smile. "And I'm in no hurry."

"You can't check it out."

"Of course not." I looked appropriately horrified.

"Do you have two pieces of identification?"

I showed my passport and my UNCC faculty ID. She looked at both.

"Are you researching a book?"

"Mm."

She pointed to one of several long wooden tables. "Wait there."

Rounding her counter, Madam Archivist crossed to a bank of gray metal filing cabinets, opened one drawer, and removed a bulky file folder. Placing the file on my table, she almost smiled.

"Take your time, dear."

The clippings had been glued onto blank pages. Scores of them. A date had been written to the side of each article, and, on many, the word "Masada" had been circled within the headline or the text.

By noon, I'd learned three important things.

First, Jake was not exaggerating. Save for brief mention at a press conference following the second season's excavation, the cave finds were never reported by the media. The *Jerusalem Post* even ran a special "Masada Section" in November of '64. In it Yadin described all the sensational finds from the first season, mosaics, scrolls, the synagogue, the *mikvehs,* the palace skeletons. Not a word on the cave bones.

Second, Yadin knew about the pig bones. A March '69 article quoted him as saying that animal bones, including those of pigs, were found among the various human remains at Masada.

Elsewhere, Yadin stated that officials from the Religious Affairs Ministry had suggested pigs might have been brought up to Masada to help with garbage disposal. Apparently, that was done in the Warsaw ghetto in the forties.

I couldn't see it. If the zealots had a garbage problem, they'd have chucked it over the side and let the Romans deal.

And Yadin didn't back off from the statement he made in '69. In an '81 interview he told a *Post* reporter that he'd advised Chief Rabbi Yehuda Unterman in '69 that he couldn't vouch for the Cave 2001 remains being Jewish, since they were commingled with pig bones.

Third, Yadin asserted that radiocarbon tests were never done on the cave remains. In the same '81 interview in which he'd discussed the pig bones, he stated that carbon-fourteen dating wasn't requested, and that it was not his business to do so. An anthropologist put it off to high cost. That was the interview Jake had remembered.

I sat back, considering.

Obviously, Yadin doubted the cave folks were Jewish zealots. Yet he never sent samples for radiocarbon dating.

Why not? The test wasn't that expensive. What did Yadin suspect? Or know? Did he or one of his staff figure out the identity of the cave burials? Of Max?

I began sliding pages back into the file.

Or *did* Yadin or one of his staff send samples for radiocarbon testing? Could someone have used a request for radiocarbon testing or some other type of analysis as a cover to get troublesome evidence out of the country?

Troublesome evidence like Max?

Could someone have sent Max to Paris to hide him? To make him disappear?

I knew my next stop.

As on my first visit, I was struck by how similar Mount Scopus is to other university campuses. On Sunday afternoon, the grounds were deader than Kokomo.

But legal parking was still as likely as an audience with the pope.

Leaving the Tempo in the same spot in which Jake had wedged the Honda, I hurried straight to the library. After passing security, I asked for the periodical section, located the journal *Radiocarbon,* and pulled every volume published in the early sixties.

Exiting the stacks, I found a carrel, and began searching, issue by issue.

It took less than an hour.

I sat back, staring at my notes, a star pupil with a breakthrough, and not a clue what it meant.

Reshelving the journals, I bolted.

* * *

It took Jake an eternity to open his gate. His eyes were at half-mast, and creases made a road map of his left cheek.

I trailed Jake to his flat, tingling with the excitement of discovery. He went straight to the kitchen. I was bursting as he filled a kettle and set it to boil.

"Tea?"

"Yes, yes. You're familiar with the journal *Radiocarbon*?"

Jake nodded.

"I did a quick check at the university library. Between sixty-one and sixty-three Yadin sent materials from his excavation of the Bar Kochba site here in Israel to the lab at Cambridge."

"Which site?"

"The Bar Kochba caves near the Dead Sea? Failed Jewish rebellion against the Romans? Second century C.E.? But the specific site isn't important."

"Uh-huh." Jake dropped tea bags into mugs.

"My point is Yadin sent materials from his dig at Bar Kochba for radiocarbon dating."

"Uh-huh."

"Are you listening to me?"

"I'm riveted."

"I've also been through the Masada folder in the *Jerusalem Post* archives."

"Busy, busy."

"In an eighty-one interview, Yadin told a *Post* reporter that it was not his business to initiate radiocarbon testing."

"So?"

"Yadin contradicted himself."

Jake raised a hand to cover a belch.

"Yadin always insisted that nothing from Masada had been sent for carbon-fourteen dating, right?"

"Far as I know."

"But Yadin *did* send materials off from other sites. And it wasn't just Yadin at Bar Kochba. During that same period other Israeli archaeologists were using other labs. The U.S. Geological Survey lab in Washington, D.C., for example."

"Cream or sugar?"

"Cream." I was fighting the urge to shake Jake into consciousness.

"You said that back in the sixties some member of the Knesset insisted skeletons from Masada had been sent abroad."

"Shlomo Lorinez."

"Don't you see? Lorinez may have been right. Some of the Cave 2001 bones may very well have been shipped out of Israel."

Jake filled both mugs and handed me one.

"The articulated skeleton?"

"Exactly."

"But it's just speculation."

"In his memo Haas reported a total of two hundred and twenty bones, right?"

Jake nodded.

"A normal adult human skeleton has two hundred and six bones. So Haas's count couldn't have included Max."

"Who's Max?"

"Masada Max. The articulated skeleton."

"Why Max?"

"Ryan likes alliteration."

Jake flicked a bushy brow, but made no comment.

"Obviously Haas never saw that skeleton," I said. "Why not?"

Jake stopped dipping his tea bag. "Because it was sent to the Musée de l'Homme in Paris?"

"Welcome to the land of the living, Jake."

"Nice alliteration."

"But why keep it secret?" I asked.

I didn't wait for an answer.

"And why the Musée de l'Homme? They don't do radiocarbon testing. And why a complete skeleton? You need only a small bone sample. And why single out that one skeleton? Yadin never talked about it. Haas never saw it."

"I've said from the get-go, there's more to that skeleton than anyone's letting on."

"You told me you were going to ask the Hevrat Kadisha straight out if they'd taken Max. Did you phone them?"

"Twice."

"And?"

"I'm waiting for a callback." Sarcastic.

Wrapping the string, I squeezed my tea bag against the bowl of my spoon.

"That'll make your tea bitter," Jake said.

"I like it strong."

"You'll get it bitter." Jake was fully awake and his argumentative self.

"I think I prefer you sleepy."

We both added cream and stirred.

"What's happening with the DNA?" Jake asked.

"I haven't checked my e-mail in days. Getting online at the hotel is a nightmare." True, but I really didn't expect results this soon. And to be honest, with nothing for comparison, I suspected any DNA data on Max or his odd tooth would be of limited use.

"When I submitted my samples from the Kidron tomb after talking to you by phone in Montreal, I asked both labs to e-mail the reports to you. Figured I'd need an interpreter."

Jake's paranoia again? I didn't comment.

"Why not give it a go. Use my computer." Jake chin-cocked the file room. "I'll grab a quick shower."

Why not? Taking my mug to his laptop, I logged on.

E-mails were in my box from both DNA labs.

I opened the reports on Jake's Kidron bones first. There was some information, but it meant little to me. I assumed each sample number corresponded to an ossuary or to a bone dump on the tomb floor.

Next, I opened the ancient and mitochondrial DNA reports on Max and his tooth.

At first I was surprised. Then confused.

I read the final section again and again. I couldn't imagine what it meant. But I knew one thing.

I'd been dead right about Max.

And dead wrong about the relevance of the DNA.

34

I MUST HAVE HAD THAT DOE-IN-THE-HEADLIGHTS LOOK.

"What are you staring at?"

The creases were gone and Jake's face was wet. Instead of sweats, he now wore jeans and a red luau shirt.

"DNA results."

"Oh, yeah?"

Jake clicked on the printer and I made a hard copy.

Jake scanned each report, face neutral. Then, "Very nice." He dragged a chair beside mine and dropped into it. "Now. What does it mean?"

"The mitochondrial DNA—"

"Slowly."

I took a breath.

"And from the top."

"The top?" I was hardly in the mood for a biology lesson.

"The penthouse."

Deep breath. Calm. Go.

"You're familiar with nuclear DNA?"

"That's the double-helix kind found in the nucleus of a cell."

"Yes. Researchers have been working for years to map the DNA molecule. Much of that mapping has focused on an area that codes for specific proteins we share as a species."

"Sounds like Atkins. No carbs, no fats."

"Do you want to hear this?"

Jake held up both hands.

I tried to think of a simpler way to put it.

"Some researchers are working to map the area of DNA that makes us all alike, the genes that give us two ears, scarce body hair, a pelvis designed for walking. Medical researchers are working to identify genes that can mutate and cause illnesses, like cystic fibrosis or Huntington's."

"So mappers look at genes that make us all the same. Medical researchers look at genes that make things go wrong."

"That's not a bad way to look at it. Forensic scientists, on the other hand, look at the parts of the DNA molecule that make people genetically different. The junk, or filler, DNA they study contains polymorphisms, variations that distinguish one person from another. But these differences are not physically obvious.

"All that said, there are those in forensic science who have crossed over from junk DNA and its variations to the genes that control physical characteristics, the differences we notice when looking at a person. These researchers are investigating what might be used to predict, from the genes, individual traits like skin or eye color."

Jake looked confused. And rightly so. I was so excited I was botching the explanation.

"Say police collect a sample left by an unknown perpetrator. Blood or semen at a crime scene, maybe. Without a suspect in mind, they have no one to whom to compare that sample. It exists in a vacuum. But if that sample can be used to limit the population of potential suspects, that's a very useful investigative tool."

Jake saw where I was going. "Predict sex, and you've cut your suspect pool by half."

"Exactly. Programs already exist that can predict biogeographical ancestry. When you phoned me in Montreal we discussed a case in which that was done."

"So the advantage is that you're not limited to comparison of an unknown sample to a known, you can actually predict what a guy might look like."

"Or girl."

"Yowza. A guy like Max or the people in my tomb?"

"Exactly. So far I've been talking about nuclear DNA. Are you familiar with mitochondrial DNA?"

"Refresh me."

"Mitochondrial DNA isn't located in the nucleus, it's located out in the cell."

"What does it do?"

"Think of it as an energy source."

"I could use a fill-up. What's its role in a forensic context?"

"The coding region of mitochondrial DNA is small, maybe eleven thousand base pairs, and shows little variation. But, like nuclear DNA, there's a part of the genome that doesn't seem to do much, but has lots of polymorphism sites."

"What's the advantage over nuclear DNA?"

"There are only two copies of nuclear DNA, but hundreds to thousands of copies of mitochondrial DNA in each of our cells. So the likelihood of recovering mitochondrial DNA from small or degraded samples is much greater."

"Small and degraded like my Kidron bone. Or two-thousand-year-old Max."

"Yes. The older the bone, the lower the likelihood of extracting a testable sample of nuclear DNA. Another advantage of mitochondrial DNA is that it's inherited only through female lines, so the genes aren't scrambled and recombined every time conception takes place. That means that if an individual isn't available for direct comparison, any maternally related family member can provide a reference sample. Your mitochondrial DNA is identical to that of your mother, your sisters, your grandmother."

"But my daughters would have their mother's mitochondrial DNA, not mine."

"Exactly."

"Let me put this into the perspective of our tomb, since that's what interests me. With ancient and degraded bone, you're more likely to get mitochondrial than nuclear DNA."

"Yes."

"Both mitochondrial and nuclear DNA can be used to compare unknowns to knowns. Like tying a suspect to a crime scene, or nailing Daddy in a paternity suit. Both can be used to show family relationships, though in different ways. But nuclear DNA can now be used to predict individual traits."

"To a very limited extent," I said. "Sex, and some indicators of racial background."

"Okay. On to the tomb."

I picked up the lab report. "Not all your samples produced results. But the nuclear DNA tells us you've got four women and three men. Keep in mind that's not gospel."

"Bad pun. Explain."

"Your standard CODIS set includes amelogenin markers for *X* and *Y*. Greatly oversimplifying, if you see both markers in a sample, it's a boy. No *Y* marker, it's a girl.

"However, things are always more complicated with ancient bone. In degraded samples, alleles, or genes, that are actually present may fail to show a signature. But if you repeat the test again and again, and repeatedly get only *X*'s, it's pretty safe to assume your sample is from a female."

"What else?" Jake glanced over his shoulder at the door. My eyes followed, as though controlled by his movement.

"At least six of the tomb individuals are related," I said.

"Oh?" Jake drew closer, throwing a shadow onto the printout.

"But that's exactly what you'd expect in a family tomb. The surprising thing is th—"

"Which six?" Jake's levity had vanished.

"I don't know. Your individuals are reported only by sample numbers."

Jake cupped a hand on his mouth for a second or two. Then he snatched the printouts, shot to his feet, and crossed the room in three lanky strides.

"Jake. That's not the most significant thing."

I was addressing empty air.

Forget the tomb bones. I wanted to talk about Max. *That* was important. Then I remembered the tooth report.

No, I told myself. It was all important now.

I found Jake in the back bedroom arranging prints on a worktable. Joining him, I could see they were the ossuary photos Ryan and I had viewed.

As I watched, Jake wrote a name on the lower border of each print. Beside each name, he added the DNA lab's reference number.

Handing me the printouts, Jake called out the first sample number. I checked the nuclear DNA report.

"Female," I read.

"Marya," he said. Mary.

Jake drew a female symbol on the Marya ossuary photo, then flipped through a set of stapled pages.

"The physical anthropologist estimated this gal was old, sixty-five plus." He jotted the figure, then read the next lab number.

"Female," I said.

"Mariameme. The one called Mary."

Jake checked the physical anthropologist's report. "Older adult." He marked the photo, then read the third number.

"Male," I said.

"Yehuda, son of Jeshua."

Jude, son of Jesus, I translated in my mind.

"Twenty-five to forty years." Jake read the next number.

"Female," I said.

"Salome. Older adult."

One by one, we worked our way through the remains that had been associated with inscribed ossuaries. Mary. Mary. Joseph. Matthew. Jude. Salome. Jesus. In each case, the inscription fit the gender predicted by the nuclear DNA. Or vice versa.

Two sets of remains from the tomb floor were determined to be those of a male and a female.

Amplification of nuclear DNA was unsuccessful for Jesus and Matthew, and for the other samples recovered from the tomb floor. No results. No information on those individuals.

Jake and I looked at each other. It was like waiting out a no-hitter. Neither of us put it into words. But even with the gaps, it all fit. The Jesus family.

"So who's related to who?" Jake asked.

"Whom." Nervous reflex. I switched from the nuclear- to the mitochondrial-DNA report.

"Remember, these results show links, or lack of links, through female lines. Mother-daughter, mother-son, siblings sharing the same mother, cousins whose mothers had the same mother, and so on. Okay. Here goes. Mariameme and Salome are related." I spoke aloud as I matched sample numbers to names. "So is Marya, the older Mary."

Jake made notations on the three prints.

"Yose is part of the lineage. So is Jude."

More notations.

"The male from the tomb floor is related."

"Meaning he shows the same mitochondrial-DNA sequencing as Mariameme, Salome, Marya, Yose, and Jude."

"Yes," I said. "The female from the tomb floor is unique. That's no big deal. She may have married into the family from outside. As a relative only by marriage, not blood, she, and her children, if she had any, would have had the mitochondrial DNA of her mother's line."

"Nothing from Daddy."

"Mitochondrial DNA does not recombine. The whole shooting match comes from Mom."

I continued with the printout.

"Matthew is also unique. But again, if his mother was from another family, he would have *her* mitochondrial DNA, not that of her husband."

"He could be a cousin."

"Yes. The offspring of a brother and his wife."

I looked up.

"The Jesus material was too degraded for amplification. Sequencing wasn't possible."

Jake began sketching a family tree, hand darting like a hummingbird.

"Everything tallies. The older Mary is the mother." Jake drew a circle, named it Mary, and sent spokes shooting downward from it. "Salome. Mary. Joseph. Jesus. According to scripture, those are four of Mary's seven kids."

The inscription. *Yehuda, son of Yeshua.* Jude, son of Jesus.

Donovan Joyce's crazy theory. Jesus survived the crucifixion, married, and fathered a child. Were we back to that?

My mind wouldn't accept it.

The hell with the no-hitter. I jumped into the commentary.

"How does Jude fit in?" I asked.

Jake raised both brows and dipped his chin. Need I say the obvious?

"Jesus with siblings, living on, and becoming a daddy? You're talking about the three fundamental doctrines of the Catholic Church—virgin birth, resurrection, and celibacy."

Jake raised both shoulders. He was so agitated the move came across more spasm than shrug.

"No, Jake. What you're inferring can't be. This Jude has DNA that links him to the other women in your tomb, to the older Mary, Salome, and Mariameme. If Jesus had fathered a son, that child would have the mitochondrial DNA of its mother's family, not its father's family."

"Fine. Jude could be a nephew of Jesus. A grandson of Mary." Jake added a circle at the end of one spoke, and sent another spoke shooting downward from it. "One of the sisters could have married another man named Jesus and had a son named Jude."

"Donovan Joyce claimed he'd seen a scroll written by someone named Jesus, son of James," I offered, almost against my will.

"That couldn't have been James of the ossuary, Jesus' brother. James's wife would have been unrelated, and James's son would have had his mother's mitochondrial DNA, not his grandmother's, right?"

"Yes."

Thoughts were whipsawing in my head. "Jake, there's someth—"

Again he cut me off.

"The female from the tomb floor is unrelated. She could be—" Jake stopped as the thought struck him. "Holy hell, Tempe. Donovan Joyce thought Jesus married Mary Magdalene. Others have suggested the same thing. That female could be Mary Magdalene."

Jake was barely taking time to breathe.

"But it really isn't important who she is. And Matthew's unrelated, right? He could be one of the disciples who, for whatever reason, ended up buried in the tomb. Or a son of one of the brothers, another nephew."

"Lot of mights. Lot of maybes." I resisted the pull of Jake's exhilaration.

Jake ignored that.

"James is missing because his ossuary was stolen. And Simon died decades later. Hot damn, Tempe, it's practically the whole family."

The same thought crossed our minds simultaneously. Jake voiced it.

"So who's the crucified man in the shroud?"

"*Maybe* crucified," I cautioned.

"Okay. The Jesus from the ossuary could be another nephew. Damn! Why couldn't that lab sequence him?"

Abruptly, Jake strode to the ossuary cabinet. Disengaging the padlock, he peered in. Satisfied, he closed and resecured the door.

Jesus alive and with offspring? Jesus dead and remaining shrouded in a tomb? Each scenario seemed worse than the next.

"It's all speculation," I said.

When Jake turned, his eyes bored into mine. "Not if I can prove the James ossuary came from that tomb."

I picked up the mitochondrial-DNA report. Marya, Mariameme, Salome, Yose, Yehuda, and the unknown male were members of a single matrilineage. Matthew had come from another lineage, and the unknown female from the tomb floor had come from yet another. The bones from the ossuary inscribed *Yeshua, son of Yehosef* were too degraded to yield DNA.

Jesus, son of Joseph. But what Jesus? What Joseph?

Had Jake really found the tomb of the Holy Family? If so, who was the shrouded man I'd found in the hidden loculus?

"There's something else, Jake."

"What?"

I started to speak, but Jake's phone stopped me.

"Miracle of miracles. Could that be the Hevrat Kadisha, actually returning my call about Max?" he said, loping to the office.

In Jake's absence I reread the reports on Max and his tooth.

The nuclear DNA told me Max was male. No biggie. I knew that from the bones. Same for the odd molar stuck in Max's jaw. Male.

The mitochondrial DNA told me Max was not a member of the matrilineage in the Kidron tomb. His sequencing was unique. If this really was the Jesus family, Max was an outsider. Or at least not a descendant of one of those females.

The mitochondrial DNA also told me the odd molar in Max's jaw belonged to someone other than Max. Okay. Bergeron said that. He was certain it came from a younger individual.

It was the next statement that made no sense. I was on my third reread when Jake returned.

"Assho—"

"Hevrat Kadisha?"

Tight nod.

"What did they say?"

"*Baruch Dayan ha-emet.*"

I curled my fingers in a come-on gesture.

"Blessed is the one true Judge."

"What else?"

"We are the spawn of Satan. They are following the greatest *mitz-*

vah. Now the self-righteous little wankers plan to put the screws to my Talpiot site."

"You've unearthed skeletal remains at a first-century synagogue?"

"Of course not. I told him that, but he didn't believe me. Said he and his storm troopers would be landing today in full force."

"Did you ask if they took Max?"

"The good rabbi refused to discuss it."

Jake hesitated. "But he also said something weird."

I waited.

"He wanted all the harassing phone calls to stop."

"And?"

"I've only contacted the Hevrat Kadisha twice."

"So who's doing all the phoning?"

"Apparently the rabbi doesn't know."

A strange silence followed. I broke it.

"You were right, Jake." I held up the mitochondrial DNA reports on Max and his tooth. "This could be bigger than either of us imagined."

"Lay it on me."

I did.

Now Jake looked like the doe in the headlights.

35

I'D REPEATED IT TWICE. JAKE WAS STILL NOT GETTING IT.

"The tooth and the skeleton show different mitochondrial-DNA sequencing. That means the tooth came from a different person than the skeleton. But we already knew that. The dentist affiliated with my Montreal lab already told us that. The tooth came from someone younger than Max.

"And Max's mitochondrial DNA is unique, different from both the tooth person and the members of the tomb matrilineage. If Max was a member of that family, his mother was an outsider."

"A female who married in."

"Possibly. But the real shocker is that the mitochondrial DNA in the molar is identical to the mitochondrial DNA in the Kidron tomb family."

"DNA ties the tooth, but not the skeleton, to the Mary lineage?"

"Sequencing links the odd tooth from Max to the matrilineally linked individuals in your tomb."

"The tooth that was reinserted into Max's jaw?"

"Yes, Jake. It means the owner of the tooth was related to the people in your tomb. He was a member of that family, a maternal relative."

"But the tooth didn't belong in that jaw. How did it get there?"

"My guess is the transfer was a simple mistake. The tooth probably slipped from the jaw of one of the individuals in the commingled remains, and became erroneously incorporated with the bones of the articulated skeleton. Maybe during recovery. Maybe during transport. It couldn't have happened at Haas's lab. We now know Haas never saw Max."

"So at least one person in Cave 2001 was unquestionably related to the people in the Kidron tomb. What the hell was a member of that family doing up on Masada?"

Jake walked to the window, shoved his hands into his pockets, and looked down. I waited while he wandered through thoughts of his own.

"Yadin's reticence to discuss the cave burials. Haas's failure to report on them." Jake's voice was hushed. "Of course. Those weren't zealots. A group of Nazarenes was living in that cave."

Though Jake wasn't really speaking to me, his hold on my attention was complete.

"What the hell have we stumbled onto? Who was this Max? Why was that one skeleton not given to Haas? Who was hidden in the loculus in the Kidron tomb? Why weren't those bones ever collected and placed in an ossuary?"

It came out sounding like the middle of a thought.

"Jesus followers on Masada, one of them with biological ties to the tomb in the Kidron. One of them a member of the Holy Family. And to prove that I've got to prove the James ossuary came from that tomb."

Jake turned, eyes burning with something that froze my response.

"I thought we had two unrelated first-century finds, each mind-blowing on its own. That's not true. It's all connected. The missing Masada skeleton and the Kidron tomb are all part of the same story. And it's mega, maybe the biggest discovery of the century. Hell, the millennium."

Jake strode back to the table, picked up the physical anthropology report, laid it down, touched an ossuary photo, then another, stacked the photos, laid the report on top of the stack, ran his finger around its edge.

"This is bigger than even *I* imagined, Tempe. And more dangerous."

"Dangerous? But we no longer have Max. And no one knows about the shroud bones."

"Not yet."

"It's time we tell Blotnik."

Jake spun on me. "No!"

I jerked as though shocked by live current.

Jake raised an apologetic hand.

"Sorry. My head's cranking up again. It's just. I— Not Blotnik."

"Jake, are you allowing personal feelings to cloud your judgment?"

"Blotnik's a has-been. No." Jake snorted. "That's being charitable. He's a never-was. And a real asshole."

"Blotnik could be Caligula, but he heads the IAA. The man must have done something to earn that position."

"He published a few brilliant articles back in the sixties, got the academic world shitting its fancy French shorts, got a lot of plum offers, then sat back and never wrote another thing of merit. Now he rides on the backs of others."

"Despite your view of Blotnik, the IAA has authority over antiquities in this country."

Outside, a car door slammed. Jake's eyes skittered to the window, to the locked cabinet, then back to mine. Sighing, he picked up and began clicking a ballpoint pen.

"I'll visit Ruth Anne Bloom this afternoon."

"Bloom is the physical anthropologist attached to the IAA?"

Jake nodded.

"You'll tell her about the shroud bones?"

"Yes." With his free hand, Jake squeezed the bridge of his nose.

"You're not just saying that?"

"I'm not just saying that." Jake threw down the pen. "You're right. It's too risky to keep the bones here."

Risky for whom? I wondered, watching Jake cross back to the window. The bones? Jake? Jake's future career? I knew my friend. He, too, had academic ambitions.

"Would you like me to go with you to the Rockefeller?"

Jake shook his head. "I've got to swing by the dig and warn my crew about the Hevrat Kadisha. They know the drill, but I want to be sure the damn bone police don't take them by surprise."

I looked at my watch.

"I'm supposed to meet Ryan at the hotel at four. But I can change that."

"No need. I'll call you in a couple of hours."

"You'll have dinner with us tonight?"

Jake nodded, thinking, no longer listening.

* * *

Ryan arrived at my room shortly after I did. I must have looked unhappy.

"You okay?"

I nodded, not wanting to go into details of my spat with Jake.

"How's your pal?"

"His head's hurting, but he's fine." I slammed the door on the minibar. "Judgmental, but fine."

Ryan let it go.

"Learn anything useful at the *Post*?"

Popping a Diet Coke, I told Ryan about the articles in which Yadin contradicted himself concerning the use of radiocarbon dating.

"So the old boy did send materials out of the country. Why wouldn't he do that with the Masada skeletons?"

"Why not indeed."

"But listen to this. I got DNA results. A number of individuals in the Kidron tomb had identical sequencing."

"Meaning they're related."

"Yes. But that's no big deal. It's a family tomb. You'd expect the people buried there to be related. What is a big deal is that mitochondrial DNA links Max's odd tooth to that family."

"Meaning someone buried in Cave 2001 was a member of the family buried in the Kidron tomb."

I love Ryan's quickness.

"Exactly. And since Jake's convinced the Kidron tomb held the members of the Holy Family, that would place early Christians on Masada at the time of the siege."

"Wow."

"Yeah. The Israelis will be antagonistic to any such suggestion."

"Jesus people at Masada, maybe even a member of the Holy Family."

"Exactly. But I still have no idea who Max is." I took a swig. "Was. His DNA sequencing was unique. If he was related to those in the Kidron tomb, it wasn't through any of the ladies Jake recovered."

"Kaplan was dancing around the subject this morning."

That got my attention.

"Claimed Ferris was on a first-name basis with Max."

"He had proof of identity?"

"The world according to Kaplan."

A tingle of excitement ran up my spine. I'd spent a month trying to attach a label to the Masada skeleton. It'd been like chasing smoke in a pitch-black tunnel. If I was honest with myself, I'd come to suspect all hope of individualization had evaporated with time.

"For God's sake, Ryan. Tell me what Kaplan said."

"Kaplan claims he never found out. But word on the street was, the bones were big."

"The street of illegal antiquities?"

Ryan nodded. "Here's the bad news. Friedman had to cut Kaplan loose."

"You're kidding."

"Kaplan lawyered up. Counsel suggested, ever so politely, that his client's rights were being violated in that he'd been held well past the legal limit. I believe the term 'constitutionally impaired' was directed at Friedman."

"What about the shoplifting?"

"Litvak dropped his complaint. And I've got zilch to tie Kaplan to the Ferris hit."

"Kaplan admitted he was hired to shoot the guy."

"He says he didn't do it."

"He planned to sell a stolen skeleton." My voice sounded shrill in the quiet room.

"Intent isn't a crime. Besides, he's now claiming he never really intended to hawk the thing. Just made some calls out of curiosity."

"Bloody hell."

"Here's another interesting development. Courtney Purviance is in the wind."

"Ferris's secretary has disappeared?"

"When Kaplan first told us about the Masada skeleton, we asked why Ferris decided to sell after hiding the bones for more than thirty years."

I'd wondered that myself.

"He claimed Ferris's business was tanking."

"That's not what Purviance told you."

"Not at all. So somebody's lying. That's why we wanted to ask Purviance some more questions. I fired off a query. Guy named Birch is working this with me."

"The blond detective I saw at the Ferris autopsy."

Ryan nodded. "Birch has been trying to contact Purviance for several days now. She's not at Ferris's warehouse. She's not at home. The lady appears to have vanished."

"Did anyone tell her not to leave town?"

"She isn't a suspect. I couldn't order her to stay put. I did suggest it would be useful to be able to touch base, but I doubt Purviance plays by any rulebook but her own."

"Any evidence of a planned trip?"

Ryan shook his head.

"That's not good," I said.

"No. It's not. Birch is on it."

Ryan came to me and placed a hand on each of my shoulders.

"Friedman and I are going to stick to Kaplan like white on rice. We'll know every place this turkey goes, everything he does, everyone he sees."

"Friedman's rope."

"We're betting Kaplan'll tie himself a noose."

Ryan drew me close.

"You'll be on your own for a while."

"I'll be fine."

"You've got my mobile number."

I broke free and gave Ryan a falsely bright smile. "Don't hold your breath, handsome. I'm dining with a tall, debonair man tonight."

"Bit bald."

"Bald is the new beautiful."

Ryan smiled. "I hate it when you get all weepy over me."

"Go." I turned Ryan toward the door. "Heart-pumping surveillance awaits."

When Ryan had gone, I phoned Jake to settle on a restaurant. No answer.

My watch said five. I'd been up since dawn, and was starting to fade.

Power nap? Why not. Jake would call within the hour.

Seconds later I was awakened by a noise at my door.

A key? A rattling knob?

Disoriented, I looked at the clock.

Seven thirty-two.

I flew across the room.

"Jake?"

No answer.

"Ryan?

Something swished on the tile at my feet. Looking down, I saw a folded paper slide through the crack.

I opened the door.

A young woman was scurrying down the corridor. She wore a *hijab,* dark dress, and oxfords.

"Miss?"

Without stopping the woman spoke over her shoulder. "This man hurt your room."

With that the woman rounded the corner, and her footsteps receded down the stone steps.

I closed and locked my door. Outside, traffic hummed. Inside, the room screamed silence.

Bending, I picked up and unfolded the paper. On it were the same words the woman had spoken. And a single name. Hossam al-Ahmed.

Was the woman a maid? Had she witnessed the break-in to my room? Why come forward now? Why in this manner?

Snatching up the phone, I asked for Mrs. Hanani. I was told the manager had gone for the day. I left a message, asking that she call me.

Placing the note in my purse, I called Jake. Still no answer. Was he still out? Had he tried to contact me? Had I slept through his call?

I tried again at seven forty-five, eight, and eight-fifteen. At eight-thirty I gave up and went down to the Cellar Bar.

Though my dinner was good, I was too agitated to appreciate the chef's efforts. I kept wondering why Jake hadn't returned my calls.

Could he still be at the Rockefeller?

But hadn't Jake planned to swing by his site first, then visit Bloom at the Rockefeller? Had he changed his mind about visiting Bloom? Maybe decided against driving alone with the shroud bones?

But he couldn't still be at the dig. It was dark.

Maybe he'd called my room, gotten no answer, and decided to dine with his crew.

Had I been so tired I'd slept through the ring? I doubted it.

The more I mulled it over, the more worried I became.

Across the bar, I could see two dark-skinned men seated at another alcove table. One was short and wiry, with skull-tight hair and a gap between his front teeth. The other was a beluga, with long, thin wisps pulled into a ponytail.

I thought of Hossam al-Ahmed. Who was he? Had he really ransacked my room? Why?

The men in the alcove were drinking juice, not speaking. A yellow candle lit their table. Shadows slid upward, morphing their features into Halloween masks.

Were the men watching me? Was my imagination in overdrive?

I snuck a peek.

The beluga removed shades from a pocket, slipped them on, and gave me an oily smile.

My eyes snapped back to my plate.

Signing for my meal, I hurried to my room and again called Jake.

No answer.

Maybe the headache had intensified, so he'd pulled the plug on his phone and crashed.

For lack of a better plan, I took a bath. My usual remedy for agitation. No go.

Who were the guys in the bar?

Who was Hossam al-Ahmed?

What had happened to Courtney Purviance?

Where was Jake?

How was Jake? Was he having a relapse? Had he thrown an embolism? Developed a subdural hematoma?

Mother Mary! I was going completely schizoid.

While toweling off, my eyes fell on Ryan's phone records, dry now, but browned and rippled from their encounter with the Coke.

Why not? It would keep my mind from worrying about Jake.

Propping myself in bed, I turned on the lamp and stared out the window. Thin wisps of fog blurred the minaret's top.

While not the full, majestic sweep of Jerusalem, my view was reassuring. Night sky. Lots of it. The same sky that had hung in this place forever.

My focus moved inward.

Arrows of light played on my dimmed ceiling. The day's heat had waned, and the room was pleasantly cool. A perfumed dampness permeated the air.

I closed my eyes and listened, the printouts lying on my upraised knees.

Traffic. The tinkle of a shopkeeper's bell. Cats meeting cats in the courtyard.

A car alarm cut the night with staccato beeps.

Opening my eyes, I took up Ryan's printouts.

I was faster than I'd been on my first go-round. I could see patterns now, and recognized more numbers.

But the bath had been more calming than I'd thought. My lids grew heavy. More than once, I lost my place.

I was about to kill the light when a number caught my attention. Was it drowsiness, or was something wrong there?

I ran the sequence again and again.

I felt blood making the rounds in my brain.

Grabbing the phone, I dialed Ryan.

36

"RYAN HERE."

"It's Tempe."

"How was dinner?" Subdued.

"Jake never showed."

Slight hitch. Surprise.

"I'll have the cad flogged."

"Turned out for the better. I may have found something in the phone records."

"I'm listening."

"When did Ferris take Miriam to Boca?" I asked.

"Mid-January." Ryan was keeping his answers short. I pictured him and Friedman folded like pretzels in a darkened car.

"Okay. Here's the sequence as I've been able to piece it together. On December twenty-eighth and twenty-ninth, calls were made from the Mirabel warehouse to the Renaissance Boca Raton Hotel. That was Ferris making arrangements."

"Okay."

"On January fourth a call was placed to l'Abbaye Sainte-Marie-des-Neiges. That was Ferris giving Morissonneau a heads-up on his plan to collect Max."

"Go on."

"On January seventh a call was made to Kaplan's home. That was Ferris contacting his middleman. Kaplan was called again on January tenth. Then, from the sixteenth through the twenty-third, there's a marked drop-off in outgoing calls from Mirabel."

"Ferris was down south with Miriam."

"Right. Two calls were made to the Boca resort. Probably Purviance with questions for the boss. But get this. On January nineteenth, Kaplan's home number was again dialed from the warehouse."

Ryan got it right away. "Ferris was in Florida. It couldn't have been him. So who's calling Kaplan?"

"Purviance?" I suggested.

"She ran the business when Ferris was gone. But why would Purviance call Kaplan? He's not a customer or a supplier. And Ferris's dealings with Kaplan weren't exactly kosher. Purviance wouldn't have been tuned into those transactions." Pause. "Could Purviance have been responding to a message?"

"I thought of that. The warehouse records show no incoming calls from Kaplan's home or shop."

"So someone phoned Kaplan's home from Ferris's warehouse while Ferris was in Florida. But Kaplan hadn't phoned the warehouse, either from his home or his shop, making it unlikely that Purviance was calling Kaplan in response to a message he'd left for Ferris. So who the hell made the call? And why?"

"Someone else with access? A family member?"

"Again, why?"

"Astute questions, Detective."

"Sonovabitch."

"Sonovabitch. Any word from Birch?"

I heard rustling, imagined Ryan seeking a more comfortable position.

"Purviance is still missing."

"That's bad, isn't it?"

"If the lady overheard or saw something, the perp might have clipped her to keep her from talking."

"Jesus."

"But ballistics caught a break on the Jericho nine-mil that killed Ferris. Piece was reported stolen by a seventy-four-year-old plumber named Ozols. Car break-in in Saint-Léonard."

"When?"

"January twenty-second, less than three weeks before Ferris was shot. Birch is thinking street thugs. Score a gun, hit a warehouse, things go south, Ferris gets popped."

Something stirred in my unconscious.

"According to Purviance, nothing of value was taken," I said, distracted by the heads-up from my hindbrain.

"Mopes may have panicked and split."

"The gun theft could also suggest pre-planning. Someone wanted a hit and needed a firearm. Also, Ferris took two bullets to the back of the head. That suggests a professional job, not a panic shooting."

"Miriam was in Florida."

"Yes," I agreed. "She was."

I heard a voice in the background.

"Kaplan's on the move," Ryan said, then disconnected.

No longer sleepy, I went back to the call records. This time, I began with the dump on Kaplan's home phone. The January and February lists were short.

Almost immediately, I got another shocker.

February first. Nine seventy-two. The international exchange for Israel. Zero-two. The area code for Jerusalem and Hebron. I knew the number.

The Rockefeller. And not the main switchboard this time.

Kaplan had dialed the office of Tovya Blotnik. The call had lasted twenty-three minutes.

Blotnik had been in the loop for at least ten days when Ferris died.

Had I seen Blotnik's number elsewhere? Was that the whisper I'd felt from my id?

I went back and checked Ferris's warehouse record for February.

Bingo. Ferris had called the switchboard of the Rockefeller on January eighth. One month later he'd called Blotnik's direct line.

Was that the signal my hindbrain had been sending? Somehow, the itch didn't feel scratched.

Then what?

Think.

It was like a mirage. The more I focused, the faster the allusion dissolved.

The hell with it.

I started to dial Ryan, stopped. He and Friedman were busy tailing Kaplan. A ringing phone could blow their cover. Or the phone would be off.

I tried Jake.

Still no answer.

Frustrated, I slammed the receiver.

Eleven-ten. Where the hell was he?

I tried returning to the records. My mind wouldn't focus.

I got up and paced the room, eyes wandering the desk, the window, the images woven into the rug. What story did those images tell?

What story would Max tell if he could speak?

Blotnik and Kaplan talked. Why? Had Kaplan called the IAA to squirrel out whatever he could on the skeleton? No, that would be for Ferris. Kaplan was only the middleman. Was Blotnik a potential buyer?

Was Jake unwell? Could he be lying unconscious on his bedroom floor?

Was he angry? Had he resented my comments about Blotnik more than he'd let on?

Was Jake correct in his assessment of Blotnik?

A terrible thought.

Was Blotnik more than ambitious? Was he dangerous?

I tried Jake again. Got the answering machine again.

"Bloody hell!"

Throwing on jeans and a Windbreaker, I grabbed Friedman's keys and hurried down the stairs.

Not a single window in Jake's flat was lit. The fog had thickened, all but obliterating the surrounding homes.

Terrific.

Leaving the car, I hurried across the street, wondering how I would gain entrance to Jake's property. Above the wall I could see treetops, their branches fuzzy claws against the night sky.

I needn't have worried. The gate was unlatched and slightly ajar.

Lucky break? Bad sign?

I pushed through.

In the yard, a single bulb threw a sickly yellow cone onto the goat pen. As I passed, I heard movement. Glancing sideways, I saw murky horned cutouts.

"Baaa," I whispered.

No response.

Animal odors joined the damp city smells. Feces. Sweat. Rotting lettuce and apple cores.

Jake's stairway was a thin black tunnel. Shadows linked to shadows, forming a rosary of shapes. The climb took an eternity. I kept looking backward.

At the door, I knocked softly.

"Jake?"

Why was I whispering?

"Jake," I called out, banging with the heel of my palm.

Three tries, no answer.

I turned the knob. The door swung in.

A tickle of fear.

First the gate, now the door. Would Jake have left the place unsecured?

Never, if he'd gone out. But did he lock up when at home? I couldn't recall.

I hesitated.

If Jake was home, why didn't he answer? Why hadn't he phoned me?

Images began free-falling in my head. Jake lying on the floor. Jake unconscious in bed.

Something touched my leg.

I jumped, and a hand flew to my mouth. Heart thudding, I looked down.

One of the toms stared up, eyes shiny globes in the dimness.

Before I could react, the door swung inward. Hinges creaked softly, and the cat was gone.

I peered through the gap. Across the room, I could see objects tossed beside the computer. Even in the dark, I knew what they were. Jake's sunglasses. Jake's wallet. Jake's passport.

And what they meant.

I pushed through the door. "Jake?"

I groped for a light switch, found none.

"Jake, are you here?"

Feeling my way through the darkness, I rounded the corner into the front room. I was searching the wall, when something crashed to my left.

As adrenaline fired through me, my fingers found the switch. Trembling, I flipped it, and the room filled with light.

The cat was on the kitchen counter, legs flexed, muscles tensed for flight. A vase lay shattered on the tile, rusty water oozing outward like blood from a corpse.

The cat dropped and sniffed the puddle.

"Jake!"

The cat's head jerked up, then it froze, one paw raised and curled. Eyeing me, it gave one tentative *mrrrp*.

"Where the hell's Jake?" I asked.

The cat clammed up like a cheat at a tax audit.

"Jake!"

Alarmed, the cat shot past me and exited the way it had entered.

Jake wasn't in his bedroom. Nor was he in the workroom.

My mind logged details as I flew through the flat.

Mug in the sink. Aspirin on the counter. Photos and reports cleared from the table. Otherwise, the place looked as it had when I left.

Had Jake taken the bones to Ruth Anne Bloom?

Hurrying to the back porch, I fumbled for a wall switch. When I found one and flipped it, nothing happened.

Frustrated, I returned to the kitchen and dug through drawers until I located a flashlight. Clicking it on, I returned to the porch.

The cabinet was at the far end. Where its doors met, I could see a black strip shooting from top to bottom. My heart clenched in my chest.

Gripping the flash over one shoulder, I crept forward. I smelled glue, and dust, and the mud of millennia. Outside my beam, shadows overlapped and forged odd shapes.

Six feet from the cabinet, I froze.

The padlock was gone, and one door hung askew. Bones or no bones, Jake would have secured the lock.

And the front gate.

I whipped around.

Blackness.

I could hear my own breath rising and falling in my mouth.

In two strides I closed the gap and illuminated the cabinet's interior. Shelf by shelf, I checked, dust twirling and revolving in the hard, white shaft.

The reconstructed ossuaries were there.

The fragments were there.

The shroud bones were gone.

37

HAD JAKE TAKEN THE BONES TO BLOOM?

Not a chance. He'd never have left the cabinet open, and he wouldn't have gone out with his passport and wallet still here, and the door unlocked.

Had the bones been stolen?

Over Jake's dead body.

Oh God. Had Jake been abducted? Worse?

Fear gives rise to a powerful rush of emotions. A stream of names tore through my head. The Hevrat Kadisha. Hershel Kaplan. Hossam al-Ahmed.

Tovya Blotnik!

A soft crunching sound penetrated my dread.

Footsteps on gravel?

Killing the light, I held my breath and listened.

Sleeve brushing jacket. Branch scraping stucco. Goat bleat drifting up from the yard.

Only benign sounds, nothing hostile.

Dropping to my knees, I searched for the padlock. It was nowhere to be seen.

I returned to the kitchen and replaced the flashlight. Closing the drawer, I noticed Jake's answering machine on the counter above. The flasher was blinking in clusters of ten.

I tallied my own calls to Jake. Eight, the first around five, the last just before leaving the hotel.

One of the other messages might hold a clue to his whereabouts.

Invade Jake's privacy?

Damn right. This looked to be a bad situation.

I hit "replay."

The first caller was, indeed, me.

The second message was left by a man speaking Hebrew. I caught the words Hevrat Kadisha, and *isha,* woman. Nothing else. Fortunately, the guy was brief. Hitting "replay," again and again, I transcribed phonetically.

The next caller was Ruth Anne Bloom. She left only her name and the fact that she was working late.

The last seven messages were again mine.

The machine clicked off.

What had I learned? Zilch.

Was Jake already gone when I first called? Had he ignored or not heard my message? Was he monitoring? Had he left after listening to the male caller? To Ruth Anne Bloom? Had he left of his own will?

I looked at the gibberish in my hand.

I looked at my watch. It was now past midnight. Whom to call?

Ryan answered on the first ring.

I told him where I was and what I'd learned.

Ryan's breathing revealed his annoyance at my having ventured out alone. I knew what was coming, and wasn't in the mood for a Q and A.

"Jake could be in trouble," I said.

"Hold on."

The next voice was Friedman's.

I explained what I wanted, and, one by one, pronounced the phonemes I'd written down. It took several tries, but Friedman's Hebrew finally mimicked the message on the tape.

The caller had been a member of the Hevrat Kadisha, phoning in answer to Jake's query.

Okay. I'd guessed that. The next part of Friedman's translation surprised me.

A number of the "harassing" calls had been made by a woman.

"That's it?"

"The caller wished your friend's hands to wither and fall off should he desecrate another grave."

A woman had been calling the Hevrat Kadisha?

I heard rustling as Friedman passed the phone back to Ryan.

"You know what I want you to do." Brusque.

"Yes," I said.

"You'll go back to the American Colony?"

"Yes." Eventually.

Ryan didn't buy it.

"But first?"

"Poke around here, see if I can scare up contact information for Jake's crew. I might find a list of those working this Talpiot site."

"And then?"

"Call them."

"And then?"

Adrenaline had my mind in overdrive. Ryan's paternalism wasn't gearing it down.

"Shoot out to Arafat's old compound, flash some leg, maybe score a date for Saturday night."

Ryan ignored that.

"If you go anywhere but the hotel, please call me."

"I will."

"I mean it."

"I'll call."

Silence. I broke it.

"What's Kaplan doing?"

"Working on Eagle Scout."

"Meaning?"

"Early to bed."

"You're sitting on him?"

"Yes. Look, Tempe. It's just possible Kaplan's not our shooter. If that's the case, someone else is."

"Okay. I won't go to Ramallah."

Ryan followed that with his standard.

"You can be a real pain in the ass, Brennan."

I followed with mine.

"I work on it."

When we'd disconnected, I hurried to Jake's office. My eyes were drawn to the objects beside the computer. My anxiety skyrocketed.

Jake's site was in the desert. He wouldn't go there without sunglasses. He wouldn't go anywhere without ID.

Car keys?

I began shuffling papers, poking through trays, opening and closing drawers.

No keys.

I checked the bedroom, the kitchen, the workroom.

No keys.

And no info on the crew. No list of names. No task rotation sheet. No ledger with check stubs. Zip.

Returning to the computer, I noticed a yellow Post-it poking from below the keyboard. I snatched it up.

Jake's scrawl. The name Esther Getz, and a phone number four digits off Blotnik's at the Rockefeller.

Sudden thought. Could the Getzster be the woman phoning the Hevrat Kadisha?

I hadn't a molecule of evidence to suggest that. Nothing. Unless you count gender. And what did calls to the Hevrat Kadisha have to do with anything anyway?

Okay. Jake had intended to see Getz or Bloom or both. Had he?

I stared at the number. Calling at this hour would be futile. Rude.

"Screw rude." I wanted Bloom to know I was looking for Jake.

Four rings. Voice mail. Message.

I stood a moment, fingers locked on the receiver.

Getz?

Why not?

Voice mail. Message.

Now what? Who else to ring?

I knew the calls were pointless, but I was frustrated and had no better ideas.

Again, the flashing cursor from my id. There. Gone. There. Gone.

Indicating what? When nothing is making sense, I often repeat known facts over and over in the hope that a pattern may emerge.

Think.

Masada skeleton. Stolen.

Shroud bones. Missing.

Jake. Missing.

Courtney Purviance. Missing.

Avram Ferris. Dead.

Sylvain Morissonneau. Dead.

Hershel Kaplan. Solicited for a hit. By a woman. Maybe. Now in Israel. Was trying to sell bones?

My hotel room trashed.

My car followed.

Ferris-Kaplan-Blotnik telephone calls.

Ruth Anne Bloom. I don't trust her. Why? Jake's early-on admonitions not to contact the IAA?

Tovya Blotnik. Jake doesn't trust him.

Cave 2001 bones linked to Kidron tomb bones.

Was there a pattern?

Yeah. Everything led back to Max.

Why the itchy id? Was there a piece that didn't fit?

If so, I wasn't seeing it.

My gaze wandered to a snapshot above the monitor. Jake, smiling, holding a stone vessel in one hand.

My mind looped.

Jake. Missing.

I dialed another number. I was stunned when a voice answered.

"I'm here." Muffled, as though spoken into a hand-cupped mouthpiece.

I identified myself.

"The American?" Surprised.

"I'm sorry to call at this hour, Dr. Blotnik."

"I—I'm working late." Off-balance. Mine was not the voice Blotnik expected to hear. "It's my habit."

I remembered my first call to the IAA. Blotnik sure wasn't working late that night.

I skipped the niceties.

"Have you seen Jake Drum today?"

"No."

"Ruth Anne Bloom?"

"Ruth Anne?"

"Yes."

"Ruth Anne has gone up north to Galilee."

Bloom had left Jake a message saying she was working late. Working late where? At home? At the Rockefeller? At a lab elsewhere? Had she changed her plans? Was she lying? Was Blotnik lying? Had Blotnik merely misunderstood?

I made a quick decision.

"I need to talk to you."

"Tonight?"

"Now."

"That's impossible. I'm—" Blotnik was clearly rattled.

"I'll be there in thirty minutes. Wait for me."

I didn't listen to Blotnik's reply.

In the car, I thought of Ryan. I should have called and given my destination, but I hadn't thought to do it before leaving, and I had no cell phone. Maybe I could call from Blotnik's.

It was a night of open gates.

I should have seen that as an omen. Instead, I assumed Blotnik had anticipated my arrival.

Driving into the compound, I circled to the front courtyard and hurried down the driveway on foot. The fog was giving way to mist. The air smelled of turned earth and flowers and dead leaves.

The Rockefeller loomed like a giant black fortress, its edges merging with the velvety night. Rounding one corner, I glanced out the gate I'd just entered.

Across the way, the Old City slumbered, a place of dark and quiet stones. Gone were the delivery boys and housewives and schoolgirls and shoppers shouldering one another on the narrow streets. As I watched, a car turned from Sultan Suleiman onto Derech Jericho, its headlights white cones sweeping the haze.

I cut to the side door, an entrance used only by museum personnel. Like the gate, it was unlocked. Putting a shoulder to the wood, I pushed, and entered.

An ancient overhead fixture bathed the small vestibule in ocher. Ahead, a short corridor ended at doors giving onto exhibit halls. To the right, an iron-scrolled staircase curved upward, a backstage portal to the staff offices Jake and I had entered from the museum's interior.

I spotted a phone on a wooden shelf beside the exhibit hall doors.

Crossing to it, I lifted the receiver. The dial tone sounded like a French horn in the night-empty building.

I dialed Ryan. No answer. Was Kaplan on the move? I left a message.

Deep breath, then I climbed, hand on the rail, weight on the balls of my feet. At the top, I turned and headed down the long corridor, footsteps clicking off walls and floor.

A single wall sconce saved the hall from total darkness. To my right, handrailed balconies overlooking first-floor halls. To my left, arch-shaped recesses, all but one disappearing into inky darkness. Ahead, the access Jake and I had used on our visit to Getz.

The fourth alcove appeared softly luminous. On entering, I saw why. Pale yellow light seeped from cracks framing Blotnik's door.

So did voices, barely audible, but sounding serene enough.

It was 1 A.M. Who in God's name could be here with Blotnik? Jake? Bloom? Getz?

I crossed the alcove and knocked softly.

The voices didn't falter.

I knocked again, harder.

Not a hitch in the conversation.

"Dr. Blotnik?"

The men kept talking. Were they men?

Leaning in, I put my ear to the door.

"Dr. Blotnik?" Louder. "Are you there?"

Funny how your mind takes snapshots. I can still see the knob, old and going green. I can still feel the coolness of the brass on my palm.

The id's lightning-quick, conjuring maps while the senses are still GPS'ing landmarks.

The hinges creaked as the door swung in.

The voices. The smell.

Some part of my brain charted.

Without knowing, I knew.

38

Reality intake. Data bytes racing into my ears, nose, eyes.

Metered talk. BBC voices. Radio on a credenza beside Blotnik's desk.

Hint of cordite in the air. Something else. Coppery. Salty.

The small hairs rose on my neck and arms. My eyes jumped to the desktop.

A banker's lamp emitting an eerie green glow. Stacked papers sheared across the blotter. Scattered books, pens. An upended pot, broken in two, the small cactus still rooted in the uncontained soil.

Blotnik's chair was swiveled at an odd angle. Though the overheads were off, behind and above I could see blood droplets, as though the wall had been mortally wounded.

High-velocity spatter!

Dear God. Who'd been shot? Jake? Blotnik?

I didn't want to see.

I had to see.

Stepping softly to the desk, I peeked behind.

No corpse.

Relief? Confusion?

To the right rear, I noticed a closet. A dim radiance spilled between the door and jamb.

Edging past the desk, I crossed and pushed with my fingertips.

More image assimilation. Dark wood, smooth from generations of too much varnish.

Metal shelving stacked with office supplies, boxes, and labeled containers. Weak light coming from an ell ahead and to the left.

I inched forward, one hand trailing the edge of a shelf.

Five steps in, my foot slid on something sticky and wet.

I looked down.

A dark rivulet was snaking around the corner of the ell.

Like the screech before the crash. The shadow before the hawk strike. The mental alarm sounded. I was too late.

Too late for whom?

I forced my legs to make the turn.

Blotnik lay on his belly, blood-soaked yarmulke driven into a hole in his skull. There was another wound in his back, and another in his shoulder. Blood was congealing in the puddle haloing his body, and in the tributaries oozing from it.

My hand flew to my mouth. I felt woozy, almost sick.

I slumped to the wall, one phrase winging through my head.

Not Jake. Not Jake. Tell me you didn't do this, Jake.

Then who? Ultra-Orthodox radicals? Christian fanatics? Islamic fundamentalists?

One second. Five. Ten.

My senses returned.

Skirting the blood, I squatted and placed fingers on Blotnik's neck. No pulse. The skin felt cool, not cold.

Blotnik hadn't been dead long. Of course not. I knew that. I'd spoken to him less than an hour ago.

Was the killer still here?

Stumbling back to the office, I grabbed up the phone.

No dial tone.

My eyes traveled the cord. Three inches from the mouthpiece, it ended cleanly.

High-voltage fear.

My gaze danced the desktop, fell on a paper.

Why that one?

It was centered on the blotter, square and neat. Despite the chaos. Below the chaos.

Before the chaos?

Had Blotnik been reading it? Might it lead me to Jake?

Crime scene! Don't touch! my left brain hollered.

Find Jake! My right brain countered.

I wiggled the paper free. It was Getz's report on the shroud. Addressed to Jake.

Should Blotnik have had Getz's report? Had he filched it from Getz's office? Or were such reports routinely routed to him? Getz worked for the Rockefeller, not for the IAA. Wasn't that why Jake had gone to her though he'd refused to talk to Blotnik?

Or *did* Getz work for the museum? She'd offered to take possession of the shroud for the IAA. Was she actually on Blotnik's staff? Did she work for the Rockefeller *and* the IAA? I'd never asked Jake to clarify.

Was Getz somehow in collusion with Blotnik? Did it involve the shroud bones? But Jake hadn't told Getz about the shroud bones. Or had he? Getz's name and number were on the Post-it in Jake's office. Had they spoken since we'd left her the shroud?

Jake hated Blotnik. He would never have given him the report.

A terrible thought.

Someone had stolen the shroud bones. Suspecting Blotnik, Jake had stormed over here to demand their return. Jake owned a gun. Had things gotten out of hand? Had he killed Blotnik in a rage?

I skimmed the report. Two words leaped out. "Skeletal remains."

I read the paragraph. Getz had found microscopic bone embedded in the shroud. Her report suggested larger skeletal remains might exist.

Blotnik knew!

I quick-scanned the office. No shroud bones. I was checking the closet when I heard a soft creak.

My breath froze in my throat.

The door hinge!

Someone was in Blotnik's office!

Footsteps crossed the office floor. Papers rustled. More footsteps. At the credenza?

Without thinking, I skittered backward toward the ell.

One shoe hit the pooled blood and shot sideways. I pitched forward.

Instinct took control. I threw out my hands, clawing for a lifeline. My fingers closed on a metal upright.

The shelving wobbled.

Time fractured.

A bundle of paper hand towels teetered then tumbled to the floor.

Whump.

Sudden silence in the office.

Total silence in the closet.

Predator and prey sniffed the air.

Then, hurried footsteps.

Departing?

Relief.

Then fear, like a fist pressing my chest.

The footsteps were moving in my direction.

I crouched, paralyzed, maxed to every sound.

My mind hiccupped some forgotten caveat.

Never yield the advantage of lighting.

Blotnik's visitor could see me better than I could see him.

Grabbing a book, I twisted and aimed at the fixture behind me. The bulb shattered, raining glass onto Blotnik's body.

A silhouette filled the doorway, lumpy bag hanging from its left shoulder, right arm flexed, pointing a dark object from chest level. A brimmed cap shadowed the face so I couldn't make out the features.

Throat-clearing, then, "*Mi sham?*" Who's there?

The voice was female.

I held rigid.

The woman cleared her throat again and tried Arabic.

In the office, a tinny voice announced the BBC news.

The woman retreated one step. In the emerald backlighting I could see she wore boots, jeans, and a khaki shirt. Her armpits were stained. One blonde tendril looped from the side of her cap.

The woman was heavy, and way too short to be Getz. And blonde.

Ruth Anne Bloom?

I felt sweat on my face. Cold heat in my chest. Had this woman killed Blotnik? Would she kill me?

One thought rose up from the base of my brain.

Stall!

"Who are you?"

"I'm asking the questions." The woman answered my English with English.

It wasn't Ruth Anne Bloom. Bloom's English was heavily accented.

I didn't reply.

"Answer me. Or you're in the frame for a lot of hurt." Hard. But agitated. Unsure.

"Who I am doesn't matter."

"I'll decide what matters." Louder. A threat of violence.

"Dr. Blotnik's dead."

"And I'll park some rounds in your ass just as quick."

Cop talk? Was this woman on the job? Or one of the millions watching too much TV?

Before I could respond, she spoke again.

"Wait a minute. I know that accent. I know you."

And I'd heard *her* voice. But when? Where? Had we crossed paths here? At the hotel? The museum? Police headquarters? I hadn't met many women in Israel.

Sudden thought. The caller to Jake's flat had talked of a woman pestering the Hevrat Kadisha.

A number of the "harassing" calls had been made by a woman.

Could this be the woman? Did she have her own agenda for Max? Had she stolen the shroud bones?

I had no idea as to motive. She spoke English, Hebrew, and Arabic. Was she Christian? Jewish? Muslim?

"Confiscating bones in the name of the Lord?" I threw out.

No response.

"Question is, which Lord?"

"Oh, please."

Wet sniffing. The woman's free hand darted to her face.

I wasn't sure how to probe.

"I know about the Masada skeleton."

"You don't know jack." Sniff. "On your feet."

I rose.

"Reach and grab your skull."

I rose and laced my fingers on top of my head. Senses buzzing, I tried a new line of questioning.

"Why kill Blotnik?"

"Collateral damage."

Ferris? Why not?

"Why shoot Ferris?"

The woman stiffened. "I don't have time for this."

Sensing I'd struck a chord, I dug deeper.

"Two bullets to the brain. That's cold."

"Shut up!" The woman sniffed, cleared her throat.

"You should have seen what the cats did to him."

"Stinking little bastards."

When things fall into place, they often do so rapidly.

I can't say what my senses took in. The cadence of her speech. The nasal drip. The blonde hair. The trilingualism. The fact that this woman knew me. Knew the cats.

Suddenly, disparate facts toggled.

The bad police dialogue.

A Law & Order *rerun. Briscoe telling a suspect he didn't know jack.*

A woman hired Hersh Kaplan to kill Avram Ferris.

Kaplan said she sounded like a cokehead.

The sniffing. The throat-clearing.

"I have sinus problems."

Kaplan was phoned from the Mirabel warehouse the week the boss was vacationing with Miriam.

"So someone phoned Kaplan's home from Ferris's warehouse while Ferris was in Florida. But Kaplan hadn't phoned the warehouse, either from his home or his shop, making it unlikely that Purviance was calling Kaplan in response to a message he'd left for Ferris. So who the hell made the call? And why?"

Ferris was shot with a Jericho nine-millimeter semiautomatic. That gun was reported stolen by a man named Ozols. In Saint-Léonard.

"That's 'oak' in Latvian. We've got an international arborist convention, right here in Saint-Léonard."

Ozols. Oak. The Latvian name I'd seen in a lobby in Saint-Léonard.

The lobby of Courtney Purviance's building.

"And here's another interesting development. Courtney Purviance is in the wind."

My subconscious blossomed into a full-color map.

Courtney Purviance had killed Avram Ferris. She hadn't been abducted. She was standing in the doorway, pointing a gun at my chest.

Of course. Purviance knew the warehouse and its contents. Probably knew about Max. Travel to Israel was a regular part of her job. Flying here was routine.

But why kill Ferris? Blotnik?

Religious conviction? Greed? Some deranged personal vendetta?

Would she kill me with equal callousness?

I felt a rush of fear, then anger, then an almost trancelike calm. I would have to talk my way out. There was no getting past the gun.

"What happened, Courtney? Ferris didn't cut you in for a big enough piece of the pie?"

The gun dipped, then the muzzle straightened.

"Or did you just want more?"

"Zip it."

"Did you have to steal another gun?"

Again, Purviance tensed.

"Or is it easier to score a piece in Israel?"

"I'm warning you."

"Poor old Mr. Ozols. That wasn't a nice thing to do to a neighbor."

"Why are you here? Why did you have to get involved in this?"

I could see Purviance's finger stroking the trigger. She was nervous. I decided to bluff.

"I'm with the SQ."

"Move." The gun waggled me forward. "Easy."

I took two steps. As I approached, Purviance backed off.

We sized each other up in the dim green glow.

"Yeah. You came to my house with that crime dick."

"The cops are liking you for the Ferris hit." I went with Purviance's Hollywood cop talk.

"And you're one of them." Sarcastic.

"You're a collar."

"Really?" Sniff. "And there's a whole squad waiting for your call or they'll storm this museum."

She'd read my bluff. Okay. I stayed with the station-house lingo, but tried a new tack.

"Ask me? You're getting a bum rap. Ferris was hawking merchandise he shouldn't have been. God be damned. History be damned. Bring on the bucks."

Purviance wet her lips, but didn't speak.

"You got wise, right? Told him not to wholesale those bones. At least not without cutting you in. He blew you off."

The conflict inside her played out in her features. Purviance was angry and hurt. And jumpy as hell. A bad combination.

"Who are we to lip the boss? We're just the secretary. The maid. The chick who irons his shorts. Prick probably treated you like a field hand."

"That's not how it was."

I pushed.

"That Ferris was one stone-cold bastard."

"Avram was a good man."

"Yeah. And Hitler liked dogs."

"Avram loved me." Blurted.

Something else clicked for me.

Purviance lived alone. All those calls from the Mirabel warehouse to her home. Ferris and Purviance weren't just coworkers. They were lovers.

"He had it coming. Bastard was running a game on you. Probably fed you the old saw about leaving his old lady."

"Avram loved me." Repeated. "He knew I was ten times smarter than that cow of a wife."

"That why he snuck south with ole Miriam? You're not dumb. You figured out he was never leaving her."

"She didn't love him." Bitter. "He was just too weak to deal with it."

"Strike one. Miriam's doing Coppertone while you're stuck in your cold-weather flat. You're his favorite squeeze, but who's left behind to answer the phones? And the cheap son of a bitch won't even cut you in on the skeleton."

Purviance wiped her nose on the back of the gun hand.

"Then, strike two. Kaplan screwed you over. First your lover, then your hit man. You were having a bad run."

Purviance jerked the gun so the muzzle was now on my face. Easy. Don't antagonize her.

"Ferris owed you. Kaplan owed you. You knew that skeleton would put you bucks up. Why not take it?"

"Why not." Defiant.

"Then the bones disappeared. Strike three. Screwed again."

"Shut up."

"You come all the way to Israel to steal them back. No bones found. Strike four. Screwed again."

"Screwed? I think this will do."

Purviance tapped her bag. I heard the hollow thunk of a plastic container.

"Gutsy. You already capped the boss. Why not Blotnik?"

"Blotnik was a thief."

"Saved you all that nuisance of breaking and entering."

A smile crawled Purviance's face. "I hadn't a clue about these bones until Blotnik blabbed. Old fool hadn't had them two hours."

"How did he know about them?"

"Some old bat found fragments while scoping the shroud they'd been in. What the hell." Purviance again tapped the bag. "This could be crap. Or it could be the Holy Grail. This time I'm taking no chances."

"What did you offer Blotnik? Did he think you had the Masada skeleton?"

Again the cold smile. "Just conning the con man."

She'd killed Blotnik, snatched the shroud bones, and gotten away. What was she doing back here?

"You were moving under the radar. Why double back?"

"We both know a relic's worth zip without paper."

We heard it at the same instant. The soft squeak of a rubber sole.

Purviance's trigger finger twitched. She hesitated, undecided.

"Move!" she hissed.

I stepped back into the closet, eyes focused on Purviance's gun.

The closet door slammed. A bolt clicked.

Hurried footsteps, then silence.

I put my ear to the wood.

A sound like surf, overridden by the drone of a radio commentator.

Stay quiet? Draw attention?

What the hell.

I pounded.

I called out.

Seconds later the office door slammed inward against a wall.

Heart plowing, I shrank deeper back toward the ell.

A strip of light under the closet door.

Rubber soles.

The bolt clicked open.

The door swung in.

39

I'D NEVER BEEN SO GLAD TO SEE ANYONE IN MY LIFE.

"What the hell are you doing here?" Jake's tone was all shock.

"Did you see her?"

"Who?"

"Purviance."

"Who's Purviance?"

"Never mind." I pushed past him and grabbed an arm. "We've got to stop her."

I tugged. We both ran.

"She's got no more than a three-minute lead."

Out the office. Down the hall.

"Who's Purviance?"

"The lady with your shroud bones."

Gripping the rail, I took three stairs at a time. Jake stayed with me.

"You drove?" I threw over my shoulder.

"I've got the crew truck. Tempe—"

"Where?" I was breathing hard.

"In the drive."

As we flew out the door, a car blew past, driver's head barely clearing the wheel.

"That's her," I panted.

The car shot the gate.

"Move!"

Yanking the doors, Jake and I threw ourselves into the truck.

Jake turned the key and flooded the engine. It roared in neutral. Jake threw the gearshift, then tacked a triangle of short turns.

As we came about, Purviance's car was disappearing from the foot of the drive.

"She's turned left onto Sultan Suleiman."

Jake jammed the gas. Our tires spit gravel and we rocketed forward.

"What's she driving?"

"Citroën C-3, I think. I only got a quick look."

We plunged downhill. Across the way, the Old City was swallowed in mist.

Barely braking, Jake jerked the wheel hard left. I lurched right and my shoulder slammed the window.

Up ahead, the Citroën's taillights were again hooking left.

Jake pounded the accelerator.

I reached back, tugged and clicked my seat belt.

Jake made the turn onto Derech Jericho.

The Citroën had lengthened its lead. Its taillights were now two tiny red blurs.

"Where's she going?"

"We're on HaEgoz at this point, but behind us it's called the Jericho road. She could be heading to Jericho. Hell, she could be heading to Jordan."

Few cars moved along the pavement. Fog swirled the streetlights.

Purviance kicked it to fifty.

Jake stayed with her.

Purviance kicked it to sixty.

"Hang on."

I placed two hands on the dash.

Jake floored it. The gap closed.

The air in the truck felt damp and close. Mist filmed the windshield.

Jake hit the wipers. I cracked a window.

Lights flicked by on both sides of the street. Apartments? Garages? Nightclubs? Synagogues? The buildings were black LEGO blobs. I wasn't sure where we were.

A tower took shape on my right, neon logo shimmying in the haze. The Hyatt. We were about to intersect the Nablus Road.

Purviance made the turn.

"She's heading north," I said. Nervous talk. Jake knew that.

The traffic signal went red. Ignoring it, Jake spun the wheel. We fishtailed. Jake muscled the back wheels into line with the front.

The Citroën's taillights had shrunk to dots. Purviance had picked up a quarter-mile lead.

My heart was doing flip-flops. My palms felt damp on the dash.

Now and then a billboard framed into view, faded. We raced on.

Suddenly signs flared out of the fog. MA'ALEH ADUMIN. JERICHO. DEAD SEA.

"She's heading for Highway One." Jake's voice was guy-wire taut.

Something was up. The Citroën's taillights were now expanding.

"She's slowing down," I said.

"Checkpoint."

"Will they stop her?"

"This one's usually a wave-through."

Jake was right. After a brief pause, the Citroën blew past the guardhouse.

"Shall we tell them to stop her?"

"Not a chance."

"They could pull her over."

"These guys are border patrol, not police."

Jake braked. The truck slowed.

"Let's ask—"

"No."

"This is a mistake."

"Don't say a word."

We rolled to a stop. The guard looked us over, bored, then waved us through. Before I could speak, Jake hit the gas.

A sudden thought.

Back at the museum, Jake never asked about Blotnik.

I hadn't given him time?

He already knew that Blotnik was dead?

I looked sideways. Jake was a black silhouette, long neck corrugated by the bony tube of his throat.

Sweet Jesus. Did Jake have an agenda of his own?

Jake accelerated hard. The truck lurched forward.

My palms slapped the dash.

The terrain turned desolate. My world narrowed to the two red blurs at the Citroën's rear.

Purviance goosed it to seventy, then eighty.

We ran hard through desert older than time. I knew what stretched to either side of the highway. Terra-cotta hills, furnaced valleys, Bedouin camps with their shoddy huts and slumbering herds. The Judean wilderness. A moonscape of bleaching bones and seeping sand, tonight all lost to the fog.

Mile after mile of stillness. Nothingness. Now and then a rare lamp bathed the Citroën in artificial light. Seconds later, our truck would blink through. I'd see my hands, salmon surreal, bracing the dash.

Purviance edged toward ninety. Jake matched her.

The Citroën rounded curve after curve, taillights winking into our vision, then out, then in again. Our truck strained. We began to drop back.

The tension in the cab was palpable. No one spoke as each of us focused on those pulsing red eyes.

We hit a bump. Jake downshifted. The front wheels went airborne. The rear followed. My head whiplashed as the truck slammed down.

When I looked up, the Citroën's taillights were disappearing in mist.

Shifting back into fourth, Jake gunned it. The lights ballooned. I stole a peek in the side-view. No one behind us.

In my memory, what happened next happened in slow motion, like an instant replay. In reality, the whole thing probably took a minute and a half.

The Citroën entered a curve. We followed. I remember glistening blacktop. The needle nearing ninety. Jake's hands, tight on the wheel.

A car appeared on the other side of the highway, headlights blurry ribbons slashing the mist. The ribbons wavered, then swooned toward the Citroën.

Purviance jerked the wheel. The Citroën pitched right, dropped two tires onto the shoulder. Purviance jerked again. The Citroën hopped back up onto the pavement.

The oncoming car crossed the center lane, illuminating the Citroën. I could see Purviance's head wagging back and forth as she fought the wheel. Steady red told me her foot was slammed to the brake.

The oncoming car veered wide, away from the Citroën. Action and reaction. The Citroën also veered wide, and again bit gravel.

Purviance cut hard to the left and regained the blacktop. Inexplicably, the car then surged back to the right. The Citroën bounced from the road, and careened off the guardrail. Sparks flew.

Panicked, Purviance fought to go left. The Citroën hit slickness, hydroplaned, and spun.

The oncoming car was now hurtling toward us, tires straddling both lanes. I could see the driver's head. I could see a passenger.

I braced for the impact.

Jake jerked the wheel. We shot right and our front tire dropped.

The car thundered past.

Our rear tire dropped.

Jake's leg pumped, his hands death-locked the wheel.

We bolted and pitched, stones and gravel peppering the guardrail.

I planted both hands against the dash and tried to keep my elbows flexed. I dropped my chin to my chest.

I heard metal slam metal.

I looked up to see the Citroën's headlights lurch sideways. They hung a moment, then nose-dived into darkness.

I heard an eruption of metal, sand, and dirt. Another. A wailing horn. Steady. Terrible.

Our speed choked back. The guardrail clicked past slower and slower.

The truck had barely stopped when Jake flipped open his cell phone.

"Shit."

"No signal?"

"Piece of crap." Jake tossed the phone on the dash and jabbed at the glove box. "Flashlights."

While I found Mag-Lites, Jake dug flares from the back of the truck. Together, we sprinted up the tarmac.

The guardrail gaped jagged and curled. We peered past, down the hill. The fog was a dense ocean, swallowing our beams.

As Jake set flares, I hopped the barrier and scrambled down the slope.

In the basin, my light picked out a trail of shapes. A hubcap. A side panel. A side-view mirror.

The Citroën was a pitch-black hump in the darkness. I probed it with the Mag-Lite.

The car had impacted, flipped, and landed on its roof. Every window was shattered. Steam or smoke hissed from under the crumpled hood.

Purviance was half in, half out the driver's-side door, twisted like a rag doll tossed to the floor. So much blood smeared her face I couldn't see skin. Her jacket was saturated.

I heard crunching, then Jake was beside me.

"Jesus Christ!"

"We've got to get her out," I said.

Together, Jake and I tried to ease Purviance free. Her body was slick with mist and blood. We kept losing our grip.

Above, a truck braked to a stop. Two men got out and started shouting questions. We ignored them, concentrated on Purviance.

Jake and I changed sides. Nothing worked. We couldn't get a good angle.

Purviance moaned softly. I grabbed my light and ran the beam the length of her body. Flecks of glass glistened on her clothing and in her blood-soaked hair.

"One foot's wedged among the pedals," I said. "I'll go in through the other side."

"No way."

I didn't wait to argue. Circling the Citroën, I sized up what remained of the passenger window. Big enough.

I dropped my light, doubled over, and squeezed through head-first. Pulling with my elbows, I wriggled to the driver's side.

Groping like a blind man, I determined I was right. One of Purviance's feet was broken and jammed behind the brake.

Using outstretched arms, I tried gentle twisting. The foot remained lodged. I shoved harder. No go.

An acrid smell was irritating my nose. My eyes were watering.

Burning rubber!

My heart thudded my rib cage.

Bellying closer, I dropped my upper body over the seat, yanked the zipper of Purviance's boot, grabbed the heel, and tugged.

I felt some give.

Another hard pull and Purviance's heel was loose. Using my fingers, I shoehorned her foot.

"Now!" I screamed when the toes slid free.

As Jake tugged, I wormed the foot through the pedals. Then I muscled back-ass out the window.

Smoke was pouring from the engine.

Voices were shouting from the highway. I didn't need a translator.

"Get back!"

"It's going to blow!"

Circling the Citroën, I grabbed Purviance under one arm. Jake had the other. Together we tugged her free and eased her to the ground.

Jake dived for the car.

"We've got to get clear!"

Jake was enveloped in smoke. I could see his lanky form darting forward and back.

"Jake!"

Jake was a madman, racing from one shattered window to the next.

"I can't do this alone!"

Jake left the car and helped me drag Purviance another five yards. Then he raced back to the Citroën and began kicking its trunk.

"It's going to blow!" I was screaming now.

Jake's foot pistoned again and again.

Something popped. The hissing grew louder, the smoke thickened.

Were we still in range? A powerful blast would turn auto parts into deadly missiles.

Grabbing Purviance by her upper arms, I turned and began inching backward. Her body was dead weight. Was she already gone? Was I doing her more harm than good?

Foot by foot I dragged.

Three yards.

My hands grew slippery with blood. My palms and fingers were cut by millions of glass slivers.

Five.

Sirens whined in the distance.

My fingers tingled. My legs were dead. But I was hyped on adrenaline. Some fierce internal energy pushed me on.

Finally I decided I was far enough. I allowed Purviance to settle to the ground. Dropping to my knees, I felt her throat.

A weak pulse? I couldn't be sure.

Ripping Purviance's jacket. I searched for the wound that was pumping out blood. A black crescent slashed her belly. I pressed a palm to it.

At that moment, a blast tore the night. I heard the awful sound of metal shearing metal.

As my head snapped up the Citroën exploded in a ball of light. Fire burst from the engine, strobing white geysers into the blue-black fog.

Dear God! Where was Jake?

I ran toward the Citroën.

Twenty feet out the heat stopped me like a wall. I threw up an arm.

"Jake!"

The car was an inferno. Flames licked its underbelly and leaped from its windows. No sign of Jake.

"Jake!"

I felt ash and sweat on my face. Mist. Tears streaming down my cheeks.

"Jake!"

A second depth charge blew metal and flames into the sky.

A sob rose in my throat.

Hands gripped my shoulders.

I was yanked roughly back.

40

I'LL TELL YOU RIGHT OUT THE GATE. EVERYONE SURVIVED.

Change that. Everyone survived but the guy in the shroud. He went from being bone to being bone ash.

Jake burned his hands and singed his brows. No big deal.

Purviance lost a lot of blood and fractured some ribs and a foot. Her spleen was removed in pieces, and she'd need hardware in the ankle. But she'd recover. And serve time.

The Citroën would not recover. Its remains were barely worth hauling for scrap.

Purviance was unconscious for a day, then the story dribbled out.

Slowly. As Ryan suggested variations based on info from Kaplan and Birch.

My mental mapping was spot-on. Ferris and Purviance had been an item. Birch found the usual at her apartment in Saint-Léonard. Man's robe in the closet. Extra Bic and Oral-B in the medicine chest.

The affair started shortly after Purviance began working for Les Imports Ashkenazim. As the years passed, she increased the pressure on Ferris to divorce Miriam. He kept putting her off. She also increased her hold on the business.

Purviance was familiar with operations at the warehouse. Read: she knew everything and was involved in everything. She overheard Ferris's call to Kaplan asking him to middleman the Masada skeleton. She overheard his conversations with Father Morissonneau and Tovya

Blotnik, and learned of the skeleton's history. She resented Ferris's working this deal on his own and freezing her out.

Not long before, she'd overheard Ferris's conversations with the travel agent. Ferris was planning to vacation in sunny Florida with his wife. It was the last straw. Ferris was working a score without her and was trying to rebuild his marriage. Purviance confronted her lover about his priorities.

Tired of guilt, or tired of the stress of maintaining the balancing act, Ferris decided to cut Purviance loose. Les Imports Ashkenazim had hit a rough patch, but, all in all, was doing well. His relationship with Miriam was improving. He didn't need Purviance. Sure, the business was riding some economic bumps, but the sale of the skeleton would take care of that. It would be better if he fired Purviance. Ferris promised her six months' severance pay, and told her to clear out.

The first call to Boca during beach week had been Purviance begging Ferris to reconsider. Ferris curtly cut her off. She'd really, truly been dumped. She was without lover and without job.

The second call to Boca was Purviance delivering a threat. She was wise to the skeleton and its value. She wanted a piece of the action or she'd enlighten Miriam about their affair and inform the authorities about the skeleton. Ferris laughed at her.

The more Purviance thought about it, the angrier she became. She'd built Ferris's business. She'd taken him to bed. And now she was being tossed like last week's garbage. Ratting him out to wife and cops would harm him but gain her nothing. And it wouldn't harm him enough. Ferris would have to pay a much bigger price. Primed on *CSI*, *Law & Order*, and *NYPD Blue*, Purviance decided to hire a hit man. Dispose of Ferris and take control of the business.

Nice Jewish girl, totally unconnected. She didn't know any hit men. Who you gonna call? Kaplan was an ex-con who did illegal work. Purviance had his number from the caller ID on the warehouse phone.

Kaplan was a felon, all right, but not a killer. He saw a real pigeon and a profit opportunity. He took Purviance's money and provided no services.

Scorned lover. Discarded business associate. Duped consumer. Purviance was seething. Driven by an obsessive rage, she decided to act. Knowing her neighbor kept a gun in his car, she stole it and killed Ferris herself.

Her fury, however, obstructed her strategic thinking. After putting two bullets into Ferris, Purviance wrapped the Jericho in his fingers and fired overhead. More TV cop show savoir faire. With a self-inflicted gunshot wound, the doc finds trace on the hand. Only, Purviance made a major blunder. She left the weapon, but collected the bullet casings, eliminating any chance of a ruling of suicide.

In the end, SIJ found a bullet fragment in the closet, created during the keyhole entry into Ferris's skull. Another bullet was dug from a wall in an outer hallway. With the earlier bullet from the closet ceiling, and the fragments recovered from Ferris's head, that demonstrated three shots. A ballistic reconstruction suggested Ferris was hit while facing the door. He was probably oblivious to Purviance's homicidal intent when she entered the closet and circled behind him.

What next for Courtney? She had quite surprised herself with her coolness in dispatching Ferris. Now to score two for one. Get out of Dodge, and recoup economic losses. Purviance booked it for Israel, using the name Channah Purviance, the pre-Canadian version on her Tunisian passport. The discrepancy allowed her to slip under the radar.

Knowing Ferris had phoned Blotnik, Purviance dropped in at the IAA, claiming to represent her boss and wanting to firm up the method of payment. More injustice awaited her. Blotnik hadn't received the Masada skeleton. Purviance bluffed, saying she knew who'd taken it. She could deliver if Blotnik had money or something of value to trade. Blotnik showed her the shroud bones. Agreeing that these had significant cash potential, Purviance struck again, and bagged the new bones.

Kaplan's story was simple. Miriam Ferris had always been kind, a friend even while he was serving time. Miriam sent him chocolates. Wrote him letters. The note we'd found in Kaplan's apartment was just one of many encouraging him to keep the faith.

Kaplan knew from Purviance about her affair with Ferris. It had been his first question when she'd contacted him to kill her boss. In their negotiations, Kaplan came to believe Purviance was treacherous and without conscience. If cornered, he figured she'd throw up a smoke screen to save herself. Who more vulnerable than the betrayed wife? Fearing Purviance might point the finger at Miriam, Kaplan slipped me the photo of Max to steer the inquiry in another direction.

Kaplan also feared Purviance might implicate him. Or worse. She'd planned to have her lover killed. If she swung into action herself, why not also off the weasel who'd scammed her three grand? And Kaplan's buddy Litvak was pissed because Kaplan had promised the Masada skeleton and then defaulted. Like Purviance, Kaplan saw the opportunity for a twofer. Make yourself scarce locally and mend fences in Israel. He, too, booked it.

Why had Blotnik stolen the shroud bones? On that one Jake was probably right.

Blotnik had been a prodigy in his grad school days in New York. Articles in prestigious journals even before completion of the Ph.D. Then the opus, three hundred pages on *Ecclesiastes Rabbah,* a rabbinic commentary from the Talmudic era. Job offers flowed like wine at Cana. Blotnik moved to Israel, married, scored permit after permit to dig coveted sites. The world was his.

A junior colleague also decided to be his. Giddy while it lasted, the affair ended badly. Blotnik's wife left him. His lover left him.

Maybe it was embarrassment. Maybe loneliness. Maybe depression. After the divorce, Blotnik largely disengaged. He organized a few excavations, published a few articles. A thin work on the ancient baths of Hammat-Gader. Then, two decades of nothing.

Ferris's call must have come like manna from heaven. Masada bones missing for over four decades? During his many years in Israeli archaeology, Blotnik had heard rumors of such a skeleton. One can only speculate what else Kaplan or Ferris told him, or what had been whispered among his colleagues. The bones were those of an important figure in first-century Roman Palestine? A biblical VIP? Blotnik must have seen his future light up like a Hollywood marquee.

Then the manna was pulled back by the death of Ferris. Lights out. Not long after, I phoned. I had the Masada skeleton. A new dawn! Cue the credits!

Seeing a way to supercharge his flagging career, or supercharge his bank account, as Ryan believed, Blotnik had researched the Masada skeleton and Cave 2001. Then Max was, again, snatched from him. Jake and I came to say the skeleton had been stolen. Blotnik was despondent. His potential comeback had fizzled. Like Purviance, the boy genius handled disappointment poorly, and was in a foul mood.

Then, more manna. A document carelessly left at a Xerox machine.

Blotnik read Getz's report and made himself a copy. First-century burial shroud? With the possibility of human remains? Discovered by Jake Drum? What was that bloke Drum's theory about a Jesus family tomb?

The explosive implications of Jake's theory and my shroud find weren't lost on Blotnik. If he couldn't have the Masada skeleton, this would work. Arming himself with a bolt cutter, he headed to Beit Hanina and waited for Jake to leave the house. It was easy.

And what of Jake?

True as stated. He'd driven to his site to find the Hevrat Kadisha causing major disruption. In the end, the police had to be called. By the time he'd left it was too late to visit Getz or Bloom. The police at the site had asked to see paperwork authorizing the excavation, which Jake kept at home.

Returning to the flat, he'd put down his pocket effects in the usual place, and dug out copies of his permits for the Talpiot site. Then he discovered the cabinet open and the shroud bones gone. Enraged, he'd stormed off without locking up. Trying to deal with both things at once, he'd first detoured to the district police headquarters to deliver his documents, then headed straight for Blotnik.

I had arrived at the Rockefeller first, and he found me in the closet.

So.

The shroud bones were incinerated to ash.

Blotnik was dead.

Kaplan was free.

Purviance would be charged with Blotnik's murder in Israel. Extradition later? Maybe.

And Max?

Representatives of the Hevrat Kadisha admitted, under pressure from Friedman, that they'd liberated and re-buried the Masada skeleton. Neither thumbscrews, garrotes, nor threats of prosecution could get them to disclose the location. They'd heard all that before. To them it was a matter of sacred Jewish law. *Halakha.* Appeals for temporary access under their watch were unyieldingly rejected.

So. Only three things remained. The original Kaplan print. The bone samples taken for DNA testing. The photos I'd shot at my Montreal lab.

Otherwise, Max was gone.

41

IT WAS NOW THURSDAY, FOUR DAYS AFTER THE CRASH. RYAN AND I would be returning to Montreal on the midnight flight. Before leaving Israel, we'd decided to make one last call.

I found myself again traveling the Jericho road. Ryan and I had passed Qumran, famed for its Essenes and caves and scrolls; and Ein Gedi, famed for its beaches and spas. On our left, the Dead Sea stretched cobalt-green toward Jordan. On our right, a tortured landscape of buttes and mesas.

Finally I saw it, stark red against the perfect blue sky. Herod's citadel at the edge of the Judean desert.

Ryan made a turn. Two kilometers later we pulled into a lot and parked. Signs reassured tourists. Restaurants, shops, toilets, this way.

"Cable car or Snake Path?" I asked.

"How rough's the climb?"

"Piece of cake."

"Why the name?"

"The trail winds a little." I'd been warned the trek was mean and dusty and took an hour or more. I was pumped.

"How about we cable up, then assess?"

"Wimp." I smiled.

"It took a Roman legion seven months to reach the top."

"They were battling an army of zealots."

"Details, details."

Masada is the most visited spot in Israel, but not that day.

Ryan bought tickets and we entered an empty cable car. At the top, we mounted a twisting staircase, then the ancient site sprawled before us.

I was awestruck. Romans. Zealots. Byzantines. Nazarenes? I was standing on the very same soil. Soil trod long before Europeans laid eyes on the New World.

I scanned what remained of the casement wall, shoulder high now, the old stones weathered and bleached. My eyes took in the playa within the wall's encompass. Mojave dry, here and there a scrub vine eking out life. Purple blossoms. Amazing. Beauty in the midst of brutal desolation.

I thought of soldiers, monks, and whole families. Dedication and sacrifice. My mind wondered. How? Why?

Beside me, Ryan checked the orientation map. Above me, an Israeli flag snapped in the wind.

"The walking tour starts over there." Ryan took my hand and led me north.

We visited the storehouses, the officers' quarters, the northern palace in which Yadin had recovered his "family." The Byzantine church, the *mikveh,* the synagogue.

We passed few people. A couple speaking German. A school group protected by armed parent-guards. Fatigue-clad teens with Uzis on their backs.

Standard circuit completed, Ryan and I reversed and headed toward the southern end of the summit. No other tourist was venturing that way.

I checked the diagram in my pamphlet. The southern citadel and wall were noted. A water cistern. The great pool. Not a word about the caves.

I paused at the casement wall, awed anew by the plain of sand and rock fading into shimmering haze. By the giant, silent formations molded by eons of scouring wind.

I pointed to a square faintly visible in the moonscape below.

"See that outline?"

Ryan nodded, elbow-leaning on the railing beside me.

"That was one of the Roman camps."

I leaned forward and craned to my left. There it was. A dark wound piercing the flesh of the cliff.

"There's the cave." My voice cracked.

I stared, mesmerized. Ryan knew what I was feeling. Gently tugging me back, he arm-draped my shoulders.

"Any theories on who he was?"

I raised my hands in a Who knows? gesture.

"Guesses?"

"Max was a man who died between the age of forty and sixty about two thousand years ago. He was buried with more than twenty other people in that cave down there." I pointed over the casement wall. "A younger person's tooth ended up in his jaw. Probably by mistake. *Lucky* mistake. Otherwise we might never have known of the link between the cave people and the family in Jake's shroud tomb."

"The one Jake believes is the Jesus family crypt."

"Yes. So Max may very well have been a Nazarene, not a zealot."

"Jake is damn sure that tomb belonged to the Holy Family."

"The names match. The decorative styles of the ossuaries. The age of the shroud." I kicked at a stone. "Jake's convinced the James ossuary came from that tomb."

"Are you?"

"I'm intrigued."

"Meaning?"

I thought a moment. What *did* I mean?

"He could be right. It's just an overwhelming concept to grasp. Of the three great religions woven through the history of Palestine, all rely more on divine mystery and spiritual belief than on science and reason to establish their legitimacy. Historic facts have been given differing spins to make them mesh with favored orthodoxy. Inconsistent facts are denied.

"The facts Jake postulates as to the Kidron tomb could potentially undermine elements of the Christian creed. Maybe Mary didn't remain a virgin. Maybe Jesus had siblings, even offspring. Maybe Jesus remained shrouded in his loculus after the crucifixion."

I tipped my head at the cave below us.

"Same goes for Cave 2001 and certain elements of revered Jewish history. Maybe Masada wasn't occupied solely by Jewish zealots during the first-century revolt. Maybe early Christians were up here, too. Who knows? What I do know is that it's tragic DNA wasn't obtained from the shroud bones. Especially since it's clear that at least one of the people in the cave up here was related to the people in Jake's tomb down there."

Ryan considered that. Then, "So, even though DNA links a tooth from Masada to the Kidron tomb, you think the resurfacing of Max and the discovery of the shroud bones within weeks of each other was pure coincidence?"

"I do. The tooth was undoubtedly from someone in Cave 2001, and mistakenly became associated with Max. But Max may have been only the messenger, not the message, in this whole saga. Funny. I'm even more curious about whose tooth it was than I am about who Max was."

"I'm not following."

"This all started with Max, but Max may simply have lucked into a prime cemetery plot."

"Still lost."

"Because Max's grave was at the back of the cave, his body wasn't disturbed by animals. It's possible he remained intact not because he was buried in a manner that differed from the others, or because his social status was more exalted than the others, but simply because he was put into the ground at a greater distance from the cave mouth. But since his was the only complete, articulated skeleton, people viewed Max as special. Someone shipped him out of Israel. Lerner stole him. Ferris and Morissonneau hid him. In the end, Max's main contribution may be that he survived intact and led us to the odd molar."

"Tying the Kidron tomb to Masada. Jake got any theories whose tooth it might be?"

"Lots of bodies in the cave. Jake's thinking a nephew of Jesus, maybe a child of one of the sisters. The mitochondrial DNA shows a maternal link."

"Not a sibling?"

"Unlikely. Inscriptions account for Jude, Joseph, James, if that ossuary's real, the Marys, and Salome. Simon died years later."

Again, we fell into silence. I spoke first.

"It's funny, Max started everything. Lerner stole him from the Musée de l'Homme because he believed Joyce's story about the scroll and his theory about Jesus living on at Masada. It turns out Joyce could have been right about Jesus, *some* Jesus, but wrong about Max. Max can't be Jesus of Nazareth, who died in his early thirties, according to Scripture. His age doesn't fit, and his mitochondrial DNA makes him an outsider to the Kidron tomb matrilineage. But Max could be a nephew of Jesus."

"Grosset's scroll was supposedly written by someone named Jesus, son of James."

"Exactly. But the tooth could also be from a nephew of Jesus. According to Bergeron, the tooth man died at the age of thirty-five to forty. If one of Jesus' sisters had married a man named James and had a son, that child would have shared her mitochondrial DNA. If these events took place around the time of the crucifixion, the age would fit. The tooth could have belonged to a Jesus, son of James. Hell, Ryan. Any male in that jumble could have gone by that name. We'll never know."

"Who was the Cave 2001 septuagenarian in Yadin's report and book?"

"Same answer. It wasn't Max, it wasn't the tooth man, but it could have been any male in that heap."

Ryan's next comment went right to the heart of it.

"The kicker is, whoever that tooth belonged to, if Jake's right about the James ossuary, and by corollary the Kidron tomb and the Holy Family, the tooth's presence in the cave places Nazarenes on Masada at the time of the siege. A fact inconsistent with Israel's accounts of Masada."

"Very much. Israeli theologians in particular would view a Nazarene connection to Masada as sacrilege. Consider their reluctance to discuss the cave skeletons or do further testing."

I turned and gestured toward the northern end of the summit.

"There's a small monument off the western side, at the tip of the Roman camp, where all the Masada remains were reinterred in sixty-nine. The Cave 2001 bones could be exhumed, but the Israelis won't do it."

"And the shroud bones?"

"We'll never know. If Jake had been able to get DNA or pursue other testing, maybe scanning electron microscopy of the calcaneus lesion, we might have learned more. As it stands, all we have are the few lousy photos I took in the loculus."

"What about the hair and bone samples Getz recovered?"

"The hair could yield something someday. The bone particles are barely more than dust. I'm amazed Getz spotted them."

"Jake hadn't set some of the shroud bones aside?"

"Never had a chance."

"Is he planning to ask for DNA testing on the James ossuary bones?"

"He submitted a request. The Israelis turned him down and they have the bones. Knowing Jake, he'll keep at it."

"The James ossuary may be fake."

"It may," I agreed.

"Jake's theory may be wrong."

"It may."

Ryan pulled me tight. He knew I was hiding feelings of guilt and disappointment. Max was gone, interred for all time in an anonymous grave. The Cave 2001 bones were gone, interred under one of Israel's most sacred monuments. The shroud bones were gone, destroyed in a holocaust of fuel and fire.

For a moment we stood gazing out at that melancholy rim of the universe. Empty. Dead.

For years I'd read and heard about this conflicted piece of our planet. It was impossible not to.

The book of Psalms called Jerusalem the City of God. Zachariah called it the City of Truth. Whose God? Whose Truth?

"LaManche phoned today." I switched back to a world in which some control over my life seemed possible.

"How is the old bird?"

"Pleased that I'll be back on Monday."

"You've only been gone a week and a half."

"He had news. There was an exhumation. Sylvain Morissonneau suffered from congestive heart failure."

"The priest at the abbey?"

I nodded. "He died of a massive coronary."

"No wild-eyed jihadists?"

"Just bad heart muscle, probably coupled with an elevated stress level brought on by the reemergence of the skeleton issue."

"Reminds me. Friedman has breaking news. He ran the maid's note past Mrs. Hanani and finally got the story on the B-and-E of your room. There was no B. Hossam al-Ahmed is a hotel cook who's been tomcatting around on his girl, one of the hotel maids. The lady-done-wrong decided to set the cad up. Trash a room, point a finger. Your door was unlocked."

"It's ironic. All our mega-theories to explain Ferris's murder and the theft of Max. Ultra-Orthodox Jews did it. Zealot Christians did it. Islamic fundamentalists did it.

"In the end, it was revenge and greed. Two of the old reliables. No state secret. No holy war. No sweeping question of doctrine or creed. We unraveled the methodology of a murder and we identified a killer. I should be elated, but somehow in the context of the last two weeks the murder seems mundane, almost like Charles Bellemare."

"The stoned-out cowboy stuck in the chimney?"

"Yes. In pursuing our small players over the large stage, I got overwhelmed by the larger context. The murder seemed almost insignificant."

"We both got caught up."

"I read something called the Gallup International Millennium Survey. Researchers sampled populations in sixty countries representing one point two billion souls worldwide, trying to learn how people feel about God. Eighty-seven percent of the respondents considered themselves part of some religion. Thirty-one percent believed theirs was the only true faith."

Ryan started to speak. I wasn't done.

"But they're wrong, Ryan. Despite the rituals, the rhetoric, and even the bombs, every religion is saying mostly the same thing. Buddhism. Taoism. Zoroastrianism. Sikhism. Shamanism. It doesn't matter. Take your pick."

"You've lost me, cupcake."

"The Torah, the Bible, the Koran. Each offers a recipe for spiritual contentment, for hope, for love, and for controlling basic human passions, and each claims to have gotten the recipe straight from God, but via a different messenger. They're all just trying to provide a formula for orderly, spiritual living, but somehow the message gets twisted, like cells in a body turning cancerous. Self-appointed spokesmen declare the boundaries of correct belief, outsiders are labeled heretics, and the faithful are called upon to attack them. I don't think it was meant to be that way."

"I know you're right, cupcake, but this working cop long ago abandoned any hope of ridding La Belle Province of crime. I don't think I'm up to reconciling the world's religions. Back home there are bodies in the morgue that deserve our attention. We do what we can. And you know what? We're pretty good at it."

One last look over the plain. So breathtakingly beautiful, so filled with strife. Then, reluctantly, I allowed Ryan to lead me from the wall.

Adieu, Israel. I wish you peace.

FROM THE FORENSIC FILES OF DR. KATHY REICHS

Most Temperance Brennan novels spring from a mixture of my real forensic cases. I start with a child's skeleton unearthed in a farmer's field, stir in a body part found in a high-rise basement, then blend. This story began with yellowed press clippings, a black-and-white glossy, a lot of bad photocopies, and a very strange tale.

Dr. James Tabor, a colleague at the University of North Carolina at Charlotte, wears two hats. He is both a biblical archaeologist and scholar, and an expert on modern apocalyptic religious movements. Wearing the latter headgear, he counseled the FBI on the Branch Davidian conflict at Waco, Texas, and advised me during the writing of *Death du Jour.* Wearing the hat of biblical scholar, he has worked on the Dead Sea Scrolls, and dug at Qumran, where they were found, excavated at the "John the Baptist" cave west of Jerusalem, and carried out investigative research on Masada, Israel's most famous archaeological site.

Monday Mourning was behind me in the autumn of 2003, and I was beginning the mental triage that would eventually culminate in my eighth book. Tabor phoned one morning, and spoke of looted tombs and purloined skeletons. He was writing a nonfiction work, *The Jesus Dynasty,* in which he intended to present the historical facts about Jesus' family, based on the latest archaeological research and discoveries. Would I like to hear the story for a possible Temperance Brennan plot?

You betcha! I'd started my career as an archaeologist. So had Tempe. Why not involve the old gal in archaeological intrigue? I agreed to meet and, over lunch, Tabor showed me pictures and clippings, and outlined the following.

From 1963 to 1965, Israeli archaeologist Yigael Yadin and an international team of volunteers excavate the Israeli site of Masada. Twenty-five skeletons and a fetus are found in a cave below the casement wall at the southern tip of the summit. Yadin does not discuss these bones with the press, though he does discuss three skeletons found by his team in the main complex of ruins at the northern end of the summit. Nor are the cave bones documented by the project's physical anthropologist, Nicu Haas. Save for mention in an appendix, neither the bones nor the contents of the cave are described in the six volumes of the final *Masada* excavation publication.

Thirty years pass. A photo surfaces of a single intact skeleton lying in the same cave from which Yadin's team excavated the twenty-five jumbled individuals. Yadin never described the intact skeleton in published reports or interviews.

Intrigued, Tabor locates transcripts of staff briefings held in lieu of field notes during the Masada excavation. Pages covering the period of the discovery and clearing of the skeleton cave are missing.

Tabors tracks down Nicu Haas's original handwritten notes. It is clear from his bone inventory that Haas has never seen the complete, articulated skeleton.

Tabor researches newspaper articles dating to the period of the Masada excavation. He finds a statement made by Yadin to a journalist in the late sixties that it is not his job to request carbon-14 testing. Tabor checks the journal *Radiocarbon,* and finds that, during the sixties, Yadin did, in fact, send samples from other sites for carbon-14 testing.

I looked at the small black-and-white photo of that single skeleton. I looked at photocopies of Haas's notes and of the transcribed staff sessions. I was hooked. But Tabor wasn't finished.

Fast-forward to the summer of 2000. While hiking the Hinnom Valley with students, Tabor and Israeli archaeologist Shimon Gibson stumble upon a freshly robbed tomb. They excavate and discover smashed ossuaries and skeletal remains wrapped in a burial shroud. Carbon-14 testing dates the shroud to the first century. DNA sequencing shows a familial relationship among individuals buried in the tomb. Ossuary fragments bear the names Mary and Salome.

Fast-forward again. October 2002. An antiquities collector announces the existence of a first-century ossuary inscribed "James, son of Joseph, brother of Jesus." The collector states that the box was purchased in 1978, but Tabor has found circumstantial evidence suggesting it was taken during the looting of his shroud tomb two years earlier. The construction matches. The decoration matches. Rumors have surfaced in Jerusalem.

Tabor considers it a serious possibility that he has stumbled onto the Jesus family tomb. In 2003, he requests bone from the "James ossuary" for mitochondrial DNA testing. He wants to compare sequencing from that bone with sequencing yielded by his "shroud" tomb lineage. The director of the Israel Antiquities Authority denies his request, explaining that the case is under investigation and in the hands of the police.

Mysterious skeletons. Missing pages. Looted tombs. The Jesus family crypt? Hot diggety! I would return to my archaeological roots and send Tempe to the Holy Land! My mind was already weaving plots as I studied Tabor's photos and maps. But how to bring Ryan and the others along?

At times, coroners and medical examiners must order autopsies despite the protest of family members. Occasionally objections spring from religious convictions.

During my tenure at the Laboratoire de sciences judiciaires et de médecine légale, a number of autopsies have been performed on ultra-Orthodox Jews who have been the victims of violence. Protocol has been modified, to the extent possible, to accommodate religious concerns.

That was it! I would start with a homicide in Montreal, then send Tempe into Jerusalem and the West Bank.

For a year I pored over transcripts, catalogs, and newspaper articles. I studied photos of ossuaries and the Masada excavation. I read books on Roman Palestine and the historical Jesus. With Tabor, I flew to Israel and visited museums, digs, tombs, and historic sites. I talked to antiquities dealers, archaeologists, scientists, and members of the Israel National Police.

And, as they say, the rest is history.

Kathy Reichs

For a full discussion of the facts behind *Cross Bones,* watch for James Tabor's upcoming book, *The Jesus Dynasty* (www.jesusdynasty.com).

ABOUT THE AUTHOR

Kathy Reichs is forensic anthropologist for the Office of the Chief Medical Examiner, State of North Carolina, and for the Laboratoire de sciences judiciaires et de médecine légale for the province of Quebec. She is one of sixty-five forensic anthropologists certified by the American Board of Forensic Anthropology and served on the Executive Committee of the Board of Directors of the American Academy of Forensic Sciences. A professor of anthropology at the University of North Carolina at Charlotte, Dr. Reichs is a native of Chicago, where she received her Ph.D. at Northwestern. She now divides her time between Charlotte and Montreal and is a frequent expert witness at criminal trials. Her first novel, *Déjà Dead,* brought Dr. Reichs fame when it became a *New York Times* bestseller and won the 1997 Ellis Award for Best First Novel. *Death du Jour, Deadly Décisions, Fatal Voyage, Grave Secrets, Bare Bones,* and *Monday Mourning* also became international and *New York Times* bestsellers. *Cross Bones* is her eighth novel featuring Temperance Brennan.